Praise for Ellery Adams's mysteries

The Secret, Book & Scone Society

"Adams launches an intriguing new mystery series, headed by four spirited amateur sleuths and touched with a hint of magical realism, which celebrates the power of books and women's friendships. Adams's many fans, readers of Sarah Addison Allen, and anyone who loves novels that revolve around books will savor this tasty treat."
—*Library Journal* STARRED REVIEW, Pick of the Month

"Adams (*Peach Pies and Alibis*, 2013) kicks off a new series featuring strong women, a touch of romance and mysticism, and both the cunning present-day mystery and the slowly revealed secrets of the intriguing heroines' pasts." —*Kirkus Reviews*

"This affecting series launch from Adams provides all the best elements of a traditional mystery . . . Well-drawn characters complement a plot with an intriguing twist or two."
—*Publishers Weekly*

"Adams' new series blends magical realism, smart women, and small-town quirks to create a cozy mystery that doubles as a love letter to books. Readers will fall in love with Nora's bookstore therapy and Hester's comfort scones. Not to mention Estella, June, hunky Jed the paramedic, and Nora's tiny house-slash-converted-train-caboose. . . . Overall this is a book that mystery fans—and avid readers—won't want to put down until they have savored every last crumb."
—*RT Book Reviews*, 4 Stars

The Book Retreat N

"[A] suspenseful and compelling read.
—*Kings River Life Magazine*

"[A] delight . . . An idyllic mansion in a quaint village complete with secret passages and books, books, and more books—what could make for a more ideal setting for a cozy murder . . . Ellery

Adams spins a new tale full of jealously, love, greed, aspirations, and poison . . . Highly recommended." —Open Book Society

"Adams . . . combines clever clues, a smart and courageous heroine and an interesting setting in a whodunit that will inspire readers to make further visits to Storyton Hall."
—*Richmond Times-Dispatch*

"Adams makes Storyton Hall come to life . . . Readers will relish the way Ellery Adams weaves together books, mystery, and fantasy." —*Fresh Fiction*

"A mystery that takes place at a book-themed resort—it doesn't get any better. The author has woven in a bunch of suspects that will keep cozy mystery lovers guessing. The story is well paced and keeps you reading until you find out whodunit."
—MyShelf.com

The Books by the Bay Mysteries

"Adams's plot is indeed killer, her writing would make her the star of any support group, and her characters . . . are a diverse, intelligent bunch." —*Richmond Times-Dispatch*

The Charmed Pie Shoppe Mysteries

"[A] savory blend of suspense, pies, and engaging characters. Foodie mystery fans will enjoy this." —*Booklist*

"A sensory delight for those who like a little magic with their culinary cozies." —*Library Journal*

"An original, intriguing story line that celebrates women, family, friendship, and loyalty within an enchanted world, with a hint of romance, an engaging cast of characters, and the promise of a continued saga of magical good confronting evil."
—*Kirkus Reviews*

"Adams permeates this unusual novel—and Ella [Mae's] pies—with a generous helping of appeal." —*Richmond Times-Dispatch*

The Secret, Book
& Scone Society

Also by Ellery Adams

The Secret, Book & Scone Society Mysteries:
The Secret, Book & Scone Society
The Whispered Word

Book Retreat Mysteries:
Murder in the Locked Library

The Secret, Book & Scone Society

ELLERY ADAMS

KENSINGTON BOOKS
www.kensingtonbooks.com

KENSINGTON BOOKS are published by

Kensington Publishing Corp.
119 West 40th Street
New York, NY 10018

Copyright © 2017 by Ellery Adams

First Kensington Hardcover Edition: November 2017

ISBN-13: 978-1-4967-1238-7
ISBN-10: 1-4967-1238-2
First Kensington Trade Paperback Printing: August 2018

eISBN-13: 978-1-4967-1239-4
eISBN-10: 1-4967-1239-0

20 19 18 17 16 15 14 13 12 11

Printed in the United States of America

For Leann Sweeney, with love

Books are everywhere; and always the same sense of adventure fills us. Second-hand books are wild books, homeless books; they have come together in vast flocks of variegated feather, and have a charm which the domesticated volumes of the library lack. Besides, in this random miscellaneous company we may rub against some complete stranger who will, with luck, turn into the best friend we have in the world.

—Virginia Woolf

The Secret, Book and Scone Society Members

Nora Pennington, Owner of Miracle Books
Hester Winthrop, Owner of the Gingerbread House
Estella Sadler, Owner of Magnolia Salon and Spa
June Dixon, Miracle Springs Thermal Pools employee

Pine Ridge Properties partners

Neil Parrish
Fenton Greer
Collin Stone
Vanessa MacCavity

Chapter 1

A book must be an ice-axe to break the seas frozen inside our soul.

—Franz Kafka

The man on the park bench stared at the empty space above the knuckle of Nora Pennington's pinkie finger.

Strangers were always hypnotized by this gap. They would gaze at the puckered skin stretched over the nub of finger bone for several awkward seconds before averting their eyes in disgust, pity, or both.

Like most strangers, the man's attention could only remain on Nora's pinkie for so long. She had other fascinating scars. He couldn't fixate on just one.

His chin jerked slightly, as though he knew he was being impolite and should look away, but was powerless to do so. His eyes slowly traveled over the bubble of shell-smooth skin on the back of her hand. It was pinker and shinier than the surrounding skin, and Nora sensed that the man had an irrational desire to touch it.

Years ago, when Nora was in the hospital, a night nurse with silver hair that flashed like fish scales when caught by the light told Nora that the burn on her hand was shaped like Iceland.

"That's where I'm from," the nurse had added proudly. Her

voice was part grandmother's lullaby, part chamomile tea, and part chenille blanket. It was the only thing that penetrated Nora's veil of pain. "You even have the two peninsulas on Iceland's western shore. See? They're like a pair of crab pincers."

Nora hadn't opened her eyes to look. She didn't want to acknowledge the nurse's presence. She didn't want comfort. She'd wanted to be left alone to sink deeper in her ocean of agony and remorse.

The man on the bench shifted, bringing Nora back to the present.

He was studying her right arm. This was her darkest, angriest scar: a Portuguese man-of-war jellyfish swimming through her skin from wrist to shoulder. And while part of its red and purple bell disappeared into the sleeve of her white blouse, there was an impression of other sea creatures reemerging above the collar. A parade of pale, glistening octopi drifted across Nora's neck and cheek, forever trapped in the ripples and wavelets the flames had carved into her skin.

The man's eyes strayed to Nora's other hand. The unblemished one.

This was unusual. Most people finished their inspection of Nora's face with a forlorn expression. She knew exactly what they were thinking when they wore that look.

What a shame. She'd be so pretty without those scars.

But this man hadn't responded with the "too bad, so sad" expression. He was clearly more interested in the scone she held than in continuing to study her burn scars.

Nora felt herself relaxing the stiff posture she held when newcomers inspected her.

"Excuse me." The man pointed at her decimated pastry. "Where did you get that?"

Nora, who'd been feeding the scone to a small flock of mourning doves, replied, "From the Gingerbread House. They're called comfort scones. The baker, Hester, makes custom scones based on what she thinks her patrons will be comforted by. You should pay her a visit."

"I love scones, but I haven't had one in forever. I used to have a chocolate-chip scone every Thursday afternoon at this little coffee shop near my office. But that was before everything changed. I couldn't look the barista in the eye after—" The man fell into an abrupt silence. He sat very still and watched the doves devour Nora's crumbs. When every last piece was gone, he asked, "Why are you feeding yours to the birds?"

"A customer dropped it on the floor while I was in the bakery buying a cinnamon twist," Nora said. "I prefer cinnamon twists over scones because they're easier to eat while I'm reading. That's my main priority when it comes to food. Other people are obsessed with calories, nutritional value, antioxidants. I look at food and wonder: Can I eat that without having to put my book down?"

This elicited a small smile from the man. He pointed at the yellow building with the cobalt blue trim and doors on the far side of the park. The former train depot, which had been converted into a bookshop, possessed an air of charming dilapidation.

"So I take it you hang out there pretty often," he said.

"I do." Dusting crumbs from her hands, Nora added, "Miracle Books is my store."

Hearing this, the man pivoted to face her.

The sudden movement startled the doves and they took off in a burst of alarmed coos and whooshing wings.

"An African-American woman working at the thermal pools told me about the resident bibliotherapist. Was she talking about you?"

Nora saw the need in the man's eyes. She'd seen it hundreds of times. But only from those who dared to look directly at her. "This woman said that the bibliotherapist was able to help people solve their problems by recommending certain titles." The man gestured at Miracle Books. "It makes sense that you'd own a bookstore."

"I have no official training," Nora said, uttering her standard disclaimer. "Before I came to Miracle Springs, I was a librarian. I haven't taken a single course in psychology. I've never done any formal counseling."

The man frowned in confusion. "This woman said that people seek you out when the rest of the services in town failed to make them feel better. But I don't get it. How can you succeed where all of the professionals—and the healing waters—can't?"

Nora shrugged. "There's no guarantee my method will work, either. I read all the time. And I listen to people. I *really* listen." She held the man's dubious gaze. "Stories don't change much across continents and centuries. Hearts are broken. Pride is wounded. Souls wander too far from home and become lost. The wrong roads are taken. The incorrect choice is made. Stories echo with loneliness. Grief. Longing. Redemption. Forgiveness. Hope. And love." Now it was her turn to point at the bookstore. "That building is stuffed with books that, once opened, reveal our communal story. And, if you're lucky, the words in those books will force you to grapple with the hardest truths of your life. After reducing you to a puddle of tears, they'll raise you to your feet again. The words will pull you up, higher and higher, until you feel the sun on your face again. Until you're suddenly humming on the way to the mailbox. Or you're buying bouquets of gerbera daisies because you crave bright colors. And you'll laugh again—as freely as champagne bubbling in a tall, glass flute. When's the last time you laughed like that?"

The man's mouth twisted. He was trying to hold his emotion in check—to keep his pain from overtaking him. His hands gripped his knees so hard that his knuckles had gone white. He looked away from Nora, and she thought he might get up and leave. Instead, he asked, "How does it work? This bibliotherapy."

"Go to the Gingerbread House and buy a comfort scone," Nora said. "Tell Hester you're coming to see me and she'll put your scone in a takeout box. I have coffee, but the fanciest thing I make with my espresso machine is a latte, so if you're used to soy no-foam mochaccinos, you're going to be disappointed."

"I confess to making decisions that have complicated my life and compromised my principles," the man said. "But I've never taken my coffee any way but black."

"Then we're off to a good start." Nora got to her feet. "While you're eating, you can tell me what brought you to Miracle Springs." She held up her hands. "This won't be like a traditional counseling session where we sit down and you talk for a long period of time. You won't need to go into detail with me. I only need a broad brushstroke—a brief glimpse into the heart of your pain. That way, I can select the right books. After that, you can start reading your way to a fresh start this evening."

The man grunted, infusing his exhalation with a feeling of dismissal. "I'm not much of a reader."

"Ah." Nora moved away a few steps and then stopped and spun on her heel. "You came to Miracle Springs to make changes, didn't you? Becoming a reader is a change for the better. Trust me. No one has ever lost by becoming addicted to stories—to the lessons learned by those who possess enough courage to put pen to paper."

"You've got a point." Another dismissive grunt. "What's the worst that could happen from my opening the cover of a book?"

For the first time since they'd begun speaking, Nora smiled. And because she was showing the man the unblemished side of her face, she saw that he was utterly transfixed.

"You have no idea," Nora said. Her smile wavered before completely vanishing. "Stories are just like people. If you don't approach them with an open mind and a healthy dose of respect, they won't reveal their hidden selves to you. In that event, you'll miss out on what they have to offer. You'll walk through life an empty husk instead of a vibrant kaleidoscope of passion, wisdom, and experience."

The man studied her for a long moment. "I don't want to be empty anymore. I came to Miracle Springs days ahead of my partners to figure out how to fix things before it happens all over again. Nothing's worked. My partners arrive on the three o'clock train, so I have nothing to lose by giving your method a shot." He grinned. "At the very least, I'll have a scone for my efforts. Where is this celebrated Gingerbread House?"

Nora gave him directions and then continued on to Miracle Books. She had things to take care of before the man returned for his session. The trolley from the lodge would be arriving soon, and trolley-loads of rich and restless souls paid Nora's bills.

Nora Pennington loved selling books. She loved talking to people about books. But what she wanted most was to heal people using books.

Four years ago, when Nora had been a patient in a hospital burn unit, she'd prayed for death. Not only were her prayers unanswered, but she was also given first-rate medical care and the perfect prescription of stories, courtesy of an Icelandic nurse with silver hair.

First, the nurse brought Nora books about physically deformed men who were capable of great genius, devout love, acts of madness, or all of the above. And while Nora refused to watch television or receive visitors, she grudgingly reread *Frankenstein.*

Next, she was given *The Phantom of the Opera*, followed by the Christine Sparks version of *The Elephant Man.*

"Are you trying to depress me? Because I don't think I need any help in that department," Nora had grumbled to the nurse.

She'd been angry. She was always angry. And when she wasn't angry, she was depressed. She felt no other emotions.

In response, the nurse had laid a copy of *The Hunchback of Notre-Dame* on her bed.

"Guess I'm ready for *Dracula* or *Dr. Jekyll and Mr. Hyde*," Nora had told her caregiver after she'd finished the Victor Hugo classic.

"You're heading in another direction," the nurse had cheerfully informed her, placing John Green's *Looking for Alaska*, Karen Kingsbury's *Waiting for Morning*, and Kristin Hannah's *Night Road* on Nora's nightstand.

Because of the narcotics, Nora hadn't immediately realized that the theme of this current set of novels was drunk driving, so she read on. As she'd turned the pages, her emotional pain became as intense as her physical pain.

"Why are you doing this?" she'd whispered to the nurse one night. "You heard about my accident. I thought you were kind."

"You have to sink to the very bottom, my child," the woman had whispered in her lullaby voice. "After that, you can push off with both feet and start swimming toward the surface. You're strong. You can get there. But it's going to hurt. You have to clean out the wound before it can heal. Let the stories be your antiseptic. Bear the pain now for a chance at a better tomorrow. Otherwise, you'll repeat the mistakes that landed you in this bed."

Nora had read every title. When she was done, the nurse had brought her a book called *The Burn Journals* by Brent Runyon. "It's about a boy who set himself on fire when he was fourteen," she told Nora. "I know you didn't burn yourself on purpose, but I thought you'd like to read about his recovery process. He might even make you laugh."

I doubt it, Nora had thought. She'd done a terrible, terrible thing. There would be no laughter in her life. Never again.

But she'd read the book. And the next one. And the next.

The night before she was to be discharged from the hospital, Nora had asked for more books.

"You're a librarian," the nurse had replied with a smile. "You know where to find them."

Nora had dropped her eyes. "I'm not going back. I need to start over—in another place."

The nurse had sat on the edge of Nora's bed and taken her good hand in hers. "What would this place look like? The place where you'd begin a new life?"

"It would have lots and lots of books," Nora had said. "I can't live without them." Gazing at the lights and omnipresent haze of the urban sprawl outside her window, she went on: "It would be in the country. Somewhere remote and lovely. A place where people still grow vegetable gardens and build purple-martin houses. Where they have quirky holiday parades and bake sales. A place where people look for the pets on posters stapled to telephone poles. A little town. Not so little that everyone will pry into my business, but small enough that the locals will eventually get used to my appearance. Eventually, they'll stop whispering."

"And what will you do for money in this paradise?" the nurse had asked.

At this question, Nora had gone clammy with fear. She'd been so caught up in her fantasy that she hadn't considered the practicalities. During her lengthy convalescence, she'd ignored visitors, phone calls, and letters. But as of tomorrow, she couldn't hide from the outside world anymore.

Her burn scars had begun to throb, which was good, because the pain kept her grounded. She wanted to feel pain. She deserved it, so she embraced it.

"I'll open a bookstore," she'd said calmly. "I have some savings, and if I find a town that needs a bookstore—"

"Doesn't every town?" the nurse had interjected, her glacier-blue eyes twinkling with humor.

Nora had smiled. Smiling hurt the burn wound on her right cheek, but she owed this woman a smile, at the very least. "If it wants a soul, then yes. Every town needs a bookstore."

Nora pushed open the door to Miracle Books to the jingle-jangle of sleigh bells. They weren't a light, melodious tinkle, but a loud clanging that erupted from a leather horse harness covered in baseball-sized brass bells. Nora had bought the harness at the flea market and hung it from a nail on the back of the door. This way, she knew when a customer entered the shop, even if she was at the other end of the labyrinth of bookshelves she'd created to funnel people from the front toward the ticket-agent's office.

Everything in the store—from the fainting couch to the leather sofa, and the assortment of upholstered chairs in various stages of degeneration—came from yard sales and flea markets. Occasionally, Nora made purchases from the local auction company, but these treasures were reserved for her home: a four-room, tiny house that had once been a functioning railroad car. The locals referred to her diminutive abode as Caboose Cottage because her refurbished train car was a cheerful apple-red.

After flipping the SHUT sign over to read OPEN, Nora continued walking deeper into the shop. She needed to brew coffee. The trolley would be pulling into the public parking area any moment now.

Nora entered the small office where train tickets were once sold to Miracle Springs travelers. In order to convert the office into a basic coffee dispensary, Nora had removed the ticket window's glass divide and hung a chalkboard next to the opening. The chalkboard listed the literary names of the beverages Miracle Books offered:

The Ernest Hemingway—Dark Roast
The Louisa May Alcott—Light Roast
The Dante Alighieri—Decaf
The Wilkie Collins—Cappuccino
The Jack London—Latte
The Agatha ChrisTEA—Earl Grey

From time to time, customers would suggest a new and complicated espresso recipe along with a suitable author name to match.

Nora, who'd learned to treat people's feelings with care since her life had taken such a dramatic turn on a dark highway four years ago, would smile and praise the person for their creativity. She would then confess that her secondhand espresso maker could barely handle steaming milk, but if she ever had the chance to upgrade, she'd keep their drink idea in mind.

At this point, the enthusiastic customer would glance around the shop and notice, possibly for the first time, the piece of duct tape on the split-chair cushion or that the reading lamp was burning one bulb instead of three. Seeing as they'd come to Miracle Springs in search of healing—from a physical or emotional injury, it wasn't always easy to tell—Nora's customers were usually empathetic people. Therefore, they'd drop the subject, order a coffee from the menu, and spend more money than they'd originally planned.

Nora made the latter especially easy to do by filling the store with impulse buys. Not only did she stock new and gently used books, but also signed books, collectible books, bookmarks, bookplates, and "shelf enhancers" as well.

Shelf enhancers were what Nora had dubbed the bookends, figurines, framed prints, paperweights, clay pots, birdcages, portrait plates, decoys, folk art, miniature needlework plaques, tea caddies, inkwells, apothecary jars, Depression glass vases, tin signs, stone busts, vintage trophies, brass scales, old game boards, and so on, which she strategically placed on every shelf.

Nora purchased every item at its rock-bottom price. She hit the yard-sale scene on certain Saturday mornings, and on occasional Sundays she combed the flea markets, examining any item captivating her interest with extreme care. The local vendors had come to respect her discriminating eye and shrewd bartering skills. They also knew that she resold their wares at a profit, but the profit margin was small and they didn't begrudge her a living.

"What else is a woman like that going to do?" some of the less charitable sellers would whisper, seeing themselves as magnanimous for giving Nora extra discounts here and there.

Of course, Nora knew exactly which vendors felt this way and didn't hesitate to accept said discounts. All she had was Miracle Books, and she'd do anything to keep her store afloat.

Almost anything, Nora thought, scooping coffee grounds into a paper filter. She hadn't been very open to suggestions from local readers, most of whom were women looking to start a book club and use Miracle Books as their meeting place. Nora was fine with that aspect, but she'd stoutly declined when asked to serve as the book-club facilitator.

"I can't" was all Nora had told Mrs. Cassidy at the time. It wasn't that she didn't like the idea of discussing a work of women's fiction as plates of homemade desserts were passed around, but Nora never put herself in the center of a crowd. She felt truly comfortable only inside the ticket booth, with a thick, wooden counter separating herself from other people. To sit in a circle facing a group of women—no, they would start asking her questions. They'd want to get to know her, and Nora couldn't allow that to happen.

She'd come to Miracle Springs to forget.

The sleigh bells jingled and jangled from the front of the

store and Nora glanced at her watch again. It was still too early for the trolley, and there was no chance the man from the bench had made it to the Gingerbread House, had a customized comfort scone prepared and packaged for him, and was now ready for his bibliotherapy session. That meant the newcomer was a customer, and Nora would let him or her wander in peace. She never approached browsers unless they gave off an air of needing help, and Nora had become adept at reading people's vibes.

Back when she was a librarian, she didn't pay much attention to vibes. Once, a patron requested a book on color auras. The title was long out-of-print and could only be acquired by interlibrary loan. As Nora was filling out the form, the patron informed her that she had a dark red aura.

"You're practical, hardworking, loyal, and honest," she'd said. "You're also a survivor. You've had, or will have to face, a serious trauma."

Nora, who'd foolishly believed herself to be content, dismissed the woman's reading as the ramblings of a New Age hobbyist.

The trauma was coming, however. It was rushing toward Nora like a runaway train. And she stood directly in its path—too busy with work and other obligations to realize that she was about to be mowed down.

Do auras change? Nora wondered, as she pressed the *brew* button on the coffeemaker. *They should. Because people change. For better and for worse.*

In the distance, she heard the whistle of the afternoon train. Nora never tired of its long, heartrending note. What other sound could convey both the romance of returning home and the ache of leave-taking? The next whistle, which would blow in approximately five minutes, meant that the train was just about to enter the narrow, dark tunnel preceding the Miracle Springs station.

Suddenly, the space where the tip of Nora's pinkie finger

used to be tingled. She stared at her hand, discomfited by the sensation. She'd never experienced the feeling before.

"Excuse me," said a soft, female voice, and Nora hid her damaged hand behind her back.

"Yes? Can I help you?" she asked, averting the burned side of her face.

Like all strangers, the woman noticed Nora's scars. However, she only gave them a cursory inspection. "Do you carry cookbooks with scone recipes? I just ate the most amazing scone at the Gingerbread House, but the baker said the recipe couldn't be duplicated because her scones are based on people's fondest memories. She told me that she uses a basic recipe and adds certain ingredients after talking to each customer."

"That's what I've heard as well," Nora said. "What did yours taste like?"

"Oranges and cream." The woman's face broke into a broad grin. "The first bite brought me back to my grandmother's house in Florida. She had orange trees. During my visits, we'd bake the most delicious things. Her kitchen was filled with clutter and sunshine. I loved every minute I spent with her."

Nora came out from inside the ticket booth. "I have several cookbooks with scone recipes. The best anyone can do is to create a scone of their own."

"I'd settle for that," the woman said. She was younger than Nora, who was edging toward forty, but had the wise and slightly guarded eyes of someone who'd experienced a decade's worth of anguish in a very short period of time. "If I could spend a few hours lost in memories of Granny, I would."

As Nora led the woman to the cookbook section, two things occurred. First, the space just above her pinkie finger tingled again. Simultaneously, the second train whistle called out the imminent arrival of more people in search of healing.

The woman, who'd paused to pluck a Vaseline-glass fox from a bookshelf, hadn't noticed that Nora had stopped walking.

"Granny had a fox just like this," the woman said, running her fingers down the fox's smooth back. "She let me touch all of her things, even when I was very young. My house was a veritable museum. It was more important to impress visitors than to be comfortable."

"What's your line of work?" Nora asked.

The woman's mouth drooped. "I'm an accountant. I'm good at it, but I hate it."

"Do you still enjoy cooking?"

"I don't know." She sounded unsure. "I might."

Nora gestured at a club chair covered in purple velvet. "I'm going to put a stack of books on that cushion. I think you need to read these books. If you read every one, in order, I believe you'll find an orange-scented, sun-filled kitchen of your own."

Twenty minutes later, the woman left with the fox and two shopping bags of books. One bag was weighed down with cookbooks, while the other held Eric Ripert's *32 Yolks*, Joanne Harris's *Chocolat*, Amy Tan's *The Joy Luck Club*, Ernest Hemingway's *A Moveable Feast*, Richard Morais's *The Hundred-Foot Journey*, Muriel Barbery's *Gourmet Rhapsody*, and Banana Yoshimoto's *Kitchen*.

Nora watched the woman walk toward the park with a light, eager step and hoped the books would do their job. If they did, the woman would make messes in her kitchen. She would buy knickknacks for her tidy, Spartan apartment. She would let her hair down and take chances. She would find joy.

Still scanning the park square, Nora wondered where the trolley passengers had gone. The lodge's green trolley was parked in its usual place, but no lodge guests strolled the sidewalks or meandered from the row of quaint shops on Bath Street to the Pink Lady Grill or the Gingerbread House.

Just then, a flash of red caught Nora's eye and she groaned inwardly as a tall, shapely woman passed in front of the bookshop window. The woman yanked the door open, ignoring the riotous clanging of the sleigh bells, and settled into the closest chair like a queen awaiting the adulation of her subjects. Her pouty lips curved into a cat-with-the-cream grin. "Consider your next bibliotherapy session canceled."

"Hello to you too, Estella." Nora picked up the stray paperbacks a customer had left on the table next to Estella's chair. "I assume you're referring to the man I met on the park bench. Why isn't he coming? Did you scare him off?"

"Me?" Estella pretended to be affronted, but Nora wasn't falling for the act. "I didn't even get a chance to meet him. I was up at the lodge wasting my time on a man I *thought* had some potential, but he's already making payments to an ex-wife and needs to send *three* kids to college. There'd be nothing left for *me*." She waved a manicured hand in dismissal.

Nora was itching to reshelve the books and check on the coffee. Though she didn't dislike Estella, she was rarely at ease in her company.

Recalling the strange sensation she'd experienced as the second train whistle blew, Nora felt an inexplicable prickle of dread. She jerked a thumb toward the window. "Where is everyone?"

Estella's grin returned. "At the train station. They've been drawn there like flies to sugar. The sheriff rolled in a few seconds ago, and since he and I have never gotten along, I made myself scarce."

Nora, who made it a point not to look people directly in the eye, forgot her rule and gave Estella an impatient stare. "What happened? Just spit it out."

Crossing her arms in disappointment, Estella murmured something about no one being any fun, but eventually complied with Nora's request. "When your man on the bench placed an order for one of Hester's comfort scones, he asked her to box it because he was heading over here to see you. He left the bakery, box in hand, but he never made it to Miracle

Books." Estella leaned back in the chair and smoothed the skirt of her white sundress. "I'm sure he'd rather be sitting in this comfy chair than where he is now."

Nora knew she wasn't going to like the answer to her question, but it had to be asked. "Which is?"

"On the tracks," Estella declared breathlessly. "Someone pushed him in front of the three o'clock train."

Chapter 2

The siren soared again, closer at hand, and then,
with no anticipatory roar and clamour, a dark and
sinuous body curved into view against the shadows
far down the high-banked track.

—F. Scott Fitzgerald

Estella Sadler had a flair for the dramatic. She behaved as if everyone watched her whenever she entered or exited a room. She wore clingy dresses, pencil skirts, and tight blouses—every item of clothing was meant to draw attention to her provocative curves—and she never appeared in public without perfume, makeup, and carefully coiffed hair. Estella invested a great deal of time, effort, and expense honing her image. She aspired to be viewed as the most desirable single woman in Miracle Springs. As far as Nora knew, Estella had successfully held this title for more than a decade. Nora also knew that plenty of local women directed their venom at Estella. They called her nasty names behind her back, fearing that she had designs on their husbands.

These fears were inane. The last thing Estella sought was an entanglement with a man sharing her ZIP code. She yearned to be whisked away by a wealthy stranger to somewhere far from Miracle Springs—the town where she was born and raised.

Once, when she'd been trimming Nora's long, thick locks of nut-brown hair, Estella had gestured around Magnolia Salon and Spa, and said, "Some women would kill to have their own business. I rent chair space to two other stylists and have part-time help in the spa too. I can take time off whenever I want, I have a cute little house, nice clothes, and enough money in the bank to pay the bills every month, but I want *so* much more."

Nora, who was accustomed to people sharing their hopes and desires with her, possibly because she was quiet, sat in silence as Estella listed all the exotic places she wanted to visit.

"But not by myself," Estella had added. "I want someone to take me *and* to take care of me wherever we go. Someone who will show me the world, but will treat me like a queen when we're watching TV at home too." Estella's scissors had stopped snipping. "Do you have books to help me get a man like that? A how-to guide on snaring a millionaire with a heart of gold?"

Though she doubted it would do any good, Nora had found such a guide for Estella. She'd also introduced her to romance authors like Catherine Coulter, Brenda Joyce, Candice Proctor, Bertrice Small, Diana Gabaldon, and Jade Lee. Estella confessed that she'd been a voracious reader as a child, but had become too focused on her ambitions to invest in reading as an adult. But with a little coaxing from Nora, Estella had renewed her love affair with fiction.

"I'm not making this up," she said now, leaning forward in her chair to impart the seriousness of her claim. "Even though it sounds like a John Grisham plot. Well, maybe not Grisham. Fill in the blank with the appropriate writer who'd dream up a scene where a clueless tourist is pushed off the ledge above the train tunnel—you know the one, the place the moms tell their kids to stay away from or else."

In an attempt to calm her tumultuous thoughts, Nora pictured the spot where the man from the bench must have drawn his last breath. It wasn't far from Caboose Cottage. Like Nora's backyard, the land leading down to the tunnel's mouth was a steep slope and though the town had erected a chain-link fence to prevent trespassers from approaching the area, bored teenagers constantly tampered with the fence. They liked to sit on the narrow swath of concrete overlooking the train tracks, swinging their legs into empty space and shouting obscenities into the black tunnel. They were amused by the echo of their voices and relished the feeling of invincibility, no matter how brief.

There was also a long-standing Miracle Springs tradition that encouraged lovers to hang a small padlock from the fence and toss its key onto the tracks. If the wheels of a passing train flattened the key, the person who hung the padlock would win the heart of the person they most desired, as long as they remembered to scratch his or her initials into the key.

"Why would he go down there in the first place?" Nora murmured to herself.

Clearly disappointed by Nora's reaction to her announcement, Estella got up from her chair and crossed to the window to see if there were signs of activity outside.

"Maybe he wasn't pushed. Maybe he jumped," Estella said while scanning the park. "Think about it. No one travels to Miracle Springs because they're happy."

Nora considered this remark. "Not every out-of-towner comes here because they're unhappy, either. Or sick. Some people like the tranquility. Miracle Springs is an oasis. A respite from a noisy, frantic, demanding life that creates stress and fatigue. Our Wi-Fi is spotty, we don't have five hundred TV channels, and the pace is slow. People can find rest here. They can be quiet."

Estella rolled her eyes. "Quiet. Rest. Ugh! That's why this town is so awful. *I* don't want slow. I want roller-coaster fast! Trendy and fascinating. Risky and scandalous. Nothing in Miracle Springs has changed for fifty years. People flock to this place because they think it's magical. Whether it's in the water, the kale smoothies, or the sunrise yoga sessions—they believe in something I don't. But your man from the park bench? Word has it he tried everything. He meditated, took long hikes, got massages, went to the hot springs and thermal pools several times—"

"*Word has it?* He hasn't been dead an hour yet. Are people lined up at the top of the slope in hopes of catching a glimpse of his corpse?" Nora asked sharply. She couldn't explain why she felt defensive on the man's behalf. She didn't know him from Adam, but he'd been on his way to see her. He'd been coming to her for help. Somehow, she felt responsible for his welfare. Not only that, but she knew what it was like to be stared at, and she didn't like the idea of a crowd of strangers gathering to gawk at the man's broken body. The heat of her anger made her burn scars itch.

"Honey, I own a salon." Estella sounded pleased to have finally gotten a rise out of Nora. "When my clients see me, they start talking. They're practically wired to tell me the latest news, and there isn't much bigger news than an out-of-towner being flattened like a penny by the three o'clock train."

Nora gave a brief shake of her head, refusing to allow her mind to dwell on Estella's detailed imagery. "Why are people saying that he was pushed?"

Estella turned away from the window. "It's a lovely summer afternoon. It hasn't rained in days. The grass leading to the drop-off is dry. The concrete slab is dry. That means your man either crept through the hole in the fence and jumped in front of the incoming train because he couldn't face the future, or someone followed him down to the ledge and gave him a shove that sent him flying. Either way, his troubles are over."

And what were those troubles? Nora wondered, recalling their conversation on the park bench and how the man had admitted to having compromised his principles. He'd also men-

tioned that his partners were arriving on the afternoon train
and that he wanted to set things straight before then.

*Did he see suicide as his only solution? Was that his way of
making things right?*

More than most, Nora understood the allure of surrendering
to an endless sleep. She'd spent countless nights in a burn unit
longing for just that, but even though her spirit had given up,
her body refused to follow. And eventually, an Icelandic nurse
and a stack of books had shown her a way out. A way through.
The stories had shown her that the only way to escape the pain
was to pull it closer. To let it burn her like a second fire.

The sleigh bells rang, startling her out of her reverie, and another woman entered the shop. Unlike Estella, whose movements were languid and catlike, this woman, who had frizzy
blond hair and freckled skin, practically hummed with frenetic
energy.

It was Hester Winthrop of the Gingerbread House.

"That man! Neil." She pointed in the direction of the tunnel.
"I just made him a comfort scone. And now he's dead!"

Hester still wore her apron. Rorschach flour shapes covered
the cranberry-colored fabric and her hand trembled. Under
normal circumstances, Nora would offer a sympathetic murmur before finding an excuse to disappear deeper into the
bookshop, but she shocked herself by saying, "Would you like
some coffee?" She included Estella in the invitation with a
glance. "We could sit in the chairs by the ticket-agent's office."

"That would be nice," Hester said, tucking a flour-crusted
curl behind her ear.

Estella arched her brows and asked, "Got any whiskey back
there? Or a jar of white lightning tucked behind the encyclope-
dias?"

It took Nora a second to understand the reference. Though
she'd seen her fair share of locals on front porches, sipping the

clear liquor out of mason jars on sticky summer evenings, Nora had never tasted the stuff.

"I don't have any booze," Nora said, walking ahead of the other women. "But my coffee is strong."

In the ticket-agent's office, she filled two mugs and placed them on the counter.

Hester reached for the mug with the chocolate-chip cookie on the front and the text COME TO THE DARK SIDE. WE HAVE COOKIES on the back. She chuckled. "That's cute." She watched Estella pick up the second mug. "What does yours say?"

"ONLY TWO PERCENT OF THE WORLD HAS RED HAIR, SO I'M BASICALLY A MAJESTIC UNICORN." Estella nodded in approval. "I like it."

"How many mugs do you have?" Hester peered through the ticket window.

"Over a hundred. There's a whole pegboard. See?" Nora moved to the side to allow Hester an unobstructed view. "One row is just for kids. For their hot chocolate. Superman, Grumpy Cat, and Snoopy are their favorites."

A shadow flitted through Hester's eyes—a darting fish that spoke of a painful memory she hadn't wanted to surface. However, it disappeared when Estella asked Nora if she set aside a special mug for herself.

"No." Nora added a splash of cream to her I LOVE HOBBITS mug. "But I never buy a mug I wouldn't want to use. I hold each one to be sure it feels comfortable in my hand."

"Speaking of comfort, the way you give everyone a unique coffee mug is a bit like my scones," Hester said once they'd all settled in the circle of chairs next to the ticket booth. "I use a basic scone recipe and add fruit, nuts, and spices after meeting and speaking with my customer."

Estella was too interested to drink her coffee. "How does that work? You don't know these out-of-towners at all, yet they talk about how your scones can awaken old memories. I don't understand how you do it."

"I get a feeling from each person. Some people can see certain colors or energy around other people. Me? I read scents and flavors. I can only do it in my shop, though," Hester explained. "And it doesn't always work. Plenty of customers have been disappointed by my scones. Instead of finding a comforting memory, they're transported to a moment in time they'd rather forget."

"There's no such thing as forgetting," Nora murmured, and absently touched part of the jellyfish scar on her arm. "But what of the man? Neil. Tell me about the scone you made for him."

As Hester took a sip of coffee, her gaze turned distant. "Even though he ordered a comfort scone, I sensed that he didn't think he was worthy of comfort. He seemed weighed down by guilt. When people with an untroubled conscience enter my bakery, their faces light up like a Christmas-tree star. If they've come to Miracle Springs to seek relief from cancer or arthritis pain or what-have-you, they still glow with that firefly light when the aroma of fresh-baked bread envelops them. That scent speaks of coming home."

"I had no idea you were a baker *and* a poet!" Estella exclaimed playfully.

"Isn't there more to all of us than what people see?" Hester asked by way of reply. She paused for another sip of coffee. "Anyway, he reluctantly ordered a comfort scone to-go and told me he was planning to take it with him to Miracle Books. I guessed he was having a session with you. Was he?"

Nora inclined her head.

"So I started in on the usual small talk. I asked where he was from, how long he'd been in town, etcetera." Hester touched her lower lip. "I'm used to folks being on the quiet side, but this guy's lips were practically zipped closed. I decided it would take a powerful flavor combination to coax a good memory to the surface, so I went out on a limb and chose a wintery recipe: Peppermint mocha."

Estella moaned. "Oh, that sounds really good."

Hester smiled at her. "Thanks. Anyway, I added dark chocolate, chocolate chips, and cold coffee to the base batter. It took about fifteen minutes for the scone to bake and another five to cool. During that time, I learned that Neil worked for a property-management firm, whatever that means. After more gentle prodding, he explained that his company is responsible for the Meadows—that housing development everyone's been so riled up over."

Nora had read about the development in the *Miracle Springs Free Press.* It didn't matter to her whether or not some cookie-cutter subdivision was built on a ten-acre tract of pastoral farmland. As long as her tax bill wasn't raised and there was a chance that her regular customer base might expand, she was fine with the project. Other locals were anything but fine with it. And though Nora wasn't interested in gossip, the development was the most popular topic among the locals. Nora couldn't buy a bunch of bananas without hearing a barrage of impassioned complaints.

"I'm not upset about that project," Estella said. "More people means more clients for me. For all the local businesses. Does it bother either of you?"

Nora shook her head, but Hester frowned. "I'm fine with Miracle Springs growing, but I don't like the idea of rows upon rows of houses crammed together like sardines in a can. I saw the rendering for the Meadows. It's an appropriate name, seeing as there won't be a tree left in this so-called neighborhood." She splayed her hands. "There was almost no green space. And the houses are too big for their narrow plots. It'll become our town's ten-acre eyesore."

To Nora, this was discouraging news. One of her favorite things about Miracle Springs was its bucolic setting. Tucked between mountains in western North Carolina, the tiny town was gifted with the best of every season. It featured an incredible foliage show in the autumn, several inches of pristine snow in the winter, and an explosion of blooming flowers during the spring and summer months. The tree-lined streets bordered lovely gardens, gracing modest houses and charming cottages. There was a clear pride of place about Miracle Springs, which was reflected in the number of house tours and garden shows.

"Did you learn anything else about . . . Neil?" Nora felt strange speaking his name. To her, he was still the man from the park bench. She thought they'd have plenty of time for introductions when he came to Miracle Books.

"Not much," Hester said. "I had other customers to serve. When his scone was cool, I drizzled it with peppermint buttercream icing and boxed it for him. The moment he took the box, his expression changed. He could smell the chocolate and peppermint. He tried to hand the box back, saying that he didn't deserve it."

Estella grunted. "That's kind of rude. You'd just spent twenty minutes making him a custom scone."

"It was his guilt talking," Hester said. "I've seen the reaction before, so I pushed the box back and gave him a dash of Maya Angelou advice. I told him, 'As long as you're breathing, it's never too late to do some good.'"

"Since he's now stopped breathing, I'd say it *is* too late for him," Estella declared with finality.

Hester turned to Estella. "Maybe not. Maybe we can help him find some peace."

Nora didn't like Hester's choice of pronoun, but before she had a chance to respond, the sleigh bells clanged and a voice boomed out, "Ms. Pennington! Are you back there? The sheriff wants to see you."

Instead of shouting, Nora made her way to the front of the

store. Estella and Hester put down their coffee cups and trailed after her.

"What's this about?" Nora asked the man in the brown and khaki uniform.

The deputy, whose face was flushed with heat, excitement, and self-importance, removed his hat and wiped his brow with his forearm. "An out-of-towner has been killed and the sheriff needs to talk to you. Pronto. You too, ma'am," he said, including Hester in the summons.

Estella, who was unaccustomed to being ignored by a member of the opposite sex, thrust out her lower lip. "What about me?"

The deputy, who was in his mid-thirties, stood a fraction taller and flashed her a boyish smile. "You don't want any part of this mess, ma'am. It's mighty ugly."

"Call me Estella. Save your 'ma'ams' for the grannies and the church ladies. I'm single and a *very* devoted sinner." Estella winked at the deputy before whispering to Nora, "After my last appointment of the day, which is to give Chelsea Phillips her regular Jennifer Aniston color and haircut, I'll put on one of my slinkiest outfits and head up to the lodge to check out Neil's partners. They're bound to be drowning their sorrows at the bar and I'm sure one of them would like a pretty shoulder to cry on. I'll let you know if I learn anything."

Estella tossed her hair over her shoulder, releasing a tendril of jasmine scent into the air, and left the shop. The deputy, whose name badge identified him as Andrews, paused to watch her walk away. He then grabbed the door before it could fully close.

"Do you need to lock up?" he asked Nora.

She shook her head. "I just put a sign up next to the register. Most of my sales are by credit card, but the honor system works whenever I have to run a quick errand."

Andrews took in his surroundings for the first time. "I don't have the attention span for books," he said. "I figure if the story's really good, someone will turn it into a movie. Movies are more my speed."

"The book is always better than the movie," Hester said, voicing Nora's thoughts at the moment.

When she finished taping her sign to the register, Nora handed Andrews a used paperback of Orson Scott Card's *Ender's Game.* "Did you see this film?"

"Yeah." Andrews held the book as though he didn't know what to do with it. "It was okay."

Nora pointed at the dog-eared paperback. "I challenge you to read fifty pages and return it to me without reading another page."

"No problem," Andrews said, giving the book a dismissive smack against his thigh. "I've never met a book I managed to finish."

When Deputy Andrews led Nora and Hester into the small, masculine antechamber just outside Sheriff Hendricks's office, another local woman was already seated in one of the metal chairs.

The woman had café au lait skin, almond-shaped eyes, and close-cropped black hair. She wore the stark white scrubs identifying her as an employee of Miracle Springs Thermal Pools. Nora immediately recognized her as a bookstore customer even though she couldn't recall her name.

"Lord, but isn't this an awful thing?" the woman muttered upon seeing Nora and Hester.

"It is," Hester agreed, sinking into a chair. "I've seen you in the bakery. You like raisin bread, right? And when you need a special treat, you order a bear claw."

The woman smiled. "Guilty as charged." She briefly covered her mouth with her hand. "Not the best expression for this setting. My name's June Dixon, and since I look like the Good Humor Man, you can probably tell that I work at the pools.

And I know you two because I frequent both of your businesses. One of these days, you should pay me a visit at the thermal pools. I can't say whether the water performs miracles or not, but it definitely eases aches and pains."

"That sounds like heaven," Hester said. "I don't think I've relaxed in five years. I can't even remember the last time I had a nice, hot bubble bath."

Nora, who'd had enough heat for one lifetime, suppressed a frown. After all, June was merely being polite by inviting her to submerge her damaged skin in one of the pools fed by the thermal springs.

She was on the verge of politely declining when the door to the sheriff's office opened and a second deputy poked his head out. This officer was far older and more grizzled looking than Andrews. Ignoring the women, he crooked a finger at the younger deputy. "Sheriff wants to see you. ASAP."

Andrews scurried into the office. As soon as the door shut behind him, June giggled. "He's like a boy being called into the principal's office."

"Have you ever met Sheriff Todd Hendricks?" Hester asked her in a low voice. "Folks don't call him Sheriff Toad behind his back for nothing."

"Can't say I've had the pleasure," June said.

Hester snorted. "*I* have. He doesn't like women. Or at least, any woman who's dared to leave the 1950s behind. Every time he comes in the bakery, I cringe. He never fails to comment on how he thinks all women should be wearing aprons."

"Why don't you burn his bun next time?" Nora asked.

Hester shook her head. "I can't mess up a perfectly edible bun on purpose. It goes against my baker's code. Can't you give him a book to make him change his opinion on women?"

"I don't think a man like that will read Gloria Steinem without a gun to his head," Nora said. She looked at June. "I recognize you from your book purchases. You like almost every genre, but you're a binge genre reader. When you're on a science-fiction kick, you stay with sci-fi for weeks. Then, all of a sudden, you'll drop that genre and turn to historical fiction." She paused for breath. "Are you the one who told Neil about me?"

June spread her hands. "I didn't know if I was right to send him your way, but it *felt* right. Once, I overheard you work your special kind of healing. I wasn't trying to eavesdrop, mind you. What I was *trying* to do was trim down the stack of books I'd picked out from a dozen to half a dozen. My budget can't match my desires." She shrugged. "While I was sitting in my chair, making my tough choices, you spoke with a woman who couldn't get over the loss of her mother. Her mama had been gone for a year, but this poor girl was stuck. I heard her tell you what she'd been going through. I heard you give her books to help get her unstuck."

"So you thought I could do the same for Neil. Get him unstuck," Nora said. "And did he tell you what was troubling him?"

"He only dropped hints, but I got a sense that something shady was going on with the Meadows and Neil regretted his part in the shadiness." June made clicking noises with her tongue. "I believe he planned on making amends, but he needed inspiration. He came to Miracle Springs days ahead of his partners in search of healing. That's what he called it. But I think he was looking for something else."

Hester cocked her head. "Courage?"

"It's not easy to face your demons," June said, her gaze falling to her lap.

Nora saw that June was including herself in that statement, and when she glanced at Hester, it was clear that June's comment had affected her too.

Outsiders flock to Miracle Springs in hopes of being made whole, but how many of its residents are hiding wounds that have never healed? Nora thought.

In the silence, which was more reflective than uncomfortable, Nora felt a fragile connection with Hester and June. It was a feeling she recalled from her previous life—a tentative warmth that could be kindled into a real friendship.

You can't do the friend thing. Friends share their secrets, Nora reminded herself. Still, the three of them were sitting here now because a man had spoken to them. He was now dead, but he'd been on his way to Miracle Books. Therefore, Nora's only tie to the dead man was now Hester and June.

"I think you're right," Nora said to June. "I think Neil made decisions he couldn't live with any longer. He wanted to make amends. He didn't strike me as a man on the verge of suicide. If I had to guess, I'd say he took those long hikes and meditated because he was trying to figure out a way to undo whatever damage he, or his company, had caused. He did say *we* more than once."

"That means he wasn't solely responsible for the wrongdoing weighing him down with guilt. One or more of his partners must have been involved," Hester pointed out. "However, if the rest of his partners were on that three o'clock train—"

"Then who pushed him onto the tracks?" June asked angrily. "And what kind of person could do such a thing?"

The two women looked expectantly at Nora. She, in turn, fixed her eyes on the bubbled scar on the back of her hand.

"Someone who couldn't let Neil follow his conscience," she said. "This person couldn't allow Neil to rock the boat. Somehow, he or she must have known that Neil wanted to change."

"The sheriff will have to investigate the Meadows from all angles now. That way, Neil won't have died in vain," Hester said, though she didn't sound very confident in this outcome.

After two minutes in Sheriff Todd Hendricks's company, Nora's dislike for the corpulent local lawman made it difficult for her to picture him investigating anything that wasn't deep-fried or covered in brown gravy. He made no attempt to disguise that he found her unattractive to look at, and he only listened to her statement with half an ear. Nora tested this theory by pausing mid-sentence now and again. The sheriff would grunt as if she'd completed her thought and he'd pretend to jot notes on the legal pad balanced on his expansive belly.

"All right, I think we've got the gist," he said after Nora reached the part about Neil sacrificing his principles. "Thank you for your time."

Though Nora was eager to leave, she didn't care for how the sheriff appeared to be looking for evidence to support a single theory.

Standing tall, she gazed straight at the sheriff and said, "I don't think this man committed suicide."

Instead of looking at her, Sheriff Hendricks shot the grizzled deputy an amused glance. "Oh? Do you have a background in law enforcement that I'm unaware of"—he consulted his notes— "Ms. Pennington?"

"No, but I spoke with this man. He wasn't without hope. He wasn't ready to give up."

"Is this your female intuition talking?" the sheriff asked with unmistakable contempt.

On another day, Nora might wonder what kind of injury had been inflicted upon the sheriff to turn him into such a prig, but she was too focused on the dead man to be distracted. "Maybe," she said, knowing how lame that sounded. "But Hester and June will say that same thing."

"Oh, good. Two more females with *vibes*. At least one of you knows her way around the kitchen. That'll be all, Ms. Pennington. We'll call if we need anything else." The sheriff jerked his enormous head in the direction of the door, causing his multiple chins to jiggle.

Nora exited the office. She walked over to where Hester and June were waiting and whispered, "That toad is going to rule Neil's death a suicide, which means no one will dig deeper into the company behind the Meadows."

"We can't let that happen," Hester said, her cheeks flushing with indignation.

June spread her hands. "But what can we do?"

Nora suddenly felt an intense pins-and-needles sensation across every centimeter of her scarred skin.

"Come to the bookstore tonight," she said, folding her bad arm under her good one. "At nine. I don't know how to make this right, but we'll have to find a way."

"I'll be there," Hester said.

"So will I," echoed June.

Nora left the station, feeling strangely electric and a little sick to her stomach all at once.

Chapter 3

*There is no greater agony than bearing an untold
story inside you.*

                                        —Maya Angelou

"What's with all the cats?" Estella jerked her thumb toward
the back door.

Nora had kept the front of the store dark, leaving only the
single bulb over the rear entrance burning. She'd also taped a
note just above the handle instructing Hester, June, and Estella
to forgo ringing the bell.

The door is unlocked. Come in, she'd written, not wanting to
explain that the delivery bell was broken and she didn't feel like
paying to have it fixed.

Hester, who'd arrived shortly before Estella, placed a pair of
cookie tins on the mirrored coffee table that sat in the middle of
five chairs. The soft lights from two table lamps reflected off the
mirror's surface, creating an ambiance of intimacy and hushed
reverence. Hester must have felt it too, for she spoke in what
Nora thought of as library volume. "I've seen that herd of cats
several times. It's the craziest thing, but they follow a man
around town in the dead of night."

"I've seen that phenomenon too," Estella said. She tossed
her beaded clutch onto a side table and dropped into a chair

with a grateful sigh. "I guess I'm not the only person awake at all hours. The only difference is, I don't wander the streets trailed by a mob of mewling felines."

"Trust me, I'm not trying to draw attention to myself. Walking is the only thing that tires me out."

Hester and Estella gaped at June as she stepped into the ring of lamplight.

"If I don't get outside and move, I can't go back to sleep," June continued. "I try to exercise every day, but I don't always find the time. Or the energy."

"I'm sorry I thought you were a man. It must be the dark clothes and that baseball cap you always wear," Estella said, still staring at June in astonishment. "What *is* the deal with the cats?"

Nora had no idea what the other women were talking about and said as much.

"Before I start explaining, would anyone else like a beer? I brought extra." June gestured at the soft cooler she'd deposited on the coffee table. Nora and Hester politely declined while Estella said that she'd already had her fill of wine up at the lodge.

"Every now and then, I like a cold beer on a sweaty summer night. The rest of the year, I don't touch the stuff," June said, opening her can. There was a *snap* followed by a hiss of air. June smiled and took a quick sip before wriggling deeper into her chair. "The only reason I could afford my house is because the crazy cat lady who lived there before me had passed on and left it in a horrible state. I'm not using the term *crazy* lightly, either. We all have our problems, but this woman had *lost* it. She dug up all the grass in the backyard and replaced it with catnip. I did my best to get rid of it, but catnip is seriously invasive. Lord, but it spreads! And when I say spreads, I mean everywhere! In the vegetable garden, in between the fence slats, under the porch. I swear it grows around the mailbox and under my car tires while I'm asleep."

Hester giggled. "Were the cats hanging around before you moved in?"

June nodded. "I didn't realize at first because they didn't show up until nightfall. Only a few are feral. I've alerted animal control a dozen times, and they keep promising to come out and trap the wild ones, but they never do. The rest of the cats wear collars. They like my house because they loved the former owner. Every Sunday, this lady fed an entire roasted chicken to the cats. She'd sit on the front steps and toss out pieces to whoever showed up for supper. So my backyard smells like catnip and my front yard smells like KFC."

Now Estella was giggling too. "No wonder cats keep appearing. They're hoping you'll be the next crazy cat lady."

"But why do they follow you when you walk?" Nora asked.

June shrugged. "My signature scent is probably catnip cologne. I swear the stuff is growing between the walls."

"You're like a reluctant Pied Piper," Hester said.

Nora had to see this for herself. She walked to the back door and slowly cracked it open. The narrow lane behind the building, which faced the abandoned train tracks, was deserted.

"They've probably gone home," said June when Nora returned to the circle of chairs. "But if you want to see the kitty parade, just get up between two and four. Chances are we'll be out walking."

"What keeps you from sleeping?" Nora asked and immediately regretted the question. She waved her hands as if she could erase her words. "Never mind. Let's talk about why we're here."

Hester popped the lids off her cookie tins. "I brought snacks. Cheddar-cheese straws and peach-pie bites."

Nora retrieved napkins, a pitcher of lemonade, and a bowl of fresh blackberries from the ticket-agent's office. She'd picked the berries after supper, washed them, and put them in a vintage milk glass bowl that had been on display on a shelf stuffed with gardening books. After tonight, the bowl would be cleaned and returned to its shelf for a future Miracle Books customer to find.

"If you want lemonade or water, help yourself to a coffee mug from the back," Nora said.

When no one moved, Estella looked at Hester and June. "Nora told me about her interview with the sheriff. Did the two of you have a similar experience?"

"Yes," Hester said. "It was obvious to me that they plan to rule Neil's death a suicide."

June smirked. "The sheriff was only interested in part of my statement. When I said that Neil seemed like a troubled soul, Hendricks immediately stopped listening. I had more to say, but he didn't want to hear it." Her jaw clenched in anger. "I don't put up with rudeness, so I refused to budge from my chair. I calmly implored the sheriff not to judge the dead man so hastily, but Sheriff Toad turned nasty like *that*." She snapped her fingers and turned to Hester. "You weren't kidding when you said that he wasn't fond of women."

"Oh, he's fond of them, all right," said Estella scornfully. "But only if they're naked and Photoshopped until they look like cartoon characters. He also pays for online sex chats. I knew the Toad was a prick even without hearing all this dirt about him from a client who has the misfortune of working for his department, but I never gave much thought about him as the leader of our law enforcement. It sounds like he's opting for the easiest ruling out of sheer laziness."

"It's also the least controversial ruling because only someone close to Neil could protest," Nora pointed out. "Could the sheriff be involved with the Meadows?"

June put down her beer and frowned. "As an investor or something along those lines?"

Since none of the group had an inkling about the sheriff's financial dealings, Hester changed the subject. "Were you able to learn anything at the lodge this evening?" she asked Estella.

Estella loved being the center of attention. While the rest of the women waited for her reply, she uncrossed her legs, languidly stretched out her hand, helped herself to a cheese straw, and then sat back and recrossed her legs.

If she were a cat, she'd be purring right now, Nora thought.

"Neil Parrish is the full name of our dead guy," Estella began. Seeing the looks of disapproval from her audience, she hastily amended her last remark. "Our victim. Sorry." She took an embarrassed nibble from the end of the cheese straw. "He worked for a firm called Pine Ridge Properties. He was a money guy. I'd like to pretend to understand more of what I heard, but what I know about commercial real-estate investment could fit in a thimble."

"Don't sweat it, sugar. I bet you did just fine," June said.

The smile Estella flashed June was so warm that Nora wondered if the town siren had any female friends. Judging from her reaction, she wasn't used to expressions of kindness from other women.

"I'll see what cyberspace says about Neil's firm while you continue with your story," Nora told Estella as she booted up her laptop. As a former librarian, Nora was adept at online research, but she'd never truly relied on technology until she'd opened Miracle Books. She now managed her inventory, balanced her budget, and showcased the store's treasures on a website she designed and maintained. What she never did was venture onto social-media sites or search for people from her former life. In Nora's mind, that woman was every bit as dead as Neil Parrish.

"Well, I stayed on the fringes of their group at the beginning," Estella said, continuing her narrative. "There are four men and one woman—all very polished and smooth. Big-city folks. Fast talkers. Used to their drink. You know Bob Loman? The head bartender at the Oasis Bar?" Estella met blank stares all around. "You three don't get out much, do you?"

"Do you have any idea how early bakers get up in the morning?" Hester asked.

Estella blinked. "No. What time?"

"I'm at the Gingerbread House by four-thirty. Except Sundays," Hester said. "That's a half day. Like Nora, I take Mondays off."

Estella whistled. "I don't see my first client until ten. I am *not* a morning person. Anyway, Bob has a way with people. He gets them to relax pretty quickly. And he's a magician at small talk, but Neil's partners barely acknowledged his existence. They took their drinks to a table and sat in these wonderful, high-back rattan chairs." She stopped again. "Assuming none of you have been to the Oasis, there's an L-shaped bar on one side of the room and small booths lining the wall on the other side. In the middle, you've got rattan chairs, brass and wooden-drum side tables, and potted palms. The black-and-white checked tile floor and the banana-leaf wallpaper add to the tropical atmosphere. Soft Cuban music plays in the background."

"Sounds like a vacation spot," June said.

"That's the idea, but Neil's partners weren't relaxing at all. Not that I could blame them," Estella added. "The train they rode in on flattened their coworker." She held up her hands in a defensive gesture. "I'm not trying to be crass. I'm only trying to point out the obvious. Neil's people should have been shocked and upset."

Nora looked up from her laptop screen. "They weren't?"

"During the first round of drinks, maybe. But as happy hour wore on, they acted more worried than upset." Estella took another bite of her cheese straw and seemed to be reflecting as she chewed.

"Do you think they were worried about their company?" Hester asked.

Estella considered this. "It's possible. I mean, two of the men had their smartphones out the whole time and were texting like crazy, but lots of people send texts after a tragedy."

June snorted. "The millennial generation, maybe. I'm in my forties, and if my coworker had been run over by a train, my phone would be the last thing I'd reach for. I'd probably want to be alone. I'd go for a walk or something. Being outside always soothes me."

"I'd be the same," Hester said. "But I'm not like most thirty-five-year-olds."

June plucked a mini–peach pie from the cookie tin and used it to salute Hester. "And for that, I sure am grateful!"

Now it was Hester's turn to reward June with a radiant smile.

"You said you were going to try to cozy up to one of the Pine Ridge men. Was your subterfuge successful?" Nora hated to ruin the warm moment, but she wanted to see if Estella had anything else to share before the focus shifted to what was on her laptop screen.

Estella shot her a wry grin. "Subterfuge? Makes me sound like Mata Hari."

Realizing that she sounded like she was plucking terms from novels, Nora blushed. The octopi scars on her cheek twitched.

"I take that as a compliment," Estella said, seeing Nora's discomfort. "And I felt like I was in a spy novel. Not a Tom Clancy or anything, but I did sit right behind their table. Only they couldn't see me because of how high the chair backs are. Plus, there was a potted palm between us. I used my compact to steal glances at them."

"Clever." Hester poured three glasses of lemonade and offered one to Estella.

Estella stared at her glass as though consuming a mixture of lemon juice, sugar, and cold water was the most ridiculous thing in the world, and then downed the contents in several swallows. "I only heard hushed murmurs and eventually, the woman decided to go to her room. That left the tall, tan, suave drink of water—Mr. Hunk—and his twitchy, spidery-looking friend. I wanted to flirt with Mr. Hunk, of course, but I knew I'd get much further with . . ." She wiggled her index finger, her lips pursed in thought. Glancing at Nora, she asked, "Who was Dracula's servant?"

"R.M. Renfield," Nora said. "The one who ate the insects?"

June, who'd just taken a bite of her second mini–peach pie, groaned in protest or disgust. Nora wasn't sure which.

"Renfield!" Estella cried. "That's exactly who the other guy reminded me of. He's a birthday cake or two away from turning sixty and was the oldest of the group by far. He was also the most anxious. He kept dabbing his forehead with a handkerchief, and he drank more than the others. So when Mr. Hunk headed to the restroom, I made my move on Renfield."

"Why am I feeling nervous for you?" Hester was on the edge of her seat. "This has already happened, but it's like I'm right there with you."

"You're a good storyteller," Nora told Estella. "And you're just getting to the best part, aren't you?"

Estella looked uncertain. "Well, I didn't have time to play it coy because Mr. Hunk wouldn't be gone long, so I just plunked down next to Renfield and acted surprised and the tiniest bit offended that he'd started drinking without me."

June barked out a hearty laugh. "Oh, Lordy, I wish I could have seen that man's face."

"He said, 'Excuse me?' and I pretended to be flustered. 'Aren't you my blind date?' I whispered, scooting my chair closer to his. I let my hand rest on his forearm, which is when I noticed the writing on his cocktail napkin."

Nora felt an inexplicable thrill of excitement. Finally: a clue.

"Don't stop now, honey," June commanded.

"The words didn't make sense to me," Estella admitted. "They might have been people's initials or a place, and I really hope I remembered them correctly. I wrote them down as soon as I put some distance between myself and Renfield." She opened her beaded clutch and removed a napkin embossed with a green palm tree and the words *Relax, Escape, Enjoy* in cursive font. Estella had written three words of her own along the bottom edge of the napkin. Unfortunately, the ink had gotten wet and was now smudged.

Hester pointed at the napkin. "Please tell me you can still read that."

"Yeah, I can." Estella squinted at the words. "*DHCB* was the first batch of abbreviations or initials or what-have-you. *A.G.* was second. The last was just one word. *Buford.*"

The other three women exchanged befuddled glances.

"Buford?" June threw her hands in the air. "Is that a person or place?"

"I don't know. I didn't have time to work my usual magic, so I couldn't get any background on the firm, the Meadows, or Neil's role," Estella said, pouting just a little. "The only thing I was able to do was catch a glimpse at that napkin before Renfield told me that his name was Fenton Greer and that he wasn't my blind date. However, he also told me that although his partner would be returning from the restroom at any moment, he'd be glad to meet me on Wednesday night for a rain check on our nonexistent date."

"Did you agree?" Hester asked breathlessly.

"Of course." Estella looked at Hester as though she wasn't right in the head. "How else would I learn more about these people?"

Estella had unwittingly provided Nora with the perfect segue to share the results of her Google search on Pine Ridge Properties. "I can fill in a few blanks," she said, swiveling the computer to allow everyone a view of the screen.

The Pine Ridge Properties homepage was comprised of simple text and colorful photographs depicting a rosy vision of the

American dream. There was a Hispanic woman tending a lush flower garden, a Norman Rockwell father pushing a golden-haired girl on a swing, a Labrador retriever sitting on a welcome mat, an elderly Asian couple sharing a porch swing, and, in the largest photograph, an African-American family posing outside their picture-perfect home.

"*Pine Ridge Properties: We Build Dreams, One House at a Time.*" June nodded thoughtfully. "That slogan has a nice ring to it. They included multiple ethnicities. And is that a link leading to more detail about their green building practices?" Her eyebrows began climbing her forehead. "This site makes them look like such a great company, but Estella described snake-oil salesmen."

"They must be engaging in shady business practices," Nora said. "It has to be big, whatever it is, because of how deeply Neil regretted his involvement."

Estella waved a hand. "Someone was willing to kill to keep these practices from becoming known, so the shadiness must be ongoing. It must involve truckloads of money. Look how slick this website is."

"The Meadows isn't their only project." Nora leaned over the laptop and clicked a map link. "This summer, Pine Ridge Properties plans to break ground on another dream community east of Asheville, and they've already begun putting up homes in a town called Bent Creek."

"Can you click on the *Meet Our Team* link?" Hester asked.

Nora complied and the four women crowded even closer to the screen.

"That's the group from the bar!" Estella exclaimed, tapping the screen with an acrylic nail. "There's Renfield, aka Fenton Greer, followed by the token woman, Vanessa MacCavity, and Neil Parrish." She studied the images for several more seconds. "We're missing the hot guy. Mr. Hunk."

"Maybe he's listed under this." Hester pointed at another link entitled *Partners*.

Nora clicked on the word and Estella immediately said, "There he is. The tan guy with the dark hair."

"Collin Stone of Stone Construction," Nora murmured aloud. "No wonder he's sun-kissed. He must spend plenty of time outdoors." She continued scanning the names and faces on the page. The other partners were investors, loan officers, Realtors, and closing attorneys in the towns of Fine's Creek and Walnut. When Nora scrolled down, the Miracle Springs partners appeared. These included Dawson Hendricks of Madison County Community Bank and Annette Goldsmith of Star Realty.

Nora glanced at the other women. "Is Dawson related—?"

"To Sheriff Toad?" Hester cut in. "Yes, Dawson's his older brother. There are three Hendricks boys. The youngest moved to the Midwest and rarely comes back to visit his folks."

Estella smirked. "Can you blame him? If I ever get out of this place, I won't come back at all."

"Why do you hate Miracle Springs?" June asked very softly.

"It's a long, sad story," Estella muttered.

Nora made a sweeping gesture, indicating the bookshelves surrounding them. "You're in good company."

Estella rewarded her with a small smile. "I guess I am. And I'm sure my story isn't the longest, the saddest, or the most unique. People have also been revising it and adding a shitload of fictional elements to it since I was a teenager. Whenever I hear the latest version, I want to laugh. Most folks in this town have no clue what they're talking about when they start jawing about me." She fixed an angry gaze on the nearest bookshelf, which featured Stephen King paperbacks and a collection of plastic Halloween pumpkins from the 1950s. "If I cared, I could set the record straight, but I don't. Neil Parrish, on the other hand, doesn't have a voice anymore. Who will tell the correct version of his story?"

Nora had never heard such an impassioned speech from Estella, but the words moved her. "We will."

"How?" Hester wanted to know. "All we have are a few initials."

"We have much more than that," Nora said. "We have Mata Hari. She already has a date with one of Neil's partners and will learn everything she can from him. June? Can you get close to these people if they come to the thermal pools for a dip?"

A big grin spread across June's face. "I sure can. Sounds echo like you wouldn't believe in the bathhouse. If any of these Pine Ridge folk so much as whisper in each other's ear, I'll know it."

"Good." Nora looked at Hester. "Tomorrow's Monday. You and I are both off. How do you feel about visiting the model home at the Meadows? We can get a read on Annette Goldsmith of Star Realty."

"I'm game, though it might seem odd for me to be looking at new construction, considering I already have a house."

Nora shrugged. "So do I, but real-estate agents are always trying to up-sell people. You watch. Annette will do everything in her power to turn our curiosity into a signature and a down payment."

"You might have to take this a step farther," Estella said. "If you pick a house plan, you can then make an appointment with Dawson Hendricks at the bank. You don't need to fill out all the paperwork. Just stay long enough to drop Neil's name and observe Dawson's reaction."

June stared at Estella. "You're one smart cookie. Anyone ever tell you that?"

"Not really," Estella whispered in a low voice.

Hoping to keep a firm hold on the positive energy that had been building among the four of them, Nora said, "The key to our success lies in careful listening. And secrecy. From now on, we can only trust each another."

Hester looked dubious. She twisted a corkscrew curl around her index finger, released it, and repeated the movement. "Please don't take this personally, but I'm way out of practice when it comes to trusting people. I like all of you. I do. But how can I know that it's safe to trust you three?"

Estella and June murmured in agreement.

Nora was silent for a long time—so long that the other women exchanged nervous glances.

Tracing the puckered edge of one of her scars, Nora felt where the smooth, undamaged flesh met the grafted skin. She was imperfect. That much she knew. She was reminded of it every time she looked in the mirror. Every time she glanced down at her arm. Every time someone's gaze lingered on her face. But she had her voice and what was left of her damaged heart.

Glancing at the closest bookshelf, Nora Pennington decided that it was time to do more than just survive. It was time to live again.

"There's only one way to gain trust," she said, turning to face Hester, June, and Estella. "We have to tell each other our stories."

Chapter 4

Peace and a well-built house cannot be bought too dearly.

—Danish Proverb

Nora sat at the café table on her little front porch and watched the sun wash over the hills surrounding Miracle Springs. Though she was up earlier than usual, she imagined dozens of hikers were already stirring along the Appalachian Trail.

Summer was the high-traffic season on the Trail, and Miracle Springs was a popular destination with hikers due to its unique overlooks, campsites, tree-house lodging, shops, and hot springs. The fact that the Trail ran very close to downtown was mutually beneficial for the local businesses. Thru-hikers—those people traveling from the start of the Trail in Georgia to its end in Maine—could often stow their gear while they dined or shopped.

Nora had often heard lodge guests marvel over how hikers were able to carry so many supplies on their backs.

"I couldn't live without my coffeemaker," one would say while watching a hiker shrug on a loaded pack.

"Or a hot shower," another might add, considering the idea with a mixture of wonder and distaste.

Nora wasn't fond of camping and understood the desire for

creature comforts. However, when it came to traveling light, she and the hikers had more in common than the tourists staying at the lodge.

Once, Nora had lived in a 1920s brick Colonial. It had nine-foot ceilings, hardwood floors, five fireplaces, a basement, a pergola, a garden with a working fountain, and a never-ending list of problems. When Nora wasn't busy with her librarian duties, she spent most of her free time cleaning the house, doing yard work, or waiting on a repairman.

Caboose Cottage made no such demands of her. With only four rooms—a kitchen, living room, bedroom, and bathroom—there wasn't an inch of wasted space. She'd also had the caboose platform leading to the front door extended into a covered deck, which gave her another place to read, eat, or to sit and reflect.

To make the winters as cozy as possible, Nora had splurged on a miniature cast-iron woodstove. Originally manufactured to be used on boats, the tiny stove was perfect for Nora's tiny house. It put out an impressive amount of heat and cost pennies to operate, because firewood in the mountains of western North Carolina didn't cost much.

Both locals and out-of-towners were fascinated by Caboose Cottage. They were interested in its diminutive footprint and design details, and never tired of asking Nora how she could possibly keep her possessions in such a tiny space.

"Where do you put your clothes?" Estella had once asked. "And your shoes, makeup, jewelry, and that sort of stuff?"

But that was just it: Nora didn't own that sort of stuff. Her wardrobe consisted of jeans and a handful of T-shirts, blouses, and sweaters. She had sneakers, two pairs of flats, and a pair of good snow boots. Other than her mother's pearl earrings, she didn't wear jewelry. And though she used makeup, Nora's entire cosmetics collection could fit inside a cookie jar, a fact that would have stunned Estella into speechlessness.

Knowing everyone's natural curiosity about Caboose Cottage, Nora was fully prepared for Hester to show up at her door that morning and launch into a predictable line of questions about Nora's lack of possessions—especially when it came to personal items like photographs, school yearbooks, or any piece of minutia that tied Nora to a family or friends.

"I know you've probably eaten," Hester said, joining Nora on the porch. "I brought you a loaf of bread for later. It's yesterday's bread, but it's still better than what you can get at the store."

Nora accepted the white paper bag. "Thanks. What kind is it?"

"Corn bread. Though I love baking it in the summer because of how it makes the whole bakery smell, I'd rather eat it in the wintertime with a big bowl of chili." Instead of taking a seat at the café table with Nora, Hester settled into the rocking chair on the other side of the front door. "I can't resist a rocker. I have a glider on my porch. It's nice, but it's just not the same. Plus, it squeaks whenever I move. Drives me crazy. I've used WD-forty on every inch of that thing and I can't find the source of the squeak. It's like a smoke-detector battery going off somewhere in your house, but you can't figure out where." She laughed. "I guess you don't have that problem."

Nora smiled. "Nope."

"It's really peaceful here. You don't have a single neighbor." Hester stared out at the railroad tracks. "What's it like when a train comes through?"

"It's loud. The whole house shakes." Nora shared the experience of her first night in her new home. "It felt like the cinder blocks wouldn't hold and I was going to roll right down the hill onto the tracks." She shook her head at the memory. "I was too wound up to go back to sleep, but I got used to the rattling and whistles pretty quickly. Actually, I don't think I could sleep without them now. Part of me listens for the freight trains at night and the passenger trains during the day. I'm not sure why."

Hester looked at her. "Well, you bought the old train station, you brew coffee in the ticket office, and you live closer to the tracks than anyone else in town. Maybe you're our unofficial stationmaster."

Nora laughed. "Do you want a tour of the stationmaster's caboose before we spend the next hour or so lying through our teeth?"

Hester did, and Nora was relieved with how the town baker behaved inside her sanctuary. From the moment she entered the living room, with its comfy couch, woodstove, bookshelves, and television hidden inside a coffee table, Hester was enchanted, but never too nosy.

"I love this!" she exclaimed in a hushed voice, her wide-eyed gaze catching sight of Nora's office nook. "Are there secret compartments in every room?"

"I'll show you a few." Nora led her into the kitchen, which had exposed beams on the ceiling, a brick arch above the cooktop, a cobalt-blue AGA electric oven, and a full-sized refrigerator.

Nora reached under one of the wooden countertops and pulled out the hidden cutting-board segment before revealing the spice-rack shelf on wheels next to the fridge. Plastic bags were stored on the inside of a cupboard door and canned goods, sauce jars, and glass bottles were stored on a shelf built between the studs. Using her foot, Nora shoved her jute rug to one side with her foot and indicated that Hester should take hold of the metal ring in the hardwood floor.

"No way!" Hester cried when she curled the ring under her index finger and gave it a yank, opening the lid to the subfloor storage cupboard.

After that, Nora showed her the storage spaces under her

bed, on both sides of her bathroom mirror, and those tucked away in her minute laundry room.

"If I lived here, I'd never get tired of putting things away. And if you knew what kind of housekeeper I was, you'd understand the significance of that statement," said Hester when the tour was over and they'd returned to the deck platform. "Your house is the perfect blend of cozy, comfortable, chic, and fun. It's a good thing Annette Goldsmith hasn't seen this place or she'd realize she could never sell you something better."

"Then let's hope I can disguise how much I love it," Nora said. After she pulled a baseball cap low over her brow—which had been covered with sunscreen, along with the rest of her exposed skin—she and Hester mounted their bicycles and rode uphill to the Meadows.

Annette, a leggy blonde in an ivory suit and leopard-print heels, was dusting the leaves on an artificial plant when Nora and Hester entered the model home.

The Realtor greeted them with a thousand-watt smile, which faltered slightly when she noticed Nora's scars, and invited them to walk around the house at their leisure.

"I'm not the type of agent who trails after you, spouting sales pitches while you're trying to get a feel for a place," Annette assured them with another electric smile. "Take your time. Open and close cabinets. Look inside all the closets. Knock on the doors to check for thickness. Make yourselves at home. If you have any questions, just holler. I'll be out on the front porch, watering the ferns."

As soon as Annette stepped outside, Hester turned to Nora. "What should we do?"

"We'd better take a quick look at the house," Nora said. "And while she's out of sight and hearing for a few minutes, we should snoop in her office."

Hester twisted a curl around her finger. "People get away with that stuff in books. But you and I will probably get caught."

"We won't," Nora said. "You'll keep an eye out for Annette, and I'll be very careful to put things back exactly as they were."

Still fidgeting with her hair, Hester proceeded upstairs. The two women swiftly viewed the spare bedrooms, baths, and attic space before returning to the main floor to check out the master suite, kitchen, and laundry room. Nora then ducked into the office, while Hester took up a guard position in the front hall. She held a folder packed with papers on the Meadows and the plan was for her to drop it on the floor as soon as Annette reentered the model home. The commotion would serve a dual purpose. It would raise the alarm for Nora and prevent Annette's immediate return to the office, as she'd feel compelled to help gather the scattered papers.

The office was pin-neat. Annette's polished wood desk held a computer, a leather penholder, a stapler, a plastic display filled with color brochures, and a brass nameplate. There was a noticeable absence of personal items—photographs, awards, knick-knacks, rubber-band balls. The most significant item appeared to be a weekly calendar attached to a clipboard. Nearly every blank was filled with surnames. Nora read each name and though she recognized a few as customers of Miracle Books, most were unfamiliar.

Nora touched the computer keyboard and was unsurprised when the screen lit up, a blinking cursor waiting for her to enter a password. Pushing Annette's ergonomic leather chair to the side, Nora opened the top desk drawer. She found the usual assortment of paper clips, staples, pushpins, postage stamps, sticky notes, and other paper-related detritus, as well as a small set of keys. Nora let those be for the moment and hurriedly examined the other drawers, but the desk was mostly a receptacle

for postcards, leaflets, brochures and a lifetime supply of Annette's business cards.

That is, until Nora tried the bottom drawer on the right-
hand side. She found that drawer locked.

"Ah!" she murmured, reaching for the small keys.

Unfortunately, her triumph was short-lived. The keys didn't
open the lock. They belonged to another lock altogether.

Nora glanced around the room, which contained no other
furniture other than a pair of guest chairs facing Annette's desk.
Her eyes fell on the double doors on the opposite wall.

What skeleton is in your closet? she thought, and immediately
chided herself for the clichéd language. *You're no Angela Lans-
bury,* she continued to berate herself as she moved to the closet.

Behind the double doors, she found that a file cabinet occupied most of the closet. She tugged on the topmost drawer, but
it wouldn't budge, so she tried the keys again. This time, she
met with success.

As Nora hurriedly read the carefully printed labels, it appeared that the hanging files contained run-of-the-mill Realtor
paperwork. There were separate files on the Meadows house
plans, black-and-white maps showing the numbered lots, lists
of available upgrades, blank contracts, HUD statements, and
more. It wasn't until Nora opened the second drawer that she
discovered a connection to Neil Parrish.

Behind a file folder marked CALLBACKS was a folder labeled
NP CLIENTS.

Just as Nora shoved the rest of the folders back in order to
peek into Neil's file, she heard a squawk of dismay followed by
a nervous giggle coming from the front hall.

Annette was finished with her watering.

Nora dug her cell phone out of her pocket, snapped a photo
of the document in Neil's folder without really looking at it, replaced the file, and closed and locked the cabinet. She barely

had time to shut the closet doors, return the key to Annette's desk, and push Annette's chair back into place before Hester barreled into the room.

"I am *such* a klutz!" she exclaimed. "I dropped this and every single paper fell out. Guess I haven't had enough caffeine yet."

Annette entered the office wearing her saleswoman smile. "We have a Keurig in the kitchen. Would you both like a cup of coffee? We can get to know each other a little."

"All right," Nora said after the slightest pause. She didn't want to seem too eager.

In the kitchen, which was easily four times the size of Nora's, Annette showed Nora and Hester the selection of Keurig pods. "There's sugar and artificial sweetener on the tray next to the machine and skim milk and half-and-half are in the fridge," she said. "Help yourselves. I'm going to grab some literature from my desk."

Nora felt a prick of unease. Would Annette notice anything amiss in her office? Had Nora accidentally moved the pen-holder or keyboard? She didn't think so, but doubt wormed its way into her mind.

"Any luck?" Hester whispered.

"I'm not sure," Nora replied in a low voice. "We'll listen to her pitch as planned, but we need to slip Neil's name in when she doesn't expect it and gauge her reaction."

The two women finished preparing their coffee and had carried their mugs to the kitchen table by the time Annette returned.

"Sorry!" she said, waving with her cell phone. "One of my clients has been going back and forth between two lots and finally made a decision. He wanted to tell me right away, but I hope I didn't keep you waiting long."

"Not at all," Hester assured her. "I haven't even had the chance to try my Fog Chaser blend."

Annette adopted a chastened expression. "Please enjoy your coffee. While you ladies are relaxing, I'll tell you a bit more about the Meadows and the kind of community we're building here in beautiful Miracle Springs."

Hester studied Annette over the rim of her mug. "Do you live in the area? I don't think I've seen you in my bakery. I own the Gingerbread House."

"I drive up from Asheville every day. That's my home base," Annette said as she turned a map of the Meadows to face Hester and Nora. "But you probably wouldn't bump into me even if I didn't live over forty-five minutes away because I've followed the Paleo Diet. And since I avoid eating wheat or sugar, I don't go to bakeries. However, I've heard lots of people talk about your delicious treats since I started working here, so you must be really good at what you do."

This time, when Annette flashed her trademark smile, Hester didn't echo the expression. "No wheat or sugar? *Ever?*" She shook her head. "If I were told that I could never again eat a slice of homemade bread—still warm from the oven—I wouldn't see a reason to go on living."

"Well, you'd have plenty of room to bake bread in a kitchen of this size," Nora said, hoping to gain favor with Annette by giving her an opening to launch her pitch.

The real-estate agent proudly glanced around the room as though she'd built it herself. "You certainly would! You could even upgrade to a commercial-grade oven. That's the beauty of working with the builder one-on-one. You'd end up with the house of your dreams." She paused. "Are you thinking about building your dream home, Hester?"

"I'm mostly curious about the cost," Hester said. "I don't think I need more space than I already have. Nora, on the other hand, lives in a train car. It's super-cute, but it's small."

Annette couldn't conceal her astonishment. "A train car?"

"A refurbished caboose," Nora said, feeling the need to defend her home. "It's part of the tiny-house movement."

"Ooooh." Annette drew out the word like a singer holding a note. Though momentarily taken aback, she swiftly recovered. "Well, if it's more space you need, we can give it to you. How many bedrooms are you looking for?"

And so Nora found herself dictating a list of false desires to Annette, who nodded encouragingly while jotting notes on a legal pad.

"I think the Cambridge plan might be right up your alley," she said when Nora was done. After opening the brochure showing an artist's rendering of a brick Cape Cod featuring all the contemporary amenities, Annette gave Nora and Hester several seconds to examine the attractive drawing before pointing out how the floor plan would provide Nora with all the space she needed. She then described which lots best suited the Cambridge plan and asked her guests if they'd like to tour the lots via golf cart.

Since Nora had yet to slip Neil's name into the conversation, she agreed, and Annette produced a set of keys from the pocket of her suit jacket. "Great! We can talk more as we drive."

The golf cart was parked in the model home's garage next to what Nora presumed was Annette's black BMW SUV. The BMW looked new, sleek, and expensive, and Nora wondered what Annette made in commission on each house sale. For a woman in her early thirties, she seemed to be doing quite well—at least, judging by her clothes and car. Nora decided to find out a bit more.

"Do you live in a Pine Ridge house?" she asked as Annette started up the golf cart.

"No," Annette replied airily. "Pine Ridge doesn't have communities in downtown Asheville. That's where I shop and work out. I also wanted maintenance-free living because I'm away from home all the time, so I bought a condo. It was a recent purchase, which is a plus because I can identify with the questions and concerns my customers have when buying a new home."

Nora made an appreciative noise and Annette proceeded to drive along the main road, pointing out certain lots that were ideal for the Cambridge plan.

"This is really exciting," Nora said after Annette paused to show them a corner lot. "But I don't know if I can afford to build, especially after seeing the base price on the brochure."

Annette was unfazed by Nora's apprehension. She'd succeeded in creating interest, which was her goal. The money matters were up to someone else. "We have a terrific partnership with Madison County Community Bank. If you call Dawson Hendricks, I bet he can show you that building a custom home in the Meadows is a *very* real possibility. And a home crafted by Pine Ridge is a great investment."

"What about the building schedule?" Hester piped up from the backseat. "Won't things run behind after that horrible accident with your associate—I'm sorry, I forgot his name."

Clever Hester, Annette thought. *She's making me say his name.*

Without warning, Annette's foot came off the accelerator and the golf cart lurched to an abrupt halt. Nora instinctively pressed both hands to the dash while Hester grabbed Nora's seat and let out a soft cry of surprise.

"I'm *so* sorry!" Annette turned to each of her guests in concern. "Are you okay?"

Nora and Hester both nodded.

After an audible exhalation, Annette resumed driving. "Neil Parrish was the Pine Ridge partner who died so tragically. What happened to him was a terrible blow to our entire team."

Though Nora took note of Annette's pinched expression and the doleful look in her eyes, she didn't believe the Realtor felt an ounce of genuine grief over Neil's death.

"I should be the one apologizing," Hester said, putting a hand on Annette's shoulder. "It must have been really traumatizing to hear how he passed. At least you weren't on the train with the rest of your colleagues. If I were them, I'm not sure how I'd ever get that moment out of my head."

Annette started driving again. "To answer your original question, we'll have no issues honoring the closing dates listed in our current or future contracts." Her saleswoman posture and false smile were back in place. "Those dates are set by our builder, and Collin Stone is a true professional. Mr. Parrish was more involved in the investment side of things. Mr. Stone runs Stone Construction, and he always tells his clients that having his name on the company letterhead doesn't mean that he spends all day in an office. He'll be out here, making sure your house is built just the way you want it."

For the first time, it struck Nora that the Meadows was rather quiet for a construction site. "Where are all the workers?" she blurted.

"Mr. Parrish's partners decided it would be in poor taste to have a normal workday after what happened," Annette said. "Construction will resume shortly."

Annette pulled the golf cart into the driveway of the model home. Nora immediately thrust out her hand and thanked the Realtor for her assistance.

"I guess my next step will be a phone call to Dawson Hendricks."

"That's great to hear!" Annette's smile blazed even brighter in the morning sun. "I'll give him a heads-up that you'll be contacting him about the Cambridge." She pressed a blue folder into Nora's hands. "Everything you need is in here, including my card. Call me if you have any questions." She then gave Hester a folder. "Just in case you want to have another look on your own. Or if you have other friends in the market for a new house, tell them to come see me."

Nora and Hester mounted their bicycles and rode in silence until they reached the sign welcoming visitors to downtown Miracle Springs.

"Come into the bakery," Hester said. "I'll fix us some lunch."

Sitting on a stool at the island in Hester's kitchen, Nora watched, entranced, as Hester made two fried green tomato grilled-cheese sandwiches.

"I don't think Annette was too broken up over Neil's death," Hester said. She deftly flipped the sandwiches in her frying pan, revealing perfectly toasted bread, gooey melted cheese, and a glimpse of green tomato.

"Neither do I," Nora agreed.

Hester plated the two sandwiches and filled two glasses with cold water. She then pulled another stool across from Nora and invited her to start eating. Picking up a half of her own sandwich, she paused before taking a bite. "Unless you found something incriminating in Annette's office, it seems like our venture was a massive waste of time."

"Her computer was password protected and I wasn't able to look through the file cabinet. I could only catch a glimpse inside the folder marked with Neil's name. There were a bunch of similar documents in there, so I took a photo of one in hopes of making sense of it later."

Nora took out her phone and put it where both she and Hester could see its screen.

"Looks like a HUD statement." Hester pointed at the photo. "The top's cut off, but I remember mine from when I bought my house. They're hard to forget when you have to read over that whopping list of fees. I don't think anyone who's endured the process of applying for a mortgage can forget what this document looks like."

To avoid responding, Nora bit into her sandwich. The blend of buttery bread, fried tomatoes, gooey cheese, and a hint of paprika was heavenly. As she chewed, Nora felt infused by warmth and comfort. The feelings allowed her to put aside the memory of how she'd never seen paperwork when she and her husband had bought their home. Nora's husband had used money bequeathed by a relative for the down payment and had handled the loan process without consulting her or asking her to be present at the time of its signing. Nora hadn't been listed as a co-borrower, and it wasn't until the night of her accident that she learned that there were very few things in her life she could truly call her own.

As it turned out, neither her house, nor her husband, numbered among them.

The first time Nora had seen a HUD statement was when she'd bought the old train depot. She'd paid for the caboose and its tiny plot with cash, but there wasn't enough left to purchase a building large enough to house thousands of books, let alone the inventory to fill it.

Nora remembered meeting with the loan officer from a big-name bank in the neighboring town. Fear and hope tumbled around inside her belly like a washing machine stuck on the spin cycle, but she'd left the bank that day with her fresh start.

Hester got up from her stool and grabbed the salt-and-pepper shakers from her spice rack. She peeled back the upper lid of her sandwich and sprinkled salt on the bed of yellow cheese. "Want some?" she asked Nora.

Nora was staring at the S on the saltshaker.

Hester waved her hand in front of Nora's face. "Hey? Where are you?"

"We didn't waste our time this morning," Nora said, digging a pen out of her purse. Using the paper towel Hester had given her, she wrote the letters *DHCB* on one corner.

"That was one of the abbreviations written on Renfield's Oasis Bar napkin," Hester said. "What of it?"

A small smile tickled the corner of Nora's mouth. "I think I know what it is. Or more precisely, who it is." As she spoke,

Nora touched each letter with the point of the pen. "I think DHCB is Dawson Hendricks of the Community Bank."

Hester inhaled sharply. "You know what this means?"

"Yes," Nora said, already feeling the weight of her decision. "I have to make an appointment with him and continue this pretense of buying a house I'd never live in. However, if Dawson Hendricks is anything like his brother, Sheriff Toad, it's going to be a very tense meeting."

Chapter 5

And when at last you find someone to whom you feel you can pour out your soul, you stop in shock at the words you utter—they are so rusty, so ugly, so meaningless and feeble from being kept in the small cramped dark inside you so long.

—Sylvia Plath

Dawson Hendricks wasn't available until Thursday afternoon, so Nora took his last appointment of the day, which was five o'clock. This was suboptimal, as Nora stayed open until six. She kept business hours of ten to six because she often netted sales from out-of-towners strolling through the shopping district before dining at the Pink Lady Grill or one of Miracle Springs's eclectic bistros. However, Estella, Hester, and June wanted to reconvene Wednesday night to share any information they'd gleaned on Neil Parrish and his suspicious death.

Nora, who wasn't used to social events, wrestled with the notion that she was getting together with the same group of women twice in one week. Not only that, but she was also looking forward to seeing them.

You told them the only way to gain trust was by sharing your stories, she thought as she rang up a young couple's purchase.

Your secrets were safe. But here you are, offering up your past on a silver tray. Why?

Nora glanced down at the books she was about to slide into a bag. The man had chosen Richard Matheson's *I Am Legend.* His pretty, fresh-faced wife had picked *The Bell Jar* by Sylvia Plath. Loneliness and isolation were themes in both novels, and anyone else might find the books odd choices for a couple who were likely still in the honeymoon phase of marriage.

But Nora knew all too well that it was possible for two lonely people to meet, believe they'd fallen in love, and marry, only to discover—years later—that their loneliness remained.

It was these feelings of loneliness and isolation that made Nora suddenly willing to open herself to the other women. Meeting with Hester, Estella, and June had stirred up memories of the times when Nora's life had been filled with social events. She'd been a member of two book clubs, volunteered at the church charity thrift shop, and had lunches, brunches, and dinners out with girlfriends. There'd also been plenty of work functions to attend, which Nora always enjoyed. Being in the library—among books and bibliophiles—was like spending quality time with family. The library was where Nora felt most at home. She'd never truly felt that way in her stately house, and no matter how hard she'd tried, she was never able to find a home in her husband's heart.

"I love this store," the young wife said as she accepted the bag from Nora. She only met Nora's eyes for a moment. This didn't bother Nora, since she was used to people looking everywhere but at her scarred face.

"If I lived in Miracle Springs, I'd come here every day," the woman went on. "I'd lose myself in this labyrinth of books and lovely knickknacks and soft chairs. Oh, and the coffee's amazing too. This is my idea of heaven."

"It's mine as well," Nora said.

The husband took the bag from his wife. "We'd better leave before you move in," he joked without much warmth.

"If I do, I'll bring my cat." This time, the woman looked directly at Nora. "His name is Mr. Mistoffelees."

"From the T.S. Eliot poem?" Nora guessed.

The woman smiled and nodded. Her husband started moving toward the door. Over his shoulder, he called out, "Come on, babe. I'm hungry."

"Go to the Gingerbread House," Nora said in a low voice to the wife. "Order comfort scones. One for each of you. It'll take Hester at least thirty minutes to make them, so it's a good thing you have something to read. Trust me, you won't regret the wait."

"Okay, we'll head there next. Thanks for the recommendation."

After the couple departed to a chorus of boisterous sleigh bells, Nora spread her left hand like a starfish and tried to remember what it felt like to wear a wedding band. It had been well over four years since she'd taken hers off, and she didn't miss the way the diamonds had rubbed against her skin or raised a callus on her palm. She didn't miss its weight or how the garish center stone had caught the sunlight.

Nora preferred the ring she now wore: an antique, silver-plated mood ring that seemed forever fixed on the color blue. According to the charts she'd seen online, her ring indicated that she was permanently calm.

Or half-dead, she thought, rubbing the ring's oval surface with the pad of her index finger.

Neil Parrish's death had jarred something loose inside Nora. She didn't understand why, because she hadn't known him. Still, her determination to prevent his being labeled a suicide had her taking chances she hadn't been willing to take until now.

That night, as she prepared for the arrival of the other women, Nora ruminated over why she'd become so invested in

Neil Parrish. Strangers with broken hearts, injured bodies, and damaged psyches came to Miracle Springs on every train, so why did she care about this stranger? Why did any of them?

It was the first question she posed to Hester, Estella, and June once they were seated in their circle of chairs.

"Did you read today's paper?" June demanded, her voice rising in anger. "The sheriff's ruling is on the bottom of the front page. It's just a blurb. A man's life reduced to four sentences. *I* care because I know what it's like to be judged, brushed aside, and forgotten. Like that." She snapped her fingers.

"Me too," said Estella. "And though I've learned not to care about what people think about me, I still like helping people. I like helping women to feel beautiful, sexy, and confident. I like seeing their expression when I spin their chair around and they see themselves in the mirror after one of my transformation sessions. It doesn't matter if they've lost all their hair because of chemo or if they have wrinkles or a double chin. I've yet to meet a woman who isn't beautiful as long as she believes she's beautiful."

Hester was staring at Estella. "I thought I had you pegged, but I was wrong. I'm as guilty as half of the women in town of misjudging you. I'm sorry, Estella."

Estella waved off the apology. "Honey, I've gone out of my way to play a part. What else could I expect but for people to see me as a money-grubbing slut? After hanging out with you gals on Sunday, though, I realized that I wanted more of this." She gestured around the circle. "We're no Fellowship of the Ring, but I haven't had girlfriends since high school. Not close ones, anyway. These days, my closest friends are all fictional."

"So are mine," Nora said. "Then again, I think my best relationships have been with someone I found in the pages of a book."

"That can only satisfy us to a certain degree," June said. She put her hand to her heart. "I felt a kinship among us on Sunday too. Our ages, skin colors, and backgrounds didn't matter one iota. We were just women with a common purpose. Period. It felt good to connect like that. It's been a while since I connected to anyone."

"Are we all loners?" Hester asked softly. "Is that why we identified with Neil?"

"What spoke to me was his regret," June said. "His desire to fix what he'd helped break—whatever that was." She turned to Estella. "Are you ready for your date? Because if you're planning to pump Renfield for information, that poor man doesn't stand a chance."

Estella wore a form-fitting dress with a bold floral print that reminded Nora of a Georgia O'Keeffe painting. Except for a few strands that had been artfully chosen to frame her pretty face, Estella's hair was swept into a loose chignon. "Before we head to the Oasis and I veer off for my date while the three of you spy on the other partners, I've been thinking about what Nora said the last time we met. About how the four of us could learn to trust each other." She paused for a long moment. "I decided that I'm going to trust you with my story. But to tell it, I need liquid courage, which is why I brought wine. Would anyone like to share with me? It's not the good stuff—just cheap red table wine—but it takes the edge off."

"With that recommendation, how could I say no?" Hester laughed. "Do you mind if I grab mugs, Nora?"

"Help yourself."

Estella uncorked the bottle with the corkscrew she took from her purse and filled four mugs. Hester had given Nora a black-and-white mug with the text PLEASE GO AWAY, I'M INTRO-VERTING TODAY.

It was one of Nora's favorites.

June showed her cardinal-red mug to the rest of the group. "Mine says YOUR SECRET IS SAFE WITH ME. I don't get it."

Hester grinned. "You will when your wine is gone. "She then turned to Estella. "I had a feeling you might tell us your story tonight, so I brought you a scone. You don't have to eat it now. You can take it home with you."

Estella took the white box Hester offered and held it as though it held a venomous snake. "Is this a trade? A baked good for my story? A scone for a secret?"

Hester looked to Nora for help.

"By showing up tonight, we've agreed to trust each other," Nora said. "With our stories. Which, I imagine, are the secrets we've been keeping from the rest of the world."

Estella opened the bakery box lid by a centimeter and inhaled. "And scones. Don't forget the scones."

"Or the books." June gestured around their space. "I feel safe here, surrounded by walls of stories."

"The Secret, Book, and Scone Society." Nora's voice was hushed and solemn. She let the name hang in the empty air between them for a moment, but was pleasantly surprised by how right it felt. "We won't be an ordinary book club," she continued. "We're all book lovers and we can always talk about books, but we came together to help a man who can no longer help himself. Whether or not we succeed, we should continue meeting until we know Neil Parrish's whole story."

Estella picked up her mug. "And to drink crappy wine."

Hester grabbed hers. "And to be among friends."

"And to laugh," June added. "I want more lines on my face—lines from laughing instead of frowning."

Estella issued a dramatic gasp. "I don't think I can toast to that one, but I'll raise my cup to the rest."

The women grinned and waited for Nora to claim her mug.

Though she hadn't touched alcohol since her accident, Nora wanted to share in this moment, so she knocked rims with the other three women and took a sip of wine.

Estella hadn't lied. The wine wasn't good. Nora had had balsamic vinaigrette with more balanced flavors. Still, she was relieved that the oaky smell and the sensation of the wine flowing over her tongue didn't raise images of that terrible night from four years ago. The night she was burned.

Somehow, the walls of books held the bad memories at bay. Protected inside her fortress of words, Nora looked at her new fellow book-club members and exchanged shy smiles with them.

"Okay," Estella said, leaning back into her chair. "Now that we have a sexy name and I've opened this bottle of shitty wine, I should get started. I don't mind going first, either. It's what I was known for in school. First girl to French kiss a boy. First girl to lose her virginity. First girl to make out with a teacher behind the bleachers."

Hester's eyes widened. "Seriously?"

Estella laughed. This time, there was humor in it. "Honey, the expression *been around the block* applied to me at a very early age—probably because the *chip-off-the-old-block* expression did too. When I was growing up, our house had a revolving door and the men came and went like a Best Buy store on Black Friday."

"Where was your daddy through all this?" June wanted to know.

The glint in Estella's eyes winked out like a snuffed candle flame. "He took off when I was knee-high without any warning. Cleaned out the checking and savings accounts before he went too."

"Bastard," Nora muttered.

"Mama married young," Estella continued. "She had me, her GED, and her looks—not much to bank on. She wasn't the town whore. Nothing that base, but she used her sex appeal to get things from men. If the men were single, married, widowed—she didn't care—and she seemed to know which guys would succumb to her charms and which ones wouldn't. When she was *entertaining* these gentlemen at our house, I was supposed to make myself scarce." Estella paused to drink from her mug. "It was a lonely childhood. I was never invited to play at other kids' houses and they never came to mine."

Hester poured a little more wine into Estella's mug. "And you lived in Miracle Springs the whole time?"

"There was nowhere else to go," Estella said, sounding defensive. "Mama had two things going for her: the roof over her head and her influence over certain men. Eventually, she got a part-time job and started looking around for a permanent replacement for my daddy. She told me never to marry for love. She told me never to forget how that had worked out for her." Estella shrugged. "So I took what she said to heart, and as soon as I hit puberty, I started using my body to get things I wanted."

June made a sympathetic noise. "I bet that kept you on the fringes, didn't it?"

"I had a few bad-girl-type friends in high school, but they all went off to college or married and left town while I stayed here. Worked my way through community college and earned my cosmetology license and a degree in business. My mom died before I graduated, so I sold our house to rent space for my salon. I had to rent because no bank would give me a loan."

"You were even younger than I was when you started your business," Hester said. "And I know all about those loan officers. They all asked if I had a husband to cosign my loan. If not a husband, a father, brother—you get the drift."

Estella raised her mug. "I do. I'm sure Nora got the same treatment."

"I actually bought this place sight unseen. I called the train company and made a cash offer. I also told them that I was ready to close right away. The other buyers weren't as attractive." Nora smiled. "On paper, that is."

"Just wait until I get a little makeup on you," Estella said. "I don't think you realize how beautiful you are." She flicked her wrist. "But let me finish. I'm getting to the hard part and this is where I need a little liquid courage."

Estella drank deeply from her mug and the other women sipped their own wine in solidarity.

"Mama remarried when I was in high school. My stepdaddy owned a car dealership and drove around town in the sleekest, shiniest, newest sports car. For Mama, who could never afford anything new, this was a true symbol of wealth. He was a fat, balding bully of a man. No other woman wanted him, but Mama thought she could tame him."

June groaned. "Lord, I don't like the sound of this."

"He started smacking her around right after the honeymoon," Estella went on. Her voice was flat and her eyes had gone glassy. She was traveling back in time. "It didn't take long before he came after me." She touched her flat belly. "He was crafty about where he hit us. Never in the face. Always in the gut or the sides. He liked to kick us when we were down too. I mean that literally. He had a pair of black wingtip dress shoes— the same kind the businessmen having their ten-dollar cocktails at the Oasis Bar wear—and he made me polish them until he could see his ugly mug grinning back at him from the leather."

Estella's gaze fell to her own shoes—strappy silver sandals that showed off the plum polish on her toenails and the thin ring encircling the second toe on her right foot. "This went on for almost two years. And then, one night, Mama fought back. She ended up in the hospital with a dislocated jaw, broken ribs, and a patchwork of bruises. My stepdaddy spent a night in the drunk tank. When he got home, he was ticked at me because I was the one who ran next door and told the neighbor that he was killing Mama. The neighbor lady called the cops."

"At least she listened to you," Nora said. "Sometimes people don't want to believe that something so horrible could be happening that close."

Estella nodded. "I should have gone back to her the next day, but I was embarrassed. My stepdaddy wasn't happy about having his behavior exposed or that he'd had to sleep it off in a cell. He started in on me with conviction. I thought I was a goner until, lo and behold, another man showed up and shot my stepdaddy right through his black heart."

"Who was the shooter?" Hester asked breathlessly.

"My daddy. He was passing through town and decided to pay Mama and me a visit. When he saw a man with his hand around my neck, he pulled a pistol out of his jacket and yelled at my stepdaddy to get his hands off me. When my stepdaddy turned to see who was hollering at him, my daddy fired."

Nora knew Estella's story was true. She could tell that Estella hadn't fabricated a single detail, but it sounded so painful that it could easily have been a work of fiction. Nora thought of how the cover might look. What font the title might have. One thing was certain: It would have to be a hardback. After what Estella had been through, there was no doubt her story must be protected by a pair of unyielding covers and a firm, unbending spine.

"Daddy went to prison," Estella continued. Her voice had turned soft and small. "He was already a wanted man before he saved me. He'd gotten into drugs and they messed with his mind. After Mama died, he was the only family I had left. He *is* the only family I have left. And he's here. In a correctional facility outside of Asheville."

Estella released a long, slow exhalation. It sounded like it came from deep in her lungs, as if she were expelling stale air and her oldest secret.

"He's the reason I can't leave Miracle Springs. He ruined my life. And then he saved my life. They shouldn't balance each other out, but somehow, they do. The end result is that I can't leave." She threw her hands out in a gesture of helplessness. "And so I escape by attaching myself to strange men for a few days. It's not the sex I'm after. Or power over them. Though that does feel good for an hour or two."

"What are you after, then?" Hester asked. Like Nora and June, she'd barely moved since Estella had started speaking.

Estella contemplated her answer for a moment. "Getting a glimpse into their worlds affords me a temporary escape. I also like how I look through their eyes. I'm always a breath of fresh air. I'm never small-town or unsophisticated. I'm their escape too. Their fantasy."

"I'm sorry, honey, but what you're describing sounds too shallow to make you feel good for long," June said gently. "I bet there are plenty of men who would offer you the real thing. A real relationship."

Estella laughed. "I don't even know what that looks like." She glanced at her watch and gasped. "We can't focus on me anymore. After I gussy you gals up, we need to get to the Oasis. For once, I plan to be on time for a date."

Nora hadn't taken such pains over her appearance since the night of her accident. She was dressed in her nicest slacks and a silky tank top in a quicksilver hue. Estella had styled her hair and applied her makeup with a deft, expert hand. The beautician was shocked to learn that Nora didn't own any high heels and insisted on stopping by her place to grab a pair.

"I feel more uncomfortable than usual, and that's saying something," Nora whispered to Hester as the trio entered the Oasis Bar. Estella, who'd gone in ahead of them, was nowhere to be seen.

"You look beautiful," Hester said.

Nora threw her a grateful smile. "Thanks. It's not my scars this time. It's actually my feet. I don't know how Estella walks in these things."

"You heard the woman," June said. "She started young. Too young. And you might feel awkward, but every man in this room is checking you out."

"Let's introduce ourselves to Bob," Nora suggested, and tottered over to the bar.

As it turned out, there was no need.

"Hello, ladies!" The middle-aged bartender beamed at them. "This is a nice treat. I've been to your places of business, but this is the first time you've been to mine." He turned his friendly gaze on June. "You work at the pools, right?"

June nodded and introduced herself.

"You get an employee discount here," Bob told June. He then leaned over and whispered, "I'll extend it to Ms. Nora and Ms. Hester too. After all, what would Miracle Springs be without our bookstore and bakery?" Standing upright again, he asked, "What can I tempt you with this evening, ladies?"

"Surprise us," Hester said before Nora or June could reply.

Bob promised to both surprise and delight them and began pouring ingredients into a chilled cocktail shaker. A waitress deposited a bowl of snack mix on the bar before continuing toward one of the booths to deliver a platter of coconut shrimp.

I should be eating instead of drinking, Nora thought. It had been so long since she'd consumed alcohol that the single glass of wine she'd had back at the bookstore was already making her smile too much.

One glance at the menu and Nora changed her mind. For the price of an appetizer, Nora could buy enough groceries to cook an entire meal.

Hester and June had the same reaction. After a cursory glance at the menu, they both began eating handfuls of snack mix. Nora followed suit.

By the time Bob presented them with their drinks—mango and basil martinis—the bowl was empty.

"I'll get you gals a bread basket," he said, flashing them a kind grin. A minute later, the waitress delivered a basket stuffed with dill rolls, corn-bread muffins, rosemary flatbread, and pimento cheese biscuits. Tucked into the basket was a bowl of honey butter and a second bowl that Bob identified as roasted red-pepper spread.

The women sipped their drinks and complimented Bob on his choice.

"Our friend Estella told us about you," Nora said. It was both unsettling and wonderful to claim Estella as her friend. Just as it was both unsettling and wonderful to be in this bar with Hester and June. Wearing makeup. And heels.

"She did?" Bob's face glowed. "I'm in love with her. I mean that. I see the real her. And I could make her happy if she'd let me. One day, when she's done playing around with these out-of-towners, she might just realize that it's true."

June reached out and gave his hand a maternal pat. "Are you sure you want to wait for her, Bob? There are other fish in the sea."

"Not for me," Bob declared firmly. "There's only Estella."

Bob briefly left them to serve another customer, but when he returned, Nora decided to steer the conversation to a safer subject: books. Bob admitted that his visits to Miracle Books were few and far between, because tending bar at both the Oasis and the garden bar left him little time for reading.

"I'd love to open a place of my own," he confided. "A little gastropub. It's a dream of mine. That, and winning Estella's heart."

"Where is she, by the way?" Hester asked.

Bob's face darkened. "With one of those Pine Ridge scumbags in the corner. Behind all the palm trees."

June glanced over her shoulder and pretended to look worried. "He's a scumbag?"

"Oh, yeah. First off, he's married. I saw him take off his ring and slip it into his pocket." Bob picked up a tumbler and began polishing it with his dishcloth. "Also, he and the rest of that group are rude to the staff. And they're terrible tippers to boot. The way you treat those in the service industry says a great deal about your character."

"Yes, it does," Hester agreed.

"That's the rub," Bob continued, warming up to his subject. "I've seen their brochures for the Meadows. They're supposed to be building a community in Miracle Springs, but they don't seem very interested in its people. When they're in this bar they spend their time with a drink in one hand and a cell phone in the other."

Like all experienced bartenders, Bob has the gift of observation, Nora thought.

"What's their mood like?" Nora asked. "Do they seem sad over the loss of their colleague?"

Bob stopped polishing. "You'd expect a little grief, wouldn't you, but I haven't seen any. These folks are all business. They're clearly on a timetable and have a fixed agenda. And they're not going to let anyone—and I'm including the sheriff, the Grim Reaper, and the Almighty when I say *anyone*—mess with that agenda."

June arched her brows. "Did the sheriff pay a visit to these lofty Pine Ridge people?"

"He sure did," Bob said, dipping his chin to acknowledge the customer who'd just signaled to him from the other side of the bar. "It was a strange visit too. When the sheriff sat down with the Pine Ridge trio, it felt more like an Irish wake than an interview. And I expected an interview. A man was run over by a train, after all. Instead, I saw five people whispering and drinking whiskey." Bob stepped away and then paused and turned back. "Here's another thing: The sheriff didn't bring a deputy along. He brought a family member instead. So unless he was off-duty, which I don't think he was, seeing as he was still in uniform, the whole event struck me as odd."

Nora's pulse quickened. "Who was the family member?"

"The sheriff's big brother," Bob said, already heading toward his customer. He tossed the name back over his shoulder. "Dawson Hendricks."

Chapter 6

They sell courage of a sort in taverns.

—Ellis Peters

"That name keeps popping up," June said.

"It sure does," agreed Hester. "And I don't have to be Perry Mason to know that something's wrong with the picture Bob just painted. Three people from Pine Ridge Properties sat in this bar and had drinks with the bank's loan officer and Sheriff Toad hours after a man was tragically killed."

Nora had a hard time imagining such a group in this tranquil setting. They must have seemed out of place among the potted palms, tropical wallpaper, and the whisper of the wicker ceiling fans, among the people who'd come to the hotel in search of healing.

"What strikes me as especially strange is that the sheriff didn't care who witnessed his behavior," she said to her companions. "The hotel and bar staff could easily identify the Pine Ridge trio. They would have recognized them as the bigwigs behind the Meadows project. Right, June?"

"Absolutely," June said. "You have no idea how fast information travels in a hotel network. News usually reaches the pools last, seeing as we're off-site, but we heard how Neil had died and that his partners were riding on the very train that struck him down within an hour of the event."

"So either the sheriff was doing no wrong during this unusual gathering involving his older brother and Neil's partners, or he didn't see that it made a difference who saw them together," Nora continued. "After all, he's *the law*."

Hester helped herself to a corn-bread muffin before passing the basket to June. "We all believe that Neil was pushed. Which means we all believe he was murdered. Why? Because he was going to make amends for the bad things he'd done. Piecing the snippets of conversation he had with you and Nora, we assume those bad things involved the Meadows. That development brought him to Miracle Springs. It also brought his partners here."

"After I'm done with Dawson Hendricks tomorrow, I hope to understand just how important he is to Pine Ridge Properties." Nora traced the rim of her martini glass and was surprised to find it empty. She hadn't even realized she'd finished her cocktail. To hide her discomfort, she kept talking. "Unless the sheriff is their hired gun and the Pine Ridge people asked him to silence Neil, I don't see why they'd want a small-town lawman on their payroll."

Before June or Hester could offer a theory, Bob presented them with a fresh round of drinks. "Compliments of the gentlemen at the far end of the bar."

Instead of looking in that direction, Nora fixed her eyes on Hester and asked, "Do you know them?"

Hester gave the men an awkward wave of thanks and then turned back to Nora. "Never seen them before. They're twice our age."

"Your age," June corrected. "But we didn't come here to flirt. Speaking of which, I'm going to visit the ladies' room. I want to check on Estella."

Hester watched June maneuver around a young couple waiting for seats at the bar. "If anyone needs checking on, it's Fenton," she said with a wry smile.

"You like Estella, don't you?" Nora asked.

"I didn't at first, but she's growing on me." Hester stared into her glass as if she could read an omen in the sun-colored cocktail. "She has an undeniable power over men. I just hope she uses that superpower for good tonight. It's obvious, from her story, this hasn't always been the case."

Nora swept her gaze around the room. The people in the Oasis Bar seemed relaxed, but subdued. The majority of the lodge's guests had come to town in search of a miracle. Estella, on the other hand, had been searching for a miracle with every new wave of guests—every group of passengers disembarking at the Miracle Springs train station. However, she'd only found a temporary respite from a painful past and an uncertain future, and that lack of connection to another human being could cause a person to act out.

"I think we all want to use our powers for good," Nora said. "But loneliness can lead people to dark places. At least we have each other now."

Hester smiled. "Yes, we do."

The two women clinked the rims of their glasses and polished off the remainder of their martinis.

I can not *have another drink*, Nora thought, despite the pleasant sensation that her body was lighter. It was as if she'd shucked off weight she hadn't even known she'd been carrying. Her brain was quieter too. All the sharp edges of her memory were softened and she felt less guarded. Less scarred.

The feeling dissipated as soon as June returned from the ladies' room. "We have to go. *Now.*" She slapped some bills on the polished wood bar.

"What's going on?" Nora asked as June shouldered her way through a knot of people.

"Fenton and Estella are getting ready to leave," June said over her shoulder. "Estella gave me a sign—just a quick one—but it was clear enough. She wants us to follow her."

Nora considered the implications of June's comment. "That could make for a very awkward elevator ride."

"Forget the elevator," Hester said. "What are we supposed to do when they reach Fenton's guest room? Tell him that we're a package deal?"

June threw a look of disgust at Hester. "Hell, no! They must be heading elsewhere or she wouldn't want us to come along. I have a feeling our crafty redhead has a plan."

Upon exiting the bar, the three women spotted Estella sashaying across the lobby toward the hotel's main door. Her arm was hooked through Fenton's and every now and then she'd lean into him, as though she felt a little unsteady on her feet. Nora didn't know Estella well enough to tell whether she was faking or if she was genuinely having trouble balancing in stilettos.

Outside, the summer night was filled with music. The soft jazz coming from the alfresco area of the restaurant harmonized with the chirping and sawing of nearby insects.

"They're getting in a golf cart." Nora pointed at the couple just as Fenton saluted one of the valets and pulled away from the curb.

"Back to my car!" June cried and the women moved as swiftly as possible in their heels to reach June's old Bronco. "I think Estella's taking her date to the thermal pools."

"Aren't they closed?" Hester asked.

June laughed. "Which is exactly the point. If Estella can find a way in, and I have a sneaking suspicion she's been inside the pool after hours more than once, then she'll have the whole place to herself. It could be very romantic. Or—"

"Very dangerous." Nora completed the thought.

June pressed down on the gas pedal, causing the Bronco to lurch forward. "Yeah. That's what I'm worried about. I think Estella plans to seduce this man in exchange for information, but she's also gotten a vibe from him. She doesn't like that vibe, so that's why she doesn't want to be left alone with him."

Hester glanced out the window at the star-pocked sky. "Fenton can't be Neil's murderer because Fenton was on the train, right? None of the Pine Ridge Property people are killers."

"Maybe they didn't commit the physical act," Nora said. "But one or all of them could have conspired to get rid of Neil."

June made a noise of agreement. "We're in the dark about lots of important things. For example, who might have told Neil's partners that his conscience was troubling him? Who lured him down to the ledge above the train tracks? Who pushed him? And who benefits the most from his death? These are all things we'll have to look at if we want to find out what happened to this man, but at the moment, there's only one crucial thing for us to do."

"Keep Estella safe," Nora said.

"Without compromising her plan," June said, holding up a finger in warning. "Luckily, not only can I get us into the pools, but I also know the perfect spot for spying. We'll be able to hear every whisper and still be close enough to knock Fenton on the head with a lead pipe if he lays a hand on Estella."

Hester chewed her thumb. "I don't like this. We're either going to overhear something terrible about Neil Parrish's murder or we're simply going to overhear things that we have no business overhearing."

June gained entrance into the bathhouse by punching a code into a side door marked STAFF ONLY. She then led Nora and Hester down a long, damp corridor to an alcove occupied by a bamboo stand filled with stacks of clean, white towels. From this position, the three women heard the sounds of splashing and giggling coming from the pool.

"Is that Estella's dress?" Hester pointed at a chair on the far side of the cavernous space.

"It sure isn't a towel," June said. "It looks like Fenton shed his clothes too."

Hidden behind the towel stand, the women were completely obscured from the bathers' view. However, June put her fingers to her lips and gestured at the ceiling. "Everything echoes in here," she whispered. "We have to be very quiet or Mr. Pine Ridge will know that he's skinny-dipping for an audience."

Hester pulled a face. "This is the epitome of uncomfortable."

June patted her arm. "Honey, I've worked here for a long time, and despite what those erectile-dysfunction commercials imply with those couples holding hands in the bathtub and exchanging satisfied smiles, I have yet to see a man who can keep it up in this water. The heat gives the guys what we at the bathhouse refer to as the *wet-noodle effect*." She held out a finger and then slowly curled it into her palm.

Something about the gesture and the smirk on June's face struck Nora as funny and she had to clamp a hand over her mouth to stifle the laugh tickling the back of her throat.

"Come and get me!" Estella called. Her words bounced off the tiles and eventually floated toward the ceiling like birds roosting in the rafters. She sounded so close that Nora was no longer tempted to laugh. Instead, she sucked in her breath and stilled her body. June and Hester did the same.

"Why are you playing hard to get?" a man's voice asked. Though his tone was light, there was an edge of impatience to it.

Estella whistled a short ditty. "Because I like games. And I like to draw out these moments. This is the best part. The buildup before that first contact. It's like the lightning before the storm. The powerful, electric part. Yes! I can *feel* how much you want to kiss me. How hungry you are to run your hands over my body."

"I am," Fenton Greer agreed hoarsely.

"But like I said, I enjoy games," Estella continued in her low, husky voice. "And if you want to play with this body and use it to satisfy your deepest desires, then you have to satisfy mine too. Do you want to know how to satisfy me, Fenton?"

"*Ye-es.*" The word was a moan.

A noise indicated that someone had gotten out of the pool very close to where Nora and her friends were crouched.

"Fenton! That's cheating," Estella scolded. "I haven't said what I want from you yet. So sit down right there on the edge and I'll tell you."

There was a slap of naked flesh against tile followed by a grunt.

"That's good. *You're* so good," Estella said. After a brief pause, during which Nora could only detect small splashes and a nearly inaudible moan from Fenton, Estella continued speaking. "The currency in this town is information. I trade in information, my sweet, suave, big-city man. And I want to know about Neil Parrish because he's the hot topic on everyone's lips. If *I* know more about him than my clients, they'll line up to hear the *juiciest* tidbits from me. Do you like juicy tidbits, Fenton?"

Nora heard a distinct *plop* as a wet piece of clothing struck the pool deck. It wasn't a loud noise because the piece of clothing probably wasn't very large and couldn't hold much water. Nora guessed that Estella had entered the pool wearing a bra and panties and that she'd just removed one of those items.

As though proving Nora's assumption correct, Fenton released an animalistic groan. Several seconds passed before he managed to find his voice, and when he did, he croaked, "What do you want to know?"

"Why would a guy like that kill himself?" Estella asked. "He had money, a successful career where he got to work with someone as interesting as you, and from what I saw in the paper, he was good-looking too. Not *my* type, though. That's why I picked you out of all the men in that bar, Fenton. I knew you were special. But back to your buddy Neil. What was his story?"

"We weren't buddies. He had his job and I had mine," Fenton said. "And I have no idea why he came unglued. No one does. Back at the office, he seemed totally normal. He left last week on a scheduled vacation and I expected to see him again at the station in Asheville. Instead, he jumped in front of the train he was supposed to be on with the rest of us."

"That's horrible! You must have been *so* shocked, even if you and Neil weren't close." Estella's voice was a velvety purr. "Didn't he reach out to anyone before he died? And hasn't his family come forward to ask for more info?"

There was a splashing sound, followed by a giggle and a chastisement of "not yet" from Estella.

After issuing a growl of frustration, Fenton addressed Estella's questions. "Neil sent a group text to all of us—his partners—about how he had to face the mistakes he'd made head-on. Well, he faced them, all right. Came nose to nose with sixty tons of steel. Crazy bastard. And Neil didn't have much in the way of family. He was raised by an aunt and uncle, and all those old codgers care about is who's going to pay their nephew's burial expenses besides them."

"Jesus!" Estella spat, momentarily forgetting her part of seductress.

"Is this your idea of foreplay? Talking about my dead partner?" Fenton asked, his voice taking on a sharpness that put Nora on edge. June and Hester had similar reactions, and the three women exchanged nervous glances. "Or are you all talk and no action? Because I can get that at home."

For the second time since they'd entered the bathhouse, the *plop* of wet cloth striking the tiles reached Nora's ears.

Estella must be baring it all, Nora thought, impressed by her friend's boldness.

"Have a drink, Fenton. That's it. Just relax and enjoy the view," Estella cooed. She fell silent for several seconds before saying, "I'm not all talk, but I'm drawn to ambitious men. To men who take what they want and don't let anyone get in their way. Men who don't like weakness. Men who will cross the line to fulfill their ambitions. Even break the law. Because sometimes, the law doesn't matter when it comes to getting what you want. What you deserve. Does this description fit you?"

"You'd be surprised," Fenton replied. "I do what's necessary to get what I want."

When Estella spoke next, she sounded so close that Nora was positive the naked couple was on the other side of the towel stand.

"Just how ruthless are you, Fenton? Would you pay someone to push your partner in front of a train?"

There was a crash of breaking glass and Nora jerked in surprise. Beside her, Hester and June shifted onto their knees. All three women were coiled like cobras waiting to strike, waiting to see if Estella needed help.

"Look what you've made me do," Fenton said. His voice was an ominous rumble.

Estella laughed. "It's only a scratch. Dip it in the pool while I grab you a towel. We can turn this into a little role-play game. You be the patient and I'll be your naughty nurse."

"I'm done with games," Fenton snapped. "I've already had enough stress this week, what with Neil and his idiotic crisis of conscience, and I'm out of patience. I want what I came here to get."

"I promised you an unforgettable evening," Estella said. "I've delivered on that promise. If you want more, then ask me on another date."

Fenton muttered under his breath and someone approached the towel stand and then retreated again. Nora hoped that both Estella and Fenton were now covered up and that their date was truly at an end.

Suddenly, Estella cried, "No! *Stop! Get off!*"

"I answered your questions!" Fenton shouted breathlessly. "You owe me a reward. That was our deal."

Nora didn't have to see what was happening to know that a physical struggle was taking place between Fenton and Estella.

Fenton's grunts and stilted speech bounced off the walls of the alcove and seemed to surround the other women.

Nora turned to June and Hester. "Let's go!"

"I've got this." June leapt to her feet and hurried over to the wall. She flicked a switch, flooding the massive space with light.

"What the hell?" Fenton bellowed.

June cleared her throat and, in the singsong voice of a flight attendant or a voicemail recording, said, "Sir, this area is closed. Please collect your clothes and make your way to the exit. Ma'am? Are you okay?"

"I'm just peachy," Estella replied. She sounded winded. "I'll let the gentleman leave first, seeing as we're not staying in the same guest room."

"Oh," June said. "I see."

Fenton barreled through the exit, leaving a stream of expletives in his wake.

"You can come out now." June beckoned to Nora and Hester.

Stepping around Fenton's broken tumbler, Nora hurried to where Estella sat on a lounge chair. She had one towel wrapped around her torso and a second draped over her shoulders.

"Are you hurt?" Nora asked, but before the words were even out, she saw angry red marks on Estella's neck. "Did he try to choke you?"

"Either that, or he was trying to hold me still. I was thrashing around too much to know which." Estella touched her neck. "He didn't have the chance to bear down and squeeze because the lights distracted him." She looked at June. "Thank you."

June folded her arms across her chest. She was angry. "You're crazy, you know that? You baited that man. A drunk and dangerous man."

"I've dealt with his type before," Estella replied. She seemed unfazed by the attack, but Nora knew that people were capable of concealing feelings of deep distress.

"We should call nine-one-one!" Hester exclaimed. "Report that bastard."

Estella shook her head. "You think Sheriff Toad will do anything? It'll be Renfield's word against mine. A few marks on my neck won't be enough to hold him."

"What about us?" Hester asked. "You have three witnesses."

"Could you see? Without lights? From where you were hiding behind the towel stand? Come on. You know what'll happen." Estella shook her head again, causing damp tendrils of red hair to cling to her cheeks. "I'd rather use the *threat* of going to the cops to get more information from that fat bastard. You heard the slime. Now we know why he and his partners weren't saddened by Neil's death. They wanted to be rid of him and the problems he might have created. With Neil gone, they can all get back to the business of making money."

June handed Estella her clothes. "Fenton said that Neil's crisis of conscience caused him stress. All that odious man seems to care about is money and himself. If you threaten those things, Estella, he'll be your enemy. And what if we're not around to rescue you the next time he gets angry?"

"I've never needed rescuing. I'm no helpless princess," Estella snapped.

Before June could reply, Nora performed a referee's timeout gesture. "You're clearly a fighter. You stepped into the ring tonight, Estella, and you were brave. But it's my turn, now. Let me follow the paper trail to Dawson Hendricks and the Madison County Community Bank."

"Hendricks," June scoffed. "The name alone gives me the creeps. I don't know Dawson, but I could see Sheriff Toad pushing Neil in front of that train and then sitting down to a nice meal of chicken-fried steak."

"Speaking of the sheriff," Hester said. "He's a regular at the Gingerbread House. I'm going to turn on the charm, toss a few treats his way, and ask him some leading questions about his financial situation." She held up her hands. "Don't worry, I'll be subtle. I'll play the dumb-woman-who-can't-balance-a-checkbook act. He'll totally eat that up."

June nodded. "I like that plan. His wife comes to the pools every now and then. I usually go out of my way to avoid her and her posse. These women must have slept through every history class on the abolishment of slavery and civil rights. And I can guarantee you that not one of them has read *The Help*."

Three of the four members of the Secret, Book, and Scone Society laughed, and though June's face had been taut with anger a moment ago, it now crinkled in amusement.

"We should get out of here," Estella said. She turned away from her friends and began to dress.

To give her more privacy, Nora, June, and Hester moved to another set of lounge chairs.

"Do you really think she's okay?" Hester whispered. "*I* wouldn't be after what just happened."

"I'll drive her home and spend some time with her," June said. "I want her to know that she's not alone."

Nora and Hester approved of this idea, and as soon as Estella was ready, the four women left the bathhouse and headed for June's car.

That's when Nora realized that she'd left her purse at the bar.

After swearing under her breath, Nora asked June to drive back up the hill to the lodge.

That's what happens when you don't have a drop of alcohol for over four years, and then you pound back three drinks.

Nora wasn't drunk. The scene with Estella had sent such a jolt of adrenaline through her body that all that remained was a lingering sense of tipsiness.

Inside the Oasis, Bob had her purse tucked behind the bar. He handed it to her with a friendly smile and asked after Estella, but Nora only mumbled something about Estella's having gone home, and turned away. As she headed for the lobby, she felt guilty for being so short with Bob. Of the men she'd recently encountered, he was the only one she'd call a gentleman.

It wasn't a man, however, but a little boy who barreled into her just as the lobby carpet gave way to the slick marble floor leading to the rotating exit doors. Pushed off-balance, Nora's right foot twisted violently in Estella's spiky heels and she toppled to the floor.

The fall hurt. Her hip and elbow struck the cold, unyielding marble and Nora squeezed her eyes shut to keep from crying out.

"Bryson! You naughty boy. Look what you've done. Apologize to the lady!"

Nora heard Bryson mutter something about a scary face. Unwilling to make eye contact with Bryson or his family, Nora decided to lie still for a moment longer. The pain surged through her right side like a storm wave.

"Just breathe, honey," a friendly voice whispered close to Nora's ear. "We've called Old Jedediah Craig. He's on the way."

Nora opened her eyes. She didn't want assistance from Old Jedediah, whoever he was. "I'll be okay," she said, feeling clammy and embarrassed. The sharpest edge of the pain was abating from her elbow and hip, though she knew bluish-plum and deep-purple bruises would bloom in both places by tomorrow.

"My friends are waiting in a car outside," she continued to explain to the elderly bellhop with the grandfatherly face.

"Your ankle's swelling like an overripe tomato," he said. "You can't put weight on that. Jedediah will have to see if it's broken. Don't you worry, Jed Craig is the best paramedic in the county."

Nora managed to sit up, but she kept her gaze lowered. She could feel far too many eyes on her.

"She'll be all right, folks," the bellhop announced, sensing Nora's discomfort. "Go on and enjoy your night, now."

There was a shuffling as the spectators moved off.

After thanking the bellhop, Nora insisted that she only

needed help getting outside. Her friends would see to her care after that.

"Well, I'll be! Here's Jedediah!" the man suddenly declared. "He must've been close by. You're a lucky lady."

Yeah, that's me. Ms. Good Fortune. Ms. Lucky Lady, Nora thought wryly, and refused to watch Old Jedediah approach. She was already imagining him as an aged Ernest Hemingway look-alike with leathery skin, a grizzly, gray beard, and a slight paunch. He'd touch her with thick-fingered, clinical hands and speak to her in a tone that suggested he had better things to do than examine a clumsy woman who, if her burn scars indicated anything, was unable to stay out of harm's way.

Nora couldn't have been more wrong.

Chapter 7

Words are a pretext. It is the inner bond that draws one person to another, not words.

—Rumi

Because Nora still had her eyes fixed on the floor, she saw Old Jedediah's boots first.

Several thoughts struck her at once. *He has big feet. He must be tall. Do paramedics wear hiking boots?*

And then, against her will, Nora's mind traveled to the night of her accident. It wasn't the pain she remembered. Some things were worse than the pain. The smell of spilled gasoline and smoke. The acrid stench of smoldering metal and charred clothing, skin, and hair. The strangled sob sounds gurgling out of her throat as she struggled to free the driver from her seat belt—to save her from being burned alive inside her mangled car. The keening of ambulance and police sirens. And afterward, the voices.

So many voices. So many questions.

Nora didn't answer any of them.

The darkness reached out to her and she dropped into its embrace.

"Are you a hiker?" the voice belonging to the boots asked her now.

The question threw Nora and she glanced up to find herself face-to-face with Old Jedediah. She took in his tousled brown hair, ocean-blue eyes, and chiseled jaw.

He can't be a day over forty, she thought, perplexed by the paramedic's nickname.

Jedediah Craig was one of the best-looking men Nora had ever seen. He possessed the rugged hands and bristle-covered cheeks and chin of a gun-toting, spur-wearing Western outlaw along with the intelligent, amused gaze of a Jane Austen hero.

"These aren't my shoes," was Nora's lame reply. She turned the scarred side of her face away from him. "I have boots like yours at home, but I don't think I'll be hiking for a day or two."

Silently berating herself for rambling, Nora waited for the paramedic to open his kit and get on with his examination. The moment he started, she planned to tell him to stop. However, he kept his hands firmly planted on his knees.

Nora could feel him studying her.

"My friends are waiting in a car outside," she said, suddenly snapping her gaze back to meet his. "Can you get me to them? I'd prefer not to sit in the middle of the lobby like a sideshow act."

"I can help you outside." He held up a finger. "But first, I'd like to be sure you haven't broken anything. Namely, your ankle. Do I have permission to touch your foot? If it isn't broken, I won't compound your embarrassment by putting you on my stretcher and wheeling you out to my rig."

Relieved, Nora said, "Just be quick, please. I'd really like to go."

Opening his kit, Jedediah pulled out a pair of gloves and laid them across his leg. He then offered Nora his hand. "Before I put these on, I should introduce myself. I'm Jed."

"Nora."

"Tell me if anything I do causes you discomfort," Jed said, his focus now entirely on her ankle, which, as the bellhop had stated, was already swelling.

With deft, gentle fingers, Jed pressed down on Nora's tissue until he met bone. From there, he worked his fingers around her ankle to the top of her foot, back to her ankle joint, and upward to her shin.

"May I take this off?" he asked, referring to Estella's shoe.

Nora nodded and Jed unfastened the tiny silver buckle. He then lowered Nora's calf until the weight of her leg fell onto his thighs. Next, he slid his right hand along the bottom of her foot, easing the shoe off in a slow, deliberate movement that had Nora hypnotized.

She was so unaccustomed to being touched that she flinched when his hand closed around her naked foot.

Jed searched her face with concern. "Did I hurt you?"

"I'm a little ticklish," she lied.

For this admission, Nora was rewarded with a lingering smile from Jed's Rhett Butler mouth.

You're no Scarlett O'Hara, Nora reminded herself. Instead of returning the smile, she looked over Jed's shoulder toward the exit doors.

"Almost done," he said quietly, correctly reading her desire to be on her way.

Jed carefully rotated her foot, checking her level of discomfort with each change in direction. Finally, he removed his gloves and dropped them into his kit.

"I doubt it's broken, but the real test is whether or not you can put any weight on it. Are you ready to try?"

Despite the throbbing in her ankle, Nora said, "yes" without hesitating.

Jed explained that he wanted her to lean into him as he lifted her, and though Nora could plainly see his well-defined biceps, she was reluctant to comply.

"I can put a hand under your other elbow if it'll make you feel better," the elderly bellhop said.

Nora accepted his offer, but it was clear that Jed didn't need any assistance. He slid his arm around Nora's waist and scooped her off the ground so abruptly that she grabbed a fist-ful of his shirt in surprise.

"I've got you," he whispered, his mouth so close that she felt the warmth of his breath on her neck. "I won't let you go," he said, squeezing her waist to reinforce his point.

Time slowed to a near halt. The seconds stretched out like the view of the mountains from one of the highest vistas on the Appalachian Trail. Nora seemed unable to release her hold of Jed's shirt. She leaned her head against his hard chest and caught hints of Honeycrisp apples, chopped wood, sunlit pine needles, and old books.

"Go on, girlie! Try putting some weight on that foot." The bellhop jarred Nora's elbow, breaking the spell. Nora felt heat rush to her face. And with the heat, came the itching. She shifted her hand from Jed's shirt to her cheek, covering up her octopi-shaped scar.

"Um. Yeah." Jed seemed to have been caught in the same daze as Nora. "If you're ready."

Nora touched her bare foot to the marble, and a sharp bolt of pain surged up from her ankle to her calf. She tried to cover her wince with a smile, feeling more foolish than she had when she'd first fallen. She had no business mooning over Jed like a teenager with a crush.

Clenching her teeth, Nora said, "It's tender, but I can make it to the car."

Though this was the truth, Jed looked at her intently for several seconds before asking the bellhop to collect Nora's shoe.

"I can handle that," the elderly man said. "And I can get the side door for you too."

Because Nora had to rely on Jed's strength more than she wanted to, her anger grew. She was not only irked with herself, but also with her friends. Why hadn't they come into the lobby to look for her? They must have realized that something was wrong. It shouldn't have taken this long for her to fetch her purse.

Outside, Nora searched for June's car.

"They're not here," she muttered crossly, glancing left and right.

"Duncan probably made them circle around," the bellhop said. "He's the head valet and he takes his job too seriously. What kind of car is your friend driving?"

After Nora told him, the bellhop removed the small walkie-talkie clipped to his belt and called to Duncan. "Help the lady driver get as close to the front door as possible," the bellhop commanded. "Her friend is hurt."

It took less than a minute for June's car to come into view. Nora avoiding making eye contact with Jed, but she was hyper-aware of his arm around her waist and of the way his fingers pressed into her lower back. She felt possessed and protected. And completely unnerved.

"You can bear weight on your foot, which is good, but you'll need to follow the RICE regime as soon as you get home," Jed said as June pulled to a stop. "Rest, ice, compression, and elevation. Ibuprofen for the pain. Do you have the supplies?"

"I do," June replied before Nora could. "I keep a whole pharmacy at my place. I like to be ready for anything." Turning to Nora, she said, "I'm sorry we weren't waiting out here, but the valet chased us off. I've dealt with him before at the bath-house. He has a serious Napoleon complex."

This made the bellhop laugh. "So that's what it's called, eh?" He opened the passenger door for Nora before retreating to his post.

Nora put her hand on the Bronco's roof to keep her balance. As she did, Jed leaned in and whispered, "You smell like honey-suckle and blackberries. It's nice."

Disarmed, Nora turned to him and mumbled her thanks. She

expected his gaze to linger on her scars, but his eyes remained locked on hers.

As he eased her into the passenger seat, he said, "You were the best part of my day."

And then, he shut the door and June drove off.

"Who is *that*?" Hester asked from the backseat.

"I don't know, but I might have to injure myself at work tomorrow," Estella said without much conviction. Her altercation with Fenton Greer had clearly taken its toll on her ability to constantly play the part of the town Jezebel.

June frowned. "Shush, you two. I want to hear what happened to Nora."

Nora gave them a brief recap, omitting the part where she momentarily forgot about the pain in her ankle as she responded to Jed's electric touch and the quiet intensity of his ocean-blue stare.

"Will you be able to keep your appointment with Dawson Hendricks?" June asked. "I've seen my share of twisted ankles in my time. It'll be days before you're walking normally again."

"Don't worry, I'll make it to the bank tomorrow," Nora said.

Using the back of Nora's seat, Hester pulled herself forward so that she could see Nora's face. "How will you get there? You won't be able to ride your bike."

"I'm going to walk softly and carry a big stick," Nora said. She then leaned her head against the headrest and closed her eyes, making it clear that she was done talking.

Nora's "big stick" was one of the first purchases she'd made after moving into Caboose Cottage. She'd spotted it at the flea market, having initially been drawn to the soft glow of the carved wooden ball on its top. When Nora had reached for the ball, it had felt at home against her palm. The wood was worn smooth from use and had a golden yellow patina. The shaft was a different story, however. In fact, it told a story. The wood-carver had created a vertical scene of a fox running through a field of flowers and butterflies. The fox ran from the bottom of the cane to the top. Here, he leaped over a stream of choppy water.

Nora had no idea how long she'd held the cane, twisting it around and around in her hands as she watched the fox move, but the woman manning the stall had finally come from behind the table to ask, "Can you see the words hidin' in the trees? They're real small. No idea what they mean, but the piece is nicely carved."

Bringing the stick closer to her face, Nora spotted the word *and* inside a tree trunk. It was well camouflaged between the lines of bark created by the wood-carver's knife. Having found one, the rest of the words suddenly jumped out at her. They were: *my, now, secret, is,* and *here.*

"You and that stick seem to go together. You want it? I'll knock five bucks off the price," the vendor had said, impatient for Nora to make a decision.

Nora had accepted the offer without additional bartering. As she settled up, the vendor asked, "Do you know what the words mean?"

It was only when the stick was safely back in her hand that Nora had answered. "They're from a book called *The Little Prince.* They say, *And now here is my secret.*"

"I don't get it," the woman had said.

"It's part of a famous quote," Nora had explained. Her fingers traced the head of the fox leaping over the river. "*And now here is my secret, a simple secret: it is only with the heart that one can see rightly; what is essential is invisible to the eye.*"

The vendor's frown had deepened.

Noting the gold cross hanging around the woman's neck, Nora said, "Take faith, for example. You can believe in it without seeing it."

This made the woman smile. "Or love. It's somethin' you feel in here." She put her hand over her heart.

Nora's heart no longer worked as it had in the past. It was a damaged organ—the most scarred part of her body. It was fine for others to believe in the wondrous nature of love, but Nora wasn't interested in the topic, so she'd simply nodded in agreement, thanked the woman for the walking stick, and left.

She was very fond of her walking stick and never hiked without it. It had saved her from walking through cobwebs and stepping into hidden holes or startling slumbering copperheads. Nora didn't think she could have made it through the day following her fall without her trusty stick.

Luckily, she hobbled the short distance from her tiny house to Miracle Books before the rain came. It started as a timid drizzle, and she thought it might be one of those short rainfalls that barely had time to wet the ground before abruptly stopping. However, as the morning progressed and the skies darkened, Nora made extra pots of coffee. Rain always brought customers. They came into the bookstore seeking something hot to drink, a soft chair, and comfort. Nora had all three of these to offer, in addition to her wonderful books.

At some point after lunch, the rain let up enough to allow the customers who'd had their fill of coffee to leave. Most of them had also purchased books, shelf enhancers, or both, so Nora was in high spirits. She'd even sold a copy of *The Little Prince* to a handsome out-of-towner who'd never heard of the book until he'd asked Nora about her walking stick.

The man returned two hours later. Holding up the slim novel, he pointed at the yellow-haired boy on its cover and exclaimed, "This story—it's awful! We never find out if the Little Prince makes it back to his rose. It was his one goal and we're left hanging. I hate endings like that."

Nora smiled. She loved talking books with animated readers. Even disgruntled readers. Whenever she delved into the plot of a novel or dissected its characters, Nora forgot about her scars. The longer she spoke with a customer about a book, the more confident and animated she became.

After inviting the man to sit, Nora and her new customer discussed some of the novel's themes.

"Exploration is an important motif," Nora said at one point. "Do you have the opportunity to travel or does your job keep you in one place?"

"Unless I'm on vacation, I stay in this part of the state," the man replied. "I design and build new housing communities."

Nora's heart skipped a beat. "Is the Meadows one of yours?"

The man nodded. "That's the latest gem in the Pine Ridge Properties crown."

Nora realized she was speaking with one of Neil Parrish's partners and silently berated herself for not recognizing him from the website. True, the photos were small, but she still should have connected the man's handsome face with the one she'd seen online during the inaugural meeting of the Secret, Book, and Scone Society.

Subtly studying the man opposite her, Nora vowed to make the most of this opportunity. Fate had provided her with a chance to investigate without having to attempt Estella's seduction methods. Even better was the fact that this suspect, which Nora silently labeled him, had come to her to talk about how he'd felt after reading *The Little Prince*. In Nora's experience as a librarian and bookshop owner, people let their guard down when discussing books. Their reactions to fictional characters often revealed a great deal about their own personalities.

"What a coincidence." Nora infused her voice with enthusiasm. "I'm closing early this afternoon to meet with a loan officer at the community bank. I toured the model home at the Meadows and was really impressed." She slumped a little and looked away. "Still, I don't want to get my hopes up. This store costs an arm and a leg to run and even though I found the perfect house plan, I'm not sure I can afford it."

"You might be pleasantly surprised by what you hear at the bank," the man said. He then extended his hand. "I'm Collin. Collin Stone."

With introductions done, Nora gestured at the copy of *The Little Prince* in Collin's other hand. "Most people don't finish a book in a day. Is your work on hold because of the accident?"

Collin stared at her blankly for a moment before he understood. "No," he hastily assured her. "Everything's proceeding as planned. Neil would have wanted it that way. He was the epitome of a go-getter." Opening the paperback to a random page, Collin shook his head. "He wouldn't have liked this book, though. It doesn't paint businessmen in the best light."

"No, it doesn't," Nora agreed. "But that's partially because the narrator loves children. He admires how they use their imagination. Adults can lose that ability. Do you think Saint-Exupéry uses the adult characters as a warning?"

Collin grunted. "Maybe, but we can't be like the prince. He has time to explore and philosophize. People like you and me need to earn money. We have bills. We have responsibilities. We can't just hop on a train and take it anywhere because this author thinks we need to focus on enjoying the journey—that the destination doesn't matter. Of course it matters."

Nora feigned a pensive expression. "Miracle Springs, as a destination, matters because of the Meadows. Is the development your metaphorical rose? Or has someone tamed you the way the prince tames the fox? That's the only way to form an unbreakable bond, according to this book."

"Tamed?" Collin laughed with genuine humor. "Not a word I'd apply to myself." He showed Nora his wedding band. "I might be married, but I'm still the same guy I was when I was single. The only difference is that I have to work harder now. I have two kids with a third on the way. My wife quit her job a year ago, which means I need to pick up the slack. I never have time to read anymore, but after I saw your stick, I decided to make a real effort to fit reading back into my schedule."

"I hope you'll take a chance on another book," Nora said, doing her best to remember that Collin may have been involved in Neil's murder. He hadn't pushed his partner in front of a train—not this debonair man in his pressed shirt and pants—but he might have hired someone else to do it. A husband and father who seemed genuinely interested in literature could still be a villain, but Nora sincerely hoped he wasn't involved. She liked this man.

With these conflicting thoughts swirling around in her mind, Nora stood and beckoned for Collin to follow her to a set of bookcases.

As she scanned the colorful book spines, she asked, "Does your next book pick have to be short or will you have more time to read over the next few days?"

Collin's eyes roamed over the shelf. "Less. With Neil gone, all the partners have more to do. Still, it would just be nice not to have to think about . . . well, you know . . ."

Recalling Estella's description of the partners in the Oasis, Nora realized that Collin was likely a master at concealing his feelings. He didn't grieve his partner's loss, so what other deceptions had he spun for her today?

"Whenever I want to take my mind off something serious, I opt for a mystery," Nora quickly said and pulled down a book.

"The Hound of the Baskervilles?" Collin sounded dubious.

"It'll make your blood race," Nora said. "Sherlock Holmes and Dr. Watson set out to disprove a curse. The book is filled with Gothic imagery, suspense, and superstition. At its heart, it's really a tale of good versus evil."

Collin flipped the book over and studied the blurb. "I always find the villains to be more interesting than the heroes. They seem more multidimensional. More realistic. I guess I can identify with the characters who make mistakes. What about you?"

The burn scar on Nora's arm tingled and she sensed that there was something leading in this seemingly innocuous question. "Life is never black-and-white," she said. "The best villains are characters we can empathize with, even if we don't condone their behavior. And you're right. They're often more complex than the heroes."

Though not in Sherlock Holmes's case, she thought.

A little grin played at the corners of Collin's mouth. "I'll give this a try, and maybe we can talk about it when I'm done. I feel like I'm back in my college days. I majored in business, but I minored in English so I could think about other things besides profit margins. It feels good to use that side of my brain for a change. The non-black-and-white part." He rapped on his temple with his knuckles. "Until I see you again, good luck at the bank. I bet you're a more attractive borrower than you realize."

Since Nora didn't know how to take this remark, she politely thanked Collin for his vote of confidence and rang up his purchase.

Later, after taping a note to the front door apologizing for closing early, Nora took a minute to stand on the sidewalk and gaze at the display window. She inhaled the rain-shower air, which held hints of cut grass and wet asphalt, and looked at the beach-read theme she'd designed. Multiple beach balls hung from the ceiling and a row of plastic buckets lined the ledge. Nora had stuffed each bucket with yellow or orange tissue paper and a book with a summery cover.

Her eyes roamed over Mariah Stewart's *That Chesapeake Summer*, Jess Walter's *Beautiful Ruins*, Liane Moriarty's *The Hypnotist's Love Story*, Elin Hilderbrand's *The Rumor*, Lorna Barrett's *Title Wave*, David Szalay's *All That Man Is*, Blake Crouch's *Pines*, Judy Blume's *Blubber*, Scott O'Dell's *Island of the Blue Dolphins*, and more.

"What would I do without you?" Nora whispered to the books before she limped toward Madison County Community Bank.

Dawson Hendricks was on the phone when Nora arrived for her appointment. The trip from Miracle Books to the bank had made her ankle sore and Nora knew that she should have iced and elevated the injured foot much more than she had throughout the day.

When Dawson came out of his office to fetch her, he gave her face the typical once-over while Nora studied the physical similarities between Dawson and his brother, Sheriff Toad. They were clearly related, though Dawson was taller and slimmer than his younger brother and had more laugh lines. Nora took this as a good sign.

"What a fine walking stick," the loan officer said. "Do you hike?"

"When I can," Nora replied. "I don't have any employees, so I spend most of my time working."

Dawson gestured for her to precede him into his office. "The life of a small-business owner isn't easy. Am I right?"

Nora nodded and waited for him to take his place behind his desk, but he hesitated. "You're really favoring that foot. Put it up on the second chair if that helps." He now sat behind his desk and reached for his computer mouse. "I've lost my balance on the trail a dozen times. Sometimes, I just forget to look down. I broke my left foot last year and I might still have an ice pack in the break room. Let me know if you need it."

Nora hadn't expected Dawson to be so solicitous. Again, she wondered how his brother had developed such a powerful disdain for women.

"I understand that you're interested in a home in the Meadows," Dawson said. "I talk to Annette frequently—she's been sending lots of business my way—and she mentioned that you were taken with the Cambridge floor plan."

"Yes, I especially loved the kitchen," Nora said. She pictured the stainless-steel appliances and knew that she could live in that house for her entire life without turning on the second wall oven.

Dawson nodded. "I hear you. I was visualizing myself as the next Gordon Ramsay after I toured the model house." He pulled out a stack of forms and folded his hands together. "Okay, let's get down to brass tacks."

Nora steeled herself. Though she'd been through this process four years ago when she'd purchased the train depot, the circumstances had been different. Back then, she'd had the whole of her savings to offer as a down payment. She'd also used a bank in a neighboring town because they'd advertised the lowest interest rate.

Now, she had to answer probing questions about her personal life and her finances. Despite Dawson's easygoing manner, Nora didn't like it. Her skin grew too warm and her burn scars itched. She willed her fingers not to stray to her cheek, but they wouldn't obey. She rubbed the shell-smooth skin and wished she could escape the hum of the fluorescent lights and the subtle clicking of Dawson's computer mouse.

The more Dawson pried, the more Nora forgot this was a ruse. She reverted to the nervous buyer she'd been four years ago, and she hated recalling her intense feelings of fear and hope. When he asked another question, Nora had to fight to keep the defiance from her voice. "I've basically put everything I have into the bookstore."

"I'm ashamed to say that I've never been inside," Dawson said, finally glancing away from his computer. "But I guess it's important to you."

"It's everything to me," Nora said fervently. She'd caught something dismissive in Dawson's last remark and it galled her.

Why did so many bankers and businesspeople look down their noses at those who devoted their lives to anything related to the arts?

Leaning forward in her chair, her eyes shining and her voice quivering with emotion, Nora said, "Virginia Woolf, an English novelist, perfectly describes how I feel about books and bookstores. She wrote, *Books are everywhere; and always the same sense of adventure fills us . . . in this random miscellaneous company we may rub against some complete stranger who will, with luck, turn into the best friend we have in the world.*"

Dawson nodded, his eyes still fixed on Nora's face. He seemed to be assessing her. Nora had entered the bank expecting to be judged, but there was something about the loan officer's gaze that implied he wasn't coming to a decision based on her previous answers.

"Do you want this house as badly as you wanted that bookstore?" he asked softly.

"I do," Nora lied without hesitation.

Smiling, Dawson stood up and closed his office door. When he resumed his seat, there was a glint in his eye that unsettled her. Tenting his hands, he said, "You won't qualify for a loan at any other bank. But if you *really* want your dream house, I'll make it happen for you."

Nora leaned forward in her chair. "How?"

Dawson wriggled his fingers. "I'm going to work some magic for you. All you have to do is add your signature to a few forms. How does that sound?"

Too good to be true, Nora thought. Aloud, she said, "Wonderful."

"Great." Dawson proffered a pen. "Then let's get started."

As Nora signed a pile of forms, she didn't fail to notice the gold script running along the length of the pen. It read, WE BUILD DREAMS, ONE HOUSE AT A TIME—PINE RIDGE PROPERTIES. On the back were the words THE MEADOWS. AGENT: ANNETTE GOLDSMITH.

The pen must have been a favorite of Dawson's, because parts of several letters had rubbed off. The *G* in *Goldsmith* for example, resembled a *C*.

Staring at Annette's name, Nora realized that she was looking at the second set of initials Estella had seen on Fenton's Oasis Bar napkin. But what did that mean? Had Annette been involved in Neil's death? Had Dawson Hendricks?

"Everything okay?" Dawson asked. He was watching her closely.

Nora forced a smile. "It couldn't be better."

Chapter 8

If more of us valued food and cheer and song above hoarded gold, it would be a merrier world.
—J.R.R. Tolkien

Nora finished signing the documents where Dawson indicated, and he concluded the meeting by promising he'd get back to her soon. He then handed her a lollipop as if she were a well-behaved child and escorted her to the front door.

Nora limped out of the bank, tossed the sucker in the trash bin, and started for home. She'd made it to the end of the block when a cherry-red Corvette pulled alongside the curb. Estella rolled down the window and called, "Hop in!"

Smiling over her friend's choice of words, Nora lurched like a zombie until she was able to drop into the low passenger seat.

"The Secret, Book, and Scone Society is meeting at the Pink Lady Grill tonight," Estella informed her. "I hope you don't have other plans."

Nora snorted. "Like what? A hot date?"

Estella shot her a sidelong glance. "What about that paramedic? He's now officially the sexiest man in Miracle Springs. And I got some dirt on him today from one of my clients. Wanna hear it?"

Though Nora most definitely did, she shook her head. "I'm more interested in how you're doing. After last night."

"I'm fine," she said. "If anything, that bastard's behavior has me even more fired up to seek justice for Neil. I know people look at me and see a slutty, gold-digging hair stylist, but I have a decent brain in this pretty head. Comes from when I was growing up, and I spent all that time hiding in my room with a pile of library books. That's what you do when you have no friends. And no TV."

"Having been to the Miracle Springs County Library, it's a wonder you found anything to read," Nora said as Estella accelerated through a yellow light.

"Papaya!" Estella shouted. She eased off the gas and grinned. "I like to think of different words describing yellow-orange. You know, the shade the light is *just* before it turns red?"

Nora laughed. "Like ochre? Or pumpkin?"

"Exactly." Estella looked pleased. "Next time, you yell out a word."

"Or you could just stop and let the light turn red," Nora said.

Estella smirked. "Where's the fun in that? Besides, I'm hungry. Borderline hangry. I hope Hester got us a table. The Pink Lady is always packed in the summertime."

The Pink Lady Grill was beloved by locals and out-of-towners alike. It was an unusual eatery, to say the least. Decorated entirely in shades of pink, the walls were covered with framed motivational quotes and letters from cancer survivors. Jack Nakamura, the owner and cook, was a Japanese-American who'd lost his mother to breast cancer in his late twenties. Back then, the diner had simply been called Jack's and offered a Southern-style breakfast menu. Nora had heard of how difficult it had been for Jack to convince the townsfolk that he could cook a mean plate of chicken and waffles and that his buttermilk biscuits were just as good as Grandma's.

Jack was barely making ends meet when his mother was diagnosed with stage-four breast cancer. As word of her illness spread and the people of Miracle Springs realized that Jack's mother wouldn't be working the cash register or showing them to their tables much longer, they flocked to the diner. No one understood how a man raised on traditional Japanese fare made the best hush puppies, fried chicken, chess pie, hummingbird cake, cheese grits, and sausage gravy in the county. In spite of their disbelief, the people of Miracle Springs continued to fill the booths of Jack's diner long after his mother passed.

To honor her memory, Jack redecorated and changed the eatery's name. He also collected funds to help local women in need pay for breast-cancer screenings and other diagnostic tests. Between his big heart and his mastery of Southern dishes, Jack soon became one of Miracle Springs's favorite sons.

He had very little spare time, but when Jack took a day off, he spent it reading. He faithfully shopped at Nora's store, where he purchased biographies, autobiographies, and books on cancer research and recovery.

"Table for two?" asked the hostess when Nora and Estella entered the diner. Nora noticed that the woman's fingernails had been painted the same shade of ballet-slipper pink as the walls. All except her pinkie nails, which were hot pink with sparkles.

"Our friends already have a table, thanks," Estella said, waving at Hester and June.

The waitress smiled cheerfully. Following Nora's glance, she splayed her fingers. "Aren't they fun? I've been using Pinterest to find new designs. You could do it too . . ." She trailed off, suddenly noticing that Nora didn't have a pinkie nail on her right hand. "What happened, hon?"

Nora wasn't about to talk about her accident with a stranger, so she gestured at the rotating pie display and said, "I was chopping apples when the knife slipped—" She shrugged haplessly and continued walking.

"How was the bank?" Hester asked as soon as Nora sat down opposite her.

June nudged Hester. "Let's give the woman a minute to look at her menu before we interrogate her. Or, you could forget the menu and order the fried catfish. Jack's is the best in all of North Carolina."

"I always have the Cobb salad," Estella said. "And a strawberry milkshake. Jack donates every cent he makes on desserts to the Susan G. Komen Foundation. But before we order, I want to tell you that I think I know the meaning of Buford, the last name on Fenton Greer's napkin."

The other women stared at her.

"It was pure luck, actually," Estella continued, her green eyes shining with excitement. "I was flipping through TV channels and stopped to watch *Smokey and the Bandit*. I love me some Burt Reynolds." She put her hand to her heart. "Anyway, the sheriff—a tubby, bumbling country bumpkin, is Buford T. Justice. I think the Buford from the napkin refers to our own tubby lawman."

"I can definitely see the resemblance," June muttered. "I remember that movie and what a cliché that character was, but the Toad is a cliché too. A lazy, short-tempered, no-good chauvinist pig." She nodded at Estella. "The 'city folk' from Asheville are making fun of our local Johnny Law. Even though they need him, they don't have to respect him."

Nora, who was too distracted to think about food, dropped her menu on the table. "It makes perfect sense for both Hendricks brothers to be involved. I'm with June. I think you're onto something, Estella. And if you're right, then we're dealing with powerful adversaries. The man in charge of decisions regarding the local people's money and the man in charge of the town's law and order."

"Was something revealed during your meeting with Dawson?" Hester asked.

The arrival of the waitress prevented Nora from answering.

Without looking at the menu, she ordered eggs, bacon, toast, and an iced tea. "I love breakfast for dinner. I could eat bacon and eggs twice a day."

The waitress lingered at the next booth, preventing Nora from talking about her meeting at the bank.

"If I never see another plate of scrambled eggs, that'll be just fine with me," June said.

Nora cocked her head. "Do you have ovophobia? A fear of eggs?"

"Is that a thing?" Hester asked.

"Alfred Hitchcock was an ovophobe," Nora said. "He couldn't stand the sight of them either."

June frowned. "I was fine with eggs until I started working at Belle Shoal Assisted Living. I worked there for fifteen years. During my tenure, I smelled scrambled eggs every morning. Powdered ones. Runny ones. Uneaten ones, mostly. The residents hated those eggs and even though those poor souls really needed their protein, they couldn't choke those nasty things down." She waved her hands. "But enough about me. Tell us about your meeting with Dawson."

Nora filled them in on her exchange with Collin Stone first. By the time she was done, their meals had arrived and she took a break to eat her omelet.

"Where was this assisted-living place?" Estella asked June as she drizzled dressing over her salad. "Not around here. The name's not familiar."

"It's in New York," June replied. "That's where I'm from."

Hester put down her fork. "Why did you leave?"

"Shame," June said, pushing away her plate even though she'd barely touched her catfish. "I was fired from my job and sued for neglect. The suit was filed against the company who owned the facility, but it also included me directly. I lost. And when I lost, I lost everything."

The other women remained silent, sensing that June needed to get her story out all at once—that it was sitting in her throat like a trapped bird desperately waiting to be set free.

"Belle Shoal was not one of these ritzy retirement communities with delicious meals and scenic walking paths," June continued. "The residents weren't entertained by magicians, karaoke machines, dance classes, or elementary kids singing carols at Christmastime. People went to Belle Shoal because they didn't have money to pay for a nice place. Most of them were without family. They didn't have visitors. Their days were filled with bland food, boring TV programs, and hours of staring at the fish tank in the main hall."

"It sounds like a setting out of a Dickens novel," Nora said.

June nodded. "*Bleak House*, maybe? Belle Shoal—*beautiful shore*—was a failed metaphor. The residents called their home Hell Hole instead. That fish tank, which was in the center of the hall and was supposed to be the 'shoal,' contained a few pathetic goldfish. Me and the other caregivers did all we could to bring a little music and color into that place. We made tissue-paper flowers, bought radios from yard sales, held bingo and Scrabble tournaments, and brought in anyone who'd visit for free. And we read aloud to our residents every afternoon. The book that ended up changing my life was *Water for Elephants*. Does anyone know it?"

The other three women at the table indicated that they'd all read Sara Gruen's novel.

"The residents loved it," June said, her gaze turning distant. "By coincidence or by some crazy twist of fate, a traveling carnival came to town days after I finished reading the book. The carnival was set up in the field down the street, and we heard the music from the rides. The residents told me that they could see the lights at night and a few even claimed to smell buttered popcorn. Suddenly, they started sharing stories of circuses, fairs, and boardwalks. They came alive talking about these things— about winning a toy for their best girl. Or eating hot dogs. Riding so high on a Ferris wheel that they felt like they were flying. Treasured memories."

Estella signaled the waitress and ordered strawberry milkshakes for everyone at the table. She then looked at June. "I counted the days to the county fair. Years ago, it was the biggest thrill a person could find in a small town. The biggest legal one, anyway. I understand why your residents were so excited."

Hester glanced from Estella to June. "But they couldn't go, right?"

June didn't respond. She picked up her fork and pushed her green beans into a neat pile.

"You took them," Nora said softly. "You wanted to do something special for them. You wanted them to have new memories that were filled with color, sound, and flavor."

June's gaze remained on her plate.

"Yes," she finally said. "I wanted them to live once more before they died. No one visited. They didn't get care packages or letters. I tried to implement a pet program, but the owners of Belle Shoal decided that animals were unsanitary and would make the residents sick." She chortled, but there was no mirth in the sound. "They were already sick! Every one of them had health issues, but I was worried about them *here*." She pounded her fist against her chest.

"How did you manage it?" Nora asked. "The logistics must have been incredibly complicated."

June whistled. "You have *no* idea. Sneaking two dozen old people out of an assisted-living facility is like breaking a bunch of serial killers out of a maximum-security prison. I had to convince certain staff members that I was taking the residents to the movies. I had to rent a bus and purchase food and ride tickets using my own money. I thought it was worth it. When I saw Mrs. Lowenthal eating cotton candy and Mr. Bloom on the bumper cars, I thought I'd made the right choice. The only choice."

"I bet they had a ball," Estella said. "No matter what happened, I don't see why you'd regret doing what you did. You were thoughtful and generous. And no matter what, those people knew how much you cared. Look what you did to prove it to them."

June's eyes sparked with anger. "But I should have been thinking about *my* family *first*. I didn't consider how my actions might affect them. I couldn't have predicted that Mr. Wayne would suffer a heart attack on the tilt-a-whirl. I couldn't have known that he would die before he reached the hospital and that anything positive that happened that night meant nothing in comparison to Mr. Wayne's accident."

The waitress appeared with their shakes. In light of June's story, the pink frozen beverages topped with crowns of whipped cream and Maraschino cherries suddenly seemed offensive in their frivolity.

"Enjoy, girls!" the waitress trilled and bustled off again.

Hester broke the silence by saying, "You don't have to go on if you don't want to."

"Yes, I do. This is how we'll know we can trust each other, remember?" June reached for her milkshake and tried to take a sip, but the shake was too thick for the narrow straw. Instead, she pulled the spoon from the bottom of the glass and popped it into her mouth. "Hmm, that's good. It has chunks of fresh strawberries."

Following her lead, the rest of the Secret, Book, and Scone Society members sampled their shakes.

Nora couldn't remember the last time she'd had a milkshake. When the cold, sweet flavors of vanilla ice cream and strawberries coated her tongue, she tried to savor the taste, but it was difficult to feel enjoyment with June's story hanging like a thundercloud over their table.

"Mr. Wayne's family filed a wrongful-death suit against the assisted-living facility," June continued. "They also sued me for neglect because I took Mr. Wayne to the carnival. They didn't care that he'd spent his last breath thanking me for the best evening he'd had in decades. They didn't tell the judge how they hadn't paid him an ounce of attention until they realized that they might profit from his death. And profit they did. They won. I lost."

She paused and Nora almost looked up—looked up to see the thundercloud that was June's story break open and release its cold, biting rain.

"I lost my job and every penny to my name," June went on in a near-croak. "My boy, who was supposed to start college the next fall, couldn't go. I couldn't afford it. I couldn't afford anything. I lost our apartment, my car, and the love and respect of my son."

"Is he still in New York?"

June moved her straw in a circular motion, blending the whipped cream into the strawberry shake. "Tyson went to live with my sister while I looked for a new job. I knew I'd have to leave the state—take any work I could get. Girls, I have done it all. I've waited tables, cleaned hotel rooms, manned a clothes press, bagged groceries. And during that time, Tyson refused to communicate with me. He wouldn't come to the phone or read a letter or e-mail. He lived with my sister for just under two years and then, they had a falling out and Tyson left. She never heard from him again."

"God," Hester breathed. "Did you try to find him?"

"Of course," June said heatedly. "As soon as I had the money, I hired a detective. He found Tyson in L.A., working as a bouncer for some nightclub. I called the club . . ." Her voice wavered and she stopped to collect herself. "Tyson told me never to contact him again—that I was dead to him. I kept trying. I sent letters and packages, but they came back unopened. Finally, I saved enough to fly to California. I showed up at the club an hour before it opened for business, but Tyson turned me away. He said that he didn't have a mother."

June let out a single, heart-wrenching sob before covering

her face with her napkin. Hester put an arm around June and squeezed. "I'm so sorry," she whispered. "So sorry, June."

Nora longed to comfort June too, but there didn't seem any words more fitting than the ones Hester repeated in a soft, soothing murmur.

"Everythin' all right?" their waitress suddenly asked in her loud twang.

Estella jumped a little in surprise and said, "We're just fine." Her reply probably sounded more abrupt than intended.

"Good thing we've eaten or she might spit in our shakes." June dabbed her eyes, sniffed, and said, "The long and the short of it is this: Though I never stop trying to connect with my son, he's made it clear that he wants nothing to do with me. Sometimes, the pain of missing him and wondering what he's doing is almost more than I can bear."

"But you bear it," Nora said. "Without letting the pain turn into bitterness."

June pointed at the window. "I found more peace here than I ever hoped to find. But I'll tell you what. It's mighty nice to have friends to talk to. I've had friendly acquaintances in other towns, but not friends." She picked up her milkshake glass. "So let's toast to sharing secrets with friends and get on with our investigation."

"To secrets," the women said in unison as they raised their glasses. "And to friends."

Nora resumed her narrative of the day's events by summarizing her meeting with Dawson Hendricks.

She finished by saying, "I can't say for certain, but I felt like he was recruiting me. My reward for whatever I would be asked to do was the approval of my loan."

Hester's eyes lit with excitement. "Under normal circumstances, do you think you'd qualify?"

"No chance in hell," Nora said. "I don't have any equity. The only thing I own outright is Caboose Cottage and selling that wouldn't give me a twenty-percent down payment on a new house in the Meadows. Plus, there's the debt I have on the store. Trust me, I'm a seriously unattractive borrower. And I'm not referring to my scars."

Estella glared at her. "People *can* see past them, you know." When Nora averted her gaze in embarrassment, Estella pressed on. "Those scars don't define you. I realize that you'd prefer to go back to your unblemished skin, but someone should tell you that those scars could never make you ugly. I don't even notice them anymore."

Surprise made Nora turn back to Estella. "Honestly?"

"Yes," Hester said. "We just see you. Not your scars."

Too moved to reply, Nora motioned for the waitress to bring the check.

After dinner, Nora had Estella drop her off at Miracle Books. She wanted to pull some titles for June and while she didn't have much in stock on estranged adult children, she had at least one nonfiction book and several novels that she felt would put June on the road to healing.

Limping around the shop, Nora realized that she'd been given a dose of healing tonight as well. This idea that people could see her—not just her scars—was an incredible notion. Nora was ruminating over this when there was a loud knock on the front door.

Nora froze. Though she'd turned on a few lamps throughout the store, she hadn't expected the light to attract any customers. Not at nine o'clock on a summer night. At this time, people were sitting on front porches or taking refuge from the humidity in dark, air-conditioned rooms.

Holding a paperback called *Done With the Crying* by Sheri McGregor in one hand, Nora hobbled to the end of a bookshelf and removed a pair of hardbacks, allowing her a glimpse of the front door. She could see the silhouette of a man, but that was all.

He knocked again, louder this time. Nora tried to gauge whether the knock sounded threatening, impatient, or just insistent.

This is my shop, she reminded herself. *If I don't like what I see when I look outside, I'll point at the* CLOSED *sign and wave the man away.*

The man turned out to be Collin Stone.

"Shit," Nora muttered under her breath. Hours ago, when the two of them had sat in the shop's comfy chairs and had an impromptu book discussion, Nora hadn't been uneasy. However, when Collin had made those cryptic remarks about Nora's plans to apply for a home loan, she'd been reminded that he might have plotted Neil's death.

And now he was here, smiling at her through the glass, as if it was completely normal for him to show up after business hours.

Nora unlocked the door and opened it, but not all the way. By blocking the space between the exterior and interior of the shop with her body, Nora made it clear that she wasn't going to invite him inside.

"I didn't mean to startle you," Collin said, still wearing his charming smile. "I was in town having dinner when a little bird told me some good news. I saw lights on in your store and hoped to catch you before you left."

Though Collin's story seemed plausible enough, Nora had the distinct feeling that this was no chance encounter. Taking a firmer hold of her walking stick, Nora met Collin's gaze. She did not return his smile.

"I've had a very long day," she said. "Perhaps we could talk in the morning?"

A shadow surfaced in Collin's eyes. Dislike. Or something even more hostile. Something like menace. "Wish I could, but I'm busy tomorrow. I won't keep you. I just stopped by to tell you that your loan was approved. You're going to be living in the Meadows by this time next year."

He folded his arms over his chest and waited. Judging from his self-satisfied grin, he clearly expected an animated response from Nora.

What little bird? she wondered. *Isn't that information confidential?*

In the seconds it took Nora to process these thoughts, Collin's smile slipped. "I thought you'd be more excited."

"I think I'm in shock," she said, forcing a closed-mouth grin. "I never expected to qualify. Did you have something to do with this? I have a feeling I owe you."

Instantly relaxing, Collin unfolded his arms and held them wide. Giving her a coy look, he said, "Other than put in a good word, there isn't much I could do."

"Well, if you *were* able to influence the bank's decision, then I'm grateful." Nora tried to widen her grin, but she found it a challenge to maintain the friendly pretense in the gloom-filled threshold. Though she hated to admit it, she felt vulnerable. The closest eatery was three blocks away and there wasn't a single passerby on the sidewalk. It was so quiet that she and Collin could have been standing on the surface of the moon.

"After we talked today, I had a gut feeling that you were just the type of person we were looking for," Collin said. He took two steps back and performed a rakish bow. "I hope you can still fall asleep after hearing your good news. I know that when I'm excited about a new project, I have trouble falling asleep at night."

Now that there was more space between her and Collin, Nora released her white-knuckled grip on her walking stick. Had she misjudged Collin Stone? Could this man—a hardworking husband and father, an insightful reader, and someone who appeared to have championed Nora's dream of buying a new house—really be involved in a murder plot?

"I have lots to think about," she told Collin. "Thanks again for stopping by."

He waved and turned away.

Nora closed and locked the front door, but continued watching Collin as he moved down the block. His stride was unhurried and he walked with his hands in his pockets. To Nora, he had the air of a man who'd checked an important item off his list.

"Was I the item?" she mumbled. Her exhalation, which fogged the door's glass panel, resembled a deformed butterfly.

Nora wiped it away with her forearm.

That night, Nora's dreams were riddled with fire. Not the car fire from the night of her accident. This fire lived in the Miracle Springs train tunnel. Like an animal waking from a long slumber, it sought to devour anything daring to enter its domain.

Nora stared at the tunnel mouth, paralyzed by horror, as the train engine burst forth into the daylight. Flames covered every inch of its surface. Tongues of yellow and orange licked the sky and lapped the ground. Behind the engine, every passenger car was ablaze. Smoke gushed from the windows, blackening the air. The train looked like a dragon that had gone insane and turned its fiery breath upon its own body.

Finally, as the train barreled closer and closer to where Nora stood, it screamed in agony and rage. The haunted, romantic whistle Nora loved was gone, and she knew that if she didn't jump out of the way, the burning train would run her down.

The train shrieked again, but the noise had lost its ferocity. The fire images began to dissolve and the next time Nora heard the sound, she recognized it as a ringing phone.

She opened her eyes, completely disoriented.

Her cell phone was in the kitchen, ringing and ringing. Nora never bothered to mute it because she didn't receive calls during off hours. Very few people had her number. That is, until recently. She'd given it to the members of the Secret, Book and Scone Society.

Through eyes blurred with sleep, Nora saw June's name on the phone screen. She answered the call.

"Nora? I'm sorry to wake you so early," June began.

Nora's gaze drifted out the kitchen window. Filaments of light bled among the tree branches. "Are you okay?"

"I couldn't sleep, so I went for a walk like I usually do," June explained. There was a hollow echo to her voice. "And I saw two cars from the sheriff's department parked in front of Estella's house. The light bars were blazing like disco balls and I heard shouting inside. I tried to get closer, but Sheriff Toad's douchebag deputy told me to get lost or I'd be arrested too."

"They were arresting Estella?" Nora croaked, her words a dry riverbed. "For what?"

"Murder," June said. "They're saying she killed Fenton Greer."

Hoping to shut out this new day and the terrible fear that had dawned along with it, Nora closed her eyes.

When she did, all she saw was fire.

Chapter 9

The worst part of holding memories is not the pain.
It's the loneliness of it.

—Lois Lowry

"Nora? Are you there?" June asked.

Nora was and she wasn't.

She was standing in the kitchen of her tiny house in Miracle Springs, but she was also kneeling on the side of a dark highway, cradling a little boy's limp body in her arms.

The toddler's clothes were burned and the places where the fire had licked his skin raw were peeping through the rents in his jeans. His face, arms, and torso were untouched, but Nora took no comfort in this. Even the light given off by the burning car, she couldn't tell if the boy drew breath. His body felt warm in her arms, but Nora didn't know if she was feeling his heat or the pain that was beginning to claw its way through the haze of shock in her brain.

After gingerly laying the boy down on the grassy shoulder, Nora began to perform CPR. She'd taken a lifesaving course at the library along with several other coworkers, and while she'd paid close attention to the instructions, she was terrified that she might be doing it wrong. However, his small lungs inflated with her exhalations and after two minutes of rescue breathing, she placed her cell phone by the boy's cheek and called 911. She didn't remember what she said or how the operator responded—some things from that night never did come back.

But the boy did.

When the paramedics arrived, he was breathing on his own. Raspy, throat-full-of-pebbles breaths.

"Nora?" June repeated, louder this time.

"I'm sorry," Nora said, speaking to June and to that little boy from her past. The hand holding the phone trembled, so she squeezed until the edges of the phone pressed into her flesh in a vain attempt to stop the shaking. "What else did you see?"

June sighed. In that sigh, Nora heard June's relief. She didn't have to bear the weight of worrying about Estella alone. Nora was willing to share the burden.

"Estella raised holy hell when they bundled her into the squad car, or whatever you call it. She screeched at those cops to get their heads examined. Even when Sheriff Todd warned her to watch her mouth, she kept on hollering. They'll be calling all of us in for statements today, I imagine, because if that girl was smart, she'll tell them that she was with us for most of the night."

Nora didn't respond right away. After filling her coffeemaker with water, she opened the canister where she kept her grounds. The rich roasted nut aroma permeated the air and Nora raised a heaping scoop directly under her nose and inhaled.

"Maybe I won't wait for their call," June went on. "Maybe I'll just waltz into the station like I'm the Queen of Sheba and announce that I'm there to prove there's no way my friend killed the wannabe rapist."

"We can't mention what happened between Estella and Fenton at the bathhouse," Nora said as she dumped rounded spoonfuls of grounds into a brown-paper filter. "The sheriff will cite Fenton's behavior as Estella's motive for committing murder. Did you hear how he died?"

June made a noise that could have been a grunt or a growl. "All I heard was that it was in the pools. Which means I won't be working today."

"You should go in anyway," Nora said. "Find out all you can. Every detail. Every bit of gossip. Who knows what will prove helpful to Estella?" She pushed the *brew* button on the coffeemaker. "Have you called Hester?"

"No. Just you."

Nora listened to the coffeemaker's comforting gurgle for several seconds. Finally, she couldn't hold back any longer. "She might have done it, June. The four of us weren't drawn to each other by accident. We're damaged women. Not bad. Not evil. But broken. The darkness wriggles in through the cracks."

"So does the light," June countered. "Show me someone who hasn't been on this earth for thirty-plus years without earning their share of scars and I'll show you someone who's spent their life in a bubble. Or on a tiny island. Or in Greenland. Anyway, Estella's no killer. I might not have the longest list of marketable skills, but I can tell when a person is ready to snap. I've seen what that looks like." She was talking so quickly that the words raced out of her mouth like horses from the starting gate, and Nora had to pay close attention to catch each one before it ran away.

"Where?" Nora asked in an attempt to slow June's pace. "When you were working at Belle Shoal?"

"Yes," June said. "Those folks might have been living inside old bodies, but their feelings were as powerful as floodwater. That was the hardest part of my job—knowing I couldn't help them escape their heads. They were trapped in stuffy, depressing rooms with the TV droning on and on. No sunlight on their faces. No music. No flowers on their bedside tables. There were thousands of rules meant to keep them safe. What those rules actually did was crush the joy out of their final days.

Some of the residents meekly submitted to their fate. Others grew angry and combative. They were usually drugged."

The coffeemaker issued a series of loud belches and beeps, signaling that it had finished brewing. "That's awful," Nora said.

"People get a caged-animal look about them when they're close to snapping," June continued. "The anger builds as they review the injustices done to them over and over again until they have to act. If Estella was traumatized following Fenton's assault, then she did an incredible job of hiding it." She paused. "I'm not saying that she wasn't shocked, scared, and pissed off. I think she was all of these and more. But plotting revenge by murdering Fenton? No way. She was the one who suggested we use what the bastard had done to her as ammunition against him and the rest of the Pine Ridge slimes to get justice for Neil. Remember?"

"I remember. For whatever reason, I needed to toss out the possibility and have you argue against it." Nora filled the largest coffee mug she had. Unlike those she kept at the bookstore, all the mugs she used at home were handmade by a local potter. She loved how the curve of the handle was a perfect fit for her fingers or how cupping the mug in two hands sent warmth deep into her palms. It was as if the North Carolina clay and homemade glaze retained more heat than a coffee mug produced in some massive factory. Nora had mugs in four different glazes. Today, she'd chosen the cobalt.

To douse the fire, she thought.

"I need to think about how we can help Estella," Nora said after taking a fortifying sip of coffee. "For now, why don't you glean as much info as possible at the lodge? I'll see if Hester can do the same at the bakery. The sheriff is a regular customer and she seems to have a way with him."

"Estella needs a lawyer. A good one," June said. "Someone from out of town. Somebody with perspective."

THE SECRET, BOOK & SCONE SOCIETY   125

Nora nodded, even though June couldn't see the gesture. "Our best chance of securing her freedom is to discover the identity of the real killer. We'll also have to gather enough evidence to convince a judge of Estella's innocence. No attorney will do that. Besides, the defense attorneys we see on TV—those that brag about their ability to keep their clients out of jail—they come with a pretty steep price tag. None of us have the kind of money it takes to hire a lawyer who has his own team of investigators and researchers. We'll have to do the legwork. The three of us."

"While keeping our jobs," June said.

"And pretending not to be interested in Estella's fate," Nora added. "For now, our book and scone society needs to truly be secret. Otherwise, people might not open up to us."

June grunted. "It's a little late for secrecy. We've been to the Oasis. And we ate at the Pink Lady last night. As soon as Estella's arrest goes public, all of Miracle Springs will be talking about how the book club for misfits drank strawberry shakes before the redhead killed an out-of-towner."

"All the more reason for us to keep our heads down."

Looking at her coffee mug, she knew that she couldn't carry both the mug and her phone to her chair. She was ready to ice her injured ankle and when she shifted her weight, a sudden jolt of pain made her remember Jedediah's instructions. She also recalled his wood-smoke voice, the feeling of his forearm pressed against the small of her back, and the scent of pine needles in his hair.

"June," she said, trying to ignore the surge in her blood at the memory of Jed's breath, warm on her neck, or his parting whisper. "See if you can find out which paramedics responded to the nine-one-one call at the lodge."

"Aha!" June cried. "Because if one of them was the hottie from your spill in the lobby, you could call him for a coffee date. Right?"

"Something like that." Heat rushed to Nora's cheeks, neck, and breasts.

What kind of woman gets turned on at the same time her friend is being processed as a murder suspect? Nora thought with shame.

Luckily, June let the subject drop. After promising to contact Nora at the shop as soon as she had useful information to share, she ended the call.

Nora spent the next thirty minutes drinking coffee, elevating and icing her foot, and thinking. Every so often, she'd jot down a thought or a question on a notepad. Finally, she picked up her phone and prepared to ruin Hester's day.

"The Gingerbread House. How may I help you?"

"It's Nora. I know you're baking, but are you serving customers yet?"

She heard the sound of a door shutting and Hester said, "That slamming noise is me putting the cinnamon rolls in to bake. They're the last things I make before I unlock the door. I love to serve them hot from the oven with the icing cascading down—"

"Hester," Nora interrupted. "Fenton Greer was murdered last night."

"What?" Hester cried. And then, "Where? How?"

Nora returned her ice pack to the freezer. "All I can tell you is that he was found at the Miracle Springs Pools and that Estella was taken into custody."

Hester drew in a shallow breath and held on to it without letting go.

"I know," Nora said softly. "I felt the same way. But we'll help her, Hester. You, me, and June. Can you work some magic with your scones? Or those cinnamon buns? Get the sheriff or his deputies to share some of the details of the crime with you? The town paper will be sniffing around those law boys too. I wouldn't be surprised if the whole gang ends up in your bakery. Keep your ears open, Hester. Our best chance of freeing Estella is by offering up the real killer on a silver platter."

"But how will Estella survive in the meantime?" Hester whispered. "In a *cell*? Think about it. I doubt she's ever been separated from her hair dryer or makeup case. She probably has satin sheets on her bed and a chenille blanket on her sofa for when she watches TV. How is she going to survive a night in jail, let alone any longer than that?"

Nora suppressed an urge to snap at Hester. At times, her younger friend seemed like an old soul. But there were other times when her curiously naïve remarks rubbed Nora the wrong way. "Estella's made of tough stuff," she said. "We all are."

Later, as Nora showered, she hoped what she'd told Hester would prove to be true. It was one thing to talk about strength, but to actually be strong in the face of hardship—that was a different story. And yet Nora had drawn courage from words before. She'd turned to books again and again to see her through the worst of days. They were waiting for her now. Rows of books. Stacks and piles of books. Just thinking of the rainbow of colored covers, myriad typefaces, leather bindings, and the occasional flash of gilt lettering allowed Nora to relax. The books in her shop weren't merely things. They were gifts wrapped in imagination, inspiration, excitement, pain, and heartache. Gifts given by thousands of writers. Gifts just waiting to be opened.

With this thought in mind, Nora dressed and hurried up the narrow path leading from Caboose Cottage to Miracle Books. She barely had time to let herself in the back entrance and unlock the front door before June called.

"For the first time since this day from hell began, I feel like we've caught a break," she began. "Jedediah was one of two paramedics who responded to the nine-one-one call from the thermal pools last night. Which means he transported Fenton's body to the morgue."

"What about the scene?" Nora asked, swallowing the unfamiliar lump that had formed in her throat at the sound of Jedediah's name. "Were you able to see anything?"

"Not a peep." June didn't bother masking her disappointment. "My manager, who is *not* a small woman, stood outside the doors with a hand on her hip. She used her other hand to wave a guest towel at anyone who dared to get too close. She flicked it at people like they were flies at a barbecue. I tried to sneak in the side entrance—I think of it as Estella's entrance now—but when I saw a deputy coming out, I hightailed it behind a bush and stayed hidden until I could get back up to the lodge. I'm waiting for Bob to come on duty. He'll want to help Estella and I think we can trust him, don't you?"

Nora hesitated. "I don't know, June. I got good vibes from him the other night, but what does that mean? Once, I knew a man so well that I could predict the words he'd speak." She felt a knife-twist in her stomach as she remembered the moment she'd found out that her husband had been living a double life. "As it turned out, I was wrong to have believed anything he said. So when it comes to trusting people, my automatic response these days is that it's better not to. Except for . . ." Nora glanced down to see that she was bending a paperback so violently that she'd not only broken its spine, she'd also crinkled its glossy new cover. She'd have to sell it as a used book now.

"I know," June said gently. "You're trying to trust the three of us. And you'll get there. As for me, I need coffee. Lots and lots of coffee. I hope Bob can make me stronger stuff than they serve at the lodge restaurants. I always hear the guests griping about how weak it is."

"Well, if he doesn't, drop by later and I'll brew you some."

Putting the phone aside, Nora ran the edge of a ruler over the book in an attempt to smooth out the wrinkles she'd made. Her efforts were fruitless. "Sorry," she said, addressing the paperback. Shoving her phone in her back pocket, she collected the book—a how-to guide on using natural supplements as a means of achieving happiness—and headed to the health and medicine section.

Nora threaded her way around the antiques, art, and coffee table categories, gathering strays while she walked. The sleigh bells rang, signaling the arrival of a customer, and Nora called out a polite hello.

She was just reaching up to reshelf the natural-supplement guide when a man's voice said, "Are you sure that belongs here?"

The book, which had been perched on the edge of the shelf like a skier facing a downhill slope, took the plunge. It skittered to the left, avoiding Nora's hand as though it were a mogul made of flesh, and plummeted to the floor. When it struck, the cover spread open and Nora was reminded of a bird preparing for flight. Only this bird was broken.

"Sorry. I didn't mean to startle you." Jedediah Craig gingerly took the paperback off the floor, cradling it by the spine like a bibliophile holding a rare tome with a vellum cover and marbled fore edges.

Nora reached for the damaged book. "I've been abusing this poor thing all morning. We're some pair." Avoiding Jed's gaze, she asked, "Why did you ask me if it belonged here?"

"Because you shelve the herbal remedies with medicine." After scanning the titles for several seconds, Jed pulled a book called *The Encyclopedia of Natural Medicine* off the shelf. "But I was just teasing." He sounded contrite. "Just because I've been trained to use certain methods doesn't mean I'm not open to other approaches to medicine. I'd never knock holistic healing or any other kind of healing, for that matter. Everyone's pain is unique. Their healing usually is too. Speaking of which, how's your ankle?"

"Tender," Nora said, feeling acutely aware of how close she and Jed were standing and of how his gaze had slowly traveled down her body to rest on her injured foot. "I can get around well enough, though." Eager to take the focus off her body, she pointed at the book in his hands. "Are you a reader? I don't think you've been in my shop before."

"Every time I drive by in the ambulance, I fantasize about pulling over and coming inside, but I suspect that my customers wouldn't appreciate that." He flashed Nora the briefest of smiles. "I moved to Miracle Springs over a month ago. Most of my stuff is still in boxes piled in my living room. I've been working crazy shifts from the moment I got here."

After replacing the book, Jed's gaze traveled to the next set of shelves, which housed an eclectic array of titles for pet owners. "I don't usually follow up on patients at their place of business, but this gave me an excuse to finally come in and browse. I was hoping you had something to help me with Henry Higgins."

Nora waited for Jed to elaborate, but he seemed distracted by a book on pet massage. "Are you referring to the doctor from *Pygmalion*?"

"What?" Jed looked at her in confusion and then laughed. "I've heard of that play. But no. Henry Higgins is my dog and I named him after the character in *My Fair Lady*. It's my mom's favorite musical. She's the one stuck taking care of my big guy until my shifts settle down. Another paramedic is supposed to join our crew next month. Until then, it'll be all work and no unpacked boxes for me."

I knew there had to be something wrong with him, Nora thought. *He's a mama's boy.*

"What kind of help do you need with Henry Higgins?" Nora liked the name. She could picture a smart, well-groomed canine like a Standard Poodle or Weimaraner sitting on his haunches next to Jed's chair, patiently waiting to go for a walk. "I guess I should ask his breed too. Not that I'm a dog expert or anything. I'm not. I had a black Lab when I was a kid, but that's the extent of my experience."

"You're missing out. Dogs are amazing. Cats too," Jed said. "And to answer your question, Henry Higgins is a Rhodesian ridgeback." Seeing Nora's blank expression, he grabbed a book on dog breeds and flipped to the Rs. "Don't be fooled by the British name mine has. These dogs originated in Africa. They were so brave that they were known to keep lions at bay. See?"

Accepting the proffered book, Nora examined an illustration of a sleek, muscular dog with roan-colored fur baring its teeth at a male lion. On the next page, there was a photograph highlighting the breed's famed ridge of hair, which ran down its back in the opposite direction from the rest of its coat, and another, larger image of a Rhodesian ridgeback running along a beach.

"They're beautiful," Nora said. "Their coats are like sand lit by the setting sun. Golden wheat and roan red."

The smile Jed turned on her was shy this time. "Your words are beautiful. But I wish you hadn't mentioned the beach. It makes me wonder if I was right to move away from the coast."

Nora saw her opportunity to engage Jed in a longer conversation. If she could coax him into small talk about inconsequential things, she might be able to get him to share a few crucial details about Fenton Greer's death.

Admit it, you're curious about this man, she thought.

"Would you like some coffee?" she asked. "While I brew a fresh pot, you could explain what's going on with Henry Higgins."

Nora was surprised by the relief that washed over Jed's features. It was obvious that he'd expected her to question him about his past and when she hadn't, he'd visibly relaxed. Nora knew the feeling all too well.

"I'd love coffee," he said. "In fact, if I could just run down to the station and grab an IV bag, I'll give myself a transfusion."

"A real addict, then?"

Jed nodded. "Not looking to be cured, either." He followed

Nora to the ticket booth. "I'll tell you about Henry Higgins if
you promise to ice and elevate after I pay for my coffee. Deal?"

"Deal," Nora agreed. "What'll it be?"

Jed studied the menu board. "An Ernest Hemingway, please."

Nora brewed a fresh pot of dark roast and listened to the
sleigh bells ring again. As Jed began his story of how he'd
adopted Henry Higgins from a rescue organization specializing
in animals with special needs, Nora served a Louisa May Alcott
and a Jack London to a husband and wife. The same couple assured her that they were in need of no assistance and planned to
browse while enjoying their coffee.

Once they'd moved off, Nora focused on Jed again. "What
kind of special needs?"

"Ice and elevate," he reminded her.

"Yes, sir." Nora collected her ice pack and joined Jed by the
circle of chairs that had become the designated meeting place
for the Secret, Book, and Scone Society. Seeing that he'd selected Estella's chair gave Nora a moment's pause. However,
she quickly recovered and took a lavender throw pillow em-
broidered with JUST ONE MORE CHAPTER in decorative plum
script from June's chair. Using the pillow to pad the coffee
table, she raised her right foot and placed the ice pack across
her swollen ankle.

Jed wasn't pleased by what he saw. "You have some significant bruising."

"I've always bruised easily. And if it starts feeling worse,
there's someone I can call." She waited a heartbeat before
adding, "Right?"

"Right," he said.

Nora repeated her question from earlier. "What kind of special needs does Henry Higgins have?"

"He sustained injuries to his eyes when he was a puppy," Jed
replied. "He has anxiety issues as well. Not the more common
ones, like fear of thunder or fireworks. Or separation issues.

His are unusual. He's more like a human in his troubles. I need to find a way to help him get out of his doggy head so he can relax."

"Was he born with the eye injuries or did they happen later?"

The muscles in Jed's jaw tensed and Nora could practically feel him clamping his teeth together. A second ago, he'd been easygoing and relaxed. Now he was stiff and guarded. "Later," he said tersely. "There was an incident. He was lucky to have survived."

Nora knew, without his having to say a word, that Jed had been present for the incident. She also knew that Henry Higgins hadn't been the only creature wounded by the event. "I have one book on using healing massage on your dog and another on the correlation between canine health and a natural diet. Both are favorites of Dr. Mack, our local vet. As for other ideas, I'd have to peruse my shelves a bit longer. Also—and forgive me if this is too forward—is there a chance that Henry Higgins has picked up additional anxiety from another source? Like you? Or your mom?"

Jed didn't respond. He suddenly became very interested in the mug Nora had selected for him. It featured the text BE CAREFUL OR YOU'LL FIND OUT WHAT MY SUPERPOWER IS.

After saluting her with the mug, he said, "Thank you for not giving me a fireman mug. Those guys get enough attention as it is. Don't get me wrong. They deserve plenty of praise. They work their asses off, but you don't see women buying calendars of shirtless paramedics, do you? We'll never be as sexy, no matter how many lives we save."

Nora knew Jed was trying to deflect her question about Henry Higgins. Somehow, he was connected to the accident that had injured his dog. Pushing him on the matter would only drive him away, and Nora needed him to stay.

"I don't know about that. Firemen have to be clean-shaven,"

Nora said casually. "I like a little bristle on a man." She pointed at his mug. "Can I top you off? I'm ready to put this ice back in the freezer."

"Let me." Jed carried the ice pack and the mugs to the ticket window. Nora served him a refill of coffee. He then promised to browse while she tended to other customers.

What Nora didn't realize until the sleigh bells began to ring more and more frequently, was that the closing of the thermal pools was driving out-of-towners through the front door of Miracle Books. With their plans to soak in the warm waters canceled, they'd headed downtown for shopping excursions instead, and Nora was loading books and shelf enhancers into bags before limping to the ticket window to serve coffee as quickly as she could.

"Do you have any help?" Jed asked her at one point.

"Can't afford any," Nora replied, shocking herself by her honesty. "Listen, Jed. I'm sorry that I don't have time to search for your titles right now. Could we meet later? I could show you what I had in mind when things calm down a little."

Jed, who had several books tucked under his arm, seemed torn. On one hand, there was something about the way he leaned close to her that spoke of his wanting to see her again. On the other hand, he was clearly reluctant to discuss his dog's injuries again. "Back here, you mean?"

"Or we could sit on the deck at my house," Nora suggested, even more stunned by this statement than by her previous one. "It's a nice spot, especially in the evening. I live right behind the shop." She jerked her thumb over her shoulder, feeling as awkward as a thirteen-year-old girl.

"That sounds good, thanks," Jed said, smiling warmly at her. "I'd like to bring some wine. What's your poison?" His smile abruptly vanished and he shook his head. "Poor choice of words. Sorry."

Nora stared at him. "I'm not sure why you're apologizing.

Does this have something to do with what happened to Fenton Greer?"

Jed's gaze slid away, but not for long. "I heard your friend was taken in for questioning. That must be really hard."

So much for keeping our society secret, Nora thought before she remembered that Jed had helped her out to June's car after she'd twisted her ankle. Because of that, he'd seen June, Hester, and Estella. The moment June had driven off, the old lodge employee had probably given Jed a biographical sketch on each of them, whether or not Jed had asked for one. That was life in Miracle Springs.

"She didn't do it," Nora said, unable to hide her fear for Estella. That fear expressed itself in anger. It filled Nora's eyes with thunderclouds and made her scars pulse like sheet lightning. "What did he die of? Greer?"

Jed was taken aback by the intensity in her voice. "I can't make that determination. The ME—"

"What did you see?" Nora pressed. "What will go in your report?"

"I can't . . ." Jed began, and trailed off. They both knew that he couldn't go around spouting theories on Fenton Greer's cause of death.

Nora could see that she'd been far too aggressive. She, who'd always kept her emotions in check, had failed to do so with Jed. There was something about him that coaxed her into honesty. That scared her.

Silence grew between them. It yawned wider and darker, forming a cave mouth, until Jed finally spoke. "If you want to cancel our plans for later, I understand. I wish I could tell you what you'd like to know, but I need this job. And in a way, I've already said too much."

The pick your poison *comment,* Nora thought. *Fenton was poisoned. But that hardly helps. There are hundreds of poisons. Maybe thousands.*

"Estella didn't do it," she repeated.

As the words dangled in the air like balloons without enough helium to rise, Nora considered how poison had long been seen as the female murder weapon of choice.

Am I trying to convince Jed of Estella's innocence? she wondered. *Or myself?*

Chapter 10

All things are poisons, for there is nothing without poisonous qualities. It is only the dose which makes a thing poison.

—Paracelsus

Nora didn't have much time to obsess over Jedediah's remark about poison.

Miracle Books was a zoo for the rest of the day, and Nora did her best to serve customers coffee, match them with the right books, and ring up their purchases.

She finally caught a break around five. By that point, her foot was throbbing and she was incredibly hungry. With no customers in the shop, she decided to run to the back for a cup of decaf and a snack.

No sooner had she filled her mug than the sleigh bells clanged.

"Damn it," Nora whispered tiredly. She knew she should be grateful for a stuffed cash register and gaps on the shelves. In addition to books, she'd sold dozens of shelf enhancers, including a tin toy with a singing bird in a cage, a vintage bowling pin, a framed silhouette of a girl and her kitten, an antique game board, a stoneware crock, a swan decoy, a leather globe, and an Art Nouveau inkwell featuring a reclining woman.

Thinking that she'd like to adopt the same posture as the inkwell lady right about now, Nora took a sip of her coffee.

"Where are you?" Hester shouted from the front of the store.

Nora let out a sigh of relief. She could sit down, after all. "In our usual spot," she called back.

Hester and June appeared at the circle of chairs.

"You look done in," June said. "Long day?"

"I've been slammed. Having the pools closed was great for business, but not so great for my foot." Though Nora hated to admit this weakness, she had to rest her injured ankle.

June frowned in concern. "I'll get ice. Hester, give that girl some food. I bet she hasn't eaten since breakfast."

Hester produced a bakery box from the bag she'd set down on the coffee table. After handing Nora a throw pillow, she patted the table. "Put your foot up first."

Nora complied and June returned from the ticket office with the ice pack. "Did you make a date with Gorgeous Jed?"

"Yes." Nora accepted the bakery box from Hester. "But I've already screwed things up with him. He stopped by the shop this morning and I didn't handle things well. I'm not Estella."

June squeezed Nora's shoulder. "Eat now. Hester and I will share our stories and you can tell us what happened with Jed when we're done."

Nora was too hungry to protest. She opened the box lid and a rush of tantalizing aromas escaped from within. The scents of melted cheese, buttery dough, and cooked ham caused Nora's stomach to gurgle, and when she scooped up the croissant resting on a sheet of wax paper, she found that it was still warm.

After biting into the stuffed pastry, she had to suppress a moan. The Gruyère cheese that had escaped from the hole at one end of the croissant had been baked a golden brown and broke off in Nora's mouth. It wasn't ham, but prosciutto, which shared the pastry's interior pocket with the cheese, and the flavor combination was heavenly. Nora could have easily devoured a second.

"You *were* hungry," Hester said. She and June had barely had the chance to serve themselves coffee before Nora was finished eating.

"You're an amazing baker," Nora said, wiping her hands on a napkin.

Hester pushed the bag toward June. "The other box is for you. I've been thinking about you since you told us your story at the Pink Lady. This is your comfort scone. You should eat it now, even if you don't feel like it. Trust me."

Though June looked nervous, she said, "That's what we're trying to do, right? Trying to trust." She steeled herself, as if she were about to stick her hand inside a box containing a puff adder, instead of a pastry. "Trust and try."

"Trust and try," Hester repeated.

The box lid was barely open before June's eyes filled with tears. "I smell apples. Reminds me of the times I used to take my son apple picking upstate. The trees always put on their best show. We'd go on hayrides, drink hot cider, and buy maple syrup. Weeks later, when that first dark, dreary winter day came, I'd make apple-cinnamon pancakes and we'd use the syrup and remember our golden, fall day." She broke off a piece of scone and, her gaze watery and distant, popped it into her mouth. "It's all in here. The apples. The maple. The cinnamon. Even the autumn sunshine." A tear rolled down her cheek. "I can smell the hay. I remember the time Tyson had a piece stuck in his hair. He pulled it out and put it between his teeth and did this crazy Southern accent. Little did he know, his mama would be living in the South one day—ha!"

It was incredible to see how deeply June had become immersed in her memory. Nora turned from her to look at Hester. Her baker friend had her hands clasped over her heart and was watching June with a mixture of anticipation and desperate hope. Nora realized that Hester gave away a tiny part of herself with every comfort scone. She desperately wanted each scone to live up to its name.

Another tear slipped down June's cheek, but she didn't appear to notice. "I just want to know that he's happy. All I've ever wanted was for him to have a good life."

"If the rest of his childhood was anything like that memory, your son was a lucky boy," Hester said.

June stared at Hester. Her eyes slowly regained focus. "Yes. He had a good childhood. I was a good mother."

"You were a good mother," Hester repeated. "Finish your scone."

"I think I will."

June relished her scone. Every bite seemed to remind her of happy moments she'd shared with her son and of how she'd done a fine job raising him. She didn't express this in words, but her tears dried and there was a new lightness about her—a sense of letting go. Though Nora knew it was only the beginning of time's healing process, it was a very significant beginning. The inability to forgive oneself could be an enormous obstacle for people suffering from an emotional wound. Nora knew this well. And she now knew that June would be receptive to the books Nora had selected for her.

"Thank you, Hester," June said after every crumb of her comfort scone had been devoured. She drank some coffee and set the bakery box aside. "It feels wrong to indulge on treats and coffee, with my backside resting on a soft chair when I know Estella is in utter misery, so let's get to it."

"Yes," Nora agreed. "For starters, I'd like to know why the sheriff was so quick to call Fenton's death a murder. Neil Parrish was pushed in front of a goddamn train, but *his* death was viewed as *suspicious* until later declared a suicide."

June produced one of her characteristic grunts. "Clearly, Sheriff Toad doesn't know his ass from his elbow. That fact aside, I got a whole plateful of tidbits from Bob. He's not only in love with Estella, but he's a keen listener and observer. Because of that, I decided to be straight with him. I told him how the three of us planned to exonerate Estella."

"Has she been officially charged?" Nora asked.

"No," Hester said. "At least, not as of three o'clock. That's when a pair of deputies came into the bakery for cookies and éclairs to take back to the station. Deputy Andrews—the one Nora loaned *Ender's Game* to—may have a crush on me. He hung around at the counter after his buddy placed their order. I think he wanted to impress me by asking if I'd heard that there'd been a second violent death in Miracle Springs, so I played the wide-eyed girl and begged him to tell me everything."

June reached across the coffee table and gave Hester a playful punch in the arm. "Look at you! And?"

"He wasted most of that time talking up his part in the investigation," Hester said. "Luckily, it was when the other deputy, Lloyd, left to use the restroom that Andrews leaned over the counter and whispered that without his sharp eyes, the sheriff wouldn't have an evidence bag with what was probably the murder weapon. Andrews spotted it under one of the lounge chairs."

Nora forgot about the pain in her foot. She jerked upright, causing the ice pack to slide to the floor. "Which was?"

"A bottle of pills," Hester said. "Unfortunately, I have no idea what the pills were, because Andrews had to leave. Lloyd told him that the sheriff was ready for them to process Fenton Greer's phone. After grabbing the box of cookies, Lloyd started walking away. When he thought he was out of earshot, he made a lewd tongue gesture and said that he couldn't wait to see if all the rumors about Estella were true." Hester shook her head in disgust. "Asshat. I wanted to bash him in the face with a frying pan. At least none of them seem to have a clue about the Secret, Book, and Scone Society."

"If there are photos of Estella on Fenton's phone, they'll have a time stamp," Nora said. Speaking Estella's name aloud filled her with guilt. "Have either of you tried to get in to see her? I haven't. I admit that Miracle Books was in charge of my life today."

"You could have waited in the station lobby from dawn 'til dusk and it wouldn't have made a difference," June said. "They weren't going to let Estella have visitors. She's being questioned. That's what I was told when I called. And I've called *six* times. On the plus side, Bob is with us. And by that I mean that he'll do anything to help Estella."

Nora wasn't sure how she felt about Bob. "I know you like the guy, but is that enough to go on? I don't know that we can trust him."

"He's already proven himself," June said. "Bob found out what kind of pills Estella supposedly mixed into Fenton's drink."

Now it was Hester's turn to sit on the edge of her chair. "Don't hold out on us," she scolded.

June was struggling to pull a piece of paper out of her handbag, but it was caught on the point of a sharp needle.

"Is that a weapon?" Nora asked in complete seriousness.

June pushed the needle deeper into her bag. "No, those are for knitting. It's how I keep my hands occupied while I'm watching TV at night, which is a healthier habit than shoving food into my mouth." She unfolded the paper. "What Deputy Andrews found at the scene is medicine. Not poison. But, of course, any medicine can become poison if you ingest too much."

"Are you familiar with this medicine?" Nora asked. "From your tenure as a caregiver?"

June nodded. "I sure am. It's nothing fancy. Just potassium pills. Potassium chloride, to be specific."

"You can overdose on that?" Hester asked. "Aren't bananas loaded with potassium?"

"Yes, but you can't die from an overdose of bananas," June

answered tersely. "We need to take a step back and first ask why Greer was taking these meds. Usually, people can get the potassium they need from food. When you can't, you have a condition called *hypokalemia*. During my time at Belle Shoal, I knew lots of patients taking potassium supplements. They all had other medical issues like kidney disease, hypertension, or complications stemming from diabetes. The medication they took to treat these issues either decreased their potassium levels or prohibited their bodies from absorbing potassium. Especially if they were on diuretics."

"So they had to take an additional pill in order to continue treatment." Nora rephrased June's statement not only for her own benefit, but also for Hester's.

"That's right," June said. "And you should have seen those pills." She raised her eyes to the ceiling. "Could choke a horse, they were so big. My poor patients. I'd have to coax those monsters down with milkshakes and smoothies."

Nora scooped up her ice pack from the floor. "How would someone use those pills as a murder weapon? I've read enough mystery novels to know that food greatly reduces the efficacy of a drug."

June nodded. "As soon as Bob told me about the pills, I thought the same thing. Another question came to me as well. If Greer had a prescription for potassium pills, would he be traveling with a full bottle or just a few pills?" She spread her hands, awaiting a reply.

"How can we know? But if Greer did have a full month's supply, he would have taken at least two pills by now," Hester mused aloud. "Leaving him with twenty-seven or -eight?"

Nora finished the rest of her coffee and examined her empty cup with a sense of despondence. Now that the pain in her ankle had subsided and there was food in her belly, it was getting increasingly harder to hold her fatigue at bay. "Unless Estella put a gun to his head, why would Greer swallow twenty-odd potassium pills?" she murmured tiredly. "Estella couldn't prove that he tried to force himself on her while we listened from behind the towel stand. That's why she decided not to march down to the sheriff's department and show them her fresh bruises. She knew damn well that Fenton Greer would deny responsibility. She also knew the sheriff wouldn't go after Greer. There's no way our chauvinistic sheriff would choose a beautician with a rep for being a loose woman over an influential businessman."

"Toad would probably tell Estella she had it coming and push her out the door. And we all know where he'd put his hand to push her," Hester muttered angrily.

June was giving Nora a strange look. "What are you saying? Are you saying that when Estella told us she was going to use what Greer had done to her as leverage, she might have actually gone back to the lodge last night and tried to worm more information out of him? Or that she somehow fed him a bottle's worth of potassium chloride?" She flicked her wrist in dismissal. "Estella's no killer."

"No," Nora agreed. And to her relief, this felt true. "However, she doesn't have many champions in Miracle Springs. Her clients appreciate her ability to make them look beautiful, but they'd hardly serve as character witnesses on her behalf. Most people would watch her ruination with glee."

"Because they don't know her!" Hester cried.

"She won't let anyone see the real her," Nora pointed out. "None of us have been willing to do that. We've become adept at hiding behind our armor. Until we found each other. I don't know about you, but this is the first time in years I've opened up to anyone."

June raised her coffee cup in a toast. "Better late than never."

Several months ago, Nora had found a dilapidated cuckoo clock at the flea market. After haggling with the vendor until he was worn out, Nora walked away with the clock for twenty bucks. She'd carefully sanded the ornately carved wood, applied a few coats of stain, and hung her treasure in the book-store.

Now the clock chimed six times and the blue cuckoo shot out of the snug compartment where he spent most of his time. He sang his merry song, capturing the attention of all three women, before retreating into his snug nest inside the wood.

Nora hated to break the spell of tranquility the little bird had cast, but she had no choice. "If we're going to figure out what really happened to Fenton Greer, we need to speak with Estella, and we must be prepared to make enemies in this town," she said. "Jedediah believes Greer was poisoned. At least, that's how I interpreted his reference to poison and his guilty reaction for mentioning the word." She described the exchange she and Jed had had earlier that day.

Hester grinned at Nora. "So he's coming over for a date? Tonight?"

"And he's bringing wine?" June added, wriggling her brows. "To drink under the stars?"

"Enough with the innuendoes," Nora replied testily. "I know he's good-looking. I know he's a newcomer. But I'm not interested in novelties. I'm interested in novels."

June gave Nora's knee a pat. "Books make excellent escapes, honey, but they can't massage your aching shoulders or whisper sexy words in your ear. Women think they want Mr. Darcy, but do we? Do we really want a man with a cravat and a top hat to take us to bed? No. We want a man who's a mixed-up mess of Othello, Heathcliff, Atticus Finch, Chief Inspector John Luther, and a Greek god or two."

"Don't forget Sherlock Holmes, Edward Rochester, and Horatio Hornblower," Hester added. "I like my Brits."

"What? No James Bond?" Nora quipped, having enjoyed June's speech immensely.

Hester shook her head. "He doesn't treat women like a gentleman should."

"Point taken," June said solemnly. "Well, Nora? Which literary man lights your fire?"

Nora knew that June hadn't meant any harm by her remark,
but the pairing of *man* and *fire* took her to a dark place. "I'll get
back to you on that one. If I don't go home and make myself
presentable, I won't get an iota of useful info out of Jed. Like I
said before, I'm not Estella. I lack both her confidence and tal-
ent when it comes to getting men to do what I want. At this
point, it's going to take all of my energy just to stay awake."

June grunted. "Honey, I was there when he helped you to
the car. You'll have no problem staying awake."

June was right. By the time Nora saw Jed's shadow stretching ahead of his body on her flagstone path, she was such a
knot of nerves that she couldn't imagine ever sleeping again.

Nora Pennington hadn't invited a man to Caboose Cottage
since she'd moved in. Not for a social call, that is. There'd been
plumbers, electricians, masons, and painters. But a paramedic
carrying a grocery bag in one hand and a bouquet of flowers in
the other? Never. Nora was tempted to go inside and lock the
door. After all, she'd sworn never to let a man get close to her
again. And having a date was letting a man get close.

*This isn't a real date. This is you extracting information from
someone who happens to be male*, she told herself as Jed as-
cended the metal steps leading to her deck. The soft light from
the Japanese lanterns lit his face and Nora caught a flash of
white teeth and glittering eyes.

Smiling at Jed, Nora reminded herself that she needed to
maintain a firm control over her emotions from this moment
until Jed left.

That proved to be difficult.

Unlike most people, Jed didn't fill silences with aimless chat-
ter. He was clearly comfortable with silence, and when he first
stood on her deck, he spent a long moment taking in the view

before he looked at her. "You live in the coolest house I've ever seen," he eventually said. "Do the trains wake you?"

"Sometimes," Nora replied.

Jed suddenly remembered the flowers in his hand. "I don't normally go for roses, but these reminded me of the flower in *The Little Prince*"—he gestured at Nora's walking stick—"so I asked my neighbor if I could cut some of hers. This variety is called William Shakespeare 2000. I have no idea why."

Nora accepted the flowers. "They're beautiful. No one's ever brought me wild roses." She touched the edge of a velvety petal, admiring the deep crimson hue before she buried her nose in the bouquet. "They smell like raspberries and cream."

Nora invited Jed inside and told him to make himself at home while she put the flowers in water. Jed didn't rush through his self-guided tour, but moved about Nora's living area and kitchen with reverence, admiring details and asking an occasional question. Finally, he scratched his chin and said, "I don't see wineglasses. Do you have them in a hidden storage compartment?"

Turning away to hide her flushed cheeks, Nora fished out two glass tumblers from a cabinet and showed them to Jed. She didn't want to explain why she didn't own wineglasses or that she hadn't touched alcohol for years until the night she'd hurt her ankle. "Most of my things serve double duty."

"Makes perfect sense," Jed said. "Corkscrew?"

Nora had no excuse for this one. "I lent mine to a friend," she lied. "But I have one for sale in the store."

Jed shook his head. "No worries. I saw your bike out there, so I'm assuming you have a bike pump."

"I do." She told him where it was. "Is that how you're going to open the wine?"

Grinning, Jed said, "Be right back."

Nora watched as Jed placed the bottle of red wine on the kitchen floor. He then pushed the bike-pump needle into the cork and began to pump. The muscles in his arms swelled under his skin like waves and he had a mole on his wrist exactly where a watch would sit. Nora imagined the mole with her finger, but her ruminations were cut short by the *pop!* of the cork.

Freed from its glass prison, it burst out of the bottle like a rocket and struck the ceiling. Jed caught the cork on its way down to the floor and set it on the counter.

Turning to Nora, he asked, "Would you prefer white wine? I guess I should have asked before I opened the red."

"Red's fine." Nora pulled out a plate of sliced cheese and dried apricots from her fridge. "Gouda and fruit. I also have this wonderful sliced bread from the Gingerbread House. It's a combination of wheat and rye."

Nora led Jed back outside. They sat down and released synchronized sighs.

Jed laughed and reached across the small café table to clink the rim of Nora's glass with his own. "I guess we both had the same kind of day."

"Except mine didn't start with a dead body and yours didn't end with a friend spending the night behind bars," Nora said crisply. She didn't know why she'd immediately gone into combat mode, but it was too late to recall her words.

Instead of responding, Jed sipped his wine and tilted his face skyward.

"Since I saw you this morning, I learned that a bottle of potassium-chloride pills was found at the scene," Nora continued in a milder tone. "Have you ever seen what a potassium-chloride fatality looks like?"

"No," Jed said.

"What if Greer was poisoned by some other means? If too much potassium shows up in his system, the ME might rule a potassium overdose as the cause of death without looking for alternative causes." Nora realized her argument sounded irrational and ridiculous.

Jed shifted in his chair. "I doubt the ME will jump to any conclusions. He'll run a whole panel of tests: blood, fluid, urine, tissue, glucose, and electrolytes. I assume so, anyway. If potassium isn't the culprit, the real one will present itself as known when the tests come back."

"While he waits weeks for those test results, what will happen to Estella in the meantime?" Nora asked without expecting an answer. "She was with Greer the night *before* he died. Not the night *of* his death. I know because *I* was with *her*. We had dinner together at the Pink Lady. Afterward, Estella went home. If Greer was poisoned, then someone besides Estella did it."

Seeing that Jed's glass was empty, Nora passed him the wine bottle. He refilled his glass and examined hers, but as she'd only taken a single sip, he put the bottle back on the table.

"When you arrived at the pools this morning, could you tell how long Greer had been dead?" Nora asked.

A veil fell over Jed's features. "Look, Nora, I'm not a forensic investigator. I've taken a few forensics courses and I did an internship with the county coroner where I used to live, but I'm no expert. All I can say is that the body was very stiff, which typically occurs eight to twelve hours after death."

Nora picked up the cheese plate and proffered it to him. "You probably didn't expect to be interrogated over Gouda and sliced bread, but this is *really* good bread."

After a brief hesitation, Jed took two pieces of cheese and a slice of bread. Nora waited for him to sample the food.

"You're right. It's really good." After polishing off the bread and cheese, Jed glanced over at Nora's untouched wineglass. He put his own on the table and brushed a scattering of crumbs off his lap. "I should get going," he said, not looking at her at all. "I'm expecting another long day tomorrow."

Nora thought of the flowers Jed had brought. Here was a man who not only recognized the quote from her walking stick, but had also searched for the perfect rose to represent the fictional flower from the Saint-Exupéry novel. A rare man indeed. And Nora had turned him off with incredible efficiency.

She regretted it too.

"Before you go," she said, stretching out her good hand, but not making contact, "I have something for you."

Ducking inside her house, she grabbed a small pile of books from her bedroom and returned to the deck. "I hope these help."

Jed shifted through the books, which included *Essential Oils for Dogs; Bad Dog (A Love Story)*; and *New Choices in Natural Healing for Dogs & Cats*. "These are great. How much do I owe you?"

"I'm lending them to you," Nora said. "That way, you can decide which ones you want to buy. Also, it'll give me a chance to order a book on canine-acupressure therapy. Maybe the next time you drop by Miracle Books, Estella won't be a murder suspect and we can talk about other things."

Jed got to his feet. He walked toward the steps and Nora wondered if he meant to leave without saying good-bye.

At the edge of the deck, however, Jed stopped and looked back over his shoulder. Holding out the books, he said, "I want to help you. Honestly, I do. But it's not that simple. I can't do anything to jeopardize my job. I really need it. More than most people need their jobs."

A curtain had lifted from Jed's features. He wore a plaintive expression and his ocean-blue eyes were entreating her to understand all that he couldn't say.

"I understand," Nora said, even though she didn't.

Jed nodded and descended the steps. At the bottom, he paused and turned all the way around. Grabbing the metal rail, he looked back up at her like a forty-year-old Romeo on the verge of a heartfelt monologue. "Nora. There was something off about Mr. Greer's body."

Though far from a lover's plea, Jed's phrase immediately drew Nora to the top of the stairs.

"What do you mean?" she asked in a near-whisper.

"You didn't hear this from me, but I could tell that he'd been moved. Postmortem lividity—you probably know from reading crime novels—shows where the blood pools. Mr. Greer's blood had pooled in the lower half of his body."

Nora was confused. "Why is that off? Wasn't he found lying on the floor?"

Jed pointed at his waist. "He was, but I'm referring to *this* lower half. From here to my feet. I don't think Greer died on his back. He died in a seated position."

Chapter 11

To live in prison is to live without mirrors. To live
without mirrors is to live without the self.
—Margaret Atwood

After Jed left, Nora called June to tell her what he'd said about the possibility that Greer's body had been moved after his death.

"That fact doesn't identify the real killer, but it supports Estella's innocence," Nora said. "After all, Estella couldn't have dragged Greer over that tile floor, even if he'd been dipped in butter. He was way too heavy." Nora recalled Greer's naked body all too well. Clearing her mind of the unpleasant image, she went on: "I also want you to know that I'm going to see Estella before I open the shop tomorrow morning. If they'll let me see her."

The slam of a screen door echoed down the phone line. Based on the chorus of the mewling of cats in the background, Nora concluded that June had stepped outside. She liked the idea that the two of them were staring up at the same stars and taking comfort from their distant, but dependable light.

"I'm worried," June said. "You, me, Estella, and Hester are smart women. We're tenacious women. But we're still just four women—three now—going up against a killer capable of pushing a man in front of a train."

"Not just *a* killer," Nora cut in. "This isn't an individual working alone."

June made a noise of dismay. "Neil's murder was bad enough. But what does Greer's death mean? Is the group turning on itself?"

"I don't know. I'm so tired that I can't think straight. Will you fill Hester in for me?"

"Of course." A cat screeched and June yelled, "Shoo!" and sighed. "This big orange tom goes out of his way to dart right in front of me when I walk. Speaking of toms, how'd your date go?"

A cloud skittered across the collective of stars above Nora, blotting out their light. "Don't ask," she said, and ended the call.

Deputy Crowder, the lickspittle who'd hovered behind the sheriff's chair the day Nora had given her statement on Neil Parrish, was more than happy to inform her that Estella wasn't free to receive visitors.

"You can't hold her indefinitely," Nora said. "I know the law. You have to charge her or let her go."

"Oh, we're charging her." Crowder's mouth curved into a smug grin. "Which is why you can't see her right now. She's meeting with her legal counsel. Who do you think is more important to her? Visiting with the used-book girl or the public defender?"

Nora refused to be goaded. "There are perks to owning a bookstore," she said pleasantly. "For example, I'm never bored. I'll sit and read until Estella's meeting is done."

The deputy shrugged. "Whatever floats your boat. You can take your smutty Harlequin novel to the lobby. Or is it a vampire story? You girls love your hot, young vampires, don't you?"

Nora didn't know what angered her more—being repeatedly called a girl or Crowder's assumption that women only read romance novels.

Pasting on her brightest smile, she said, "Vampires are alluring for many reasons. They exhibit an appreciation for art and literature. They also display a code of chivalry rarely shown by contemporary men. The vampires' supernatural beauty, charismatic personality, ability to manipulate weaker minds, and superior lovemaking skills render them utterly spellbinding."

Crowder's mouth hung open. "Huh?"

"Perhaps your wife can explain the phenomenon better than I can. I believe she's a diehard Anne Rice fan," Nora said as she pulled Alice Hoffman's *Faithful* from her handbag. "I'll be in the lobby. Reading my *smutty* vampire novel."

Crowder's confusion was amplified by the absence of a half-naked babe or a bare-chested vampire on the book cover.

Nora's satisfaction over having one-upped the deputy was short-lived, for as much as she loved Hoffman's writing, it was impossible to focus on her exquisite prose. Nora's thoughts were caught on an endless loop between the shock of learning that Estella had been formally charged and that she was currently meeting with a public defender.

Back when she'd been a librarian, Nora had carried a notepad in her pants pocket. She used it to jot down work-related tasks, to write grocery and errand lists, and to add to her ever-expanding TBR pile. While she'd left many behaviors and habits from her old life behind, she still liked to keep a notepad handy. She took it out now and, using her open book as a shield, wrote the following list of questions:

How could the medical examiner determine the cause of death so quickly?

What evidence does the sheriff have on Estella to satisfy the three Ms? Means, motive, method.

Is the public defender capable?

Is the public defender honest?

If the sheriff is in bed with Pine Ridge, what evidence will we need to present to a higher authority to exonerate Estella?

Is something off on my loan application?

Nora nodded to herself. This last question was an excellent starting place. No other bank would risk lending her several hundred thousand dollars. If Miracle Books folded, she'd have no means of paying her debt. Nora had been completely transparent about her finances. She'd told Dawson Hendricks that she was barely squeaking by. He'd examined her records, so he knew exactly how things stood.

Where would we plead our case? Nora added to her list of questions. *To the feds? Which department?*

Nora decided it would be unwise to conduct Internet searches on mortgage fraud while sitting in the sheriff's department, so she used her phone to send a group text to Hester and June. She hated to deliver bad news to her friends while they were at work, but she had no choice.

"Ms. Pennington?" Nora was relieved to find Deputy Andrews standing before her. Andrews was preferable to Deputy Crowder any day of the week. "You're waiting to see Ms. Sadler?"

Nora shot to her feet. "I am."

"Follow me, please."

Andrews had Nora fill out the visitor's log. She then presented her driver's license and surrendered her phone to the clerk.

After she followed Andrews through a warren of hallways, they reached an area marked with the signage: INMATE VISITATION.

"The sheriff would have put Ms. Sadler behind the glass and made the two of you talk using the phones, but seeing as she just finished meeting with her lawyer, I figured she might as well stay here," Andrews said. As if regretting the wisdom of his choice, he added, "Don't make me be sorry I let you two meet like this. No touching. Not even a hug. Got it?"

"We got it." Estella's voice, which rang out like a song in the big, empty room, seemed incongruent with her bedraggled appearance. Her flame-red hair hung in limp strands and her face, free of makeup, was milk-pale. Nora stared into Estella's bloodshot eyes and saw a single emotion residing there. It was rage. It sparkled like winter stars on a frozen lake. Beautiful, cold, and dangerous.

Nora waited until Andrews took up his sentry post by the door before saying, "Jesus, Estella. How the hell did this happen?"

Estella barked out a dry laugh. "Damned if *I* know! I went from feeling pretty good about the world—what with the four of us having our bonding time at the Pink Lady followed by two episodes of *Outlander* on Netflix—to being jarred out of a lovely dream about a group of men in kilts bathing in a stream. They—"

"Honestly?" Nora put out her hand in protest, torn between annoyance and amusement. "Tell me, Estella. Did you go to the lodge the night before last? Maybe for a drink before bed?"

"No," Estella said before lowering her gaze. "I wasn't feeling lonely. Loneliness is what always lands me on one of Bob's bar stools. But I'd just been with my friends. You gals filled the void that night. Can you believe that?"

Nora studied Estella. She could believe it. After all, it had taken over four years for loneliness to coax her into lowering her guard. Otherwise, she wouldn't be sitting across from a woman in an orange jumpsuit right now. And her eyes wouldn't be reflecting Estella's rage.

"You're being framed," Nora said. "June and Hester think so too. June was out walking when the sheriff's men loaded you into their cruiser. She heard you yelling." Nora glanced over to where Andrews stood before lowering her voice to a whisper. "What did you say when you were questioned?"

"I told the sheriff what I could," Estella said. "That I'd been on a date with Fenton, but not on the night he died. I said that Bob and Julia, an Oasis waitress, would corroborate my story. I didn't mention the three of you because I didn't want to get you involved."

Nora nodded. "We've been trying to keep our distance in order to help you, but my cover is definitely blown. Probably June's too. I think she called here twelve times yesterday, asking when you'd be released or allowed visitors."

"General June." Estella smiled for the first time since Nora's arrival. The smile served as a buffer against her anger. "Anyway, during the questioning part, Sheriff Toad said that he didn't need a *hairdresser* telling him how police work was done. He also said that he had proof I'd been with Fenton last night at the pools and that I'd poisoned him."

"What proof?"

"Don't you think I asked him?" Estella snapped, and then immediately raised her hands in apology. "Sorry, but I'm terrified that prison orange is going to be my only color for the next twenty years and it's not a flattering shade. Besides, I do *not* plan on following in my daddy's footsteps. Two Sadlers in prison? It's a good thing my mama isn't alive to see this." Unsure of what to do with her hands, she tucked them under her armpits. The gesture made her look like a frightened child. "I never went to Fenton's room, so what kind of proof could they have? And what poison did I supposedly give him? Acetone? Nail-polish remover? I have plenty of potent chemicals at the salon, unfortunately."

Nora put her finger over her lips. "Don't give them any ideas. And in answer to your question, Jedediah Craig told me that Andrews found a bottle of potassium-chloride pills under a lounge chair. Poolside. That's the murder weapon."

After repeating what June had said about the medication, Nora added, "Hester overheard another deputy mentioning

Greer's phone. Did you let him take photos the night the two of you were down there?"

Estella rolled her eyes. "Yeah. It was all part of the game. They were sexy, but tasteful."

"I doubt Greer's wife would agree," Nora said.

"Okay, Mother Teresa. This isn't helping." Estella jerked her head at the clock. "They're only going to give us so much time. What else can you tell me?"

Whispering so softly that Estella had to lean forward to hear her, Nora shared what Jed had said about Greer's body having been moved.

"Well, I couldn't budge that lard-ass," Estella whispered back. "And if he was sitting up, wouldn't he also have to be tied to something? You wouldn't let someone shove a bunch of pills down your throat without putting up a fight. The lounge chairs at the bathhouse wouldn't work unless someone wrapped ropes around his whole torso. What was he wearing when he was found?"

It was a good question, and one Nora hadn't thought to ask Jed. Had Greer been found fully clothed? In a swimsuit? In the nude? If his wrists had been exposed, then Jed would have noticed marks on the skin. However, if he'd been dressed for dinner in a suit and tie . . .

"Time's up, ladies," Andrews announced, and began to approach their table. "Say your good-byes."

Nora looked at Estella. "Do you need anything? What about your lawyer? Is he trustworthy?"

"My lawyer is a she. And yes, I can trust her, though I'm not sure how much she can do for me. I doubt I'll make bail."

Andrews waved impatiently at Nora. "If you want to help Ms. Sadler, you can add money to her commissary account. She'll need to buy things since it looks like she'll be with us for a while."

Though there'd been no emotion behind this statement, Nora wanted to slap the deputy in the face. How could every person in the sheriff's department blindly follow such corruption?

Crowder appeared to take Estella back to her cell.

"They allow computer calls here," Estella blurted as she passed Nora. "Get in touch with me soon, okay?"

"I will," Nora said. "I promise."

Nora followed Andrews through the same maze of corridors, but to her, they seemed even gloomier than before.

He took her all the way to the main entrance, and Nora assumed that he intended to see that she left the building. To her surprise, he not only held open the door leading outside, he stepped out into the summer sunshine with her.

Shielding his eyes against the glare, he spoke to Nora while keeping his gaze on the sidewalk in front of them. "You were right about the book," he said. "*Ender's Game*. It's good."

This was so unexpected that Nora stopped and stared at him. "What?"

"It's way better than the movie." Almost shyly, Andrews added, "Thank you for getting me to read it. I'm going to buy another Orson Scott Card novel, if you have one."

Nora felt like she was in an alternate universe. And yet she couldn't help but wonder if Andrews had mentioned the book as a way of telling her that he wasn't like Sheriff Toad.

"I do," Nora said quietly. "Listen, Deputy, what's happening around here is wrong. Estella didn't kill Fenton Greer. Please don't stand by and let an innocent woman be framed for a crime she didn't commit. You swore an oath, and I believe your word means something. I believe you're an honorable man."

Andrews acted as though she hadn't spoken. Glancing at his watch, he said, "Have a nice day, ma'am."

"Wait!" Nora cried softly. She decided to gamble on the assumption that the ME's report included postmortem lividity results. "Just check the coroner's report! See if it matches what you found at the scene. You're a smart man, Deputy Andrews. You'll spot the discrepancy. And when you do, you'll know that Estella Sadler shouldn't be in that cell."

Nora hurried away before the deputy could fully process her words. She'd taken a serious risk, she knew. He could have detained her—dragged her in front of the sheriff—but he didn't. Nora took hope from his lack of action. At this point, she'd draw hope from any source.

Entering Miracle Books was like diving into the waters of a mountain lake after walking for miles across barren desert.

Nora ran her fingertips over the spines of book after book, inhaling the familiar scents of old leather and paper. The sheer presence of so many books was a balm, and by the time the aroma of freshly brewed coffee drifted through the shop and wooed customers into dropping into the closest chair or sofa, Nora was ready to face the rest of her day.

Considering the thermal pools had reopened, Nora was surprised by how many out-of-towners came into Miracle Books that morning. Unlike yesterday, they were subdued. The murder of a fellow guest was no longer a source of excitement. One woman told Nora she'd barely slept and had been plagued by horrible nightmares.

"I'm an anxious person anyway," she admitted. "I came to Miracle Springs looking for peace. Instead, I feel more rattled than ever."

After serving her a cup of chamomile tea, Nora led her to the section where the meditation books were shelved. The woman was immediately drawn to the display of mala beads.

"These are beautiful," she said. "What are they?"

"Malas have been around for a long time." Nora removed one of the necklaces from the display. Though the beads were displayed in double loops to save space, Nora stretched out the mala to show her customer its full length. "They're also called Buddhist prayer beads. A traditional Tibetan mala consists of one hundred and eight beads. There are all kinds of ways to use these beads, but I couldn't tell you a thing about Buddhist mantras or prostrations."

The woman seemed discouraged. "Prostrations?"

"My understanding is that you're supposed to turn each bead as you whisper a prayer or a single word. Some people prefer to do this silently. And it doesn't have to be a prayer. It could be a thought you're trying to focus on. There really aren't any rules to prayer or meditation, are there? Whatever works for one person might not work for the next. What I love about malas is that every bead has a meaning. See this chart?" Nora pointed at a laminated printout affixed to the display. "This explains what each bead is and its meaning. For example, the mala I'm holding includes rosewood beads. These beads are meant to help you, and those around you, find healing. Over time, the oils from your skin will change the appearance of the beads. This represents the changes you're making as you wear your mala—a visible sign of transformation."

"So I can wear it as a necklace?" the woman asked.

"Or as a bracelet." Nora demonstrated how to loop the beads around her own wrist. She then removed the mala and proffered it to her eager customer.

The woman stroked the beads with her fingertips. "I love these. The beads have different colors and textures."

Nora nodded. "A woman in Virginia makes them. She cleanses every mala she creates in a Tibetan singing bowl before she ships them to me. She'll cleanse any mala you purchase before you use it because your mala should only hold your energy—no one else's. She also includes an instruction card and an individual bead chart so you'll know exactly what the beads in your mala mean."

"I am buying one for my best friend and my sister," the woman gushed. "I feel so much better just holding these." She turned to the bookshelf by her elbow. "Do you carry books on meditating with malas?"

Nora showed her what she had in stock before heading to the ticket booth to make two Jack Londons and serve another customer an Agatha ChrisTEA.

"Do you serve food too?" one of the men who'd ordered a Jack London wanted to know.

Nora directed them to the Gingerbread House and then made a mental note to get copies of Hester's menu to put on display for peckish customers.

Maybe I could sell a few of Hester's pastries here, Nora thought. *Something unique to the bookstore. Something she doesn't offer at the bakery. We could split the profits.*

Nora wrote this idea in her notepad to bring up with Hester another time. Today was not a day to discuss pastry. Today was a day to be figuring out who murdered Neil Parrish and Fenton Greer.

At noon, Nora did something she rarely did. She flipped the OPEN sign to CLOSED. Instead of eating a salad or soup in the ticket-agent's office, she limped down to the Madison County Community Bank and asked to see Dawson Hendricks.

"He's on his lunch break," said a perky little woman with glittery nails and platinum-blond hair styled into a pineapple-shaped puff. "May I help you?"

"I sure hope so," Nora said. Having seen Dawson's desk calendar when she'd met with him, Nora knew that he took lunch break every day from noon until one. "Mr. Dawson was kind enough to tell me that I qualified for a loan, so I've stopped by to get copies of my paperwork. I'm eager to start building my dream home at the Meadows."

The blonde mimicked a golf clap. "Good for you, sugar! I wish I could move up there, but a teller's salary isn't gonna get me one of those fancy houses. Still, I'm glad our town is growin'!" She smiled at Nora. "You own the bookstore, right?"

Nora nodded and the blonde clapped her hands for real this time. "I haven't been in since Christmas, but I did some serious damage to my savings account when I was there, yes, ma'am! My family has a long-standin' tradition of exchangin' children's books for Christmas and I found some real treasures on your shelves."

"Thank you." Nora instantly warmed toward the woman. "Yours is a lovely tradition."

"I'm Melodie. Have a seat, and I'll see if I can rustle up your paperwork."

Nora sat on a deep sofa next to an elderly man who appeared to have fallen asleep. When Melodie returned bearing a file folder in her hands, she smiled at the man. "Mrs. Clark is in the vault." She pointed to where the safety-deposit boxes were located. "She comes every week and takes her sweet time back there, but Mr. Clark doesn't seem to mind. He loves that sofa. Falls asleep almost as soon as he sits down. He says that he has trouble getting his eight hours at night because he hears cats crying outside his bedroom window. Mrs. Clark says it's all in his head."

Glancing at Mr. Clark, Nora wondered if he and June were neighbors. However, the thought was fleeting, since she was far more interested in the folder Melodie held. "Were you able to find a copy of my loan?"

"*Welllll*," Melodie drew out the word so that it sounded like a musical note. "I found *some* of your paperwork, but not all of it. I'm real sorry. I know it can't be easy to get down here, what with your hurt foot and all."

Nora hid her disappointment behind a phony smile. "Would it be okay to take what you have? Mr. Hendricks could fax me the rest when it's convenient. I might not even need anything else right now."

"I don't see why not. Hold on a sec." Melodie bustled off to a room behind the counter and returned a few minutes later with several sheets of paper, still warm from the copy machine.

"I hope you don't wait until Christmastime to come back to Miracle Books," Nora said. "Maybe you could start a whole new tradition—one just for you. You could buy books about feisty, independent women for the Fourth of July. Or how about reading about really cold, snowy places during those awful August days? When the air is so thick it just hangs over the town like a wet sponge."

Melodie's fingers strayed to her hair. "I hate those days. I can't go from my air-conditioned car to an air-conditioned store without lookin' like somethin' the cat threw up." She laughed at her own joke and Nora politely joined in. "My trouble is that I've never been a good reader. Long books put me off. I like stories. And I love the colorful pictures in kids' books. I buy them for myself—not for the kids. Plus, they always have happy endings."

"Lots of adults read and collect children's books," Nora said. "I love them too. And the reason you like them makes me think you'd also enjoy manga books. Did you like reading the comics in the newspaper when you were a kid?"

"I did then and I still do," Melodie said. "What's manga?"

Nora explained that manga was a Japanese comic book with a specific style. Judging from Melodie's dubious expression—especially when she heard that the books were to be read from right to left and not from left to right—Nora realized that her sales pitch could use some tweaking. However, Nora thought of how Deputy Andrews had been hooked by *Ender's Game* and decided that she might convert Melodie into becoming a full-time reader of graphic novels by presenting her with a free manga book.

After taking out her notepad and writing herself a reminder to pull out the first book in the series, Nora told the bubbly

teller to drop by Miracle Books the next time she had the opportunity. "Because you've been so helpful, I'd like to give you
a manga book. If it's not your thing, you can return it to me and
I'll put it back on the shelf. No harm done. I want you to read
a book about a girl who thinks she's fated for an ordinary life
until a talking cat named Luna tells her that she's really Sailor
Moon, and it's her job to defend the just and fight evil. She has
blond hair and blue eyes, just like you."

"Oh, I like the sound of this story already!" Melodie cried.
"I'll be over when the five o'clock whistle blows!"

Pleased that she'd retrieved her loan paperwork and, hopefully, acquired a new customer, Nora left the bank to return to
Miracle Books.

She unlocked the door, flipped the CLOSED sign to OPEN, and
limped back to the ticket-agent's office to examine her paperwork
while eating an egg-salad sandwich. It didn't take long before
Nora knew that she didn't have enough to go on. Her HUD
statement was missing and she would need that piece of paper if
she had any hope of proving that there was a corruption scan-
dal involving Pine Ridge Properties, Dawson Hendricks, the
sheriff, and whoever had killed Neil Parrish and Fenton Greer.

*Since I'm officially approved, should I continue pursuing my
building project?* Nora wondered. *Or will I end up in a financial entanglement I won't be able to wriggle out of if I take this
ruse too far?*

Nora looked down at her half-eaten sandwich and thought
of Estella. What kind of food would she be served in the county
jail?

*This is the risk of having friends. There's a price to pay for
making yourself vulnerable.*

Having decided she was willing to pay that price, Nora picked
up her cell phone and dialed Annette Goldsmith's number.

"You were on my list of people to call," Annette said after
Nora had identified herself. "I heard the fabulous news that

your loan was approved. Congratulations! Are you ready to move ahead on that dream house?"

Nora decided it wouldn't hurt to string the Realtor along for a few days. After all, if Nora could avoid signing a legally binding contract stating that it was her intention to purchase a new house at the Meadows, or putting down a deposit, then she might be able to keep her hands clean.

"I think so," she said after a pregnant pause. "I don't mean to sound flaky, but this *is* a big decision and I want to make sure I'm doing the right thing. Can I walk through the model home again and take a second look at the available lots?"

"Of course," Annette said so pleasantly that Nora was certain she meant quite the opposite. "But I just want you to know that two of the premium lots were sold since you were here last. I'm not telling you that to pressure you. I just don't want you to miss out on the lot you liked the most. When will you be coming by?"

Oh, she's good, Nora thought with a wry smile. She heard the sleigh bells bang against the door and decided to wrap things up with Annette. "It'll have to be after business hours. Are you ever there past five?"

"Not usually," Annette said. "I have to drive back to Asheville every day, but I could stay open for fifteen minutes or so to accommodate you."

"No, no. I'll figure something out. Maybe I can ask a friend to watch the shop for an hour tomorrow. Let me make a few calls and get back to you."

A familiar figure appeared in the window of the ticket booth. It was Collin Stone. Nora managed to smile at him and signal that she'd be with him in a minute. In response, he gave her a thumbs-up and walked off.

"Sorry," Nora said to Annette, who'd started talking. "A customer came in and I didn't catch what you said just then."

"I was advising you not to wait too long. Good things *don't* always come to those who wait."

Though Nora longed to tell the real-estate agent that she should dial it back a notch when it came to aggressive salesmanship, she refrained. She wanted Annette to view her as meek and unthreatening. That way, no one would suspect her of breaking into the Meadows model home.

Nora thanked Annette for her advice and hung up.

She spent a moment in the sanctuary of the ticket-agent's office, shaking off the previous conversation in preparation for the next. She also decided to finish her lunch, which took less than two minutes. When she was done, she searched for Collin.

But Collin was no longer in the bookstore.

Nora didn't see how this was possible, but he was gone. She meandered around the stacks until she returned to the checkout counter. Collin was nowhere to be found.

I didn't hear the sleigh bells.

The thought chilled Nora and she took another turn around the store.

She'd just turned the corner of the mystery bookshelf when a woman entered the shop and asked for books on overcoming insomnia.

Happy for the distraction, Nora helped the woman select half-a-dozen titles and then invited her to peruse them at her leisure. It didn't take long before the woman was ready to check out. She put three books and a brass music box that played the title theme from *Love Story* on the counter.

The woman was digging in a voluminous handbag for her wallet while Nora moved behind the counter, so she didn't see the shock on Nora's face when she discovered the single rose placed on a diagonal across her cash register.

It was a bright pink rose. A wild rose. A William Shakespeare 2000. The same rose Jed had given her.

Nora grabbed the beautiful flower and then jerked as the sharp tip of a thorn pierced the skin of her thumb. Angry now, but unable to show her feelings in front of her customer, Nora wiped the blood beading on her fingertip on the flower's velvety petals and then tossed the mangled, bloodied mess into the trash can. Staring at the crushed bloom, she asked herself, *How had Collin known?*

Chapter 12

Thieves respect property. They merely wish the property to become their property that they may more perfectly respect it.

—G.K. Chesterton

The trouble with planning a break-in on a summer night was that darkness didn't fall until after eight o'clock, which gave Nora plenty of time to question her sanity.

After a supper of cold fried chicken and green beans, Nora felt restless and irritable. June and Hester wouldn't arrive for another hour, so she put on her hiking boots, gathered her berry basket and walking stick, and headed out into the fading light.

Despite the steepness of the slope behind her tiny house, she didn't have to rely on her stick as much as she feared. Her injured ankle was healing, and Nora could put weight on her right foot without wincing.

When she reached the train tracks, she paused. She stared westward, to where the trains roared through the tunnel before having to slow down at the Miracle Springs station platform.

Though she couldn't see the tunnel, an image of its black maw filled Nora's mind. She thought of Neil Parrish's death, and in thinking of him, she forgot her restlessness. Mostly, what she felt was grief. Before Neil Parrish had joined her on that park bench, Nora's life in Miracle Springs had been private and peaceful. She'd exchanged that privacy for friendship. That peace for danger.

Still, tranquility could be found at the edge of the woods, and as Nora crossed over grass stippled with buttercups to where the raspberry and blackberry bushes formed a wall of leaves, thorns, and insects, she could almost pretend that her biggest worries were increasing the bookstore profits and when to find time to buy more shelf enhancers.

Nora loved berry picking. She loved the cloyingly sweet perfume surrounding the bushes, the fervent buzzing of bees, and how her basket slowly filled with the jewel-toned berries.

Her fingertips were stained indigo by the time she was done and the first of the evening's fireflies were sparkling among the trunks of the pines.

"Hey."

The voice almost startled Nora into dropping her basket. She swung around, preparing to defend herself, but suddenly realized she'd left her walking stick on the grass several feet away.

"Sorry." Jed raised both hands. A plastic grocery bag hung from his left wrist. "I didn't mean to scare you."

"I wasn't scared," Nora said tersely. "I just didn't expect you to creep up on me like that. Why didn't you say something earlier?"

Jed picked up Nora's stick and offered it to her. As she reached for it, his hand covered hers. "I wasn't going to talk at all. I was going to come back later, but my feet just kept moving toward you. Not that I can blame them. You look like a fairy queen, out here in the twilight." He took a step closer to her, still holding the walking stick. "With that moss-green shirt, you almost blend into the background. Except that you could never blend in. You'd stand out anywhere."

Nora slid her hand out from under Jed's and touched the scar on her right cheek. "Because of these?"

"Your scars make you different, yes," Jed said, his eyes locking on hers. "But they're not all I see when I look at you. To me, they just add another dimension to your beauty."

This time, he handed Nora the walking stick without trying to touch her. She accepted it reluctantly. Because now, she wanted him to touch her. The brief brush of Jed's fingertips against hers had ignited a spark.

In the purple half-light, Nora stood inches away from him and wondered how much electricity could be generated if their lips met. Or if their bare bodies were pressed together, skin to skin?

"Did you visit your friend today?" Jed asked as he moved away. He pulled a plastic bag from his pocket and approached the berry bushes. He didn't start picking, however, but waited for Nora to reply.

"I did," Nora said, trying to sound casual.

Jed plucked a fat blackberry from its stem and popped it in his mouth. He chewed slowly, savoring the tart sweetness, and then licked a droplet of juice from his palm. The next berry went into his bag. As did the next.

Nora knew she had to get going. She needed to change before June and Hester arrived and she didn't want Jed to witness the three of them sneaking through the back door of Miracle Books for what was, in fact, a secret meeting.

"I should head home," she said. "Time to elevate and ice."

Jed stopped what he was doing and turned to her. "I wish I could help. What I mean is that I wish I could help your friend. I came to Miracle Springs because of the job. And because I was looking for a sleepy town."

"Two murders is somewhat the opposite of a sleepy town, isn't it?"

Jed nodded. "Yeah. I didn't think that kind of violence occurred here." He tilted his face toward the surrounding hills and then higher, to the darkening sky. "It doesn't seem right. People *need* this place to be unlike other places."

"It's not the place," Nora said, feeling defensive of Miracle Springs. She loved her town. After all, Miracle Springs had allowed her to start over again. The empty train depot had been waiting for her, as had the little plot of land behind the depot. Nora liked to think the people had been waiting for her too. Waiting for her to open a bookstore. To fill in that missing piece of the town's soul.

"Most of the people living here want to help the out-of-towners searching for healing," Nora continued. "But there are always exceptions. Clearly, not all those visiting our town have come to be healed. Some of our guests have other goals. They plan to taint this place, but I don't have to stand by and watch that happen. I can do something about it."

She left Jed then, even though she sensed he had more to say. She would like to have heard whatever it was, but she had to go.

It was fully dark by the time she got in June's car. Hester was in the backseat, looking queasy.

"You don't have to do this," Nora told her. "You know what's at stake if we're caught."

Hester cracked her window. "Why are you focusing on me? We're all taking the same risk."

"No, honey," June argued in a gentle voice. "You and Nora have businesses that rely on your reputations. I keep watch over people at the thermal pools so they don't drown. And when they're done bathing, I give them a towel and show them to the changing rooms. I'd lose a job, not a business."

"If we wind up in jail with Estella, then we're all screwed, so let's *not* get caught. That's my role. Right, Nora?" Hester asked, sounding far younger than her years again. "To be the lookout."

"That's right. June and I will handle the snooping." Nora shot June a questioning glance. "You have the tools?"

June jerked a thumb over her shoulder. "In the trunk."

As it would seem odd for three women to be checking out house sites in the dark—especially since the Meadows had yet to install streetlamps—June drove past the entrance and parked behind a row of Leyland cypress trees on the opposite side of the road.

After June handed out flashlights and pairs of disposable gloves from the Gingerbread House, she grabbed a backpack and locked the car.

"What's in the bag?" Hester whispered.

"A crowbar, broom, and dustpan," June said. "Just in case Nora's credit-card trick doesn't work."

Before Hester could ask, Nora said, "I found an online article on breaking into your own home. It's supposedly for people who frequently lock themselves out, and it only works on doors with spring bolts. If there's a dead bolt in place, it won't work. Plan B is the crowbar."

The women fell silent as they jogged across the road and skirted behind the Meadows sign. They made it to the model home without seeing another car and crept up to the garage service door. Nora peeked through one of the glass panes and froze.

"Annette's car is still here," she hissed to her friends.

"What?" Hester and June whispered in unison.

Nora briefly glanced into the garage again. "There are two cars. Annette's and a pickup truck."

"Doesn't Annette live in Asheville?" Hester whispered.

Nora nodded and pointed toward the back of the house.

The women moved slowly along the wall until they reached the bay window in the kitchen. This time, June took a quick look inside.

She jerked away from the window and signaled for Nora and Hester to drop down. When all of them were on their knees in the new sod, June spoke so softly that it was a challenge for Nora to hear her.

"Wine bottle. Takeout boxes. Candles." She pointed at the house. "We're not going in there tonight."

But Nora didn't think they should leave. Discovering the identity of Annette's lover might prove useful. This was obviously a clandestine meeting, and Nora didn't think Collin Stone would approve of his model home being used as an assignation place.

"We can't go home. We need to see who owns that pickup," she said sotto voce.

Nora's friends didn't speak. In the gloom, their black clothing merged with the shadows, but the whites of their eyes lent them a spectral look.

"It's probably Dawson," Hester whispered. "Annette's and Dawson's initials were on Greer's cocktail napkin. They're both in on this thing—whatever it is—together."

Decoding those initials from Fenton's napkin hadn't clarified anything. Nora and her friends still didn't understand why Fenton had written a list including Annette, Dawson, and the Madison Valley Community Bank.

Nora frowned. "We'll wait for them to leave. After they're gone, we conduct our search. We have to go through with our plans. Estella's in a room with bars. We're not."

"I'm with you," June whispered. "Besides, this beats wandering around town with my merry band of cats."

Hester suddenly shushed them.

In the silence, Nora heard voices on the other side of the

kitchen wall. The words weren't clear, but a woman spoke in rapid, staccato bursts. Whenever she paused for breath, a man injected short, quick responses like a boxer throwing jabs.

Lovers' quarrel, Nora thought. She tried to pick out specific words, but the voices were being thrown in various directions as the couple moved about the room. Nora guessed they were cleaning up the evidence of their meal.

Nora put an arm around each friend. Pulling them in close, she whispered, "One of us needs to see Annette's boyfriend. The other two should stay here until both cars are gone and we're positive that we're alone."

"I'll go," Hester volunteered. "You're still hurt, Nora. I can run fast if somebody spots me."

"Hey. I might be fifteen years older than you, but I'm no slug," June said.

This was not the time for June and Hester to debate their levels of fitness, so Nora gave Hester a little push and said, "Go."

It was less than five minutes before a light went on in the garage, causing Hester to duck down. Nora could feel June tense beside her as the garage door began to open. In addition to this mechanical noise, Nora heard the slam of a car door.

Look now, she willed Hester.

Hester hesitated for what felt like far too long. Finally, she popped up and glanced in the window.

By this point, all the members of the Secret, Book, and Scone Society had visited the Pine Ridge Properties website and had memorized the names and faces of the main players, so when Hester rejoined Nora and June, she said, "The truck belongs to Collin Stone. He leaned into Annette's car and kissed her."

"Another Pine Ridge family man," Nora muttered acidly.

Headlights seared the darkness at the front of the house and the women instinctively froze. Annette backed her SUV out of the garage first, followed by Collin in his pickup. Within minutes, they were both gone.

"We should have stopped the garage door before it went all the way down," Hester said, switching on her flashlight and pointing the beam at the ground.

June shook her head. "No. Annette or Collin might have noticed and stopped to see why the door didn't close."

Nora headed for the side door leading into the garage. "Let's see how accurate that article on breaking into your own home proves to be. June? Can you train your light on the area next to the doorknob? Hester? This is when your lookout duty begins. You should create a little distance between yourself and the house."

"I know you told us that the signal for us to get out in a big hurry is an owl call," June said. "But all I hear right now are night critters. Bugs and raccoons and Lord knows what else? I might not be able to tell your owl noise from a real owl."

Hester scowled. "If you hear an owl, just get out."

June flashed her a smile. "All right, sweet pea."

Something came over Hester's features. Even with the flashlights creating weak pools of washed-out illumination, Nora could see that something had caused Hester great distress.

"Don't call me that." Her eyes glittered with anger and pain. "Don't ever call me that again."

Taken aback, June reached out to her. "Okay, honey. I'm sorry."

Hester avoided June's outstretched hand and ran to a large maple tree on the far side of the model house's driveway.

"What was that about?" June sounded stricken.

"We'll find out later." Nora knew she appeared callous, but whatever was bothering Hester could wait. Finding evidence that certain Pine Ridge Properties employees had a strong motive for getting rid of Neil Parrish and Fenton Greer was paramount.

June didn't argue. She held the light steady over the doorknob and watched, fascinated, as Nora pulled a laminated card from her back pocket and began wriggling it into the space between the door and the frame.

"I hope that's not your only credit card," June said. "It's going to be really banged up, whether this trick works or not."

Nora was razor-focused on what she was doing. "It's a gym membership card, and it's not mine. An out-of-town customer dropped it in the shop a few weeks ago. I called to tell him I'd mail it back and he never answered. I'll cut up whatever's left of it when we're done here."

Working the card slightly back and forth as she moved it higher up the door, Nora was able to determine that the dead bolt hadn't been turned. She exhaled in relief. She now worked it back down to where the spring lock connected to the doorframe, explaining her maneuvers to June as she went. "This is the moment of truth. I have to hold the card flush against the frame and try to slide it under the triangle-shaped spring bolt. The bolt has a pointy side and a sloped side. This is only going to work if the pointy side is facing us."

Nora could feel the card contacting the bolt. She could also feel the card cracking right down the middle. She'd been applying too much pressure in its center and it had begun to give.

"Take a breath," June whispered. "You can do this. You walked through fire and it didn't kill you. This won't, either."

"I didn't walk through fire. The fire walked through me," Nora whispered back. Still, she redoubled her efforts, and when she felt the card slide deeper into the space than before, she grabbed hold of the knob and twisted. The door opened and cool air from inside the garage rushed out to greet them.

"Hallelujah! I was sure we'd be smashing a window tonight," June cried softly. "Actually, I'm feeling a little disappointed. I liked the idea of breaking glass, but I guess it's smarter for us to come and go without leaving a sign. Good thing Hester thought of these gloves."

The two women hurried into the garage.

"No alarm," Nora said. "How long will this luck hold out?"

"I don't think the four of us became friends because Lady Luck has been especially generous to us," June said. "Let's not push it."

Murmuring her agreement, Nora led June to Annette's office.

June went straight to the double windows on the rear wall and opened them as wide as they would go. This way, they could hear Hester's warning hoot and make a quick exit should the need arise.

As for Nora, she opened Annette's desk drawer. "It would have been nice if she'd left the keys here," she said, taking out the second tool she'd brought along. "You'd think a woman so focused on security would have turned the dead bolt in the garage."

"She clearly had other things on her mind tonight." Joining her at the desk, June directed the flashlight beam on the locked drawer. "Was this on the Internet too?"

"There are dozens of videos on lock picking," Nora said. "I was able to practice this one on a lockbox I keep in the store."

"Really? Using nail clippers?" June looked dubious.

Nora unfolded the nail-file tool attached to the clippers and held it up to the light. "This is all you need." She slid the tool into the keyhole and jimmied it around until she felt the tip connect with the locking mechanism. Applying downward pressure, she twisted the nail file clockwise and the lock released. Nora pulled the drawer open and flashed June a triumphant grin.

June was too focused on shifting the flashlight beam so that it would illuminate the drawer's contents. "In the movies, folks always hide a bottle of liquor here. Or a gun."

Annette didn't keep booze or a weapon secreted in her desk. What she hid from the world was a framed photograph of her and Collin Stone. Annette's athletic body was accentuated by a form-fitting black cocktail dress. Collin looked dapper in a dark suit. The pair stood in front of the Meadows sign. Collin had a champagne bottle in his hand and Annette held two flutes in hers. Instead of facing the camera, they were turned toward each other. Collin had been captured mid-laugh and Annette was gazing at him with unadulterated affection.

"I wonder if he likes her as much as she likes him. She's got it bad for that builder, but he might just be another married man having a fling. They're a dime a dozen, those men," June said, making *tsk, tsk* noises with her tongue.

Nora tensed and gripped the frame so tightly that it would easily snap into pieces if she were to apply a little more pressure.

"Annette might be in love with Collin," she said when she'd mastered her anger. "Then again, she could be keeping this—" she paused, realizing that there was another photograph tucked behind the first. Pinching it by the edge, she only had to pull it out halfway before she recognized that she was looking at a black-and-white image capturing Annette and Collin in fla-grante delicto.

"Damn, that woman is flexible." June declared. "But who *took* this picture?"

Since this was an excellent question, Nora removed the photo and brought it closer to the flashlight beam. "It's kind of grainy. I'm thinking it might be a still frame from a video."

June's eyes widened at this. "So *Annette* could have filmed herself with Collin and then printed this?"

"Exactly. Which means Annette Goldsmith is either smitten with Collin Stone or she plans to blackmail him. Unfortu-nately, since we couldn't hear their argument, we don't know how she feels." Nora placed the photographs back in position and brandished the nail clippers. "Want to give the file cabinet a shot?"

"Yes, I most certainly do," June declared, and followed Nora over to the closet. Nora held the flashlight while June engaged in her first lock-picking experience. It took her a little longer to open the file drawer, but when she succeeded, a slow smile spread across her face. "Why does that feel so good?"

"It's a useful life skill. Now let's see what's inside this Pandora's box."

Nora remembered reading the file-folder labels during her tour of the model home. Removing Neil Parrish's file, she placed it on the floor and snapped photos of the HUD statements. She repeated this with the papers inside the folders designated *F.G.* for Fenton Greer and *V.M.* for Vanessa Mac-Cavity.

Collin had a file as well, but his paperwork seemed to consist of the endless sheaf of documents required to turn a piece of farmland into a housing development. Neither Nora nor June knew enough about land surveys, zoning, easements, right-of-way, utilities, permits, site photos, or the environmental-impact statements to determine whether everything was aboveboard.

"Look how many Miracle Springs officials had to give their stamp of approval to this project," Nora said, pointing at several names and signatures. "They can't all be corrupt. There just wouldn't be enough money to go around. I'll take images of a few of these, but my gut says that this file is in order."

June murmured her agreement. "I hope we find something in Fenton's. He obviously screwed up or his body wouldn't be in a human-sized file cabinet right now."

The rest of Annette's files were filled with blank sales forms, homeowners' checklists, and contracts. Nora took copies of each to peruse later on.

"We have to replace everything exactly as we found it," she told June. "Annette is a serious neat freak. She'd notice if her stapler was moved by half an inch."

Satisfied that they'd returned the files to their correct positions, Nora tried to lock the file cabinet with the nail file. She struggled for five minutes before conceding defeat.

"She's going to know someone was here now," June said.

Nora replicated one of June's customary grunts.

The women shut the closet doors and faced each other.

"We should search the rest of the house," Nora said.

"I'll go upstairs. No sense your putting more strain on that ankle." June tapped her watch. "But this is a cursory search. We've been here long enough and in my experience, the things people don't want others to see are either thrown away or kept under lock and key."

As Nora entered the kitchen, June's comment about throwing things away stuck in her mind. She decided to peek into the trash can, which she knew was located in the cabinet under the sink. Considering how much time had passed since Fenton's death—let alone Neil's—Nora expected to find only the detritus of the lovers' takeout meal. Grateful for the gloves Hester had given her, she dug under the food-sticky boxes, balled-up napkins, and plastic cutlery until she saw that the lower layers of garbage comprised mostly paper coffee cups and plastic water bottles.

Nora noted at least four water bottles at the bottom of the can. *Not very eco-conscious, are you, Annette?* she thought, and unintentionally dislodged a takeout container with her elbow. The box teetered on the edge of the can before falling into the gloom behind it.

"Shit," she muttered.

Getting down on her knees, she used the flashlight to retrieve the box and to make sure food hadn't splattered out of it and made a mess. It hadn't, but she did spy a wadded paper behind a bottle of glass cleaner. She retrieved the paper and began to smooth it out, and her pulse quickened as she realized that she was unfurling a train schedule.

It was the current month's schedule and included timetables for multiple towns in western North Carolina. Miracle Springs was one of the towns.

This could have easily belonged to a potential buyer, Nora thought, but she didn't believe that. Her instincts were firing, and when she saw that the date penciled in the corner coincided with Neil Parrish's death, she felt that the schedule was somehow significant.

Nothing else on the first floor was of interest, and when June came down from upstairs, she told Nora that she'd found nothing useful.

"Are you ready to go?"

"Yes," Nora said. "We can review everything when we get back to Miracle Books."

Hester nearly leaped on them from behind the tree trunk when they approached. "That took forever!" she cried softly. "I kept imagining all of these horrible scenarios, from Sheriff Hendricks kicking in the front door to a horde of zombies coming out of that copse of trees back there." She pointed. "Can we please get the hell out of here?"

"Absolutely," Nora said.

It was only when they were safely settled in June's car and en route to the bookshop that the three friends breathed normally again.

"I can't believe we did it," Hester said, sounding giddy with relief. "We just broke into a house. We are badasses. We came and went like ninjas!" She shadowboxed in celebration.

Nora and June exchanged nervous glances and then Nora swiveled in her seat to face Hester. "We weren't exactly ninjas.

Annette will know that someone was in her office because I wasn't able to relock her file cabinet or desk."

Hester's hands fell heavily to her lap. "Do you think they'll suspect us?"

Nora tried not to think of the Shakespeare 2000 rose placed on her cash register. "No," she replied, hoping that neither of her friends heard the lie in her voice.

Chapter 13

Promises make debt, and debt makes promises.
                                                —Dutch Proverb

Worn out from a full day's work followed by a nighttime B-and-E stint, the three women reconvened at Miracle Books only long enough for Nora to print copies of the images she'd taken of Annette's files.

After distributing the copies, she said, "We should all try to research these documents. I don't know if we'll find any-thing—most of the info focuses on the personal and financial data of buyers—but something might strike us as suspicious. We need evidence of a crime. Hard proof to present to another law-enforcement agency."

"Like what?" Hester asked.

Nora had no answer. She was a bookseller and a bibliothera-pist, not a financial guru. Still, she didn't want their group to separate on a low note, so she showed June and Hester the train schedule.

"I wonder whose handwriting is on here." June put her fin-gertip to the wrinkled paper and looked at Nora. "Just touching this thing gives me a bad feeling. Did Annette kill Neil?"

"It's possible," Nora said. "She wasn't on the train with the others from Pine Ridge. She drives to Miracle Springs every day."

"I could see a woman luring a man to the edge of the precipice," Hester said. "Maybe Annette told Neil about the lovers' padlocks. After telling him about our local legend, she asked him to take her to see it."

June looked pensive. "Once there, she could have played damsel in distress. She'd need help getting down the slope in heels. And then." She mimed a pushing motion. "No one would be the wiser if she left the model home for fifteen minutes or so. Especially since she parks her car in the garage."

"Do Annette's numbers look like the ones on this train schedule?" Hester asked Nora.

Nora shook her head. "Everything she gave me was printed from documents on her computer. There were no pencils on or in her desk. She uses a Montblanc pen. Our Realtor has expensive tastes."

"Which she might kill to defend," Hester said. "And if not her, the sheriff. Or Dawson. Our suspect list has several names."

"Neil handled the financial side of Pine Ridge Properties." Nora gestured at the printouts each of her friends held. "That's why I think the mystery behind his murder lies in the numbers. Neil wanted to come clean about his company's shady dealings. Something financially shady. Let's find it and regroup tomorrow."

Hester pointed at the train schedule. "Do you have a safe place to keep that?"

"Yes. Here." Nora tapped the top of the eglomise-style Asian coffee table positioned in the middle of the circle of chairs.

While June stared at Nora in befuddlement, Hester bent over the table and studied the chrysanthemum flowers painted on its mirrored surface. Two were ballet slipper–pink, two were pale peach, and two were cotton-candy blue. There were also two figures on the table—a man and woman—dressed in courtly robes. The man stood on a bridge. The woman, on a rock. Both figures held scrolls and at first glance, they looked like strangers seeking a quiet place to read. Upon closer inspection, it was clear that the man and woman were only pretending to read. Their coy gazes were fixed on each other.

"Where?" Hester asked impatiently. "I don't see a drawer or anything."

Nora moved to one end of the table, gripped its mirrored edge, and tugged. A narrow slit appeared in the center of the table between the man and woman. Nora pushed her fingers into the aperture and continued widening the gap. When she was done, she revealed a letter-sized space with a keyhole staring back up at them like a brass eye.

"Ooohh," June breathed. "Where's the key?"

Smiling, Nora said, "You know how people read different books in different places? I keep a book here at the shop to read during my downtime."

Hester looked at her like she'd lost her mind. "Yeah. What does that have to do with the key?"

Nora ducked into the ticket-agent's office and retrieved *The Storyteller* by Jodi Picoult. She pulled out her bookmark—an aubergine-colored satin ribbon trimmed with white lace. Dangling from the bottom, like the charm from a bracelet, was a tiny brass key.

Fitting the key into the lock of the secret compartment, Nora raised the hinged panel and showed her friends the velvet-lined storage cavity so skillfully hidden by the table's maker.

"What's in the box?" Hester asked.

"I'll show you when Estella can sit in her chair," Nora said, pointing at the chair Estella had chosen when the Secret, Book, and Scone Society had last met as a foursome.

June picked up the train schedule and laid it in the nook with the reverence of one placing a rose on top of a coffin. "Then let's do our damnedest to get her out."

In the haven that was Caboose Cottage, Nora stripped off her clothes and tossed them in a heap on the floor. She put on pajama shorts and her *Book Lovers Never Go To Bed Alone* tank top and shuffled to the kitchen for a glass of water.

As she was turning off the tap, she spied the vase of roses Jed had given her. She put down her glass and drifted over to the vase. The blooms were completely open now, like sails filled with wind, and the roses breathed a heady perfume into Nora's living room.

Nora thought of the rose left on her cash register by Collin Stone. She thought of Jed, and of how he knew something was incongrous about Fenton Greer's body, but had remained silent so as not to risk his new job. She thought of Neil Parrish, a man who'd made mistakes, but had committed to making amends, no matter the cost. And though she tried not to—and fought against it—she thought of the man who'd once been her husband.

Anger made the jellyfish-shaped burn scar on her arm pulse and Nora glanced at it in disgust. Her mouth drawn into a taut line, she grabbed the roses and yanked them out of the vase. Ignoring the water dripping onto her bare thighs and cascading down her calves, she carried the flowers to the kitchen window and tossed them out into the night.

The next day, Nora got up early to research the documents from Annette's file cabinet. While the coffee brewed, she opened her laptop and spread out the HUD statements on her coffee table. She began by reading several articles on obtaining home loans written so that even a Luddite could understand how the process worked. Though these detailed pieces reinforced what Nora already knew, it wasn't until she stumbled across a piece from the crime section of a Midwestern newspaper that she felt she'd discovered a new and noteworthy term.

Because the focus of the article was primarily on the sentence given to an Indiana man accused of mortgage fraud, it was relatively short, but Nora was particularly interested in the reference to *straw buyers*. She opened a new window and entered those words into Google's search box.

The first result was a link to a government page hosted by the Department of Insurance, Securities and Banking. According to the site, straw buyers were people with good credit who allowed other people or companies to use their names and personal information to obtain mortgage loans. These straw buyers didn't intend to occupy the home for which the mortgage was taken and were usually paid money for their role. Nora also learned of a second type of straw buyer. Unlike the first type, each of whom was complicit in the mortgage fraud, this straw buyer was unaware that his or her personal details were being used to apply for a loan. Without his or her knowledge, this buyer became the victim of a mortgage-fraud ring.

These rings can be made up of a group of people such as a lender, appraiser, broker, land developer, builder, settlement attorney, real estate agents, etc., who are all taking part in a scheme. The participants then split the proceeds, Nora read. She glanced out the window, her mind turning over everything she'd just read.

"How can I tell if I'm looking at mortgage fraud?" she asked aloud, addressing the pile of HUD statements.

Returning her attention to the screen, she scrolled to the bottom of the page where she saw a paragraph inviting District of Columbia residents who suspected they were victims of mortgage fraud to call a toll-free number.

"North Carolina must have a similar agency," Nora murmured, and felt a thrill of hope. If she failed to draw any solid conclusions from the statements in her pile, she could call her state helpline and report that she believed her name and personal details were being used in a mortgage-fraud ring. She knew she'd be asked to supply a copy of her HUD statement before a federal agency would consider her claim, which meant she needed to make an appointment to see Annette Goldsmith as soon as possible.

After examining the statements over another cup of coffee and a breakfast of vanilla yogurt topped with wild raspberries and blackberries, Nora found only one anomaly. According to the Federal Housing Authority, the minimum down payment home buyers were expected to come up with was approximately 3.5 percent of the total purchase price. Most banks, however, preferred a 20-percent down payment. For a house at the Meadows, that meant putting down a whopping 60,000 dollars. And yet, none of the approved buyers in Neil Parrish's file had been required to put more than $15,000 down.

Perplexed, Nora did a little more reading on down payments and learned that lower percentages could be obtained by applying for a home loan through government-sponsored companies. But Neil's clients had all gone through Madison County Community Bank.

Nora scanned over rows and columns of numbers. She had no idea if the appraisal fee or title-insurance fees were fair or grossly inflated and when she saw how many hits she got after starting a search on fair closing costs, she knew she didn't have time to read the results.

Instead, she unplugged her cell phone from the wall charger and dialed Annette's number.

Annette answered with her customary greeting, but a new, guarded note had entered her tone.

"I hope I'm not calling too early," Nora said. "But I was thinking about what you told me about the best lots being snapped up, and I thought I should come by sooner rather than later."

"What time did you have in mind?" Annette asked, sounding more cordial.

Nora hesitated. "If it's not too much trouble, I'd like to head over now. It'll take me at least fifteen minutes because I'll be on my bike."

"Your bike?" There was a slight pause. "Ah, that's right. I'd forgotten that you don't drive."

Nora found Annette's reply a bit odd. It was as if she'd just been discussing Nora with someone else.

Gooseflesh erupted on Nora's arms as she recalled the rose on her cash register.

Had *Annette been talking about me? To Collin? Or Sheriff Hendricks? Did she suspect me of breaking into her office?*

Despite the knowledge that no one could see into the living room of Caboose Cottage, Nora found herself shoving the printouts into a file folder and glancing wildly around her tiny house for a place to hide the folder. On a whim, she tucked it between two boxes of cereal on her highest kitchen shelf.

"Lots of people in Miracle Springs get around by bicycle," Nora said placidly. "It's one of the things I love about this town."

"What will you do when you move to the Meadows?" Annette asked. "Won't that be a tough commute when it rains or snows?"

Nora had to hand it to Annette. She was a shrewd woman. "I may upgrade to a moped. They reach speeds of thirty miles per hour and I can add a cargo carrier for groceries and books. But I should only focus on one major purchase at a time, and at the moment, a house at the Meadows tops the list."

"In that case, I'll see you in fifteen minutes," Annette said pleasantly, and ended the call.

Nora couldn't leave immediately. Because she'd be exposed to direct sunlight, she had to apply a generous layer of sunscreen and wear a baseball hat beneath her bike helmet. Her scars were now old enough that she was in no danger of pigmentation changes, but her grafted skin was thinner and more susceptible to sunburn, so she never went outside without protection.

Waiting for the sunscreen to dry put Nora at risk of being late, so she couldn't call Hester and June from her house. That meant calling one of them on the way to the Meadows.

Nora had never had a reason to buy a cell-phone mount for her bike, but today, she wished she owned such a gadget. It was extremely difficult to hold her handlebar with her left hand and her cell phone with her other.

"You could plug headphones into your phone and leave it in your basket," Hester suggested when Nora explained why their conversation had to be brief.

"I don't have headphones," Nora said. She gritted her teeth as her front tire dipped into a pothole and tried not to take her vexation out on Hester. "I'm on my way to the Meadows to see if I can get the rest of my loan paperwork by signing a contract. Did you review your printouts yet?"

"No," Hester said. "I have to take care of my baking first. But I'll call June and ask if she found anything. Be careful, Nora. Annette will be on high alert if she's aware of last night's incident. Don't do anything to make her suspect you. Just stick to the subject of your future house. Got it?"

Hester's bossiness made Nora grin. "Okay, Mom."

Without warning, Nora's call was dropped.

Nora couldn't dwell on the abrupt ending because she needed both hands to make an upcoming turn, so she let her phone gently fall into her bike basket and focused on the road.

Her ankle was sore by the time she reached the model home at the Meadows. When she saw a brown sheriff's cruiser parked at the curb, she was half-tempted to turn around. Instead, she dismounted and walked the bike to the front porch. Annette, Vanessa MacCavity, Collin Stone, and Sheriff Hendricks stood on the top step and watched her approach. It was extremely un-nerving.

This was Nora's first glimpse of Vanessa, and though it was nothing but a brief glance, her impression was one of arrogance. Taking a longer look, Nora noticed other details. Short, dark hair. Power suit. Arms crossed over her chest. Impatient drum of manicured nails. A forty-year-old woman who knew exactly what she wanted from the world and expected to get it.

"You're favoring your right foot, Ms. Pennington," the sheriff said. "Did you injure it?"

"It's stupid, really." Nora looked down at the offending limb. "I'm not used to wearing high heels and I caught the tip of my right shoe on the carpet's edge. You can probably imagine the rest—'down goes Frazier!'"

The sheriff eyed her with interest. "A girl who knows sports. I like that. Are you buying one of these nice houses?"

"I hope so," Nora said. She then adopted a concerned expression and made eye contact with Annette before returning her gaze to the sheriff. "Why? Is something wrong?"

"We had a break-in last night," Annette said, pointing at the house behind her.

Nora followed Annette's gesture as if she expected to see a shattered window or another sign of destruction. "That's terrible. Was anything taken?"

"No, nothing's missing," the sheriff answered. "It was probably kids. They get bored in the summer and dare each other to do moronic things."

"The sheriff believes the thieves were deterred when they discovered that our flat-screen TVs and computers were props. As if we'd leave an unoccupied house loaded with expensive electronics." Vanessa shook her head and then adopted a bored expression.

"That's why I didn't bother installing a security system in this house," Collin said, addressing Nora. "And also because I'd done my research on the crime rate in Miracle Springs. One of the reasons I was attracted to this town was its lack of crime." He smiled warmly. "You don't need to be concerned about this isolated incident, Ms. Pennington. I agree with the sheriff. This break-in was nothing more than a bunch of teenagers acting out a scene from one of their video games."

Nora nodded. "I'm sure you're right. Will you install a security system to discourage future incidents?"

Collin mulled this over before saying, "I don't think so. We offer them as options, though."

"Well, *I* don't want one," Nora said stoutly. "I feel a bit isolated in my current house. Here, I'll be surrounded by neighbors. I'll have a community. People looking out for each other. Especially in light of . . ." She trailed off and darted a nervous glance at Sheriff Hendricks, who immediately cleared his throat and waved at Annette.

"You two should go on inside now. You don't want your makeup to run," he said. "I know how much you gals hate that. And I guess you really need to stay out of the sun, don't you, Ms. Pennington?" he rudely added.

Vanessa covered her mouth with her hand, but not before Nora saw a flash of teeth.

Nora couldn't refrain from responding. "Actually, burn victims are encouraged to seek exposure to a moderate amount of sun. As long as it's been at least a year since our initial injury and we've taken certain precautions. Going outside is good for everyone."

Annette hurried to open the front door for Nora before the conversation could continue, and Nora entered the house. She could feel several pairs of eyes on her back as she moved.

"Would you like coffee or water?" Annette asked once they'd settled in her office. "You must be hot after your ride."

Removing her Carolina Panthers cap—another flea-market find—Nora shook her head. "I'm fine. I need to be at the bookstore by quarter of ten and I'd love to see which lots are still available before I make a decision."

"Certainly." Annette retrieved the site map from the bulletin board and explained that a red sticker represented a sold lot, while a green sticker meant that the lot was available.

"That corner lot is my favorite," Nora said, pointing at a lot near a designated green space. "There won't be any houses behind that one, right?"

"No, it'll be all woods back there."

Nora touched the map. "And when could I expect my new house to be ready?"

"If you signed a contract today, your move-in date would be mid-January."

"Which would give me plenty of time to sell my house," Nora murmured as if speaking to herself. In a louder voice, she said, "Okay, so what's the next step?"

A satisfactory gleam entered Annette's eyes and she moved from the table to her desk. "Let me get a copy of your loan-approval documents. As you know, Madison County Community Bank is our preferred lender. They're offering a three-point-seven-five-percent financing for thirty years for our first twenty-five buyers. Mr. Hendricks told you about their incentive program, right?"

Nora couldn't remember if Dawson had, but such a program would explain the low down payment amounts listed on the HUD statements in the file folder tucked between the cereal boxes in her kitchen.

"Yes," she said to Annette. "Without that incentive, I wouldn't be here today."

Annette made a noncommittal noise and returned to the table with a blank sales contract. While she summarized the legalese, Nora pretended to listen, but her mind was elsewhere. If the bank's incentive was legit, then last night's break-in was useless. Had she and her friends failed to obtain a shred of evidence to incriminate Pine Ridge?

Nora tried to focus on what Annette was saying. She knew it was important to act interested in every element of the purchase, but her thoughts drifted to Estella. Nora had desperately wanted to give her a shred of hope for when they next spoke.

"You'll sign here and here and initial here." Annette placed a pen within Nora's grasp.

If I sign this, I might be complicit in an illegal fraud ring. Nora scanned the contract without absorbing a word. *But if I don't, what chance do we have of securing Estella's freedom?*

Either way, Nora Pennington didn't have enough money to meet the down payment. Not without selling Caboose Cottage. And she had no intention of doing that.

"Are you all right?" Annette asked.

Nora released a heavy sigh. "To be honest, I'm nervous. You see, I went to the bank to get a copy of my loan because I wanted to be sure that I had enough funds to cover the down payment. Mr. Hendricks was out to lunch, and a teller gave me a copy of my file. However, some of the paperwork was missing, so even though I'm here now, I haven't reviewed my loan agreement, and I don't want to sign this contract until I do."

Annette smiled. "That's a fixable problem. I can give you all the time you need to review your loan agreement." Again, she crossed the room to her desk, retrieved the loan papers, and placed them next to the sales contract. "I'm going to make coffee. Give me a shout if you have any questions."

As soon as Annette left the room, Nora started reading her HUD statement. It looked the same as those in Neil's file and she learned nothing by examining every line.

"Damn it," she muttered under her breath. She felt completely trapped.

And then, Nora heard the front door open and Annette's bright hello as she welcomed potential customers.

"Please make yourselves at home," Nora heard her say. "I'm with a client, but I'll be available shortly."

Nora folded the copy of her loan agreement, pushed back

her chair, and hurried to the office door. Annette was just about to enter when Nora nearly barreled into her. "I'm sorry. I have to go. There's a delivery waiting for me at the shop." She held up her papers. "I'll look these over at work and call you later this afternoon."

Without giving Annette a chance to reply, Nora stepped outside into the glaring sunlight.

She didn't even bother with her bike helmet, but pulled her baseball cap down low over her forehead and mounted her bike. The rush of air over her skin as she descended the hill toward town felt heavenly. However, the tree-lined road was curvy, so as soon as the Meadows was out of sight, Nora stopped to put on her helmet and to check her voicemail messages.

Seeing she'd missed a call from June, Nora dialed her number.

"Did you find something in your stack of printouts?" she asked.

"Not a thing." June sounded crestfallen. "Hester said you rode up to the Meadows to sign a contract. Did you get to see Annette's handwriting?"

"Yes, but it doesn't look like the numbers on the train schedule." Nora sighed. "June, let's face it. We're doing a crap job at this detective work. How are we going to free Estella?"

"Don't you get down on us," June commanded firmly. "We're all Estella has. Get your ass to work. We'll figure out how to give her a morsel of hope—anything to keep her going another day. Hester wants us to come to her place tonight. I don't know about you, but I'm not used to all this socializing. My neighbors will think I've found myself a boyfriend."

Nora laughed. "Heaven forbid!" She was about to tell June her plan to contact the North Carolina branch of the Department of Insurance, Securities and Banking, when June announced that her manager was heading her way and that she had to go. Suddenly, the line went dead.

"That's twice in one day that my friends have hung up on me," Nora mused aloud and dumped the phone in her bike basket.

Several cars had zipped by her during this conversation, so Nora was careful to glance behind her before continuing forward along the shoulder. She was now approaching the most treacherous part of her ride, being that there was a sharp bend in the road that created a significant blind spot for any car coming up behind her. If the driver took the bend too close to the shoulder, he could clip Nora with his mirror or worse, sideswipe her with a trailer that swung out over the lane line.

Many of the locals drove this stretch of road faster than the posted speed limit. Because the road led from the downtown shopping district, through a hilly residential area, and eventually to a large, scenic lake, it was common to encounter trailers carrying boats, jet skis, horses, ATVs, motorbikes, and pop-up campers along this route. Nora didn't want to get too close to any of these.

She'd made it halfway around the bend when she heard the gunning of an engine directly behind her. Instinctively, she knew she should be afraid.

Nora didn't have to turn to sense a car bearing down on her.

She cast a frantic glance to her right. A low guardrail was the only thing separating the road from a steep drop into dense woods. Nora knew that if she flipped over that rail, she could very well die.

This left her one choice. An insane choice.

And she took it.

Instead of slowing, she pedaled as fast as she could.

Behind her, the car also accelerated. It sounded like it had a powerful engine. A V-6 or V-8. A truck or SUV. Nora couldn't register any details beyond that. She could only pedal, pushing her legs faster, faster, faster.

She could feel the car closing in on her, but before it could box her in on the right-hand side of the road, she veered violently in the opposite direction, crossing over the double-yellow line and desperately fighting to stay in control while hitting the brakes.

Nora felt, more than saw, the car roar past. She caught a blur of a dark paint—midnight blue, charcoal gray, or black—before she fell.

After then, there was nothing.

Chapter 14

*On days when warmth is the most important need of
the human heart, the kitchen is the place you can
find it . . .*

—E.B. White

"We really have to stop meeting like this."

Nora opened her eyes to find Jedediah Craig staring down at her. Above him was not the wide canopy of the summer sky, but the interior of a car cabin. A car. Not an ambulance.

Despite the pounding in her left temple, Nora tried to sit up.

"Not yet," Jed commanded softly. "You had a nasty crash. Thank God you have a decent helmet. Without that, I'd be driving you to the hospital right now."

"My bike—"

Jed put a hand on her shoulder. "No worse for wear. I loaded it in the back."

Now that she was fully awake, Nora recognized a host of subtle sounds: an idling engine, air-conditioning whispering through vents, the steady clicking of hazard lights.

"Did you see what happened?" she asked Jed.

He shook his head, his eyes straying to her temple. "No. I was on my way to the lake when I noticed you on the side of the road. It's my day off. That's why you're lying on the back-seat of my Blazer instead of riding in the Band-Aid bus."

"Did you see the car?" Nora propped herself on her elbows. "The one that tried to run me off the road?"

"Are you serious?" Suddenly, his phone was in his hand. "I'd better call this in."

Nora grabbed the phone. "*No!* It's better if they think I'm too scared to talk."

Jed looked at her in alarm. "Who is *they*? What's going on, Nora?"

"I can't tell you." Nora wanted to escape from her current position. She felt too vulnerable, stretched out on Jed's rear seat while he knelt on the floor, his wide shoulders wedged between the two front seats. Not for the first time since she'd met Jedediah Craig, Nora felt inexplicably aroused. Part of her wanted to be anywhere else, but another part of her—a side she'd managed to keep dormant until now—wanted to run her fingertips over the bristle covering his jawline and chin. She wanted to curl her palm around the back of his neck and coax his mouth toward hers.

To stop herself from doing something stupid, Nora sat up. However, the movement was too abrupt and she instantly felt nauseated.

Desperate for fresh air, she cracked the door and took in several long, slow breaths through her nose.

"Hey," Jed said. He pressed something cold against her forehead and the nausea instantly receded. "Look, I won't ask any more questions if they're going to upset you. Okay? But I seriously want to make sure you're not concussed. Can I take you in for an examination?"

"No," Nora replied. "I'm fine. Really. I think the bump on my temple is actually from the end of my handlebar. It's going to leave a bruise, but other than some throbbing, there's no pain. I can live with that." She made small movements with her arms and legs, testing to see if she'd sustained other injuries. "I feel pretty normal."

Jed raised his brows. "Sure. Which is why you were dizzy and nauseated from sitting up." He raised his hands in defeat. "I can't make you see a doctor, but if you refuse to be treated for the second time since we've met, then you'll have to agree to a different condition."

"Which is?"

"A doctor would keep you under observation," Jed said. "Since that's not an option, *I'd* like to keep you under observation. Do you have to open the shop now?"

Nora nodded.

"I figured as much." Jed smiled. "Well, you now have an unpaid employee for the day. I can do all the heavy lifting."

"That's really nice of you, but I can't accept." Nora pressed his hand in gratitude. "You were headed to the lake for some much-needed time off. You should hike and swim and enjoy the sunshine. Being in a bookstore all day will be dull in comparison to all that action."

Jed's eyes smiled in amusement. "There's nothing dull about you. You are, by far, the most exciting bookselling cyclist I've ever met."

Nora laughed. "You've met many of us?"

"Dozens. I'm a very cosmopolitan paramedic." A sports car zoomed past, and Jed seemed to suddenly remember that they were parked on the side of a winding road. "Time to go."

Despite Jed's protests, Nora insisted on joining him up front. "You've already rescued me," she said. "I'm not going to sit in the back and let you play chauffeur."

"I'm learning that it's fruitless to argue with you, Nora Pennington."

As Jed pulled away from the shoulder, Nora examined her torn blouse and shredded jeans.

"You have some minor lacerations," Jed said. "You'll need to clean them when we get back. It's a good thing you were wearing long sleeves and pants. They saved you from a serious road rash."

"An added bonus of having burn scars," Nora said acerbically. "Protective clothing shields me from both sun exposure and road rash after a homicidal maniac tries to run me off the side of the mountain."

Jed shot her a worried glance. "Are you sure you don't want to talk about this? I'm a good listener. You can ask any one of the grandmothers I've transported through the years. I listen raptly to everything they say about their grandkids, cats, craft projects, aches, pains, and bruises. But my favorite thing to ask the ladies is if they could go back in time and do it all again, who would they most want to kiss?"

Nora turned to him in surprise. "Seriously? That's what you talk about when they've broken a hip?"

He shrugged. "It takes their mind off their pain. And the ladies always have a name for me. Always. Sometimes, it's a man who died in a war. Or a boy they never had the guts to speak to. Every now and then, they say they married that guy and never regretted a moment. And once in a blue moon, they whisper that it's not a guy at all, but a girl."

Realizing that Jed had just successfully distracted her from both her pain and her distress over being targeted by a driver trying to run her off the road, Nora smiled.

The smile didn't last though. For as much as she'd like to listen to more of his anecdotes, she couldn't have Jed hanging out at Miracle Books all day. Not only would it be difficult to concentrate on regular tasks, but she also couldn't make a Facetime call to Estella knowing that he might overhear their conversation.

However, Jed made it clear that he wouldn't be chased off. After unloading her bike, he followed Nora into Miracle Books and began turning on lights.

"Do you want to go home and change clothes?" he asked. "I

can't operate the register, but I can say hello to people and brew a mean pot of coffee."

Nora glanced down at her shirt and jeans. "I don't know. I might sell more books in this outfit. People might feel sorry for me."

Jed started to laugh, but Nora didn't stick around long enough to hear the sound of his merriment drift into the stacks. Deciding that it would be prudent to clean out the dirt and dust from her road rash while it was still fresh, Nora hurried to Caboose Cottage, stripped off her ruined outfit, and examined her injuries in the bathroom mirror.

She saw a large area of raw, red flesh on her thigh and two smaller patches on her arm. It looked like someone had rubbed her with sandpaper. The skin was tender to the touch, but Nora suspected it would heal completely in a week or so.

You're lovelier than ever, she thought sardonically, and went into her bedroom to retrieve another long-sleeved shirt and a pair of jeans.

The loss of an outfit she couldn't afford to replace, along with the outrage over having nearly been killed, had Nora in a foul mood by the time she returned to Miracle Books. At least Jed had made good on his promise to make coffee and several customers had already entered the shop.

An elderly gentleman asked Nora for help finding books on alleviating joint pain. However, after she showed him to the section, she had a feeling that his rheumatoid arthritis wasn't the only thing troubling him.

Nora exchanged small talk with the man, whose name was Roger. When she felt he was sufficiently at ease, she asked him why he'd come to Miracle Springs.

"There's more to it than your RA, right?" she prodded in a gentle voice. "Maybe I can help."

Roger hesitated. "My daughter has cancer, and I don't know how to handle it. She does. She can handle *anything*. But we've never been close." He glanced down at the book he'd selected on joint pain. "I worked too much when she was growing up, so I never really got to know her. And now, when she needs me, I don't know how to talk to her. I don't know what it means to be a good father."

Nora knew how difficult this admission had been for Roger and thanked him for trusting her enough to share it with her.

"Come with me." She led Roger to the circle of chairs near the ticket-agent office and suggested he choose a drink from the menu. "While you're relaxing, I'll find what you need."

Roger ordered an Ernest Hemingway, which Jed volunteered to pour, leaving Nora free to peruse the fiction section. After much deliberation, as well as having to stop twice to assist other customers, Nora returned to Roger's side carrying *Empire Falls, To Kill a Mockingbird, The Sweetness at the Bottom of the Pie, Little House on the Prairie,* and *America's First Daughter: A Novel.*

"Do I read all of these?" he asked.

Nora nodded. "If you do, I think you'll be ready to talk to your daughter the way you've always wanted to talk to her. These authors will help you find the right words."

Roger wiped a solitary tear from his left eye. "Thank you. I'll write you and let you know how things go."

"I'd like that," Nora said.

She left Roger to enjoy his coffee and examine his books in peace. Jed was waiting for her in the ticket-agent's office. The gaze he turned on Nora was filled with unspoken questions.

"That sounded a bit like therapy." His tone wasn't judgmental. Merely inquisitive.

Nora was reluctant to explain her role of self-trained bibliotherapist, but since Jed had already told her that he was open to nontraditional forms of medicine, she said, "Sometimes, I recommend certain titles to help people find healing."

Jed mulled this over. "But you gave that customer a stack of novels. How does fiction heal?"

"Not all injuries are physical," Nora said, and moved off to ring up a customer waiting at the front counter.

Later, she taught Jed how to use the espresso machine and gave him a quick lesson on spotting and reshelving stray books.

"Where do you find all the cool antiques and vintage knick-knacks?" Jed pointed between a cast-iron castle doorstop and a Raggedy Ann penny bank.

As Nora described the local flea markets and auctions, Jed's eyes lit up. "My mother used to work for an auction gallery," he said. "When I was a kid, I had unique toys. I used to want all the new stuff I saw on TV, but that was before I realized how much better my antique metal soldiers were than the mass-produced plastic ones. Even when other kids teased me, I knew my shit was cooler than their shit."

"So is your mom retired now?" Nora asked, and saw the light in Jed's eyes snap out.

"You could say that." He turned away, but not before Nora caught the brief grimace.

There's a story behind that twist of his mouth, Nora thought. *A painful one. A story involving his mother.*

But Nora wouldn't dream of prying. Not all secrets were meant to be shared.

For lunch, Nora treated Jed to takeout from the Pink Lady, insisting that he accept a meal in exchange for giving up his day at the lake. He agreed, but only if she'd take a pain reliever for her headache.

"How did you know I had a headache?" she had asked in surprise.

"You've touched your temple multiple times. I'm an obser-vant guy."

Nora had swallowed some Bayer and called in their lunch order.

By day's end, Nora had to admit that she'd enjoyed Jed's com-pany. More importantly, she'd felt comfortable with him for a long period of time. He'd unobtrusively fallen in the flow of

Miracle Books. When the shop was filled with customers, he made coffee or directed them to certain areas of the store. During slow times, he read or examined Nora's shelf enhancers with such delight that she almost considered inviting him to join her the next time she went treasure hunting. She didn't, however. Because although Jed's presence had been the highlight of Nora's week, it had also prevented her from contacting Estella or working out what to do next to prove her friend's innocence.

Walking Jed to the front door, Nora thanked him with as much warmth as she was capable of, which meant she met his gaze and handed him a book wrapped in brown paper.

"What's this? You already treated me to lunch."

"And you coerced every other customer into buying a coffee or a shelf enhancer in addition to at least one book. You were very good for business."

Jed puffed out his chest. "That's the best compliment I've gotten in ages. Usually, the most I can hope for is, 'You found my vein with your first stick. You might actually know what you're doing.'"

Nora smiled and said, "Coming from someone with lots of experience being stuck with needles, it's a relief when a person slides that needle in nice and smooth on the first go-round."

"Keep turning me on with that medspeak and I'll be back tomorrow." Jed's mouth curved into a rakish grin, but it vanished as quickly as it had appeared. "Seriously, Nora. Call me if you feel any dizziness or nausea." He hesitated. "Or if you want to talk about why I found you on the side of the road in the first place. If someone deliberately hit you with a car, you shouldn't be alone tonight. Or at all."

"I agree," Nora said.

Jed searched her face, clearly nonplussed by her answer, but Nora didn't say anything else. She was ready for him to leave so she could contact the other members of the Secret, Book, and Scone Society.

Sensing the shift in the atmosphere, Jed gave Nora a parting smile—one that didn't reach his eyes—and left.

Hester's house reminded Nora of a tea cake. A pale pink Victorian cottage with icing-white trim, it was surrounded by hydrangea bushes bearing plump, white flowers and flower beds overflowing with daisies, marigolds, and impatiens.

It was clear that Hester's kitchen was the heart of her house. Every inch of space was covered with cast-iron molds, tin cookie cutters, and reproduction advertising signs.

June sat beneath a tin Hershey's sign and Hester gestured for Nora to take the chair under the Royal Baking Powder sign.

Hester looked like a fifties housewife in a polka-dot apron with a matching headband.

"What is that amazing smell?" Nora asked. She inhaled deeply and immediately began to relax. The warmth of the kitchen, combined with the scent of baking dough and the presence of her friends, gave Nora a sense of homecoming. It was a feeling of comfort she hadn't experienced since she was a child.

Hester ignored the question and pointed at Nora's hand. "Are those for us?"

Nora looked down. She'd entered Hester's house carrying a bag of food and three tiny keys affixed to three aubergine-colored ribbons. "I figured we couldn't truly be a society of secret keepers if only one of us had access to the secrets. So here." She flattened her palm, inviting June and Hester to take a bookmark. The lone bookmark on her hand was a grim reminder of their missing society member.

"Thank you," said June. "We'll come to every meeting with these tucked into the pages of our current books."

Nora got to her feet. "Let's go into the living room and connect with Estella. I set this up with the powers-that-be at the jail after work. You can't just call inmates on a whim, unfortunately, as an outside company actually handles the communication and requires that you create an account and put a credit card on file. Also, we'll have to watch what we say to Estella until we know who's listening in on her end of the conversation."

June and Hester responded with somber nods and Nora figured out how to make her inaugural phone call using her laptop. Surprisingly, the call went through smoothly and within five minutes, Estella's face filled Nora's screen.

Nora had placed the laptop on Hester's coffee table, which was actually a large steamer trunk, and taken a seat on the sofa at a slight distance from the screen. This way, Hester and June could sit on either side of her, allowing Estella a view of all three of them.

"It's so good to see you!" Estella cried. "I was worried you'd forgotten about me. Or worse. That they'd somehow scared you off. Or shut you up."

"No one's going to stop us," Nora said. "And I'm sorry that we left you hanging for so long. I just wish I had better news. How close is your audience?"

Estella glanced over her shoulder. "Not too bad," she said before lowering her voice. "Keep it down for the juicy bits."

Nora choked out a laugh. "It's *all* juicy, though that's not the word I would choose to describe what's happened since I last saw you."

She managed to summarize her morning visit to the Meadows as if it were a trip to the grocery store and Estella adopted a bland expression throughout. Only her eyes betrayed her shock over hearing how Nora was run off the road.

June and Hester weren't as passive in their reactions, however. Both shouted expletives.

"You *must* have found something," Estella said after Nora had shushed Hester and June. "Otherwise, why else would they be motivated to give you a lethal nudge?"

Nora shook her head and spoke in a near whisper. "If we did, we're all stumped as to what it was. I qualify for a home loan based on a special incentive from the bank. And yet Dawson Hendricks has seen my financial statements. He knows I can't cough up the down payment without selling Caboose Cottage first, but I still got the distinct impression from Annette that Pine Ridge Properties would allow me to sign a contract based on the fact that I was preapproved at the bank. It makes no sense. Doesn't Collin Stone need capital to build these houses?"

"How many homes have actually been completed?" Estella asked. "I haven't been up to the Meadows since they broke ground on the model home."

"None are finished." Nora turned to June and Hester. "How many would you say have been started?"

Hester tapped her chin. "Four. Maybe five."

"No other lots have been cleared. And my guess is that only three houses have been framed. The development isn't very far along," June said.

"Especially in light of how many lots have been sold." Nora described the site map in Annette's office. "Either that map is bogus, or a rash of contracts were signed within a short time period."

Estella made a pensive noise. "That puts a ton of pressure on Collin." Checking to see if the guard was overtly listening, she added, "He might be an ass, but I'd still like to see him working out in the sun. Shirtless and sweaty."

"It's more than a personality flaw, Estella. We're talking about murder," Nora pointed out sternly. "This is a Scott Turow, *Presumed Innocent*, kill-your-colleague type of murder."

June shook her head in disagreement. "Nah. It's more like Patrick Bateman of *American Psycho*, murdering his coworker."

"Bateman didn't care about money, his reputation, or other human beings," Nora argued. "I think Collin Stone cares about at least two of those. We have no idea how he feels about Annette. Is Collin in love with her or is he using her?"

Estella made a time-out gesture. "Wait a sec! Is your builder a bad boy?"

"Yeah," Hester said. "And from what we saw in the model house, it looks like the badness happens regularly."

"Saw?" Estella leaned closer to the screen. "Was it hot?"

Nora was tempted to slam her laptop lid shut. "Do you want to get out of there, Estella?"

"*Nora*," Hester scolded. "Be nice."

But Hester hadn't been pushed off her bike. Collin hadn't left a rose on Hester's cash register. And Hester didn't understand why Nora didn't feel like entertaining Estella by describing the lurid details of a married man's affair.

Glancing sideways at her friend, Nora snapped, "Sorry, Mom."

She started to turn away, but Hester's hand clamped down on her shoulder like a vise. "Don't call me that."

June, who was on Nora's other side, peeked behind Nora's back to get a look at Hester's face. "Honey, what's wrong with you? You sounded just like that when I called you *sweet pea*."

Nora pried Hester's fingers loose. Even in midair, her hand was curled inward like a talon.

"Hester?" Estella pleaded from a stark room across town. "Talk to us. Is it . . . does this have something to do with your secret?"

After a lengthy pause, Hester whispered, "Once, I was your average high school girl. I studied hard, hung out with my friends, and played the flute. My dad called me *sweet pea*." She swallowed and then spoke a little louder. "In the winter of my junior year, I got pregnant, and I was sent off to live with an aunt in Michigan until the baby was born. I wasn't allowed to leave her house for any reason. Around Halloween, I gave birth to a little girl. I never saw her. I never held her. She was taken away while she was still crying. My parents said that if I breathed a word about what had happened, they'd never speak to me again."

"Jesus," Estella murmured.

There was a banging noise off-screen and a man's voice announced, "Ten minutes. You're only getting this long because I want to finish this article."

"Thank you, Officer." Estella gave him a winsome smile. "You're such a gentleman." She continued staring in his direction for several seconds before she was able to focus on her friends again. "Hester, plenty of young women have had to give a child up for adoption. You don't have to be ashamed, darling."

Now, Nora understood why Hester's personality vacillated between old soul and naïve innocent. She'd been through a traumatic ordeal. Instead of helping her recover, Hester's parents had forced her to remain silent. They'd forced her to pretend that her pregnancy hadn't occurred. They'd told her to suppress her memories and feelings.

But memories and feelings don't disappear like a bad dream. Nora knew this. They'd twist Hester's future into knots, possibly preventing her from ever forming a healthy relationship with a man. Or with anyone.

Nora guessed that Hester's shame had eventually morphed into anger and that she'd come to Miracle Springs to seek the independence she desperately craved.

"Did you become a book lover then?" she asked Hester in a soft voice. "During your time at your aunt's house?"

"I'd always been a reader," Hester said. "But books were all I had when I was with my aunt. She was a horrible woman and she called me terrible names. I don't know how such a bitch could have such beautiful books." Hester closed her eyes and shook her head at the memory. "She had a whole room lined with books, but I had to do a chore just to borrow one of them. I would have done anything, though, because those stories took me away from my thoughts and her nasty words." She blinked back tears. "They saved my life."

June reached across Nora's lap and took Hester's hand. "Is that where you learned to bake too?"

Hester's mouth formed a wobbly smile. "Yes. My aunt couldn't defrost a bag of frozen peas, but she owned dozens and dozens of gorgeous cookbooks. I begged her to let me try a recipe. Just one. I was dying of boredom."

"What was it?" Estella asked. "The very first thing you made?"

A torso in a sheriff's-department uniform blouse appeared behind Estella's head. "Time's up, Ms. Sadler. Say good-bye now."

"Wait!" Estella protested. "What was it, Hester?"

Hester's gaze had turned dreamy. Distant. "Can't you guess?" A tiny smile flitted at the corners of her mouth. "The very first thing I baked was a scone."

Chapter 15

*It's always that way when you're looking at books.
An hour goes by in a minute: you don't know where
the hell the time went.*

—John Dunning

When the connection with Estella was terminated, Hester began to cry.

"I shouldn't have taken up her time," she said, sniffling. "That was so selfish of me. She's sitting there, waiting for our call—waiting for us to get her out of there—and I talk about my stupid past."

Nora grabbed a box of tissues from the side table and handed them to Hester. "Estella will understand and she won't hold this against you. June and I understand too. Sometimes, things happen in the present that trigger our most painful memories. Sometimes, we can't stop them from breaking through. They're like floodwaters and we're powerless to stop the flow."

"It's better to let it all out," June added. "Here, where you're safe. Here, in this wonderful, cozy house. With your friends."

Hester wiped her tears and blew her nose. She stuck the tissue in her apron pocket and made a visible effort to gain control over her emotions.

"Are you still in contact with your parents?" June asked.

Hester's shoulders rose in a semblance of a shrug. "I call every Monday and tell them about the bakery. They talk about my brother and his family, their dog, and the trips they have planned. I always wait until nighttime so I can have a glass of wine before I dial their number. I have another glass after we're done talking." She tried to smile but failed. "We never say anything real. We've been strangers since they shipped me off to my aunt's."

Nora now searched June's face. Was it difficult for her to hear the child's point of view in a case of familial estrangement? There was hurt in June's eyes, but there was sympathy too. And because June had such a generous heart, she was able to focus on Hester's pain instead of her own.

"Hester." June walked around to Hester's side of the sofa and knelt in front of her like a suitor. "There isn't a teenager on God's green earth who hasn't made a mistake. Big ones. Small ones. Mistakes that hurt others. Mistakes that hurt themselves. The whole point of your teenage years is to figure out what sort of adult you're going to be, and you can't do that without screwing up along the way. It's just like that saying about omelets and breaking eggs." She laid her hands on Hester's knees. "Your family made you feel like a bad person because you got pregnant. You boarded the shame train at seventeen and never got off. Am I right?"

"It's not just the pregnancy," Hester said in a small voice. "It's the baby. I had a *baby*. A daughter." She jerked her head toward the window. "Somewhere, out there, I have a daughter."

Nora recognized the true cause of Hester's shame. "You never tried to find her."

Hester lowered her gaze and remained silent.

"Do you want to find her?" Nora asked. "After we conquer our current mountain, June, Estella, and me will help you however we can."

"Thanks." Hester sounded withdrawn. Almost shy. But

Nora understood her friend's behavior. She'd seen it dozens of times at Miracle Books. After her customers confided in her, they always went quiet. Often, they'd have her ring up their purchases right away so they could flee the store, but Nora knew that no matter where they were headed, they would end up finding a place to stop and read one of the books she'd recommended.

"I think we should start our uphill climb with a meal," June said, smiling up at Hester. "I always think better on a full belly and Hester, you need to get something warm in yours. Your hands are like ice and it's summertime in the South!"

Hester examined the gooseflesh on her arms. "It's because I put on air-conditioning for you two. I don't use it. I prefer open windows and ceiling fans. I also love being barefoot, so I'm probably cold because my feet are cold."

"Well!" June exclaimed with a delight that seemed at odds with the conversation. "I can fix that."

Getting to her feet, she performed a little jig en route to her purse. She was humming as she dug around inside the voluminous tote. Eventually, she withdrew a pair of mango-colored socks and carried them back to Hester.

"This is the first decent pair I've made. Put them on and see if they fit."

Hester raised the socks to her cheek, caressing her skin with the soft wool. "They smell really nice. What's that scent?"

"I use essential oils at home for lots of things," June said while motioning for Hester to hurry up. "I thought I'd add a few drops of rose oil to these."

Hester released a long, slow sigh of contentment once her feet were covered with her new socks. "Thank you, June." She smiled, looking more like her sunny self. "Okay, ladies. Let's move into the kitchen and figure out what Nora did to worry someone to the point where they'd push you off a cliff."

Over a meal of cucumber salad and white chicken enchiladas, the three friends reviewed Nora's activities immediately following Neil's death. Not one of them could determine where she'd aroused the suspicion of the murderer or the people involved in the killings of both Neil Parrish and Fenton Greer.

"It isn't only me," Nora said as she carried her dirty plate to the sink. "They went after Estella first, remember? She was arrested immediately after Fenton Greer's body was found. As though the whole event had been carefully prearranged."

Hester went pale. "With Estella out of the way, the puppet master painted a target on your back next. But why? Because the killer somehow knows that the four of us are looking for him? Or her?"

"That's the feeling I'm getting," Nora said. "And I believe the puppet master might be Collin Stone."

Though reluctant to do so, she told June and Hester about the rose left on her cash register following Collin's visit to Miracle Books.

"Why are you just sharing this with us now?" June was angry. She tossed her flatware in the sink and put her hands on her hips. "We're *supposed* to trust each other! What else have you not told us? We can't figure this out if we aren't seeing the whole picture."

"I'm sorry. I've gotten so used to keeping my distance that I'm no good at the give-and-take relationships require." Nora touched the burn scar on her right forearm. "I'm still holding on to my secret. I know damned well that until the three of you hear it, I'll continue hiding parts of myself."

Hester walked over to the oven and turned off the timer. She picked up a pair of oven mitts and looked at Nora. "Are you ready to tell us?"

Nora nodded. "But Estella has to be with us. In person. Not as a face on my laptop screen."

"I agree," Hester said. She opened the oven door and a current of peanut-butter-and-chocolate-scented air flowed through the kitchen.

Nora and June watched as Hester removed a tray of golden scones from the oven to the cooktop.

"If that's our dessert, then I'm mighty glad that you're my friend." June inched toward the hot tray. After inhaling deeply, she moaned and said, "Your aunt must have been as round as a Thanksgiving turkey by the time you left her house."

Hester giggled. "She *was*! After those first scones, she was totally hooked on my cooking. I knew she had a sweet tooth, but I had no idea how much it would control our lives. It got so bad that she started rejecting any dish that wasn't a baked good. If I didn't plan on baking a cookie, pie, cake, muffin, bread, scone, cobbler, bagel, éclair, cream puff, macaroon—well, you get the picture—then I wasn't allowed to cook."

At Hester's request, Nora and June resumed their seats at the kitchen table while Hester made preparations to plate their scones. Unlike Nora, who owned a total of eight white dishes, Hester's cabinets were stuffed with plates of all shapes and sizes. She deliberated for several minutes before choosing porcelain bread-and-butter plates with a pale yellow border and delicate pink and yellow flowers. After sliding a scone onto each plate, she gave two plastic condiment bottles a shake and created zigzags of chocolate and peanut-butter sauce on top of the pastry. Observing her at work had a hypnotizing effect on Nora. She couldn't remember the last time she'd felt so relaxed.

"Dessert is a peanut-butter cup scone," Hester said. "It's my comfort scone, because the last kindness I received before I left for my aunt's came from my younger brother. He didn't know why I was leaving. He was only told that I'd done something unforgivable and that I was being sent away as a punishment." She paused, shook her head in anger, and continued. "My brother snuck in my room that morning—against my parents' wishes—and hugged me. He also slipped a peanut-butter cup into my coat pocket in case I got hungry. When I ate it that night at my aunt's house, I swore I'd repay him for that gesture one day."

"And now?" June asked while cutting off the corner of her scone. "Are you and your brother close?"

"No," Hester said sadly. "It must have been so hard on him with me gone. My parents put all their eggs in one basket, you know? The pressure got to him and for years, he couldn't seem to hold down a job. I used to send him money, but things are better for him these days. That's what my parents say, anyway. My brother and I don't talk much."

Nora popped a bite of scone into her mouth, reveling in the smooth, rich blend of melted chocolate and peanut butter and the springy texture of the dough. The warmth traveled down her throat, spread through her chest, and stretched to the tips of her fingers.

"You were born to do this," she told Hester. "To make food that seems so simple, but has an incredible complexity of taste and an ability to stir the heart? That's a gift."

Beaming with pleasure, Hester spoke of how her aunt had died relatively young and had surprised the whole family by leaving Hester a significant chunk of change under the provision that she would use it to first attend culinary school and, after graduating, to open her own bakery.

"The mean aunt?" June was astonished. "Didn't you say that she was a shrew?"

Hester gave a hapless shrug. "There was no explanation. My parents resented the gift, of course. They made snide comments about it the whole time I was in school and for months after I hung my Gingerbread House shingle. But by then, they no longer had the power to hurt me as much."

Nora chewed, considering what Hester had just said. "That phrase—*the power to hurt*—makes me think of Neil and Fenton. Those two men were capable of hurting our killer or the people who orchestrated the murders. Judging by their positions in Pine Ridge Properties, these crimes are motivated by money."

June put down her fork. She had yet to finish her scone, but she'd clearly been struck by a thought. "Put that theory together with the number of sold lots and what I assume is a pile of home loans doled out by Dawson Hendricks down at Madison Community Bank, and I'd agree with you. So let's make a list of all the people who could possibly benefit from this real-estate scheme and then try to work through how they set it up and how Neil could have unraveled the whole scheme."

Hester grabbed pen and paper. Together, the women came up with a list of names including Sheriff Hendricks, Dawson Hendricks, Collin Stone, Vanessa MacCavity, and Annette Goldsmith.

Nora tapped Vanessa's name with her index finger. "She's been remarkably invisible. Other than the night Estella saw her at the bar with the rest of the Pine Ridge gang and the day I saw her at the model home, what has Vanessa been doing?"

"If I'm remembering correctly from your website research, Vanessa handles the firm's PR," June said to Nora. "I'm not sure what that entails when it comes to real-estate development, but I picture her walking around with a phone stuck to her ear."

"She certainly hasn't done much in the way of advertising." Hester still had last Sunday's newspaper folded on her countertop. She brought it over and turned to the real-estate section. There, under the HOMES FOR SALE heading, was a modest ad for the Meadows. "This is the only ad I've seen."

June frowned. "So what is the woman doing all day?" She looked at Nora. "Didn't Neil say that his partners were coming in for a group meeting? Why leave their home base in Asheville in the first place?"

Nora nodded absently. Though the question of how Vanessa had been spending her time in Miracle Springs was worth investigating, she was also concerned that more names needed to be added to their current list.

"There are other possibilities," she said, returning her attention to the paper. "The title agent. Closing attorneys. Other members of the sheriff's department. And what if other people who applied for loans were like me? They knew they couldn't afford a house at the Meadows but signed a contract anyway, even though something feels *off* about it, because that's how badly they want to improve their station in life?"

A weighted silence followed Nora's words. She wondered if June and Hester felt like she did—that this problem was too big for three women to tackle.

But when she glanced first at June and then at Hester, Nora reconsidered her initial feeling of defeat. Her friends were survivors. Not only had they risen above their painful experiences, but they'd also gained a level of kindness, generosity of spirit, and a deep compassion that many people wouldn't come to know should they live three lifetimes. Nora knew that every member of the Secret, Book, and Scone Society possessed the inner strength to see this thing through to the end.

"I'll talk to Bob tomorrow. Ask him to find out what Vanessa's been doing," June said.

Hester raised her fork and spun it around so that it caught the light. "I'm going to work some magic on Deputy Andrews. I'm a terrible flirt. My dating experience is limited and my track record with men isn't good. But I think he likes me and I'm going to use that to our advantage. Have either of you ever read M.F.K. Fisher's *The Art of Eating*?"

"Never heard of it," June said.

"Fisher was a well-known food writer," Hester explained. "She once said that 'sharing food with another human being is an intimate act that should not be indulged in lightly.'" Pointing at the remains of June's scone, Hester said, "I'm going to bake something special for Andrews to try. In the Gingerbread House. After closing. That's as intimate as I'm willing to be."

Nora's thoughts strayed to her day at Miracle Books with Jed. Though she was undeniably attracted to the paramedic, she couldn't seduce him in exchange for his help. To begin with, she wasn't convinced that Jed would respond. Not only that, but Nora didn't think she was ready to be intimate with a man. She might never be ready. On any level.

As if she'd read Nora's thoughts, June pursed her lips. "What about your Jedediah? We're going to need him if Deputy Andrews ignored your request to check out the coroner's report. Jed's the one who brought up the notion that Fenton's body had been moved. How can he turn a blind eye to an inaccurate ruling? EMTs take an oath. I don't know exactly what it says, but if he's a decent man—and my gut tells me that he is—then we should remind him of his oath."

Hester collected the dessert dishes and carried them to the sink. "What does the oath say?"

Nora retrieved her laptop. It took her less than a minute to pull up the oath. She read it first before passing the computer to Hester.

"This line might be a problem," Hester said. "The one that discusses entering homes and *never revealing what I see or hear in the lives of men unless required by law.*"

June stared at the screen with a pensive expression. "I don't think that line can trump this one: *I shall also share my medical knowledge with those who may benefit from what I have learned.*" She glanced between Hester and Nora. "Maybe Jed doesn't think his medical knowledge was relevant once he'd delivered his patient to the morgue, but I beg to differ."

"He likes you, Nora. There's no way he'd volunteer to be your unpaid employee if he didn't. Possible concussion or not." Hester gave Nora a coy grin. "Could you call him up and tell him that you have another book recommendation? Have him swing by during closing time and, I don't know, take him to a secluded reading nook and see if you can guilt him into paying a visit to the medical examiner?"

Nora shook her head. "He won't do it. Despite the words he spoke when he first became an EMT, he made it crystal clear that he can't afford to lose his job. Something happened to him. Something that caused him to move here and start over. Just like the rest of us. I can't force him to tell me about that event. I already know that he isn't willing to talk about it. Not yet. And if I push him, he'll only regret that he decided to trust me with that detail about Fenton in the first place."

"You like him too," Hester said, her grin widening. "*That's* why you don't want to push him."

June raised a hand, forestalling Nora's protest. "We all have to step out of our comfort zones. They're going to come after you again, Nora. That rose was a warning. Think about it. How did Collin know about it in the first place unless he'd already been watching you? Think of the effort it took to locate the bush that wild rose came from. You got a serious warning from a dangerous man." June pointed a stiff finger at Nora. "You didn't heed that warning, so someone decided to push you off the side of a mountain. There were two people in that car: the driver and the person who shoved you. This confirms our theory that we're not dealing with a single murderer."

"The witness is the key," Nora said, looking at Hester. "We need to know who they are and what they think they saw Estella do."

She'd patiently waited for June to finish, but she was angry now. Not at June, but at herself. Instead of coercing Jed into helping them, she'd shut down. She'd hidden behind her bookshelves and safe subjects like her shelf enhancers and food. Always books. Books were her way of staying connected to other people without letting any individual person get too close.

"Even if I learn the name of the witness from Deputy Andrews, I don't see how that changes things," Hester said. "We'd have to discredit him. Or her. How can we do that if the sheriff is in on the scheme?"

"We use the newspaper to expose them," Nora said. "And we start a social-media campaign as a backup. But this can only happen if we get the witness to admit that they fabricated the story about seeing Estella the night of Fenton's murder."

June grunted. "There's the rub. No one's scared of us."

"That's their mistake," Nora said. The space where her pinkie used to be started to tingle. "They have no clue what we're made of. If they did, they'd be seriously frightened."

The next evening, Hester sent Nora and June a group text. It was short and to the point.

ANDREWS IS STILL HERE. I SNUCK TO THE BACK TO SEND THIS. THE WITNESS IS VANESSA MACCAVITY. SHE SWORE SHE SAW ESTELLA AND FENTON TOGETHER IN THE GARDEN AROUND 10, KISSING. SHE ALSO SAYS SHE SAW AN EMPTY MARTINI GLASS NEAR FENTON BUT ESTELLA WASN'T DRINKING OR HAD NO GLASS.

"How convenient," June said to Nora when she called less than a minute after Hester's text came through. "There are no security cameras in the garden. The paths are illuminated at night, but the gazebo isn't lit because the management doesn't want to attract bugs to the structure."

"Any luck finding out how Vanessa has spent her time since she arrived in Miracle Springs? Other than lying about Estella's movements?" Nora asked in a tight voice. Her blood was already rising in temperature as it surged through her veins. She wanted a piece of this woman—Vanessa—for possibly precipitating Estella's arrest. Nora also wanted to know who tried to kill her on that mountain road. And she wanted to look into the face of Neil's murderer and feel that she and the Secret, Book, and Scone Society had sought—and achieved—justice for a stranger.

"According to Bob, who's been collecting gossip for us like a truck-stop waitress since I asked for his help, Vanessa divides her time between lounging at the pool sipping cocktails, receiving massages and facial treatments, and talking on the phone in her suite. The housekeepers can't tidy up while Vanessa's inside because she always hangs the DO NOT DISTURB sign on her doorknob. Her suite has three rooms. She could easily move from one to the other while the staff cleaned, but she won't let them in. They can hear her on the phone. Apparently, she has a short fuse and a nasty tongue."

A plan began to take shape in Nora's mind. "One of my customers mentioned a party taking place tomorrow night at the lodge. An alfresco event with food, music, and fireworks." She looked to June for confirmation. "Is this right?"

"It is," June said. "Are you thinking of going?"

"We all are." Nora smiled. "The three of us are crashing this party. And by the end of the night, we'll have what we need to take care of the vermin infesting our town."

June hooted in enthusiastic agreement. "Pass me the rat killer, sister. I am ready to do some exterminating."

Chapter 16

Green was the silence, wet was the light, the month of June trembled like a butterfly.
                                                    —Pablo Neruda

"Jedediah Craig. It's a pleasure to officially meet you." Jed shook hands with Hester and June on a wide veranda overlooking the lodge grounds. "The night we first saw each other, I was on duty."

Nora gave a self-effacing shrug. "That wasn't my finest hour. But don't worry, I'm not wearing heels tonight."

"That's because your fairy godmother can't lend you any," Hester muttered softly, referring to Estella.

Nora gave Hester a pointed look. This was not the time to raise serious subjects. There would be opportunities for that later. For now, Nora wanted Jed to relax and enjoy himself. Hopefully, he'd have a few drinks—enough to leave him open to suggestion—and then Nora could convince him to take a risk in the name of justice.

"No fairy godmother? It sure looks like someone waved a magic wand." Though Jed spoke to Hester, his eyes were on Nora. He was drinking her in. He stared at her face for a long moment before his gaze slowly moved down the length of her body and back up again. "If you brought yours from Ollivander's, what do you think it would be made of?" he asked Nora.

Nora's skin was prickly with heat from watching Jed caress her body with his appreciative glance. During those long, slow seconds, she fantasized about Jed leading her to a secluded garden nook. He'd stand behind her, sweeping her long hair to one side as he untied the strings at the base of her neck—the strings holding the top of her coral sundress in place. Nora would welcome the kiss of the moist night air on her skin, just as she'd welcome the feel of Jed's fingertips sliding down her naked shoulders, over the smooth ridge of her collarbone and the swell of her breasts.

"Ollivander's?" Hester cocked her head. "Isn't that from *Harry Potter*?"

Nora was still caught up in thoughts of how she would like Jed to put his hands and his lips—anywhere and everywhere on her body—but she managed to reply in a normal, if slightly hoarse voice.

"The wand chooses the wizard, Mr. Craig," she said. "I took one of those online quizzes, and the results were that my wand would be dogwood with a phoenix core."

"Phoenix. Born again through fire." Jed gently covered Nora's scarred hand with his own. "That sounds about right."

Jed could have reached for either hand, but he'd chosen her disfigured hand over the unblemished one. Nora didn't know what to make of this. She was so surprised by her feelings for Jed that she couldn't think clearly at all.

"Have fun, you two!" June suddenly said, looping her arm through Hester's. "We're off to do some damage at the buffet. My employee discount really helped with tonight's tickets, but I'm still going to eat every penny's worth of that steep price."

Nora feared Jed might offer to reimburse her for the tickets. Instead he said, "Let me take care of the drinks tonight. Maybe we can grab some cocktails and find a quiet corner where we can see the sky. I really like that about your house. Because you have a view of the train tracks, it feels like your place could be sitting on the edge of anywhere."

"There were tons of lightning bugs when I was out on the deck waiting for June to pick me up," Nora said as they headed for the outdoor bar. "They were hovering around the berry bushes, which made me think about running into you there. And of the other times we've bumped into each other. We've had some unusual encounters."

"It's better than meeting through some online dating site," Jed said. "Makes for a better story."

"Stories matter," Nora replied with a smile.

When they reached the bar, Nora saw that Bob wasn't on duty, and she wondered if he was working his usual shift at the Oasis. After looking over the alfresco bar menu, Nora and Jed decided on mojitos.

"Make mine a virgin, please," Nora whispered to the barkeep when Jed was distracted by the sight of two burly chefs in starched white coats carrying a wood board bearing a roasted pig.

They were greeted with applause by a throng of expectant diners who parted to allow the chefs to place the board in the center of the buffet. As soon as the men retreated, the guests began collecting plates and scooping food onto them before the lodge manager could finish his welcome speech.

Someone made a comment about the film *Babe*, which made Nora think of sheepdogs. That thought reminded her to ask after Jed's dog.

"How's Henry Higgins doing?"

Jed handed Nora her mojito and raised his own in a toast. "To summer nights and excellent company." He and Nora drank from their glasses. Jed took a second sip before replying to Nora's question. "Henry Higgins is about the same, but I like the idea of changing his diet, so we're starting with that. My mom can't do the massages—it's just too much for her to handle. I'll give the hands-on stuff a go once Double H is here."

They continued talking, sticking to safe subjects like work, books, food, and films. Though Jed hadn't been to a movie theater in ages, he confessed that he had a large collection of movies on DVD and tended to watch them over and over. As he was telling Nora the plot of a war movie she hadn't seen and was unlikely to watch, she spotted Vanessa MacCavity heading their way.

"Ready to grab some dinner?" Nora asked, interrupting Jed's description of the storming of the Normandy beach.

Jed glanced at the buffet. "Sure. It looks like there's a break in the action. And I promise not to talk about that scene while we're eating."

Nora knew he wouldn't have the chance anyway. The plan was for Hester and June to give them a few minutes alone before sitting down at their table. Since the tables were oversized picnic tables, this wouldn't seem out of place.

At this point, June, who had more medical experience than Nora and Hester put together, would ease into reminiscences of her encounters with paramedics during her tenure at the assisted-living facility. Once she had Jed engrossed in a dramatic rescue tale featuring an elderly gentleman and the frozen pond near the facility, Hester would pretend to receive a disturbing text. She'd begin to cry and would rush off in distress. After signaling Jed that she'd be right back, Nora would chase after her friend.

June would act concerned for a minute or two. Then, she'd order a round of drinks and raise the subject of potassium-chloride poisoning and her belief that it was unlikely Fenton Greer would have consumed a cocktail mixed with enough potassium to set off a cardiac arrest. June's task was to raise doubt about Greer's cause of death, and to inspire Jed to speak with the medical examiner.

Nora was so focused on what was supposed to happen after she and Jed sat down that she barely paid attention to the bounty of food on the buffet. She selected a spinach salad, corn on the cob, bacon-wrapped tenderloin, and a slice of watermelon without giving the items much thought. She'd had a few bites of salad and tasted her meat when her friends appeared.

"Mind if we join you?" June asked Nora.

After the briefest pause, during which she shot Jed an apologetic smile, Nora made room on her side of the bench.

Five minutes later, she was trailing Hester across the lawn toward the main building.

"It felt good to cry," Hester said once they were alone in the stairwell. "I'm so nervous that it was nice to have a release, even if I was pretending. You should try it."

Nora increased her pace. "I'm not the crying type."

She was nervous, though. The Secret, Book, and Scone Society was pinning their hopes on gathering enough incriminating evidence from Vanessa's room to turn the tables on the collective who'd murdered two people, framed Estella, and tried to silence Nora.

At the fourth-floor stairwell, Hester held open the door and waited for Nora to walk with her, side by side, down the carpeted hallway. They passed no one on the way to Vanessa's suite. As Nora watched Hester pull out a plastic key card from her handbag, she whispered, "Are you sure you want to do this?"

Hester nodded firmly, waved the key card in front of the magnetic reader, and shoved open the door. Together, the two friends darted into the suite and let the door shut behind them.

Thanks to Bob, they knew the layout of the suite by heart. For Estella's sake, Bob had procured the key card and a floor plan. He'd given these items to June during her lunch break.

All Nora had to do now was affix the recording device she'd bought from a flea-market vendor to a wall of Vanessa's suite. This was Nora's first purchase from the man's actual shop, which was two train stops away from Miracle Springs. The

Bunker specialized in "guns, ammo, and war-related items." Nora knew the motto well because the owner, Denny, had it emblazed on the banners festooned all over his flea-market booth. It was also stitched into the back of his leather vest, along with various skulls, flags, and crossed-rifle patches.

Denny's booth had never interested Nora. She had no need for camo outfits, weapons, or war-related items in her line of work.

Until now.

And when she'd visited the Bunker, she knew that she'd come to the right place. Denny listened closely as she explained that she was on the hunt for an unobtrusive recording device that wouldn't break the bank.

"I've got just the thing," he'd said and led her over to the covert-ops section of the store. "Lots of choices, here. Smoke detectors with built-in cameras and recording devices. Alarm clocks. MP-three players. That's my favorite." He'd pointed to what looked like an electrical outlet. "All you've got to do is stick it on the wall. Nobody will notice an extra outlet behind a table or a chair."

Especially a guest in a hotel room, Nora thought. The housekeeping staff would most certainly notice, however, so she'd have to place the outlet out of sight.

Denny had showed her how the outlet face slid off to reveal the camera and recorder. He'd then briefly described how to operate the device, accepted her cash payment, and wished her a nice day.

Thinking that the world had become a very strange place, Nora had thanked him and headed for the train station.

Now she surveyed the suite's spacious living room and tried to decide where to affix the outlet. The obvious choice was near the table where Vanessa kept her laptop, appointment book, and cell-phone charger. As Hester hurried into the adjacent bedroom to have a look around, Nora grabbed a wing chair covered in a silk-floral brocade fabric by its arms and shimmied it forward. Judging from the imprints its feet left in the carpet, the chair was seldom moved, so Nora dropped to her knees and pressed the spy gadget against the wall directly behind the chair. After pushing the chair back into place, she decided to risk another minute taking photos of Vanessa's appointment book.

Hester returned to the living room and nodded. Nora responded with a thumbs-up before peering out a crack in the suite's door.

The hallway was clear.

The women exited the suite and made for the stairwell.

"Anything in the bedroom?" Nora asked in a hushed voice.

"Vanessa MacCavity likes to shop," Hester said. "And she has expensive taste. Some of her clothes still have the price tags attached. I'd have to save for a month to pay for a single item in her wardrobe." On the landing between the third and second floor, Hester stopped. "I know she's a guest at a four-star hotel and it's summertime, but Vanessa has a ridiculous amount of resort wear."

Nora gave a little shrug. "Bob said that she spent most of her time at the spa or on her phone by the pool. I guess she doesn't need to wear skirt suits to do her job."

"She has to be doing *something* besides placing newspaper ads to merit a salary that allows for three swimsuits at two hundred dollars apiece."

Nora whistled. "Hopefully, we'll learn soon enough." She glanced at her watch. "Not bad. All told, we've been gone fifteen minutes. Jed should be squirming, but not suspicious."

When they returned to the table, however, Jed was gone.

"He told me to tell you that he was sorry," June said. "His pager went off. He had to go."

Since the other diners had gathered around a huge fire pit to roast gourmet s'mores, June had the oversized picnic table to herself. Nora and Hester began picking at their uneaten meals.

"Did you know that he was on call?" Hester asked. She buttered a piece of dill roll and popped it in her mouth.

With a nod, Nora turned to June. "Did you have any luck?"

"We had a polite argument and Jedediah raised a good point." June lowered her voice. "If Greer had a preexisting heart condition, consuming that much potassium chloride on an empty stomach might have killed him. Naturally, I asked your man to check on that for us."

"He's not my man," Nora said.

June shrugged. "I think he'd like to be. He—" She stopped and leaned closer to her plate. "Don't look now, but Vanessa has her phone to her ear and she's making a face like she just tasted sour milk. Oh, there she goes. No dessert or dancing on the lawn for her. She's leaving the party. Were there any dead bodies in her closets?"

"Just expensive clothes," Hester said.

Nora pulled out her phone. "And her day planner. I took photos of at least twelve weeks of entries. I thought it might help to get a glimpse of her past, present, and future."

"Send them to us. We can divide the weeks and study a chunk right now," Hester suggested. "Maybe we won't need to go back into her room for the device."

June gave Hester a pointed look. "You know we can't leave it there."

"I know," Hester mumbled before focusing on her cellphone screen. "I'll take March and April."

"I'll go for May and June. Seems appropriate," June said with a smile. "You gaze into the future, Nora." She squinted at her phone. "Good Lord, I've seen doctors with better handwriting."

Nora studied the cryptic scrawl in Vanessa's planner while finishing her meal. She wasn't one to waste food, especially when it was pricey and delicious. Beside her, Hester also ate and read.

"Look at us. We're like teens having lunch at the mall—faces glued to our screens," June said after a few minutes. "I'm getting some dessert before the vultures devour it all. Any requests?" She pointed at the laminated s'mores menu on their table.

Hester gave it a quick glance. "I'd like the Grasshopper, please. I've never had a s'more made with a Peppermint Pattie."

Nora looked over the menu. "I'll have the dark chocolate and strawberry s'more. Thanks. Which one are you ordering?"

"Either the Banana Split or the Samoa. I have a soft spot for toasted coconut."

June had barely gotten up from the table when Nora was finally able to decipher two words of Vanessa's spiky handwriting. "Little Switzerland," she murmured.

"Sounds like a town," Hester said without looking up from her phone.

Nora called up Google Maps and sure enough, Hester was right. "It's not much bigger than Miracle Springs." An idea began to germinate in Nora's mind. "Can you pull up the Pine Ridge Properties website and see where their other new development is being built? I can't remember the name of the town, but it wasn't Little Switzerland."

"It's Bent Creek."

Nora ran a Google search on the other two towns. "All three towns are similar in population, are within an hour's drive of Asheville, and feature a community bank. Can you click on the Pine Ridge development at Bent Creek and tell me which bank they're working with?"

Hester stared at Nora. "I think I see where you're going with this."

By the time June returned with three plates of warm s'mores and twice as many packets of moist toilettes, Nora believed she had an inkling of how the Pine Ridge Properties scam operated.

*   *   *

After asking her friends to hand over their phones, she put them in a neat row and then tapped on the May, June, and July planner photos.

"Three housing developments in three small towns in western North Carolina," Nora began. "Two of the three, the Glades in Bent Creek and the Meadows in Miracle Springs, have a model home and several houses under construction. According to the site maps, fifteen lots have been sold in Bent Creek and fourteen in Miracle Springs. Is that right, Hester?"

Hester licked melted chocolate from her fingertips and nodded.

Nora was too engrossed in her theory to be distracted by the s'more. She glanced at June, who was eating her dessert with a look of rapture.

"Go on," June prompted. "I might be having a foodgasm, but I'm listening to every word."

"Okay, so Pine Ridge Properties has gotten backing from the local banks in Bent Creek and Miracle Springs. In turn, buyers are funneled to those banks for their home loans. From the outset, the banks and Pine Ridge collectively stand to make a tidy profit once all the lots are sold."

Hester frowned. "Where's the illegal activity?"

"I don't think Collin Stone plans to build any of these houses," Nora said. "Which would explain the rush to have all these developments out as quickly as possible."

June wiped off her hands and reached for Nora's phone. As she studied the month of July, her eyes went wide. She was just about to speak when bluegrass music tripped out of the speakers positioned around the perimeter of the lawn.

The party's MC, a rotund, jolly man wearing a straw hat, white pants, and a Hawaiian shirt, waved a glow stick in the air and announced that the dancing would begin shortly. He asked everyone to vacate the picnic tables so that the staff could move them off to the side. He then invited the guests to purchase glow-stick jewelry from the table near the bar and suggested that they all refresh their glasses while they had the chance.

"Let's find a private place in the garden." Hester pocketed her phone, grabbed her dessert plate, and reached over the table to touch June's shoulder. "They're coming to move our table."

Nora, who couldn't care less if another table had to be moved first, walked around to June's side and gazed down at her phone screen. "What is it?"

June pointed. "I used to live in New York, remember? We had several major airports, and this is the code for one of them. *EWR* stands for Newark. And I'm pretty sure the four-digit number following the airport code is a flight number."

Nora was in the middle of searching for the flight's destination when a young man in khakis and a Hawaiian shirt, with a name badge pinned to the breast pocket, gave the three friends a polite smile. "Excuse me, ladies. Would you mind if we scooted this table closer to the bushes? You can sit back down afterward."

Hester motioned for Nora and June to hurry up. "That's okay. We have another spot picked out."

June led them down a path and under an Asian arch flanked by a sign that read, WELCOME TO THE JAPANESE ZEN GARDEN—ZEN IS A JOURNEY. TAKE YOUR FIRST STEP.

The sign almost made Nora hesitate. It felt like a commitment to pass under the wooden arch, but to what? And yet as they approached a rectangular rock garden with a gravel river and raked sand, Nora was infused with calm. There was something incredibly soothing about the patterns in the sand.

"The flight goes to the Cayman Islands," she whispered, feeling a sense of reverence for this place. "Specifically, George Town."

"That would explain the extra outfits," Hester said. "Vanessa needs more than five days' worth of resort wear if she's heading to the Caymans for a vacation."

June shook her head. "Not a vacation. I think she's leaving the country."

"Me too," Nora said. "After making a last-minute transfer of Pine Ridge Properties funds to an offshore account."

In unison, the three women glanced up at the illuminated guest-room windows. They'd walked to a point where they had a clear view of Vanessa's suite. Every light blazed.

"If that's true, the sheriff will have to release Estella," Hester said. "Vanessa is the key witness and her word won't be worth shit once she takes off with . . ." She turned to Nora. "How much money are we talking about?"

"Several million," Nora said. "Enough to purchase a leisurely life in the islands."

June folded her arms over her chest. "But for how many people? Who else will be on that plane to George Town? Vanessa doesn't strike me as the sharing type."

"I can tell you who won't be there," Nora said. The old bitterness seeped out of her pores like stale sweat, but she couldn't stop it.

Hearing the cold anger in Nora's voice, Hester moved a little closer to her. "Who?"

Nora knew that Hester was offering her comfort, but it was all she could do not to shove her away. Instead, she snapped a dead twig off the closest tree and began drawing figures in the sand, deliberately ruining the perfectly spaced pattern of waves.

As her friends looked on in silence, Nora drew a stick-figure man. To his left, she drew a woman. On his right, she drew another woman and three children. She pointed to this group with her twig. "They're not going to George Town—Collin Stone's wife and three kids."

"Should we tell his wife what he's been doing?" Hester asked.

Nora stared at the people in the sand. "It's too late to save them," she whispered. "We can only hope they'll recover from what Collin's done to them." Squatting down, she slowly and tenderly erased the woman and children.

"Nora—" June began.

"We're going after Annette Goldsmith," Nora interrupted. She picked up the twig and drew a circle around the other woman. "Tomorrow. And by the time we're done with her, she'll be more than willing to help us set a trap for Collin Stone. No one is taking that flight to the Caymans." She drove the point of her twig through the center of the man's head. "Because we're not going to be victims. Never again. The hunters are about to become the hunted."

Chapter 17

You've got to jump off cliffs and build your wings on the way down.

— Ray Bradbury

"I see you brought a few friends along, but signing a contract on your dream house *is* a big deal," Annette Goldsmith said when Nora, June, and Hester entered the model home at the Meadows the following afternoon.

It was half past five, and though Nora disliked having to close Miracle Books early again, her desire to initiate the plan she and her friends had devised far exceeded her concerns over losing a few sales.

"They're my backup. In case things go off-track," Nora said, breezing past a confused Annette toward the kitchen. June and Hester waved politely at the real estate agent and trailed after Nora.

Nora heard Annette shut the front door. When she entered the kitchen, her saleswoman smile was back in place. "I'm glad that you—"

"Sit down, Annette." Nora cut her off while gesturing at the closest chair. "I'm not here to buy a house. I'm here to give you the chance to save your skin."

The smile morphed into a sneer. "What are you talking about?"

Regardless of how composed she appeared, Nora knew that Annette Goldsmith's life was about to be unalterably changed. Nora almost felt sorry for her. Almost.

"You and Collin Stone are having an affair," Nora said, and watched color flood Annette's cheeks. "Sit down, Annette. We have lots of things to discuss and limited time."

"You broke into my office, didn't you?" Annette asked.

Nora released an exasperated sigh. "I'm giving you one more chance to sit down. If you don't, we'll leave and share our story with a reporter friend of mine. And that story includes far more than your secret photos of Collin or your sex tape. *Far* more."

Annette sat down. "What are you talking about?"

"Cut the clueless act," Nora snapped. "It doesn't suit you and it's insulting to us. We might actually help you avoid the harsh prison sentence the rest of your partners are bound to face. But that depends on you. Were you aware of the penalties for committing mortgage fraud before you got involved in this mess?"

Nora slid a piece of paper across the table. Annette instinctively reached for it. "Examples of recent cases," Nora explained. "Look at the sentences these criminals received. Six years' imprisonment. Fines of over a million dollars. Do you have that kind of money, Annette? Or does Collin have an Annette in every model home? You're already sharing the man with his wife. How many other women does he have? Do you even know?"

This elicited an immediate reaction from Annette. "He loves me," she said, pressing her shoulders against her chairback and raising her chin like a defiant child. "I don't care if you expose us. I want his wife to find out."

"Did your builder boyfriend share his plans for the rest of the summer?" June spoke for the first time and Nora let her. She knew she had to do a better job concealing her anger. "Is he doing something special in July, for instance?"

Hester jumped in next. "Did he ask if you had a current passport?"

"Because he's leaving the country," Nora said. "With *all* the money. He's not traveling alone, either. Vanessa booked their tickets. One for her and one for Collin."

Annette fought to maintain control over her face, but she failed. Her brows furrowed, her lips drew back, and her eyes glittered with fury.

"That's right." Nora dropped the triumphant tone she'd previously adopted. Her voice became gentle and sympathetic. "They're bound for the Cayman Islands. Next month. We have the flight number. And if they're going together, where does that leave you?"

Annette didn't respond, but her rage was almost palpable. It rolled off her body and tainted the air. and Nora struggled to avoid being swept up by the familiar feeling—to not be pulled back into the past by Annette's pain. Nora knew that the emotion behind Annette's anger was pain. Sorrow would come later. For now, she'd want vengeance. Nora was banking on that.

"Don't let them win," Nora said in a near-whisper. "They think they're better than you—that they'll collect one more major chunk of change before jetting off to paradise. And my guess is that this chunk is coming from the investors at the bank in Bent Creek." Nora waited. "Just how involved are you, Annette? Did you commit murder because Collin asked you to get rid of his problem partner?"

"*No!*" Annette shouted. "I had nothing to do with Neil's death. Or Fenton's. I barely knew those guys."

Though she sounded sincere, Nora couldn't take Annette at her word. "Why should I believe you? You're a criminal. You've been misleading the people of this town all along—people whose only fault was a desire to own a new house."

"Which they couldn't afford," Annette retorted. "The buyers Dawson selected were like *you*. You'd sell your soul for three bedrooms, a jetted tub, and stainless-steel appliances."

June and Hester exchanged brief, victorious glances. Though every member of the Secret, Book, and Scone Society suspected Dawson of playing a major role in the fraud ring—especially since his initials had been written on Greer's napkin and he was the loan officer at Madison County Community Bank—it was a relief to hear Annette confirm their theory.

"*You* sold our souls without our knowledge or permission," Nora said, pointing at Annette. "You're a Realtor. You know full well that straw buyers can be penalized, even if they don't receive a cent for the use of their names or credit ratings. Besides, no one would ever move into your houses because Collin wasn't going to build them. Surely, you were aware of this fact."

Annette's shoulders drooped a little. Nora had been waiting for such a sign, because it spoke of resignation and defeat. The real-estate agent was tempted to confess everything, but she wasn't quite there yet.

Nora spread her hands. "The whole venture must have seemed harmless enough, right? You'd earn some easy money. As would Dawson. But the Pine Ridge partners received a way bigger cut than you."

"It's their brainchild," Annette said with a shrug. "I just work for them."

"Not for long," Nora reminded her. "Collin and Vanessa obviously put enough by to fund a whole new life in the tropics. That leaves you out in the cold. Literally. What will you do when all the buyers come to you, asking why their houses aren't being built?" Recalling Arthur Miller's play, *The Crucible*, Nora pressed on with more vehemence. "When they form an angry mob, who'll be left to take the blame? You. You'll be burned, Annette. Like a witch at the stake."

June and Hester directed surprised glances at Nora—probably because she'd used fire imagery to threaten Annette—but there was approval in their glances as well. June and Hester believed in Nora, which made her feel stronger than Samson.

"Why did Neil have to go?" she asked Annette.

"He and Vanessa were in charge of securing investors for each development," Annette said. Her gaze was fixed on the napkin holder in the center of the table. "You need major capital to start a new community on the scale Collin and Pine Ridge planned. The idea was to build in three or four towns in western North Carolina. By focusing on towns in the same region, Pine Ridge could establish credibility. Quickly. Things were going fine until Neil got the necessary capital from Madison County Community Bank. According to Collin, Neil started acting weird after that. It was like he drank the Miracle Springs Kool-Aid, and it changed him."

Nora smiled. "This place has that effect on people. That's why Neil spent a few days here before the rest of his partners arrived by train. He wanted to make things right and he was trying to figure out how to do it. Did he speak to you about his intentions?"

"No," Annette said. "But I did hear him talk a potential buyer out of a sale."

"And you told Collin about the incident, didn't you?" Nora shook her head in disapproval. "You helped to seal Neil's fate."

Annette looked up. "He sealed his own fate! He should have kept his mouth shut and finished what he'd started."

"Fenton Greer played *his* part to the letter, and he's just as dead as Neil. I don't think your boyfriend was ever going to split the money . . ." Nora trailed off and held up her fingers. "How many ways? Seven? Vanessa, Fenton, Neil, Collin, Dawson, the sheriff, and you. Am I forgetting anyone?"

Ignoring Nora's question, Annette asked her own. "What do you want? Money?"

"Tell us how it works," Nora said. "Walk us through the scam."

Annette rolled her eyes, as if they were wasting her precious time. "Why? You've obviously figured it all out. Vanessa and Neil acquired a large sum from investors at the local bank. Using some of that money, Collin purchased tracts of land in three towns, got the necessary permits, and cleared enough lots to build a model home and start a few houses. We have an inside person at each bank—a loan officer. The other real estate agents are just country bumpkins happy to be making commissions. Some of our buyers are legit, but many are like you. They can't afford these houses, but the loan officers push their loans through so we can collect as many down payments as possible. The loan officers and me get paid under the table from that kitty. Collin and his Pine Ridge partners skim money from the funds acquired from the investors. I don't have access to those, so I don't know how much was raised or how much each partner received."

Hester released an exasperated groan. "How were you going to dodge the shit storm that was bound to hit once people realized their houses weren't going to be built?"

"Easy," Annette said. "I'd quit. After all, I'm just the real-estate agent. I'm not the builder. Besides, Collin and I were—"

"Going to drive off into the sunset together?" Nora guessed. "He never mentioned a Cayman Island sunset, did he?"

Annette's eyes blazed with renewed anger. "No."

"Don't let him play you, honey." June pushed her cell phone across the table. On the screen was the U. S. Attorney's Office, Western District of North Carolina website. "There's a number listed under the *about* link. If you tell them everything, you might just get a slap on the wrist. Otherwise, Hester can show you the alternative."

Hester pulled a sheet of paper out of her pocket and unfolded it. "The first case is the most recent. The real-estate agent was sentenced to forty-six months in prison." She slid the paper over to Annette. "There are more examples, but you get the idea. Forty-six months in prison."

Annette scanned the printout before flicking it back toward Hester. Nora felt her patience evaporating.

"Our friend was arrested for a crime she didn't commit. You, on the other hand, are actually guilty. So take out your phone and make the call. This is your one chance. And I kind of hope you don't do it because I'd love to see you in an orange jump-suit. Maybe, if you behave yourself, you'll be allowed out for litter collection. If so, I'll make sure to throw a greasy cheese-burger wrapper and a handful of leftover fries your way. I can ride by, nice and slow, on my bicycle. It still works, despite your trying to run me off the road."

"It was my car, but I wasn't there!" Annette cried. "Collin asked to borrow my keys, which I thought was weird because he had his truck, but I didn't want to ask him in front of Vanessa and the sheriff, so I just gave them to him. I'm telling you—I'm *not* a killer!"

Nora recalled how she'd rode up to the model home that day to find Annette, Collin, Vanessa, and Sheriff Hendricks to-gether. They looked like they'd just finished a meeting.

"Who rode in your car with Collin? The sheriff?" Nora asked.

Annette grimaced. "That pig left after you and I came inside to take care of your paperwork. Collin and Vanessa had things to discuss, so they talked in the garage. They were still there when you pedaled off."

"Your boyfriend's a murderer," Hester said. "And the woman he's going to run away with is his *real* partner in crime. *They're* the Bonnie and Clyde of this story. You've been used."

With a trembling hand, Annette picked up June's phone and cradled it in her palm. Her eyes were moist with unshed tears. "Collin didn't kill Neil. He sent me a text, with a photo, from the train minutes before Neil died. And the night of Fenton's death, Collin was with me. It was the first time we'd ever spent a whole night together."

"Smart," Nora mused aloud. "You serve as Collin's alibi and Vanessa serves as the witness. Not that due process of the law matters, because the sheriff is already in the Pine Ridge pocket."

"So Sheriff Toad or Big Brother Dawson is our murderer," June said.

Nora kept her eyes locked on Annette, silently willing her to make the right choice.

"I know you're hurting," Nora whispered. "And there's more hurt waiting ahead. Listen to me, Annette. The only way out is through. We all have to pay for our mistakes, but you don't have to go through this alone. We'll go through it with you. All four of us—Estella included—know what it's like to face a trial by fire. Some of us more literally than others."

The kindness of Nora's offering cracked the last of Annette's defenses and she began to cry. June moved to her side and soothed her with soft words and a gentle touch. "You're stronger than you know, honey. You're stronger than Collin Stone believes you to be. Show him what you're made of."

Wiping her eyes, Annette nodded. "That asshole. He'll be sorry he used me."

Focusing on June's phone again, she frowned.

"My password screen came on. Hold on a sec." June punched in some numbers and returned the phone to Annette. "There you go, hon. Let's get this party started."

"So the party's in the kitchen?" a man called out from the front of the house.

Nora's blood turned to ice. She hadn't heard a car engine or the sound of anyone approaching the model house. But the heavy tread of boots moving over hardwood floors was unmistakable.

And there was more than one set.

Collin Stone appeared in the kitchen. Sheriff Hendricks followed closely behind.

"Put that down, sweetheart," Collin said, moving to Annette's side. When she hesitated, he stroked her cheek with his index finger.

His touch was clearly tender, but Annette flinched like she'd been slapped. Nora wondered if, all this time, Annette had been waiting for Collin to touch her this way, and now that he had, it was too late.

She made to slide the phone across the table to June, but Collin snatched it out of her hand and examined the screen.

"Oh, Annie." His voice was soft and sad. "I thought you cared about me."

"I *did* care!" Annette snarled at him. "You lied to me. About *everything*!"

Behind Collin, the sheriff chuckled and tapped his temple. "The light bulbs are coming on, eh, blondie?"

Collin cast a backward glance at the tubby lawman. "There's no need to insult Annette, Sheriff. We wouldn't have made it this far without her. These other ladies are a different matter. They seem determined to cause trouble in your peaceful burg."

The sheriff hooked his thumbs through his utility belt and swayed on the balls of his feet. "I know how to handle women who don't know their place."

"Shut up," Nora said, too exasperated to remain silent. "It's over for both of you. Do you actually think we'd come up here without making our own phone calls first?" She stared down the two men. "You've been so busy manipulating, deceiving, and underestimating women that you couldn't possibly conceive that a group of women could ruin your plans."

The sheriff removed a plastic wrist tie from his pocket. "The only thing you'll be doing is remaining silent. I'm taking the three of you in."

"On what trumped-up charge?" June demanded coolly.

"I've got quite a list." The sheriff's mouth curved into a self-satisfied grin. "You three, plus Ms. Estella Sadler, murdered Mr. Parrish and Mr. Greer. After Ms. Sadler was hauled off to jail, the rest of you committed B-and-E by letting yourselves into Annette's office as well as Ms. MacCavity's hotel room. I've got you on multiple thefts too. Hotel key cards, confidential documents, etcetera." He placed another wrist tie on the table. "You sure you made those phone calls, Ms. Pennington?"

Nora's thoughts were racing. She'd missed something.

Not something. Someone. *Another local fed this collection of scumbags information on the Secret, Book, and Scone Society's every move. A person who'd gained Neil Parrish's trust while ratting on him to his partners. A man others viewed as sincere, friendly, and wholesome. A hard and humble worker. An everyman's man.*

"Jesus." Nora closed her eyes and pressed her fingertips against the lids as if she could block out the terrible truth.

The sheriff began to laugh. "Now the brunette is having a light-bulb moment! You gals are always a step behind, aren't you?" He cast a nervous glance at Collin, who was staring at him in disapproval. The sheriff's mirth dissipated.

It was all Nora could do not to punch the sheriff in the face, but her anger made it difficult to concentrate and her friends were now frightened. Nora couldn't allow that. She couldn't let them down after they'd come this far.

"We left a name off our list," she said to June and Hester before turning back to the sheriff. "I suppose Bob did the dirty work. I really can't picture you squeezing through that hole in the fence above the train tracks. Bob's much leaner than you."

Next to Nora, June sucked in a shocked breath.

Sheriff Hendricks refused to be goaded. "Everyone loves a bartender with a kind face and a generous pour. Neil was deep into his cups the first two nights of his stay."

"That's enough—" Collin tried to cut in, but Nora talked over him.

"He told Bob lots of secrets and Bob decided to profit off of them. But he couldn't kill a Pine Ridge partner without your blessing, Sheriff. Especially with your brother's involvement in the fraud ring."

The sheriff moved his face so close to Nora's that she could see every pore. Sweat glistened on his forehead and dampened his sideburns. "Most men can't get ahead acting like Boy Scouts. We have to make real hard choices. We try to do right by our families. We pay the bills. We save for houses, schools, cars, clothes, vacations. There's never enough. We can never work enough hours or bring enough money home to make anyone happy."

Behind the sheriff, Collin was nodding in agreement.

"Is that why you hate women?" Nora asked. "Because a woman made you feel like your efforts weren't enough?"

"Not just one woman. My mama, my wife, my daughters— they're all the same." Raspberries of heat mottled the sheriff's neck and cheeks. "Nag, nag, nag about everything I'm *not* doing. Never a word about anything I've *done*. All that I've given them. No thank-yous. Nothing. My only escape is going online. But in the end, I have to go back to three generations of sour faces and complaining."

Nora was stunned by this revelation. Because the sheriff felt unloved and unappreciated by his family, he treated all women like second-class citizens. She hadn't expected him to bare this secret side of himself. "But you found a way to make that extra money. Through Pine Ridge. Did it make a difference at home?"

"I'm not going to share a cent of it," the sheriff said with a triumphant gleam in his eyes. "I'm going to buy myself a sweet fishing boat and spend my free time on the lake. No women allowed. I'm done letting them run my life." He backed away from Nora and shook his head, as if he'd divulged more than he'd intended. Pointing at Annette, he narrowed his eyes.

"Speaking of time, the ball is over for you, Cinderella. Go home. And you know what'll happen if you talk. So don't talk."

Annette paled and looked at Collin. "Why did you do this to me?"

"I'm sorry," Collin said. "I didn't think you'd take it so hard. In my defense, I never made you any promises. I only offered you a chance to make some extra money and to have a little fun too."

"But why did you have to use me? If you never wanted me in the first place . . ."

Collin spread his hands. "I had to keep you under my thumb. I'm sorry. Really. But you'll be okay. You're young and pretty. Plenty of men will line up to share stir-fried bok choy with you." When Collin spoke next, his voice was hard. "Don't get dramatic."

Nora willed Annette to go without protest. Once she was back in Asheville, Annette's fury over being used and betrayed would override whatever fear she felt now, and Nora believed that the real-estate agent would willingly turn herself in if it meant getting revenge against Collin Stone.

Sheriff Hendricks pointed at the wrist ties on the table. "Well, Cinderella? Should I get out another one?"

Annette threw Collin a look of pure loathing before she hurried out of the kitchen. Moments later, Nora heard the sound of the garage door going up. Then down.

"Maybe we shouldn't have let her go," Collin said.

"She can't say anything without incriminating herself," the sheriff replied. "How would she explain where she got the cash for that Beamer?" He turned to Nora again. "It was Ms. MacCavity's idea to push you off the mountain, by the way. She said you were the head of the snake. Guess she was right."

June laughed. "Honey, your metaphor's all wrong. All of our heads are covered in snakes. We're all gorgons. Like Medusa."

She wriggled her fingers in the air. "And we're going to turn you to stone."

The sheriff glared at June. "Are you threatening me?"

Hester barked out a laugh and Nora knew there was no humor behind it. Her friends were angry. "Sheriff Toad has no clue who Medusa is. He's a man who used his badge to betray the people who voted for him. I wonder if he realized that his amphibian appearance earns him ridicule throughout the county."

The sheriff's doughy face was now the color of ripe cherries. He whipped his gun from his holster and pointed it at Hester.

"I will not stand for disrespect. Not from you. Not from anybody." The sheriff's eyes were manic, and Nora realized that he was out of his depth. The small-town lawman was fine with bending the rules in exchange for a quick buck, but he clearly preferred to leave the plotting and the dirty work to others. The amount of perspiration beading his brow and soaking into his uniform blouse collar spoke volumes. Sheriff Hendricks was uncomfortable with this situation. And he wasn't really in charge. Collin was.

Nora waved her arms, forcing the sheriff to look at her. Baiting him was the wrong way to go. She needed to try to reason with him.

"What will you do now?" she asked. "Shoot three unarmed women in cold blood? How will you explain that? There can only be so many murders in a town this size before the media gets wind of what's happening and descends. And where will Collin and Vanessa be when they arrive?"

Collin put a hand on the sheriff's arm. "Can we wrap this up, Todd? I'd like to call it a day."

Sheriff Hendricks snorted. "That makes two of us. Okay, gals, stand up and put your hands behind your backs. Move nice and slow now. I don't want to get rough."

"You can't frame us for Neil's murder or paint us as accessories for Fenton's," Nora protested. "It won't work. We have no motive for killing those men."

"She has a point, Sheriff," Collin said mildly. "Maybe we need to tie up our loose ends here and now."

Nora, who couldn't keep her eyes off the black maw at the end of the gun, felt her panic rising. She could talk circles around Hendricks, but Collin Stone was another matter. He was a sly charmer who would do anything to achieve his goal. The combination of those traits made him extremely dangerous.

Sheriff Hendricks looked unsettled. "I'm not shooting three women in this kitchen."

"I'd never suggest such a thing." Collin gave the sheriff's shoulder a brotherly squeeze. "Let me help you secure the ladies and I'll tell you what I have in mind."

Collin plucked a wrist tie off the table and walked behind Hester's chair. "Ms. Winthrop, if you would?"

After shooting a frightened glance at Nora, Hester put her arms behind her back. Collin wrapped the tie around her wrists and pulled. There was a high-pitched *zip* as the plastic tightened. Hester winced, but she made no sound.

"Your turn, towel lady," the sheriff cackled.

"How does it feel, Sheriff?" June's mouth asked wryly as she offered the sheriff her hands. "Having to do whatever the boss man says? Because we all know who's in charge here, and it ain't you."

Collin wagged a finger in front of June's face. "If you keep disrespecting the sheriff, I'll have to gag you."

June fell silent.

Collin stepped up to Nora. With disconcerting gentleness, he moved her arms until her hands met behind her chair. After he'd finished binding her wrists, he leaned in close and whispered, "I enjoyed our time together in the bookstore. You're like Vanessa, you know. Smart, intuitive, and easy to talk to. Unfortunately, you still have to die. And I want you to know that the method I've chosen isn't personal. It's just the best one for several reasons."

While Nora took this in, Collin gestured for Sheriff Hendricks to join him on the other side of the room. Nora watched as the sheriff's expression registered overt surprise.

After a long hesitation, he nodded and cast a sympathetic glance at Nora. When she saw the dread in the lawman's eyes, she knew what Collin had planned for them.

"It *is* personal, you bastard." Infusing her voice with all the venom she could muster, Nora locked eyes with Collin. "And it's cruel. But you're a cruel and selfish man. Look at the future you're inflicting on your wife and children."

Collin dropped his gaze and Nora believed she might have actually gotten to him, but when he faced her again, she could see the determination in the set of his jaw. "My wife won't miss me. Neither will my kids. They've built a life that doesn't include me. Like the sheriff here, I've been a good provider, but somewhere along the way, I became an outsider in my own home. When I met Vanessa, we connected on every level. We could talk about books the way you and I did in your shop, Nora. But we could also talk about real estate, food, wine, the places we wanted to travel to, and so much more. She's my other half. I just didn't know it until we met." He smiled. "I'm going to live life for myself now, and no one's going to get in my way."

Collin left the room.

"What's he going to do?" Hester asked. She sounded like a scared little girl.

Nora didn't reply. She watched Sheriff Hendricks move to the cooktop. He turned on the burners. Once all five were ringed with a high flame, he spoke.

"Remember those bored teenagers? The ones who broke into this place just to see if they could?" The sheriff wasn't looking at the three women, but at the dancing flames. "They came back.

Only this time, they upped the ante from breaking and entering to arson. Dumbass kids. They didn't know people were inside. No one was *supposed* to be in the house this late." He sighed. "The aftermath will create lots of wagging tongues. Folks will make up all sorts of tales about what you gals were doing here. Drinking? Taking drugs? Selling drugs? It doesn't matter. Eventually, the good people of Miracle Springs will forget you. They'll find something else to talk about and we'll all move on."

Collin reentered the kitchen carrying a red gas can. He unscrewed the cap and stared at Nora with doleful eyes. "I wish you hadn't gone and played the hero. Things don't end nice and neat like they do in books. In real life, heroes die. In real life, guys like me get away. And the scarred, sensitive, once-beautiful, bibliotherapist"—he paused as if his emotions had momentarily gotten the better of him—"she has to burn."

Chapter 18

The wound is the place where the light enters you.
—Pablo Neruda

"I'm going to my office," the sheriff told Collin. "I have to be seen by people before this fire gets called in."

Collin dipped his head in acknowledgment. "Go ahead. Bob should be here any minute. After I leave, I'll head to a public place too. That Pink Lady Grill, maybe."

"Best burger in town," the sheriff said. His expression turned dreamy, but he blinked as if he suddenly remembered that he still had a role to play. Jerking his thumb at the three women, he asked, "Is Bob handling them? Like he handled our other problems?"

"That's the plan," Collin said.

Sheriff Todd Hendricks paused in the doorway, and Nora wondered if his conscience made him hesitate. But he didn't look at any of the women. He simply waited for several long seconds before he finally left.

Following his departure, June issued a derisive grunt. "I knew Greer didn't die from a potassium overdose. Bob must have slipped something more potent in his drink."

"You didn't quite have it all figured out, did you?" As Collin settled into the chair opposite Nora, his boot made contact with the red canister on the floor and the pungent odor of gasoline immediately tainted the air.

Nora met Collin's eyes with a cold stare. She refused to let him see her fear. And she was afraid. She felt like she was on the verge of being turned inside out.

"The lab results will reveal another medicine or a type of poison," June said, reclaiming Collin's attention. "Unless you're paying off the medical examiner too."

"There was no need," Collin said. "The sheriff told the doc to look for potassium in Greer's body, and the doc found it. By the time lab results come back that could raise questions about the cause of death, I'll be long gone." He raised his hands. "And before you ask me to explain what happened to Greer, don't. This isn't a novel where the bad guy confesses everything. You don't need to know every detail."

The doorbell rang and Hester let out a tiny shriek. Collin smiled at her. "Speaking of books, it sounds like the wolf-in-sheep's-clothing character has arrived. Tonight, however, he won't bother with his disguise. You'll get to see his wolf side."

"I don't know about that," Bob said as he stepped into the kitchen. "These ladies aren't like that slut, Estella. She'd dirty herself with any Tom, Dick, or Harry as long as he was rich enough. I wanted to punish her, but these ladies haven't done anything to me. I'm not onboard with this."

Collin leapt up and got into Bob's face, his mouth twisting in anger. "Is that so? You'd best get *onboard* or I'll make an anonymous phone call describing how you prepared cocktails mixed with potassium chloride stolen from Greer's hotel room. After Greer drank your special drinks, you saw that he was close to passing out, so you helped him to a hotel golf cart and drove him to a maintenance shed. There, you put a dust mask over his face—a mask connected by plastic tubing to a canister of carbon monoxide—and waited for him to die. Finally, you dumped his body in the bathhouse."

"You know I did everything because of *her!*" Bob shouted. "I pushed Neil for the money. To impress *her*! And that *still* wasn't enough—after all the years I've listened to her, given her free drinks, and watched her make a fool of herself with loser after loser. I was *done* being the nice guy!" He gestured at Nora, June, and Hester. "I was willing to spy on these three for money. Why wouldn't I? I sold my soul the day I killed your partner. But there's a difference between bumping off scumbags who wanted to dupe the people of this town and burning three women alive."

Collin nodded in sympathetic agreement. "I know. I wish it hadn't come to this, but there's no other choice. Get your—"

"Bob does have another option," Nora interjected. "He can stop taking orders from you right now. He's his own man."

Bob seemed pleased by this notion. Jabbing a finger near Collin's face, he said, "The lady's right. You want to come after me? Go ahead. If I go down, you go down. You see me as a dumb, small-town bartender—a sheep—but I have proof of our *transactions* hidden away. If anything happens to me, that proof will surface. Down the swift dark stream you go. Remember that, city boy."

Collin opened his mouth to reply, but Bob marched out of the room.

"Hey!" June cried. "*Bob!* Don't leave us alone with him!"

"Down the swift dark stream you go!" Bob shouted from the hallway.

Though the phrase made no sense, it was familiar to Nora. She repeated the words to herself and tried to place them.

Collin broke her concentration when he scooped up the open gas canister, causing gas to slosh over the sides and onto the floor, and took off after Bob. As he ran, he left a liquid gas trail in his wake.

"Bob! *Look out!*" Nora yelled, lurching to her feet. Her

chair slammed against the floor with a dull thud. Beside her, June and Hester sat frozen in fear.

Nora moved to the cabinets, hoping to find scissors or a sharp knife in one of the drawers. An animalistic scream echoed down the hall, and Nora knew that she was too late to save Bob. Suppressing a sob of terror, she pulled open a drawer containing plastic cutlery.

Bob screamed over and over. His voice turned from a high-pitched wail to a horrific keening. Underlying these terrible sounds was the distinct *whoosh* of flames. The trail of gas leading from the kitchen to the hallway had ignited and was now racing back toward its origin point like a fiery bullet train.

When the trail crossed the threshold into the kitchen, it divided, forming narrow rivulets of flames. The polished hardwood floor and white toe-kick boards blackened and an acrid smoke permeated the air. Nora saw that the gas had also splattered the cabinets and oven. It would be foolish to try to turn off the cooktop burners, so she retreated toward the table.

"We have to get out!" Nora shouted at her friends.

June and Hester had been so transfixed by the progression of the flames that they were still seated. But Nora's urgent cry broke the fire's spell and both women jumped up.

Nora hurried to the sliding-glass door leading to the back patio. She spun around, facing the kitchen, her blind fingers fumbling for the lock. As soon as she felt the lock release, she grabbed the handle and shuffled sideways, pulling the door partially open.

"Go!" Nora yelled.

June and Hester were so focused on escaping the tainted air and infringing heat, that they didn't see the shape hurtling toward them through the smoke.

But Nora did.

The moment she was outside, Nora screamed for June and Hester to split up and run. She had just enough time to believe that her friends would get away before Collin's hands clamped around her forearms like two vises.

"Not you," he snarled, squeezing hard. "You're not going anywhere."

Nora twisted her shoulders and cried out as Collin yanked her back toward the house. Toward the fire. No matter how she tried, she couldn't free herself from his iron grip.

Inside the kitchen, the smoke had thickened into a pewter fog and the flames were hip-high. Nora could hear the room succumbing to the fire's hunger. The crackling, sizzling, and popping noises were different from those she'd heard the night she'd been burned. This smoke couldn't rise into the crisp January air of a wide, winter sky. It hung low, like a heavy tomcat waiting to spring. It stung Nora's eyes and tried to claw its way down her throat.

Collin pushed her deeper into the room, and she was engulfed by heat.

Instinctively, Nora hunched her shoulders and bent her head. She fought the urge to cough and again tried to wrench herself loose from her captor's grasp.

Collin was raging at her—hurling curses about how she was ruining everything as he dug his fingers into her flesh—all the while maneuvering her so that she faced the stove. He then gave her a mighty shove, sending her careening into the stainless-steel refrigerator.

Nora pivoted to avoid striking the metal with her cheek, which meant her shoulder took the brunt of the contact. She bounced off the appliance like a rubber ball. The pain and smoke stole the oxygen from her lungs and the world began to tilt.

Suddenly, Nora was on the floor. The impact of falling chased off her dizziness enough for her to be aware of the fire encroaching near her back. She rolled away from it, moving toward what she prayed were the sliding doors.

She couldn't see much. Her eyes were watering and dozens of tiny black dots hovered at the edge of her vision. Shapes shifted and danced, so she kept her eyes tightly shut and rolled over again. And again.

Chancing the briefest peek, she nearly sobbed in relief at the sight of the sliding door. Naturally, Collin had closed it. Nora thought she saw him standing on the other side, watching her, but she couldn't tell. His hulking figure seemed to divide into two shadows, but Nora didn't know what she saw because she had to close her throbbing eyes against the smoke's persistent sting. She couldn't even think about Collin's next move. She could only focus on rolling to the door.

Nora turned her body, fighting against the blackness coaxing her to surrender. With no more oxygen reserves in her lungs, she was forced to draw in a shallow breath through her nose. The air was now completely polluted, and she began to cough.

The action pulled in more tainted air, and she felt like her throat was being seared. The pain startled her into opening her eyes. She caught a glimpse of summer sky through glass.

As if from a great distance, words drifted into her mind. She couldn't remember where she'd heard them before.

Float beyond the world of trees.
Out into the whispering breeze.

And then the darkness took her.

Nora woke in an unfamiliar, yet all-too-familiar place. Even with her eyes closed, she recognized the steady beeping of the machine by her head as well as the upward tilt of the bed. She moved her hands and there it was: the expectant tug of the IV's plastic cannula from where it was taped to her right wrist.

A voice near the foot of her bed said, "It's okay, Nora. It's not like the last time."

This was such an odd remark that, despite not wanting to see the new scars she'd acquired at the Meadows, Nora opened her eyes.

Jedediah Craig sat in a plastic chair beside her bed. He had something curled inside his fist, and when he saw Nora's gaze land there, he unfolded his fingers like a flower to reveal a set of mala beads.

Jed's voice had been hoarse, which had made him sound like a different man. Keenly aware of the significance of this, Nora forgot about her own condition.

"Did you pull me out?" she asked. Her voice was a dry riverbed.

Jed poured two cups of water. He gave one to Nora and they both drank. When she was done, he put the cups on the nightstand.

"I wish I'd been there sooner," he said. "I'm sorry."

Nora stared at him in surprise. "You saved me. The last thing I remember is smoke burning my throat and eyes. And the sky. I think Collin Stone was watching me. And there was something else. Something important."

Jed silently waited for her to remember, but Nora couldn't.

With a frown, she brought the hand free of the IV tubing to her throat. "I should be sore. How long have I been out?"

Instead of answering her question, Jed took Nora's hand and let the mala beads spill onto her palm.

"Concentrate on these while I talk. They're not from Miracle Books, but I thought they'd bring you comfort anyway."

When Nora took the beads between her fingers, Jed began to speak. "You were admitted to Mission Hospital in Asheville three days ago. Sending you to Mission was my call. I didn't think the medical center at Miracle Springs would be good enough if you woke up and exhibited symptoms of PTSD. Burn victims are trauma survivors, and there was no telling how facing a second fire would affect you." He smiled. "But you seem incredibly unshaken for someone who hasn't had a painkiller for over four hours."

Nora's gaze followed her IV line from her wrist upward to the metal pole. The only bag hanging from the metal pole was filled with fluids. There was no morphine drip. No intravenous narcotics. "What are my injuries?" she asked.

"The primary concern was smoke inhalation," Jed said. "You were treated with oxygen and steroids. There's a significant risk of infection after such an injury, so it's common to keep patients for up to three days for observation. The Mission staff has been very thorough. Your chest scans are clear and your white blood count is good, which means you should be able to skip out of here tonight or tomorrow morning."

"Skip?" Nora dumped the mala beads on the blanket and fished around for the bed controls. When she found them, she raised herself to an upright position and examined her arms. Her left arm was redder than usual. It looked like she'd spent a day at the beach and had forgotten sunscreen.

"That's as bad as it gets," Jed said.

Nora found his matter-of-fact tone reassuring. "Am I this lovely shade of lobster elsewhere?"

"Pretty much from fingers to hairline," Jed said. "You'll need a haircut when you get back to Miracle Springs too, though I like how the shorter pieces frame your face."

The compliment threw Nora off-guard. She reached up to touch a strand of chin-length hair. "Thanks," she whispered. She lowered her hand and her fingers automatically sought the burn scar on her forearm. Looking at the shell-smooth skin, Nora said, "You're right, this is nothing like the last time. So why don't I remember anything?"

Jed reached for their water cups again. "You had to be sedated."

Nora accepted hers with a small "Oh."

"It's nothing to be ashamed of. You were reliving your first fire, which isn't uncommon for survivors," he said. "You kept going in and out of consciousness, and the staff couldn't treat your injuries while you kept taking out your breathing tube or IV line, so they sedated you."

Nora suddenly noticed the dark circles under Jed's eyes and his uncombed hair. "You volunteered to watch over me. Is that why I'm not restrained?" When he didn't respond, Nora grabbed his hand. "What about your job?"

Jed grinned. "No one's going to give a pink slip to the guy who runs into the burning building to save the girl. I'm safe, unless the crew from station nine convince my boss that it's wrong for a paramedic to steal the firemen's limelight."

Nora laughed. It felt good to hold Jed's hand. She had so many questions that they were tripping over each other in her head, but the man caressing the skin of her palm with the pad of his thumb was worthy of patience. Not only had he risked his life for her, but he'd also sat vigil at her bedside for countless hours.

"I'll never be able to tell you how grateful I am that you found me inside the model house, but I can't figure out how you came to be there," Nora said.

Jed looked aggrieved. "I moved to Miracle Springs because I wanted a fresh, new, quiet life. I didn't expect to meet someone like you, but after I did, I wanted to know you better. Then you hit me up with the whole murder-theory thing and it totally threw me. I told you that I can't afford to lose this job. I need it because I'm responsible for my mom's care. I've already screwed up once and she paid the price for my mistake. If I spent the rest of my life trying to make it up to her, it wouldn't be long enough."

He paused. There was only the sound of the machines, and the sense of Jed's shame and regret, filling the room. Nora wanted to comfort him, but she knew it was best to stay silent.

"Despite my desire to toe the line, I couldn't stop thinking about my responsibility to my profession. Having seen Mr. Greer's body, I knew I couldn't forget about what you'd told me, so I asked the ME, Dr. Lou, out for a beer. We talked about sports and a bunch of other cases before I raised the subject of Mr. Greer's postmortem lividity."

Nora almost forgot that she was in a hospital room. "And?"

"The discrepancy between how the blood pooled in Mr. Greer's body and how Mr. Greer had been found didn't escape the doc's notice. He wasn't going to rule Mr. Greer's death an overdose by potassium chloride just because the sheriff pressured him to do just that. Dr. Lou is built like a linebacker. He's also gay." Jed grinned. "Over our third round, he shared some unforgettable stories about being one of the first men in his med-school class to come out. Believe me, this man is *not* easily intimidated, and he's a stickler for detail. He told me that Mr. Greer didn't have a preexisting heart condition, so the good doc already had a gut feeling that something was off about the cause of death. Don't worry, Nora, he'll wait for the lab results before making a ruling."

Nora was about to voice her relief when a nurse entered the room. She had the clipped, efficient gait Nora had observed dozens of times with dozens of nurses.

"How are you feeling?" the nurse asked while withdrawing a thermometer from her pocket. Approaching Nora on the left, she glanced at Jed. "If you don't mind."

Taking the hint, he scooted out of the way.

The nurse dropped a blood-pressure cuff on the bed and offered Nora the thermometer.

"I feel calm and clearheaded and I'm not in any pain," Nora said. She then opened her mouth wide and lifted her tongue.

After placing the thermometer in Nora's mouth, the nurse wrapped the blood-pressure cuff around Nora's upper arm. "Good" was her simple reply as she began inflating the cuff.

While the nurse completed her tasks, Nora thought about

another nurse with glacier-blue eyes and the tender touch of a grandmother. Not for the first time, she wished she'd made more of an effort to thank that woman for the books. And the kindness.

"The doctor's on his rounds. He should be here shortly," said the present-day nurse. "Are you experiencing any discomfort at all?"

"No discomfort. But I'm hungry." Nora wanted to recover her strength. She was eager to earn her walking papers and return to Miracle Books. And to her friends.

The nurse assured Nora that lunch would soon be served and left. Nora immediately motioned for Jed to return to his spot.

Smiling, Jed obliged. Once settled, he continued his narrative.

"Deputy Andrews is the real hero of this story. After you, that is. And June, Hester, and Estella. When I pulled up to the model home, Andrews had Collin Stone pinned to the ground. He was trying to secure his wrists while Stone fought like the fish in Hemingway's *The Old Man and the Sea.*"

"Nice literary reference."

Jed was pleased. "Thanks. I had three days to come up with it. Anyway, when Andrews spotted me, he yelled for me to check the kitchen. He'd heard what had been said from the moment you, June, and Hester had entered the house—I guess Hester's cell phone was in her pocket on speaker mode. Andrews was listening on the other end, and he jumped in his car when it sounded like you ladies were in danger."

Nora gripped Jed's arm. "Are they okay? June and Hester?"

"Yes." Jed covered Nora's hand with his. "They're fine. Other than worrying about you. They haven't had much sleep, but after your release, all four of you can rest in your own beds."

Nora stared at him. "Wait. You said *four.*"

Jed squeezed her hand and Nora's mouth stretched into such a wide smile that the burn scars on her right cheek twitched. She didn't care. She was too happy to worry about how she looked. "We did it? We did it! We freed Estella and nailed ..." She trailed off. "Have those Pine Ridge pricks taken her place in jail?"

"The feds took Sheriff Hendricks, Dawson Hendricks, Vanessa MacCavity, and Collin Stone into custody. They're in a cell, just not in Miracle Springs."

Nora recalled the shrill screams of agony echoing down the hallway of the model home seconds before the fire had begun. "And Bob?"

"No one could have saved him, Nora," Jed said in a subdued tone. "The fire investigator thinks he was gone before Andrews and I had even parked our cars."

Up to this point, Nora had been leaning forward, completely captivated by all that Jed had told her. Now she fell back against the pillow and stared up at the ceiling.

"Bob killed two people," she murmured. "He pushed Neil in front of a train for money. He served Fenton Greer a potassium-chloride cocktail chased by a killer dose of carbon monoxide because the money didn't get him the girl and he decided to punish the girl by framing her for murder." She released a pent-up breath. "Bob did reprehensible things, so why don't I feel like the scales of justice have been balanced?"

"Is it because you know that Bob's death was far worse than incarceration?" Jed guessed.

After considering this, Nora shook her head. "His screams will probably haunt my sleep for many nights to come, but it's more than the horrible way he died. It's more than the fact that he was burned." With her gaze fixed on the ceiling, Nora continued: "Bob thought he loved Estella. He built a fantasy life around her, and when she didn't want to take her place in his fantasy, he punished her. I understand the power and allure of fantasy—of becoming so attached to what *might be* that you pay no attention to reality. Before I moved to Miracle Springs, I made the same mistake. And like Bob, I lost my mind when my fantasy world fell apart."

"You didn't kill anyone, though," Jed said.

"I almost did." Nora took his hand and pressed it to the burn scar on her face. "That's how I came by this."

Though Jed seemed shocked by Nora's admission, he didn't pull away.

"One day, after I tell my friends, I'll tell you my story," Nora promised. "If you want to hear it."

"I do," Jed said. "And I—"

He was interrupted by a shriek of delight from the doorway. Estella burst into the room.

She rushed to Nora's side, swerving around the IV pole, and planted a kiss on Nora's forehead.

"Your hair looks like a squirrel's nest," she said, frowning in disapproval.

June and Hester appeared at the foot of the bed, but Nora only had eyes for Estella. Other than being a trifle pale, she was as lovely as ever. She wore a yellow dress trimmed with white, lipstick the color of a ripe persimmon, and an abundance of jasmine perfume.

"It's nice to see you too." Nora gave Estella a wry smile.

"You're still beautiful!" Estella jerked a thumb at Jed. "Why else would this stud spend the last three days in this awful room?"

Averting his face, Jed rose from his chair. He then indicated that June or Hester should take it. Hester accepted, while June opted for the recliner in the corner. Estella remained where she was.

Nora asked her friends to bring her up to speed on the investigation.

"The media has dubbed the whole mess 'The Meadows Murders,'" Hester said. "And we have a very recent update from Deputy Andrews."

"*You* have an update," June corrected. "Because he's sweet on you."

Ignoring June, Hester went on, "Sheriff Toad, Dawson, Vanessa, and Collin are being charged with mortgage fraud. There's enough proof to land them in prison for a couple of years, but sticking them with a conspiracy or accessory to commit murder charge is harder. The authorities need concrete evidence and no one knows where Bob hid his insurance."

"*If* he was telling the truth," Estella added caustically.

Nora remembered Bob's last words verbatim. "*Down the swift dark stream you go.*"

She let the words hang in space for a moment before repeating them. She had no doubt she recalled them with such ease because they'd come from a book.

And then, she began to smile.

"Is something funny?" Estella asked.

"I used to work with a wonderful children's librarian," Nora explained. "She could really bring characters to life when she read aloud. If a book included a song, she'd sing it. With gusto. The kids adored her."

June was the first to understand. "Bob's words are from a song?"

"Yes," Nora said. Very softly, she sang the two lines:

Down the swift dark stream you go,
Back to the lands you once did know!

Other lines from the song flowed through Nora's mind like the river from its lyrics, infusing her with energy. She felt her blood course through her body. Her stomach rumbled with hunger. She was alive and filled with purpose. And the Secret,

Book, and Scone Society had another important task to complete.

Nora turned to Estella. "Can you work your magic on my doctor? I want to get out of here right now."

"I'll do my best." Estella took out her compact and examined her reflection. Satisfied by what she saw, she shoved it back in her bag. "June, you'd better come with me. You speak better 'medical' than I do."

As soon as her friends were gone, Nora looked at Hester. "Will you call Andrews? I'd like to go straight from here to Bob's house. I think I can help find the evidence Bob hid away."

Hester gaped at her. "Because of a song?"

"Yes," Nora said. "I've always been a fan of Tolkien, but never so much as now."

She was about to throw off her sheet and blanket when she realized that she was clad in a scanty hospital gown. "Do I have clothes?" she asked Jed as Hester stepped into the hallway to make her phone call.

Jed removed a white plastic bag stamped PATIENT BELONGINGS from the wardrobe and placed it on the bed. He then touched her hand with his fingertips. It was a good-bye touch. "I should be going too, but I'll see you in town. I need something new to read, and I'm hoping you can recommend a book or two."

A different nurse bustled in before Nora could answer, her clipboard catching the light.

The wink of silver reminded Nora of another nurse in another hospital. A woman who had saved Nora from darkness. Books and kindness had saved her.

Nora thought of her beloved bookstore, of the hundreds of books waiting to be placed in empty, scarred, and imperfect hands. Young, smooth, unblemished hands. Old, wrinkled, age-spotted hands. Deserving hands, all of them. Every time Nora passed a book from her hand to another's, she knew that she was doing far more than selling a stranger a story. She was offering them a new beginning. Just as she had been offered a fresh start all those years ago. By turning pages. By absorbing words, images, emotions, and dreams.

"Recommend a book or two?" Nora smiled at Jed. "I couldn't think of anything I'd rather do."

Afterword

As soon as healing takes place, go out and heal somebody else.

—Maya Angelou

It was late in the afternoon by the time Nora and the other members of the Secret, Book, and Scone Society met Deputy Andrews at a log cabin in the middle of the woods.

"It's so peaceful here." June gazed around. "So quiet."

Estella smirked. "It's both too isolated and too close to the Trail. I'd worry about hikers knocking on my door, asking to use the bathroom or something."

Nora was too focused on getting inside to offer an opinion on Bob's house. She headed straight for Andrews, who immediately offered her his hand. "I'm so glad that you're okay, Ms. Pennington. Without you and the rest of these ladies, there wouldn't be an investigation at all."

"Thank you for trusting us, Deputy," Nora said. "You took a major risk, going against your boss. It couldn't have been easy."

Andrews shook his head. "No, but like my mama says, doing the right thing usually isn't easy. It's damned hard. And I'm not innocent, either. I didn't start reviewing the files after you asked me to. The doubt had to work its way in. *Ender's Game* helped."

Nora stared at him in surprise. "How?"

"There's a line in the book about lies being more dependable than truth," Andrews said as he unlocked Bob's door. "I'd become so used to the sheriff's lies that I believed them. They felt dependable. If you and Orson Scott Card hadn't made me question things, I doubt I would have chanced losing my job without more evidence."

"I hope we'll find that today," Nora said. "Otherwise, the risks we've taken won't amount to much. Fines and a few years in prison are hardly a just punishment for two murders and a plot to commit mortgage fraud in multiple towns."

Andrews waved for Nora to precede him into the cabin. "Collin Stone will be charged with at least one count of murder."

"Bob's," Nora whispered.

As she stepped into the silent house, she felt unexpectedly cold. It was unsettling to see the signs of Bob's life: the leather club chair by the fireplace, the crocheted afghan on the sofa, the collection of books and knickknacks on the shelves of a painted hutch, the framed maps and travel posters on the walls.

Estella, who'd entered the cabin behind Andrews, rubbed her hands over her arms. "Is it just me? Or is it chilly in here?"

June gave her a quick, one-armed hug. "We need to turn on some lights. The trees are blocking the sunshine." She steered Estella in the opposite direction. "Let's check out the kitchen."

"I'm going to see if the tool shed's unlocked," Hester said, and darted back outside.

Andrews watched her leave and then showed Nora his phone screen. "After Hester told me about the song, I bookmarked a website on Tolkien. Bob's hint about where his insurance is hidden came from the Wood-elves' Barrel song."

"It's from *The Hobbit.*" Nora gestured at the travel posters. "Like Tolkien, Bob clearly dreamed of faraway places. Both men also liked maps." She moved closer to the bookcases. "Bob owns all of Tolkien's titles."

Andrews joined her. "Do you think he hid the proof inside one of these books?"

"I'm not sure," Nora confessed. "There's a reason he picked a song about wine barrels floating downstream. This was how the barrels were delivered to the men of Lake-town in order to be refilled, but it was also how the dwarves and one Hobbit escaped from the Wood-elves. They *hid* in the barrels."

Andrews turned away from the bookcase, his eyes scanning the dim living room. "A barrel. Could it be that literal?"

As it turned out, it was. Nora and Andrews found a vintage Coca-Cola advertising bank shaped like a barrel in Bob's bedroom. This room, with its heavy wood furniture and dark bedding, was even colder and less light-filled than the downstairs spaces, and the lamp on the nightstand only served to emphasize the gloom.

"I always imagined a log cabin as being cozy. Quilts, crackling fires, snow on the sill, coffee laced with whiskey—that sort of thing," Nora said. "This one's depressing."

Andrews, who'd poked his head into the bathroom, glanced back at Nora. "A friend of mine lives on the other side of the ridge. His cabin has a totally different feel. It's bright and colorful. Probably because his family lives there—a wife, two kids, and a dog."

Nora realized that Bob's house had slowly developed a patina of loneliness and longing. He'd tried to escape these feelings by pinning all his hopes on winning Estella, and when that had failed, he'd become unstable and destructive.

Again, Nora felt conflicted over Bob's death. Drawn to the dresser, she reached for a black-and-white photograph of a man, a woman, and a little boy in denim overalls. The adults each held one of the boy's hands and were gazing down at him with such affection that Nora guessed they must be Bob's parents.

There were two other photographs of the same family. In both scenes, the subjects had aged, but their love for each other shone from their eyes and lit their faces. Behind the third photograph, Nora spied a wooden barrel bank.

"Deputy Andrews," Nora whispered. She knew better than to touch the bank. "This might be what we're looking for."

Andrews pulled on a pair of gloves. After examining the barrel's underside, he produced a pocketknife from his utility belt and pried open the base.

Nora half-expected a shower of coins to fall to the floor. However, whatever had been hidden inside the barrel seemed to be stuck. Andrews pinched the edge of the object with his forefingers and carefully withdrew an envelope from the round aperture.

"There's writing on the front," Nora said.

Flipping it over, Andrews read the text aloud: "'False hopes are more dangerous than fears.' Forgive me, Estella."

"Another line from Tolkien, I think." Nora pointed at the second phrase. "It's as if Bob knew Collin and the others would turn on him."

Andrews stared at the envelope. "I should take this straight to the lab, but you four deserve to know what's inside. Let's go down to the kitchen."

They descended the stairs to find Estella sitting in the chair by the fire, her gaze fixed on a poster of the Greek island of Santorini.

"He never talked about any of this," she said quietly. "Traveling. Maps. Books. He'd compliment me on my dress or ask after my clients. We'd compare notes about working service-oriented jobs or complain about the weather. The only deep conversation we ever had was when he asked why I wouldn't date local men. I told him a bit about my past. Not much, but more than I tell most people."

Though Nora was dying to see the contents of Bob's envelope, she knew why Estella's voice was tinged with grief and guilt. "You aren't responsible for Bob's actions. Even if you'd gone out with him, he would have doubted your sincerity. He wasn't looking for something real. He was looking for an escape. That's what you were to him. A fantasy. His life was probably a succession of shattered fantasies." Nora gestured at the doorway where Andrews patiently waited. "Estella. We found something."

This declaration brought June into the room.

"Praise Jesus! I'm going to call Hester." June rushed outside and shouted for Hester, who raced into the kitchen with her eyes shining. Turning an electric smile on Andrews, she asked, "You did it? You found what you needed?"

Though reluctant to disappoint her, Andrews said, "Not me. Nora."

"We found it together," Nora clarified, and made a hurry-up gesture.

Using his pocketknife, Andrews cut a neat slit along the envelope's seam. He then pulled out a letter and a flash drive. The flash drive went right back into the envelope, but Andrews unfolded the typewritten letter and began to read.

"This USB drive contains the communication between myself and Collin Stone of Stone Construction. Stone and the senior partners of Pine Ridge Properties paid me to kill Neil Parrish. They wanted Parrish's death to look like an accident, so I asked Parrish to meet me near the train tracks. Neil and me had gotten pretty friendly. I knew he was having second thoughts about ripping off the good people of Miracle Springs. I couldn't trust him to do the right thing, so I told him a different version of the padlock legend. I said that if he hung a padlock and the incoming train flattened his key, it meant that he could change his destiny. The guy was so caught up in the idea that he never sensed danger coming. I almost felt bad for him. But I know greedy city types. They don't ever change. My parents lost everything in a real-estate scam to a city guy just like Parrish. Getting suckered like that drove them to an early grave and changed

the course my life was supposed to take. I could have been so much more.

"But I'm more than people think I am. I sure had the Pine Ridge assholes fooled. I told Collin Stone that I wanted money to impress Estella, but that was a lie. I wanted to get back at the scum who look at people like me—at the regular Joes—and see us as disposable. My only regret is what I did to Estella. I knew she'd be released when Stone and his partners ran off with the profits, but I hated the thought of her being in jail. Tell her I'm sorry. I know she'll understand. She is the finest woman I've ever known."

A loud sniffle from across the table gave Andrews pause. He glanced at Estella over the top of the letter.

"This changes everything, don't you see?" She wiped away a tear. "Bob didn't give a crap about money. And I don't think he was in love with me, either. We were genuinely fond of each other. It was almost . . . better than being in love. It was something we could both count on." Another tear rolled down her chin. "I'm not saying that he's a good guy or anything. He killed *two* people. But he was trying to protect his neighbors. He—"

"He went about it all wrong," June pointed out.

Nora held up her hand to keep June from saying anything else. "And he paid a terrible price. Let's give him a chance to redeem himself. After all, isn't that what we were trying to do for Neil?"

The other women nodded.

Andrews, sensing the floor was his again, continued reading.

"I was paid to take out Parrish. But later on, Stone, that harpy Vanessa MacCavity, Sheriff Hendricks, and his snake of a brother, Dawson, were worried that Fenton Greer had overshared with Estella in the bathhouse, so Stone hired me to kill Greer.

"I never trusted Stone or his pals, so I recorded conversations and both murders using my phone. There should be plenty on

that USB to nail the bastards. I knew I was right when I saw Greer's cocktail napkin. Greer was making a list of the people who'd need extra incentive to keep their mouths shut about Parrish's untimely death. Dawson and Annette had both heard Parrish complain about what Pine Ridge was doing, and Sheriff Toad would need whatever payoff his brother got or he wouldn't be happy. I wish I had that napkin as extra proof, but Greer took it when he left the bar.

"Anyway, that's my story. And if you're reading this, it hasn't had a happy ending. That's okay. It's what I expected. And what I deserve. Just know I did what I did because I couldn't stand by and do nothing while good people got hurt."

Andrews placed the letter back in the envelope and slipped the envelope into an evidence bag. "I need to get this to the techs." He looked at each woman in turn. "Thank you."

Estella pretended to examine her newly polished fingernails. "It's nothing. Seriously. What's a few days in a jail cell or hospital room? I bet we'll never get a speeding ticket in Miracle Springs again, will we?"

Andrews barked out a laugh. "I can't make that promise, Ms. Sadler." His smile faded as he added, "After all, the sheriff's department has a soiled reputation to restore."

Estella followed Andrews and her friends outside. "Reputations are overrated, Deputy. Take it from me. People will believe what they choose to believe. All you can do is wake up and try to be a better person than you were the day before."

"Is that from a book?" Andrews asked.

Estella looked at Nora and smiled. "Probably. Isn't everything worth repeating from a book?"

Nora couldn't stop touching her hair. It had been years since she'd worn it shoulder-length with layers framing her face, and she felt so much lighter. In losing her heavy, long side braid in the model-home fire, she'd gained a sense of freedom. Of newness.

"Does it hurt?" June asked, pointing at Nora's left arm.

Nora glanced down at her angry-looking skin. "Not really. I'm using prescription lotion to take away the sting. I should be back to normal in a few days." She gave a self-effacing shrug. "In other words, I'll only be burned on my right side."

Estella, who'd been in the ticket-agent's office pouring cups of decaf, called out, "You'd better get used to being the face of Miracle Springs. Do you realize what'll happen when people find out that you survived a second fire? All in the name of justice?"

"Hopefully, they'll pour into Miracle Books and leave again with a bag in each hand," June said. "After that, they can go to the Gingerbread House. And your appointment book will always be full, Estella."

"Sorry I'm late!" Hester shouted above the slam of the back door. She entered the circle of chairs and handed Nora a bakery box. "Are you ready?"

Nora pulled the box closer to her chest. She could feel the scone's heat right through the box. "Yes. It's time."

The members of the Secret, Book, and Scone Society distributed cups of coffee and puff pastries Hester had shaped to resemble open books. She'd embellished the treats by adding lines of melted chocolate to each book, creating the effect of text.

"I thought you might like to sell these here," Hester said. "I could make them once the morning rush is over or teach you how to bake them. You could offer a chocolate version or ones with raspberry text. Or a blank book sprinkled with powdered sugar."

Nora was stunned. "I was going to ask you about making something special for Miracle Books, but I thought I'd wait until I was sure we'd both still have businesses to run. For a while there, I wasn't sure if we'd make it through this ordeal."

"Girl, please." June flicked her wrist in dismissal. "Can't you read my mug?"

June's mug featured the outline of a sheep and the text I WOOL SURVIVE.

The women shared a companionable laugh, but when the laughter had drifted into the rafters, the bookstore held a quiet expectation, so Nora pulled on the ends of the mirrored coffee table and exposed the hidden compartment. Using the key affixed to her bookmark, Nora opened the lock, raised the lid, and removed a shoe box from inside the cavity.

Instead of resuming her seat in one of the soft chairs, she dropped to her knees.

"In my first life, I was an upper-class suburban housewife and librarian," Nora began. She curled her fingers around the edge of the box in a protective gesture. "I thought I loved my husband when we got married, but I think I loved the idea of marriage more than the person I stood next to at the altar. Because of what I'd read in books, I wanted a friend, lover, and partner in crime. I wanted a fantasy man who was a blend of Atticus Finch, Nick Charles, Fitzwilliam Darcy, Rhett Butler, Jack Reacher, and Noah from *The Notebook*."

"If you ever find a man like that, send him my way," Estella said.

Nora shook her head. "That's my point. He doesn't exist. And I didn't know how to love the man I'd chosen. I was an excellent librarian. I was a devoted friend. I'm not sure if I was a good wife. I took care of the house. I cooked. I picked up the dry cleaning. I attended his boring work functions. I made our weekend plans. But as the years passed, our lives were nothing but a predictable orbit. A good marriage needs collisions. Meteorites and solar flares. Fights, laughter, passion, sex. Stars dying and being reborn. What we ended up with was as distant and cold as space. Only I didn't see it. I was too busy with my routine to see that we had died almost from the beginning."

Nora paused for a sip of coffee. Earlier that day, she'd told her friends that she didn't want alcohol at tonight's meeting. No one had asked why.

"My husband found a different way of filling the void," Nora continued with her narrative. "He started having an affair."

June muttered, "Damn."

"It went on for over a year without my knowledge. My husband became an adept liar. He also pretended to care more about me during this time. He wrote me sweet notes and brought me flowers. I thought our marriage was improving, but these tokens were signs of its impending finale. My husband didn't love me. He wanted to be with this other woman, but guilt caused him to waffle between the two of us. He had sex with both of us. He went on dates with both of us. He made promises to both of us. But his two worlds collided on New Year's Eve when he snuck out to meet her."

"On a major holiday?" Hester asked. "Didn't you two have plans?"

Nora took another sip of coffee. She needed its warmth to make it through this next part. "I'd gone to bed early—hopped up on cold meds—and was suddenly jarred awake by some noise on the downstairs TV. When I realized that my husband was gone, I called his cell. He didn't pick up. Worried and confused, I looked on his computer and saw . . . well, what I saw turned my world upside down."

"Of course it did, honey," June whispered.

"What I remember most is the rage," Nora continued. "My whole body shook with fury. I broke, tore, or bashed lots of his stuff, but it didn't help. I wanted to hurt *him*. I wanted him to feel the pain I was feeling." Nora's voice grew tight with the old anger. "I wanted to smash his face with my fist. I wanted to take a golf club to his car. I wanted to do all of those things, but I was trembling too much to drive, so I started chugging wine to calm myself. When that was gone, I went for the bourbon. As for finding my husband, that was easy. I used the Find My Friends app on my phone, drove over to his lover's house, and waltzed right in. Guess they'd been too excited to remember to lock it."

Hester's hand flew to her mouth. "Uh-oh."

Nora forced herself to go on. "They were snuggled up together, making plans for the future, and I stood in the doorway with rage shooting out of me like lightning bolts. I'd carried in the golf club, but my husband grabbed it and yelled that his lover was pregnant. She was crying. And something inside me broke. Because I realized that I wanted a child. I'd wanted one for years. I'd foolishly assumed that a baby would happen in due time. A family. My husband would have both. Just not with me. The hurt was so engulfing that I couldn't breathe. I ran out of the house, got in the car, and drove off."

Nora stopped to gather her courage. Without looking at her friends, she opened the shoe-box lid. "I drove recklessly, like I wanted to die. And of course, I'd had too much to drink. I'd barely gotten on the highway when I lost control and struck a car traveling in the opposite lane. I don't remember the impact. I only remember coming to and seeing the other car on fire."

Nora removed a pair of charred sneakers from the box. They looked incredibly small in her palm. "The passengers in that car were a woman and her toddler boy. I pulled the mom out first because the fire was coming from the engine. She was unconscious. Carrying her must have taken its toll because I blacked out again."

As if from a great distance, Nora heard one of her friends sniff. She knew someone was crying, but she couldn't look up. Not yet. She had to get through this. "When I opened my eyes, I saw flames engulfing the car." It was so hard to get the words out. Nora had to push each one from her throat. "I glanced at the mother and realized that the boy was still inside the burning car. God, it was so horrible when that sank in . . ."

Nora shook her head. She had to master her emotions in order to finish. "The flames were already chewing on the front seats when I flung open the back door and started fighting with the boy's car-seat latches. I had no experience with those things. They were a total enigma to me. Like the hardest puzzle I've ever had to solve. The seat was on the passenger side so I pivoted my body to block the flames from reaching him. That's why my right side is burned." Nora briefly raised her scarred arm. "But I got him out. I started rescue breathing. I also called for help."

Nora waited for someone to ask the obvious question.

Estella obliged. "Did they make it? The mother and son?"

"Yes," Nora said. "The mom suffered minor burns from the airbag and lacerations. Her son's injuries were more serious. He'd inhaled too much smoke and he had burns on his feet and lower legs. He was in the hospital for over a week. Luckily, children have an incredible capacity to heal, and this boy was no exception. There was a chance he might have minor scarring on his calves, but no one could say for sure. The boy's father sent me his shoes to serve as a reminder of what I'd done."

"That's cruel."

Nora looked at Hester and said, "No. It was necessary. And I've kept them ever since. The shoes and the secret. I almost killed that boy and his mother because my pain mastered me. I would have gone to jail if I hadn't been so injured. As it stands, I have a record. I don't have a driver's license. I'll never drive again." Nora set the shoe box aside and reached for her coffee cup again. She knew the liquid would be tepid at best, but she needed to moisten her mouth. "I never saw my husband again. Or the house we shared for over a decade. I've never searched for him online, or anyone else, from my former life. In my mind, I died that New Year's Eve. I'm still figuring out who I am now, but so far, I like this me better."

Nora smiled at each of her friends and released a long, steady sigh. She was done.

Hester pointed at the bakery box. "Eat your scone."

Nora was tired. Telling her secret had drained her. She wasn't hungry, but she had the feeling that the comfort scone Hester had baked would help her recharge.

She was surprised that her scone appeared to be plain. It didn't contain berries, nuts, or toffee chips. It hadn't been drizzled with a special glaze or sprinkled with finishing sugar. However, when Nora picked it up, she could see that it had been cut in half and filled with a red berry jam.

Nora inhaled the buttery scent of the golden scone before taking a healthy bite out of the pastry. Immediately, her thoughts were flooded by a memory of her mother reading aloud from Nora's favorite childhood book: *Bread and Jam for Frances*.

It was the earliest memory Nora had of falling in love with a story. Recalling it now filled her with such a pure joy that she felt like her veins no longer carried blood to parts of her body, but particles of nourishing light.

After she shared the memory with her friends, Nora locked the hidden compartment in the coffee table and put her finger on the keyhole. "This is no longer a place for my secret. However, if any member of the Secret, Book, and Scone Society needs to hide something away, you have a place. The rest of us will keep it safe."

"I guess we should use these pretty keys as bookmarks in the meantime," June said.

Nora watched Estella, June, and Hester glance at the surrounding bookshelves. A radiant grin spread over her face as she asked, "What should we read, my friends?"

A month later, the Secret, Book, and Scone Society met to wrap up their discussion of *A Man Called Ove*. However, there proved to be more urgent things to talk about, so Backman's endearing novel was shelved until the next meeting.

"It's awful!" Hester cried as she dropped into her chair. "The

Madison Valley Community Bank has folded. All of the employees arc out of work."

"There's more bad news," Estella added gravely. "The bank could only insure up to a certain dollar amount, so anyone who entrusted them with more than that has lost their money."

June grunted. "I hope those bastards we helped to indict choke on a chicken bone in prison. I know Dawson got a lighter sentence because no one could prove his involvement in the murders, but I can still imagine his life after his release. I like to picture him cleaning septic systems or public toilets."

Nora nodded. "I like that visual too. And even though we'll have to wait a little longer for Sheriff Toad, Collin Stone, and Vanessa MacCavity to be sentenced, at least we know they've been found guilty for conspiracy to commit murder and mortgage fraud."

"Miracle Springs will need a new sheriff," Estella said, and nudged Hester. "Is your boyfriend thinking about campaigning?"

Hester blushed. "He's not my boyfriend. We've had one date. I've been crazy busy." She glanced at Nora. "It's the same for you, right?"

"Total insanity," Nora said. "Some days, I can't eat lunch. I sneak in nuts or raisins while running credit cards. It doesn't surprise me that Miracle Springs has gained national attention. What surprises me is that the story isn't dying. The media keeps digging up fresh dirt on the Pine Ridge partners and the Hendricks brothers."

Estella flicked a lock of hair off her shoulder. "It's the peak season on crack. I had to hire part-time help for the spa and I'm still turning people away. I like the extra money, but I'm wiped."

"Me too," June said. "Ever since my promotion to manager I feel like a wrung-out mop." She sank back into her chair. "At least we have jobs. We have an income. Unlike those poor souls from the bank. I wish we could help them."

Hester kicked off her shoes and started to massage her right foot. Suddenly, she froze and stared into the middle distance.

"Hester?" Nora put a hand on her friend's lower back. "Are you okay?"

"We *can* help!" Hester cried, startling Nora. "We can't give people their jobs back. We can't give them money. But we *can* lift their spirits. What if we made an anonymous delivery to each person in need of a boost? A paper bag filled with simple treats? I could put in a loaf of farmer's bread, for example."

June nodded enthusiastically. "I could add a pair of my aromatherapy socks."

"I have lots of books about hope." Nora gestured around the shop. "I could also add a tea tin or a bag of coffee."

"And I could put together relaxation-themed baskets including a candle, hand lotion, and a loofah sponge," Estella said. "Hester, I really like this idea."

"Me too," Nora agreed. "Now we just need to find the time to assemble and deliver these secret bags."

June jerked her thumb toward the front of the bookshop. "I thought you were going to hang a HELP WANTED sign in the window."

Nora turned to her with a frown. "I did. I put it up this afternoon."

"It's not there now."

Still frowning, Nora told her friends to continue their anonymous brown-bag planning while she checked her display window.

As she wound her way around the bookshelves, she suddenly had the unsettling feeling that she was being watched.

Nora didn't head directly for the front door, but moved behind the checkout counter. She curled her hand around the Louisville Slugger she kept tucked between the box of register tape and a case of paper used for wrapping fragile shelf enhancers.

"Okay," she said calmly. "Come on out now. You obviously waited for me to close, but why?"

Nora caught movement off to her left. A very thin, girlish-looking woman stepped out of the shadows of the fiction section. She approached the checkout counter slowly, almost fearfully. Nora noticed that her cheap flip-flops and floral housedress were several sizes too big. She held the HELP WANTED sign in her hand. Encircling her bony wrist was a plastic hospital-identification bracelet.

"Please," she whispered. "I need a job."

Nora came out from behind the counter. Very gently, so as not to spook her visitor, she said, "What you need is something to eat. Follow me."

When Nora rounded a corner, she glanced back to catch the girl caressing the spine of a particularly colorful book. She knew right then that the stranger would be staying for more than just a scone.

THE SECRET, BOOK & SCONE SOCIETY

Ellery Adams

ABOUT THIS GUIDE

The suggested questions are included to enhance
your group's reading of Ellery Adams's
The Secret, Book & Scone Society.

DISCUSSION QUESTIONS

One of the best things about finishing a book is discussing it with a friend. Or even better, a group of friends. When we share our thoughts and feelings about characters, plots, and settings, even an old book can gain fresh life. So pour the coffee, pass the scones, get comfy, and use this reader's guide to help spark a fun and lively discussion.

1. What kind of miracles does Miracle Springs offer?

2. What brings Nora, Hester, Estella, and June together and why are they able to form a friendship and open up to each other at this particular time in their lives?

3. Do you believe in "Bibliotherapy"? Can you heal by reading about others in similar circumstances?

4. What do you make of June and those cats?

5. Would you like to live in Nora's Caboose Cottage? Why or why not?

6. There are many literary references in *The Secret, Book & Scone Society*. Did any hold particular meaning for you?

7. Some of the most famous works of literature involve a scarred man. His damage is often romanticized. How do you feel about stories that involve less-than-attractive women, scarred and/or deformed women?

8. Have you ever been treated differently because of your gender?

9. Which of the villains seems to have more depth? Were you able to feel sympathy for any of them? If so, why?

10. How do you feel about Nora and Jed as a couple? Do you think they have a future together?

11. Did any of the Secret, Book and Scone Society members say or do something that surprised, delighted, or angered you? Please share.

12. What kinds of activities do you consider therapeutic?

13. Every scone starts with the same basic recipe. Do you have a favorite flavor?

14. Did you feel differently about Nora after she shared her secret?

15. What predictions could be drawn from the final scene involving the stranger and the Help Wanted sign?

Don't miss the next Secret, Book & Scone Society mystery,

THE WHISPERED WORD

by *New York Times* bestselling author
Ellery Adams

Now on sale.

Read on for a preview.

Hide until everybody goes home. Hide until every-
body forgets about you. Hide until everybody dies.

—Yoko Ono

"That girl's got one foot in the grave."

Nora Pennington, proprietress of the only bookshop in Miracle Springs, North Carolina, glanced from her friend to the empty chair where she expected to find the fragile slip of a girl who'd hidden in the stacks until past closing time. However, the girl wasn't there.

Recalling the hospital ID bracelet encircling the girl's bony wrist, Nora returned her attention to her friend. "June, did she say anything to you? Or to Hester or Estella?"

June grunted. "Oh, sure. She told the three of us her whole story. Yes, ma'am. She donated a kidney to the love of her life and the surgery took place without a hitch, but when the sweethearts woke up, Miss-Skinny-as-a-Broom-Handle found out that Mr. Right was Mr. Seriously Wrong. According to a news report, he was an escaped serial killer. No, that wasn't it. He ran a cult. So she bolted from the hospital when the nurses weren't watching, snatched a housedress from a clothesline, and hopped a train to Miracle Springs."

A woman issued a throaty chuckle behind June.

"June Dixon, I believe you could write fiction if you had the notion," declared Estella Sadler in an exaggerated Southern accent. Estella uncrossed her shapely legs and stood up. Jerking a thumb toward the back of the bookstore, she said, "Unless you need help evicting your bubble-wrap refugee, I'm calling it a night. You know I live for excitement, but even *I* need a break. Besides, if I'm planning to add Good Samaritan to my resumé— a title I *never* thought I'd add—then I could use a decent night's sleep. Sweet dreams, ladies."

Nora turned to Hester Winthrop, the fourth member of the Secret, Book and Scone Society, and arched her brows. "Bubble-wrap refugee?"

"You'll see," Hester said as she picked up her handbag. "I need to get going too. The bread won't knead itself at five in the morning and I'll be baking extra loaves starting tomorrow to put in our secret gift bags."

June shook her head. "I don't know many people who wake up when it's dark out and work all day long without taking a break. With your freckles and endless energy, you remind me of Pippi Longstocking."

Hester grinned. "Except Estella's the redhead, not me."

June grunted again. "Estella's no Pippi. She's catlike. She moves with slow grace until it's time to pounce. Who does she remind me of?" She tapped her finger against her chin. "Shere Khan. That's it! The tiger from *The Jungle Book*."

"And what book character are you?" Nora asked, unable to avoid being drawn in by the subject.

June put her hand over her heart. "When I worked at the nursing home, one of my favorite patients called me a black Mary Poppins."

Seeing the shock on Hester's face, June burst into laughter. "Honey, I wasn't offended. This lady meant it as a compliment. She wanted me to know that she could see how I tried to find ways to put a little magic into the residents' lives."

Hester gestured in the direction of Nora's small stockroom. "I don't think there's been much magic in that one's life lately. What are you going to do about her, Nora?"

Nora shrugged. She'd moved to Miracle Springs in search of peace and privacy. She hadn't wanted a single responsibility beyond owning her tiny house and her one-of-a-kind bookstore. She hadn't wanted any pets. Or close relationships. She refused to join a place of worship or participate in charity events. She didn't sponsor children's athletic teams, enter bake-offs or gardening competitions, or take sides in local politics. She didn't seek out anyone's company. Despite her reclusive nature, people sought her out.

Strangers came looking for her. People from other states and sometimes, other countries. People with skin of every color. People with an array of stories to tell. People carrying a burden they were incapable of putting down. These weary souls came to her, the "woman who might have been beautiful, had she not been burned," or "the bibliotherapist with the burn scars." These were examples of how the Miracle Springs Lodge staff members referred to Nora. They made these remarks without malice, for the majority of the hotel and spa employees liked her. Or, more accurately, they liked her bookstore. It was difficult not to. In fact, it was virtually impossible not to fall in love with the place.

Meandering through the bookshop was like falling in love for the very first time.

In the beginning, Nora's customers would hesitate near the front door in case they wanted to beat a hasty retreat. Many entered fearing the store would be stocked with only New Age titles and crystals—a reasonable concern in a town built upon the premise of healing.

People had been traveling to the region's hot springs and thermal pools for nearly two centuries in search of pain relief—whether of body or spirit—and the waters continued to draw the broken, injured, and spent to the remote hamlet every day. Because Nora had never bathed in the hot springs, she couldn't say if the waters had restorative powers. But she believed books had the power to heal. She believed that the experiences of an author, rendered into carefully chosen words, gifted readers with the ability to let go of their painful past and continue their story anew.

Because of this, Nora's store was stuffed with books of every imaginable format and genre. There were the latest bestsellers with glossy hardcovers. There were dog-eared, yellowed, used paperbacks. There were first editions, signed books, and beautiful, leather-bound books with gilt lettering. Some books had no words at all, but were filled with exquisite illustrations or paper sculptures. To Nora Pennington, every book had value. Every story had meaning.

Faced with this overwhelming cornucopia of books, Nora's first-time customers needed a minute to get their bearings. After all, there was so much to see. A warren of shelves immediately invited them to wander—to become lost in a labyrinth of colorful spines. And yet, something close at hand also tempted them to pause. This temptation was often a beautiful book cover. At other times, it was a shelf enhancer.

Nora created the term "shelf enhancer" before ever opening Miracle Books. One day, when she was still assembling her initial inventory, she'd been rummaging through a box of books at the local flea market when she'd come across a pair of bronze owl bookends. They weren't in perfect shape. There was minor flaking to the bronze in several places, undoubtedly due to age. Regardless of their flaws, Nora liked the owls. Their gaze was stern, almost severe. And their talons were hooked over a stack of thick tomes, lending the impression that they were guarding the knowledge held within the books.

"If you buy the set of Nancy Drews, I'll give you a discount on the owls," the vendor had said to Nora while overtly studying her burn scars.

Though Nora was used to being stared at, she wasn't used to bargaining. Still, she knew that she'd have to buy every book at rock-bottom prices if she wanted her business to succeed, so she turned the bookends over in her hands and thought of how much more interesting her future store would be if her shelves were enhanced by unique, eye-catching, vintage items. And then, she'd begun to haggle.

The shelf enhancers became impulse buys for locals and visitors alike. Now, as Nora moved deeper into the stacks, she walked by a wooden mortar filled with crushed lavender, a marble and brass letter holder, a picture frame in pink Lucite, a Victorian child's porcelain tea set, and an art nouveau trumpet vase. And those were just some of the treasures displayed in the Contemporary Romance section.

As Nora rounded the corner of a bookcase crammed with pulp fiction novels toward the back of the shop, she heard the loud clang of brass bells smacking against wood. The bells, which had once been attached to a horse harness, now hung from a strip of leather behind Nora's front door.

The sound meant that her friends had left.

Nora was alone with her books and the pale, thin girl.

And there she was, curled into a fetal position on top of a layer of bubble wrap and white packing paper in Nora's stockroom. She looked like an undernourished Goldilocks who'd passed out after a night of too much partying.

Nora studied the stranger in the dim light. Though her lithe figure and pallid skin made her appear childlike, Nora guessed that she was well out of her teens.

"What am I supposed to do with you?" she murmured under her breath.

Nora had intended to live an uncomplicated life in Miracle

Springs, but despite her attempts to keep people at arm's length, she'd recently become friends with three remarkable women and had formed The Secret, Book, and Scone Society. In the middle of their investigation into the murder of a visiting businessman, Estella, June, and Hester had each shared their deepest secret with Nora. And eventually, she'd entrusted them with hers—the terrible truth behind the jellyfish burn scar swimming up her right arm and the pod of tiny bubbly octopi scars floating up her shoulder and neck to caress her cheek with their puckered tentacles.

I've already risked enough, Nora thought, staring down at the sleeping girl.

Miracle Springs was still reeling following the abrupt closing of the community bank. Dozens of people had lost their jobs. Others had been jailed. The town needed to recover. So did Nora.

But she was torn. Part of her wanted to shake the girl awake and tell her to move on.

"This is a bookstore, not a hotel," she could hear herself saying.

The other part of her remembered how the girl had caressed the book spines when she thought no one had been watching. There had been such tenderness in that touch. And longing. There'd been loss too.

Nora had seen herself in that moment. Because of that, she strode to one of the shop's many reading nooks, grabbed the throw blanket from the back of the fainting couch, and draped it over the slumbering girl.

I wish I could sleep that soundly, Nora thought. But the girl's hospital bracelet and ill-fitting clothing hinted at a sleep that was anything but sound. This young woman's sleep was of the bone-weary kind. It was the sleep of someone who'd been running and running and had finally run out of steam.

Nora lingered for a moment to consider why a person would

run away from a hospital before she decided that she didn't want to discover the answer to that question. She didn't want to get involved. She would give the girl food and shelter. For now. That was all.

After writing a brief note, Nora locked the girl in the bookstore for the night.

The next morning, Nora woke early. She hadn't slept well and her thoughts were focused entirely on coffee.

She was well into her second cup when she remembered her stockroom Goldilocks.

"Damn it," she muttered. She showered, dressed, and made a plate of food for the girl.

Nora walked the short distance from her tiny house, affectionately dubbed Caboose Cottage by the townsfolk, and unlocked the back door to Miracle Books.

"It's Nora! The shop owner!" she called out upon entering. She didn't want to scare the girl and it was possible that she was still sleeping.

However, the stockroom was empty.

Nora stood in the doorway and tried to comprehend what she was seeing. The room had been completely altered. The boxes had been flattened and lined up neatly along one wall. There wasn't a shred of bubble wrap or packing paper in sight.

Moving through the store to the ticket agent's booth, Nora glanced around for signs of life. Had the girl used one of the hundred coffee mugs hanging from the pegboard to make herself a cup of coffee or tea? If she had, she'd already washed it and hung it back up.

"I have fresh bread. It's lightly toasted and buttered," Nora said, her voice resonating through the stacks. "Hester baked it. You met her last night. She's the one with the freckles and the frizzy, blonde hair." Nora continued on to the checkout counter. "I also have blackberries that I picked yesterday morning. And farmer's cheese. I could make you a cappuccino or a latte if you'd like."

By this time, Nora had reached the register. She set down the plate of food on the counter and stopped to listen. The girl was still here. She could feel her presence. But why was she hiding?

Nora threaded her way to the front of the store. She was immediately struck by the foreignness of the display window. It had not looked like that last night.

"What the—?"

Digging the brass skeleton key that unlocked the front door of what had once been the train depot for Miracle Springs, Nora rushed outside to view the window from the sidewalk.

What she saw was so magical that she could hardly believe it was real.

The scene had been created entirely out of packing materials. The central figure was a woman sculptured using clear packing tape. The transparent tape woman held a string fastened to an enormous balloon made of bubble wrap. Both woman and balloon were surrounded by hundreds of origami birds of various sizes fashioned from white paper. The birds swayed and spun, coaxed into subtle movement by the air exiting a nearby duct.

For a moment, Nora felt as if she were in motion. She almost glanced down, half expecting the concrete slabs under her feet to have transformed into a moving sidewalk.

When she looked at the window again, she saw the books. Books with blue covers dangled from the ceiling. White string dug into each gutter, forcing the books to flap open and creating an illusion of wings. Nora found herself shifting left and right in an effort to read every title.

The girl—for she must be the artist behind this masterpiece— had selected books from a variety of genres. There was *Cat in the Hat*, *Go Set a Watchman*, *Wonder*, *All the Light We Cannot See*, *The Great Gatsby*, *Eragon*, *The Mystery at Moss-Covered Mansion*, *A Brief History of Time*, and a dozen more. On the bottom of the window, a whimsical set of cardboard letters spelled out the phrase MY BLUE HEAVEN.

Nora reentered the store and found the girl standing next to the plate of food. She hadn't touched it, but was hovering so close to it that her hunger was almost palpable.

"It's beautiful." Nora gestured at the window behind her. "Did you spend all night making that?"

The girl took a long time to reply. When she finally spoke, her voice was a faint whisper, like a breeze winding through reeds. "It took a few hours."

"I think you've earned your breakfast," Nora said, indicating the plate. "Come on. I'll make you a coffee while you eat."

Though the girl said nothing, she picked up the plate and followed Nora to the circle of chairs near the ticket agent's booth.

Nora tapped the chalkboard menu affixed to the wall next to the ticket window and asked, "What would you like?"

The girl stepped up to the menu. Her lips moved as she murmured every word aloud.

> The Ernest Hemingway — Dark Roast
> Louisa May Alcott — Light Roast
> Dante Alighieri — Decaf
> The Wilkie Collins — Cappuccino
> Jack London — Latte
> Agatha ChrisTEA — Earl Grey

Nora turned away. She knew that people who had previously struggled with or continued to struggle with reading often read words out loud or tracked words with their fingers. If this was the case with this girl, Nora didn't want to embarrass her by gawking at her while she tried to process the menu. Instead, she searched for the perfect coffee cup for her guest.

The majority of Nora's mugs, which were purchased at yard sales or flea markets, bore book-related sayings or humorous one-liners. Glancing at her collection, she decided that none of them were a good fit for this girl. She wished she had one of her handmade pottery mugs covered with a thick cobalt glaze from home, especially since the girl seemed to have an affinity for blue. Nora could give her one of the mugs she kept for when children asked for hot chocolate, but Cookie Monster, Batman, Snoopy, or Harry Potter fan didn't feel right either.

Nora selected a white mug with a donut covered in pink icing and rainbow sprinkles. The donut was flanked by the words, I to the left and CARE to the right. Giving the girl a questioning look, Nora wished, for the first time, that she owned an innocuous kitten or puppy mug.

"Anything tempt you?"

"A latte would be great, thanks."

Nora nodded and moved behind the espresso machine to make the drink. She hadn't asked the girl if she wanted sugar or special milk because she didn't make a habit of giving her customers too many choices. If they wanted sugar, they could stir it in themselves. If they wanted soy, almond, or coconut milk, they were out of luck. Nora didn't stock a range of items. She was neither a Starbucks nor a grocery store. Her espresso machine was a refurnished model that ran on a wing and a prayer, and Nora was always relieved when her customers stuck to a standard cup of coffee or herbal tea.

"What's your name?" Nora casually inquired over the hiss and sputter of the machine. She'd already made the espresso and was now frothing the milk for the girl's latte.

There was no answer, so Nora finished preparing the latte. When she was done, she set down the donut mug next to the dish of food.

The girl kept her eyes fixed on the offerings. "It's . . . Abilene. My name's Abilene."

Given the slight pause, Nora wondered if the girl had just

made up a name. But if she had, it didn't matter to Nora. She would call the girl whatever name she wanted to be called.

"That's a pretty name." She gave the girl a friendly smile. "I don't like it when people watch me eat, so why don't you grab a seat and enjoy your food? I'm going to head to the front and take care of things I need to do before opening for the day. I don't need to mess with the window display, thanks to you. I won't want to change that for months. It's really amazing."

Abilene returned Nora's smile with a small, shy smile of her own. "Thanks."

Later, Nora was behind the checkout counter, circling promising yard sale ads in the paper when Abilene silently appeared. "Thanks for the food. The bread and berries were really good. And thanks for letting me stay last night. I'll show myself out."

She turned toward the front door.

Nora knew the girl couldn't show herself out because the door was locked and the heavy brass skeleton key was inside the cash register. As she watched Abilene and tried to decide what to do about the young woman so clearly in need of help, something occurred that would keep her from leaving Miracle Books anytime soon.

Without warning, the rubber strap on Abilene's left flip-flop snapped, causing her to lose her balance. She pitched forward, colliding with a floor spinner stuffed with paperbacks. The display was made of acrylic, and Nora gasped in dismay as an entire side gave way in a series of violent cracks. Abilene cried out in pain.

By the time Nora dropped to her knees beside the girl, she was cradling her right hand with her left. She tried to hide the blood seeping from between her fingers and the tear tracks wetting her cheeks, but failed.

"Don't move," Nora ordered and ran to get a dishtowel from the back.

When she returned to Abilene, the girl refused to let her look at her hand.

"I'm fine," she insisted stubbornly.

Nora scowled at her. "Bullshit. You're bleeding all over my floor. Come on. I need to see it."

Averting her gaze, Abilene offered Nora her injured hand.

Gently, Nora pried away the girl's fingers. Blood immediately welled from a deep gash across her palm. It was deep enough to require sutures. This was not a wound that would heal on its own.

"You need stitches," Nora said, balling up the towel and pressing it against Abilene's palm.

The girl drew back so abruptly that she nearly knocked Nora over. "No. I'm fine."

Nora realized that there was no way she'd get Abilene to an urgent care center or doctor's office. "Listen. I have a friend who can patch you up. He won't tell anyone about you. I'm going to call him. You're going to stay with me today. No arguments. You're going to rest and eat. No one will ask you questions. And if they do, you don't have to answer them."

Abilene shook her head and Nora feared that the girl would bolt the second she turned her back. She'd have to find another way to coerce her into staying put, which wouldn't be easy. It was obvious that Abilene was incredibly on edge.

Why? Nora silently wondered as she held the girl's hand. *What happened to you?*

"Look, Abilene." Nora adopted the firm, no-nonsense tone she'd employed during her previous life as a librarian. Pretending that Abilene was an unruly high school student, she said, "You broke my spinner and you've made a mess that needs to be cleaned up before I open at ten. The way I see it, you have two choices. You can run out through the back exit, leaving a trail of blood, and pass out in some field a few miles away. Your left foot will be wrecked because you have only one shoe that clearly doesn't fit. But what happens to your foot doesn't matter because your hand will likely get infected and you'll run a fever. Whoever finds you *will* call for an ambulance. Or they'll call the police. Is *that* what you want?"

Abilene refused to answer.

"Your other option is to let my friend patch you up. You can regain your strength, change into clothes that actually fit, and do a few light chores for me to earn your keep." Nora cocked her head. "Do you like books?"

Judging by the window display, the girl most certainly did, but Nora wanted to see if her question would elicit a response. It did.

Abilene whipped her head around. Her eyes were lit with twin sparks. Not the sparks of enthusiasm, but of anger.

"I love them," she declared in a voice that was almost loud.

Nora was relieved by this evidence of Abilene's passion. Whatever else the girl was, she wasn't weak. There was a layer of steel under that translucent skin. And Nora guessed it was strength that had carried Abilene this far. From wherever it was that she had come.

"I love books too," Nora whispered reverently to the girl. "In fact, they saved my life." She held Abilene's gaze. "So believe me when I tell you that this is a safe place for you. Here, among the books. With me, a woman who was rescued by them."

Abilene glanced around the shop and Nora recognized the girl's expression of longing. How long had she been running? Who was she afraid of, and was Nora being a fool for inviting more danger into her quiet world? After all, she'd just risked life and limb for a complete stranger and had vowed never to repeat such ridiculous behavior. She'd barely been released from the hospital and yet, here she was, offering shelter to a young woman who was undoubtedly being hunted. But by whom?

The thoughts churning around in Nora's head were interrupted by a buzzing noise outside the bookstore. Putting the towel in Abilene's left hand and forcing her to press it against the wound on her right palm, Nora stood and walked over to peer out the glass panel over the front door. What she saw made her breath catch in surprise.

A crowd had gathered on the sidewalk. The faces of men, women, and children were all turned toward the display window of Miracle Books. This collection of locals and out-of-towners were pointing, smiling, and snapping pictures of Abilene's creation with their cell phones.

Nora looked at her watch. It was nine thirty, which meant the trolley from Miracle Lodge had arrived early and delivered Nora's favorite kind of customers: the wealthy kind.

"There's a group of people out there admiring your work," Nora told Abilene. "You see? I'm not the only one who thinks it's beautiful."

The compliment brought a rush of color to Abilene's cheeks and she seemed to glow with delight. The reaction was so powerful that Nora could see that the girl was unaccustomed to being praised.

"So? Should we see to that hand?"

After a brief hesitation, Abilene reached out with her index finger and held it over Nora's pinkie knuckle—over the empty space where the rest of her finger should have been, but wasn't.

"Did the books save you? After you were burned?" she asked in a timid whisper.

Nora snatched her hand away. "We all have a story. We all have secrets. But we don't have to share them. Not with everyone."

Someone knocked on the front door and Abilene gave a start.

Since Nora didn't recognize the man, she ignored him. He'd have to wait until she opened at ten.

"How did it get so late so soon?" she muttered to herself. Abilene's indecision was making her irritable. Not only did she have things to do, but she was also annoyed with herself for welcoming this strange girl in the first place.

"I like his poems too," Abilene said. "You were quoting Dr. Seuss, weren't you?"

When Nora gaped at her in surprise, the girl responded by smiling.

Finally, Abilene got to her feet and said, "Yes. I'd like to stay. For a little while, if I can. Here with you. And the books. These wonderful, wonderful books."

Connect with Us

Visit us online at
KensingtonBooks.com
to read more from your favorite authors, see books
by series, view reading group guides, and more.

for sneak peeks, chances to win books and prize packs,
and to share your thoughts with other readers.

facebook.com/kensingtonpublishing
twitter.com/kensingtonbooks

Tell us what you think!

To share your thoughts, submit a review,
or sign up for our eNewsletters, please visit:
KensingtonBooks.com/TellUs.